Don Kuhn was born in London in 1922. He was educated at an elementary school in Romford, and at St Martin's School of Art in London.

A physical disability prevented him from serving in the armed forces during the War and was the cause of a long sojourn in hospital. During this time he met Pat, a nurse whom he married in 1942.

In 1956 they moved to their present home in Somerset where they both now teach music. Don has written several successful one-act plays for local amateur dramatic societies, one of which has been published.

"The More We Are Together" is his first novel.

THE MORE WE ARE TOGETHER

To Janet
With Very Best
Wishes.
Don Kuhn

August, 2001

Don Kuhn

The More We Are Together

Vanguard Press

VANGUARD PAPERBACK

© Copyright 2001
Don Kuhn

The right of Don Kuhn to be identified as author of
this work has been asserted by him in accordance with the
Copyright, Designs and Patents Act 1988

All Rights Reserved

No reproduction, copy or transmission of this publication
may be made without written permission.
No paragraph of this publication may be reproduced,
copied or transmitted save with the written permission or in
accordance
with the provisions of the Copyright Act 1956 (as amended).

Any person who does any unauthorised act in relation to
this publication may be liable to criminal
prosecution and civil claims for damage.

A CIP catalogue record for this title is
available from the British Library
ISBN 1 903489 16 4

*Vanguard Press is an imprint of
Pegasus Elliot MacKenzie Publishers*
www.pegasuspublishers.com

First Published in 2001

**Vanguard Press
Sheraton House Castle Park
Cambridge England**

Printed & Bound in Great Britain

Dedication

To Pat, with Love

> "Oh! The more we are together,
> The merrier we'll be."
>
> **Irving King**
>
> *(The Official Song of the Ancient
> Order of Froth Blowers)*

Chapter 1

This Boxing Day it is the turn of the Stilwells to entertain the Scallys.

The left-overs of yesterday's turkey and Christmas pudding have been eaten and the two wives have retired to the living room, where they sit resplendent amid the tinselled decorations and wilting Christmas cards, while their men folk, in time-honoured fashion, do the washing-up. On the television, Royalty are busy distributing gifts to children in hospital, but the sound is turned down and neither lady is watching.

Elsie Stilwell is reclining on the settee with her legs up, popping chocolate liqueurs into her mouth as fast as she can go, and recalling nostalgically happier Christmases spent in Australia in years gone by.

Nora Scally sits by the fire, her dumpy figure lost in the depths of the huge armchair. She is thinking about her 'Big Move', away from the Eastland Estate to Webbley Park, the smarter part of Brockbury, and is hoping that by this time next year she will have achieved it.

But what with the food and wine, the warm room, the dim December light and the unaccustomed silence, by the time the two men come in with the coffee they have both drifted off to sleep.

"Come along now, ladies!" cries Colin Stilwell in his policeman's voice. "Make room for us gents!"

Elsie Stilwell reluctantly puts her feet to the floor so that Len Scally can sit beside her on the settee. Furniture is shifted to accommodate the coffee table. Colin produces the brandy bottle and glasses and pours each of them a generous measure. Len takes a packet of panatella cigars from his jacket pocket and gives one to Colin. Nora adjusts her skirt and replaces her paper hat, which has fallen off during her snooze.

"Take a dekko at these," says Colin as he takes a number of holiday brochures from his 'G-Plan' bookshelf and hands them round.

It is a solemn moment, the moment when the Stilwells and the Scallys try to make up their minds where they want to go for their holiday together in the forthcoming year.

"So what's it to be this time then?" grins Colin as he drops his big frame into the armchair opposite Nora. "Hang-gliding or windsurfing?"

No one responds. Pages flap. Brandy is sipped.

"What about Disneyland?" says Elsie after a bit.

"Which one?"

"Paris is the nearest."

"Not a bad idea," concedes Colin with a hint of reservation. "but why not go the whole hog and go to America – California or Orlando?"

"Can't afford it," says Nora promptly. "Don't forget we're moving next year, so we don't want to spend more than we can help. Best to stay in this country this time."

"Just as cheap to go abroad as stay here – cheaper in fact." Colin flaps the pages of his brochure. "Here you are, fortnight on the Costa Brava for two hundred and thirty-five quid."

"Don't fancy Spain," says Nora.

"Somewhere else then. Plenty of places to choose from."

"Still rather go to Disneyland," says Elsie.

"Paris is too dear," insists Nora.

Elsie glares across at her friend. "You going to be bloody awkward about it this time, or what?"

"Course not! Just that we don't want to spend more than we can help. No point in looking at things we can't afford."

Elsie snorts. She's fed up to the back teeth hearing about Nora's move.

"Let's keep to the matter in hand," cuts in Colin hastily. "Let's look a bit further. Try to find something we all fancy."

More page flapping and sipping of brandy.

But Elsie gets side-tracked by the decor of the bedrooms illustrated in her brochure, trying to visualise how she would like their bedroom to look when Colin redecorates it in the spring.

Colin is distracted by the golden beaches and exotic swimming pools, inspecting the photos closely to see if any of the bikini-clad girls are topless, but no such luck.

Len Scally inspects the hotel bars and other drinking facilities illustrated, and comes to the conclusion that none look so homely or inviting as the good old British pub.

Nora scrutinises the price lists. She finds the presentation by hotel, date, single and double rooms, with all the supplements and exceptions, confusing, and doesn't bother to try to sort it out. She already knows what she wants to do. She is biding her time, letting the others have their say first before coming out with it.

"What about Minorca?" says Colin. "That seems cheap enough."

"Oh, I'm not flying," says Nora. She's never flown in her life and has no intention of starting now.

Elsie takes another liqueur. "I still say Disneyland."

"Well, we don't need to fly if we go to the Paris one," says Colin. "We could go by boat."

"And I'm not going by boat either." (Nora hasn't forgotten when years ago she went by boat on a weekend trip to Denmark with a party of women from work. She was tossed all the way there and all the way back – never again.)

Colin is inspired. "Hey! What about the Tunnel?"

"You won't catch me going through that bleedin' Tunnel," says Elsie. She shudders at the very thought and takes a sip of her brandy.

"No worse than going under the Thames in the Underground," Colin protests.

"That's different."

"Then how the bloody hell are we supposed to get there?" he demands.

"No need to get shirty, Colin," Nora says equably. "I told you, Paris is too dear. It's got to be cheap and cheerful this time."

Colin wheezes like a concertina with frustration.

"Course," adds Nora, "there's nothing to stop you and Elsie going to Paris on your own."

"Not having that," cuts in Elsie. "You know what he is. He'll be bunking off to the Folies-Bergère or summat."

Something Colin wouldn't mind doing. Sighing, he pours himself another brandy. "So what *do* you want to do?"

"*I* think," says Nora, "we ought to stay in England this time, like I said. Perhaps do something more exciting the year after." She has no intention of doing that either.

"Well, what about going to Bournemouth again?" Elsie loves Bournemouth.

Colin groans. "Not *again*!"

"Hotels are dear in Bournemouth," objects Nora.

"Why do we have to keep going to the same old places all the time?" Colin's had enough of marching up and down seaside promenades, following the women around shops. "Can't we do something different for a change?"

"Such as?" challenges Elsie.

"Well…like hiring a boat or summat, going on the canals. Tell you what, Norfolk Broads is the place!"

"Bloody boring, if you ask me, floating along in the pouring rain with nothing to do."

"It's not just floating along. Have to stop to work the locks and that, tie up and see places, visit pubs, have nice meals."

"Do a spot of fishing too," pipes up Len. He's partial to a spot of fishing providing it's not too cold.

"All right for you men. We want something to do too, don't we, Nora?"

"Course we do," nods Nora.

"Like shops, I suppose," sneers Colin.

"It's our holiday as well as yours. What we want is a bit of fun, good food, nice accommodation, shows and that."

"Better go to London then. All the shows and shops you want there."

"London's too dear," says Nora.

"Well, I dunno." Colin scratches the balding spot in his otherwise abundant fair hair. "Suppose we'll have to go to one of the same old places again then. But can't we go somewhere we haven't been?"

"Scarborough!" cries Elsie. "We haven't been to Scarborough."

"Bit breezy up there." Len feels the cold something chronic.

"Mavis liked it. Plenty of nice walks she says. Fishing for you men, coach trips to the Yorkshire Dales."

"Tell you what," cries Colin, smitten by a brainwave. "If

you want a *really* cheap holiday, why not rent a caravan?"

"Not bloody likely!" Elsie's not having that. "Have enough cooking all the year, ain't that right, Nora?"

"That's right," nods Nora, trying to pull down her skirts over her plump knees. She thinks Colin is staring up her legs.

"Len and me, we'll do the cooking, won't we, Len?"

"Um," says Len, without enthusiasm.

"Oh sure," says Elsie, "beans and bloody chips all the time."

Nora agrees. "Must have decent meals. What I enjoy most on holiday is nice meals in decent surroundings, nicely served and that."

"Can always eat out," protests Colin.

"Then it adds to the cost. Might as well go to a decent hotel and be dry and warm, and be done with it."

"Well, I dunno." Colin reaches for the bottle and pours another brandy.

"You going to guzzle all that or can you spare a drop for us?" demands Elsie sharply.

"Sorry, sorry." Colin leaps to his feet and dispenses more brandy all round.

During this brief intermission Nora shifts her chair further from the fire and makes another futile attempt to pull down her skirt. Len lights up another panatella. The chocolate liqueurs are handed round.

"What about the south coast?" suggests Nora, spotting her chance.

"Warmer on the south coast," says Len as he looks at the end of his cigar to see if it's alight.

"Been everywhere on the south coast," objects Colin, "all the places worth going to, anyroad."

"Eastbourne!" exclaims Elsie suddenly.

"Been there."

"Nice, though."

"Can't we go somewhere *different*, for Pete's sake?"

"Well, *where*?" demands Elsie.

Colin appeals to his old mate for support. "You ain't said much, Len. You got any bright ideas?"

"Um…" Len leans forward to pick up his brandy and puts his foot over the ash he's dropped on Elsie's carpet, hoping she hasn't seen. "Well...um...what about Torquay?"

"Been there, mate. Lost your raincoat there, left it on the bloody beach – remember?"

Len prefers not to. "Well, what about Clacton then?"

"Clacton's not on the south coast," says Nora, who knows her geography better than that.

"Yes, it is."

"No, it's not!"

"I'll get the map," says Colin, leaping up again to go to his 'G-Plan' bookshelf.

"Leave it," snaps Elsie. "Don't want to go there anyway."

He subsides into his chair again with a sigh.

"Bognor's on the south coast," resumes Len. "So is Southsea and Folkstone and Portsmouth and...um...Brighton and...um..."

"Brighton!" cries Nora. "We haven't been to Brighton."

"True." Colin's interest is aroused. "Went once for a day on a coach trip. Interesting. Got them onion domes and that."

"Like to see them," nods Nora. With Colin all for it she feels she's almost home and dry.

"Course," he goes on, "got to be a bit careful there, securitywise. Get the yobos down from London." Being a security man Colin knows all about that.

"Trouble is, hotels in Brighton will be expensive," continues Nora. "Probably have to stay in a guest house."

"Plenty of them in Brighton, I should think."

"Course, it'd be cheaper to stay just outside Brighton." She feigns sudden dramatic inspiration. "Now why didn't I think of that before?"

"What?"

"I heard of a nice little place not far from Brighton, just the other day. Now who told me about that?"

"What place?" asks Elsie suspiciously.

"Forgotten for the minute. I know it's a nice little resort – quiet and peaceful – with a small beach and little harbour. Nice little private hotel there, too."

"Who told you that?" Elsie's wondering how it is she hasn't heard about it.

"Can't remember for the moment." She doesn't want to

reveal her source in case it puts Elsie off. "It'll come to me later, don't worry."

"And it's really close to Brighton?" asks Colin.

"Just a short bus ride away."

"I'll get the map."

"Leave it," snaps Elsie again.

"Anyhow," resumes Nora, "seems to me it's the ideal place. What d'you say I find out more about it and let you know?"

"Suits me," says Colin.

"I'm easy," says Len. He usually is.

"No harm in finding out more, I suppose," agrees Elsie. "But don't go booking nothing without telling us."

"Course not!"

"Right then! Meeting adjourned pending further information." Colin reaches for the brandy bottle. "Reckon that calls for another drink."

"No it don't," says Elsie, "you've had enough. You put on that video you said you've got for us."

"Oh! Ah!" He'd forgotten all about the video.

"What is it?" asks Nora.

"You'll see."

There is a general shift round. Nora goes to the bathroom followed by Len. Colin fiddles with the leads and plugs. The furniture is rearranged so everyone can see the telly screen. Elsie takes out the tray of dirty crocks and returns with a box of figs and a plate of nuts, draws the curtains across and puts on a table lamp. Len loosens his belt and swaps places with Nora who has become overheated from sitting close to the fire. When they are settled Colin switches on the video and the once familiar music of *The Thorn Birds* issues forth.

"Oooh lovely!" exclaims Nora. "I love the man who plays a priest, and he's got such an angelic face."

They settle back to watch. The chocolate box is handed round. Nuts crack. Fig seeds creep behind dentures. Eyes droop. Before long all four are asleep.

*****

"I don't think them videos are worth the money," says Nora

as she scrambles into bed that night. "I wouldn't waste money on one, myself. You've not only got to buy the machine, you've got to buy or hire the films as well. No point to that when you've already seen 'em on the telly umpteen times, anyway."

"Um," says Len as he ties his pyjama cord over his beer belly. He has to tie it pretty tight otherwise the bottoms are liable to end up around his feet without warning.

"Anyway," Nora continues as she adjusts her hair net and reminds herself she has a hair appointment on Tuesday morning, "it wouldn't surprise me if Colin only bought it so he could watch video nasties when Elsie isn't about. And I reckon that's why he's so keen to get on this Internet thing."

"Shouldn't think so."

"Don't know so much. Didn't you see him looking up my legs this afternoon? He's a bit that way you know. All the girls at work say so. It's his age. What is he – fifty-two, three? Must be the male menopause. Anyhow, don't let him talk you into watching any of them nasties."

Len's reply is lost in the grunts he makes as he bends down to pull off his socks, but is to the effect that he's not in the least bit interested in that sort of thing. Which is true. Now he is hitting sixty it's far too much like hard work. On the odd occasions when Nora happens to feel the urge he does his best to oblige, but only in the interests of marital harmony. Even as a young man Len was never an ardent lover. He didn't marry for sex, or love, or even money, but for a housekeeper to tend his everyday needs. If truth be told, he doesn't care that much for women. He's a man's man, his main pleasure being gossiping to his cronies at his local, The Mason and Magpie.

"Don't forget the curtains," Nora reminds him just as he heaves himself into bed. She likes a little fresh air at nights. She burps involuntarily. "I wish Elsie wouldn't make her cakes so rich, it gives me terrible wind. I think I'd better have some Bisodol."

Len needs no prompting. He leaves his bed and pads down to the kitchen to collect the remedy, his feet freezing in the process.

"Not a bad Christmas on the whole," observes Nora when he returns. "Bit of a come down with the Stilwells today after yesterday, but at least we've got the holiday settled. And I enjoyed the singsong at the end. Elsie's very good on the organ. Got a natural talent for it."

"Trouble is, she don't know when to stop," grunts Len.

"I wish you hadn't looked so bored, though. You ought to sing up, you know. You'd enjoy it. Good for you."

"No good at singing." He hates it, in fact.

"Well, I enjoy it. But it's a good job Boris came home when he did, or we'd still have been singing away there now."

Boris is Colin's twenty-year-old son by a previous marriage.

"I'm surprised at Colin letting him go roaring off on that motorbike of his, coming home at all hours, disturbing the neighbours. On Boxing Day too!"

"You ready?" Len is anxious to get to sleep.

Nora signals that she is by placing the tumbler on her bedside table. Len reaches up and presses the light switch dangling over the bed.

"You'd have thought being Boxing Day Boris could have stayed in just for once," she resumes in the darkness. "Mark you, I'm not sorry he didn't. He's such a great lump of a chap, lolling about all over the place. But it's surprising Colin hasn't better control over him, having been a policeman and that."

"Um." Sleep is already descending on Len.

Nora snuggles down, and deposits her cold feet on Len's, but finding them colder than her own, changes her mind. "I did enjoy myself at the Blooms' yesterday. That's a lovely house they've got. En-suite bathrooms, I ask you! We're not going to be able to afford things like that when we move up there. We'll have to make do with a nice two-bedroomed bungalow. Still, it'll be a good deal better than this place, don't you agree?"

No answer from Len. He's already zizzing.

Nora's not bothered. She's content just to lie there thinking about her fabulous Christmas Day spent with the Blooms.

Oliver and Marsha Bloom are the parents of Georgina, a nurse, who Len and Nora's twenty-three-year-old son Gavin succeeded in taking to the altar, or rather the registry office, as recently as the beginning of last November, an unprecedented event which gave Nora an enormous boost. And then, when the Blooms invited herself and Len, along with the newly-weds, to join them at their magnificent house in Webbley Park for Christmas Day, she was sent into an orbit of ecstasy from which she hasn't yet completely descended.

Everything had been so perfectly done, she recalls euphorically, doilies under the coffee cups, that kind of thing, and such nice people. They'd gone out of their way to make them feel at home.

"*Do* call me Marsha," Mrs Bloom had said in her deep cultured voice as she gently relieved Nora of her coat upon arrival. Nora hadn't found it easy to use first names on such slender acquaintance, but by the end of the evening she was calling her Marsha on the slightest pretext.

And Oliver Bloom, who is a very highly paid executive with some international chain of hotels, took Len to his bosom like a long lost friend and showed him his wine cellar. Luckily Len, although a beer man by habit, also knows a bit about wines from occasionally serving behind the bar at the Sports and Social Club, so he was able to display some knowledge of the subject, and acquitted himself with merit.

As for Gavin, thinks Nora, as she floats on her soothing sea of happy recollection, he behaved with a charm and easy confidence as if to the manor born. She couldn't be more proud of him if he'd been awarded the VC. He is a very bright lad, and she is firmly convinced he takes after herself rather than Len. He worked hard at school, passing his exams with flying colours, and then got himself accepted for a job with a bank in the face of fierce competition.

And now, to cap it all, he has married Georgina Bloom!

At first Nora had been alarmed. The night he came home and announced his intentions he also said they wanted to get married as quickly and quietly as possible. She immediately thought he must have put Georgina in the family way, as she always calls it, but Gavin quickly put her at her ease by explaining, as if to a five-year-old, that they had been exceptionally fortunate in being offered a flat by a nursing colleague of Georgina's who'd taken a job in America and was leaving immediately. This meant they would have to start paying rent right away if they were to take the flat over. They saw no point, Gavin informed his parents, in paying rent on it for six months or so during a long engagement and not living in it, so they had decided to get married as soon as possible and take up residence immediately afterwards.

The suddenness of it all was a shock for Nora, but it gave her untold consolation when it occurred to her the young couple were set on getting married rather than just living together as so many couples preferred doing these days. Of course, she muses, a girl of Georgina's breeding would never dream of doing such a thing. She has been too well brought up. The Blooms are people of high moral principles, and regular churchgoers.

Yes, Nora reflects happily as she lies wakefully in bed staring at the lampshade above her head bathed in the orange glow of the sodium lamp outside the window, things couldn't have worked out better. It is her duty now, for Gavin's sake, to move off this dreary estate and up to Webbley Park just as soon as she can. She is well aware that this is an ambition she would never have achieved had her old dad not died recently and left his old terraced house down on the London road to herself and her brother, Cyril, the proceeds of its sale to be divided equally between them. It probably won't amount to much, she realises, but it will make all the difference.

Nora burps again. The Bisodol has done its work. She turns and settles down to sleep. The next thing she has to do, she thinks as slumber descends, is to sort out Dad's house and put it on the market...

*****

In the Stilwell household lights still blaze.

Colin lies in bed fuming. He's just had a row with his son Boris over drinking and driving. In his eight-by-ten bedroom Boris is flaked out on the bed, still in his motorbike clobber. The light is still on, and so is Radio One.

Elsie is soaking away her Christmas cares in the bath, idly shifting about icebergs of foam on the surface of the water with her finger. In her mind she is going over yet again the phone call she made on Christmas Eve to her two sons in Australia. It was that woman who'd answered the phone, Maisie or whatever her name was, the woman with whom Elsie's former husband, Cliff, had replaced her. Bloody bitch. Still, she had allowed her to speak to Andy and Martin. They seemed to be happy enough. Elsie finds it hard to believe Andy will be eighteen in June and Martin sixteen next November. It doesn't seem ten years since they were all celebrating Christmas together in the heat of the sun. If only they still were!

As she heaves herself out of the water Elsie wonders if Colin is expecting what he calls his 'innings' tonight. Normally Friday night is sex night, but being Christmas and that, he may not think it fitting. She hopes so. Her stomach is grinding and she keeps farting. She blames the salmon and cucumber sandwiches she made for Nora and Len before they left, either that or the Change of Life. She is tortured by that in all sorts of ways, doesn't know what she's up to sometimes.

"If he does it again I'll arrest the bugger myself," growls Colin as Elsie comes into the bedroom.

"Who? Boris?" asks Elsie absently.

"No, the Vicar." He can be sarky when he feels like it.

"You can't arrest your own son."

"Oh yes I can! He's got to learn. I'm no longer a copper, I know, but I still believe in respecting the law."

Elsie has deliberately put on her nightdress before coming into the bedroom, but as she climbs into bed her hopes fade as she sees Colin is naked. Keep him talking, she thinks. "What Boris needs," she says, "is a job."

"Don't I know it! Trouble is, he can never keep one. Look at the trouble I went to get him that job down at the Plant. And what happened? Had the place in an uproar within a week and got himself fired. I dunno. You do your best to bring your kids up right and proper and that's how they repay you."

"It's a shame," says Elsie.

Colin suddenly jerks himself upright and bangs on the wall behind the bed. "Turn that bleedin' thing off!" he bawls.

There is no response, so he leaps out of bed and rushes naked out of the room.

"You'll catch your death," warns Elsie.

The radio stops. Colin returns, flings himself back on the bed. "He's flaked out. Light full on. Little sod. I dunno."

"Try not to upset yourself," says Elsie.

Colin lies prone in the bed, staring at the ceiling. Elsie feels sorry for him. She feels sorry for Boris as well, having no job, being on the Social Security and all. But then, Elsie often feels sorry for everyone, including herself. She is inclined to be too soft-hearted at times, she knows that only too well; it was being soft-hearted that got her into trouble in Australia.

"I'd make him join the Force if I thought they'd have him, or the Army," Colin laughs bitterly. "My God, he wouldn't last five minutes! I'd have to buy him out."

"Pity he can't find a nice girl. Settle down and that."

"What – and have *two* of 'em here under our feet? And that's another thing, Els', he's not interested in girls. All he thinks about is bikes, bikes, bikes – and booze. It's not natural. I hope to God he's not gay, that's all. I couldn't stand that. He's a real worry, I can tell you."

"Never mind," says Elsie. Overwhelmed by compassion she turns towards him and puts her hand on his bare stomach, which is getting a bit puddingy these days. It'll be as bad as Len's if he doesn't watch it. "Well, there's one thing," she continues, wanting to get his mind off Boris, "it looks as if we've got the holiday sorted. You'll enjoy seeing Brighton again."

"Not if Nora's going to pennypinch all the time. What's the matter with the bloody woman, getting all stuck up just because Gavin's married that nurse? Suddenly, we're not good enough for her."

"She'll get over it," soothes Elsie.

"She'd better for her own sake. She's crazy to think she can afford to move up Webbley Park. Doesn't she realise the cost of places up there?"

"Well, she reckons now her dad's died she can sell his house and add the money to what she gets for hers."

"That dump on the London Road? She'll be lucky if she gets enough from that to buy a Mars bar."

"That's *her* problem," says Elsie with an element of relish. Truth be told, she's as much pissed off with Nora's 'Big Move' as Colin.

"It's crazy. I mean, it won't be long before they have to retire and neither of them earns all that much down at the Plant. How does she think they're going to live up there with the high rates and that?"

Colin rants on. Elsie wants to get to sleep. Only way to stop him is to get on with the lovemaking, so she takes to pulling gently at his short and curlies. But Colin isn't moved. He just lies there, like a beached whale.

"Don't you want it tonight?" she murmurs.

"Eh? Oh, I dunno. Might as well I suppose."

Thanks a lot! thinks Elsie.

He turns towards her, pulls up her nightie. She's glad she has it on. She likes something between her skin and his sweaty body. Despite his eye for the girls Colin's lovemaking is pedestrian at the best of times, and clearly tonight isn't likely to be a sparkling exception.

Never mind. Close your eyes and think of England, Elsie tells herself. Or better still, of Australia.

No one could equal Cliff in bed. Torrid, he was. Colin may be the better looking, with his fair hair, blue eyes and John Wayne figure, but Cliff knew how to arouse a woman, always coming up with a fresh, tantalisingly erotic approach that titillated Elsie into an intolerable frenzy. She still mourns Cliff, still loves him passionately, if she is honest, and hates that bitch whom he brought into her home, taking over her own boys and all. It was all her own fault, Elsie knows, having felt sorry for Brig, that chef from Wagga Wagga, when he came to work in Sydney at the same restaurant as herself. He'd pitched her some yarn about how suicidal he'd felt after his wife's tragic death. Elsie was the only person he'd met, he told her, who understood how he was feeling, and to whom he could really let his hair down. That wasn't all he'd let down, she thinks grimly. Soft-hearted Elsie, that's me.

Suddenly Colin rolls off her and on to his back, exhausted, embarrassed, worried. He's unable to rise to the occasion.

"Sorry Els', sorry Els'. Dunno what's wrong. Never happened before. Reckon I must be getting past it."

"Never mind." She soothes his brow. "It's them cucumber sandwiches I 'spect."

Chapter 2

Nora is at the hairdresser's having a colour rinse and set in readiness for the 'Big Do' at the Regal Chemicals Sports and Social Club on New Year's Eve, which is the day after next.

She is very fussy about her hair, especially after having observed Marsha Bloom's luxuriant coiffures, so she doesn't mind spending a little money on it. She has been hoping the rinse will bring back the deep chestnut colour of her youth, but it has turned out to be coppery. She isn't altogether displeased. At least the grey has disappeared and she feels she looks years younger.

Her hairdresser, Delphine, owner of the establishment, is a tall willowy lady with a swan-like neck, which enables her to bend right over her clients' heads and inspect their scalps, as if for nits, which Nora finds disquieting. But Delphine is good at her job. She has deft fingers that go like bobbins and work miracles.

Inevitably Delphine asks, "Did you have a good Christmas, Mrs Scally?"

"Oooh, lovely!" Nora's cue to tell her all about the wonders of her Christmas Day with the Blooms, and how she had a quiet but pleasant Boxing Day with the Stilwells. Delphine knows Elsie, of course. At least, she recalls her rather greasy hair and split ends.

"By the way," says Nora once the subject of Christmas has been exhausted, "didn't you tell me you went to Brighton this year for your holiday?"

"Not Brighton," answers Delphine. "Benthaven."

"It's near Brighton though?"

"Just a few miles further along the coast."

"What's it like there?"

"Oh, *very* nice. Pleasant, peaceful…you know."

"You stayed in a guest house, didn't you tell me?"

"That's right. Well, a private hotel really."

"Nice was it? Comfortable and that?"

"Oh, *yes!*" Delphine warms to the conversation. "Very homely. And such nice people, a Scottish couple, ever so friendly, you know. And the hotel is as clean as a new pin. I said to Dick, you could eat off the floors."

Nora isn't contemplating doing that. "What about the food?" she asks.

"Oh, *fabulous*! Not a lot of fancy stuff, mind, just plain wholesome home cooking. I said to Dick, you get much better value for your money in a guest house than in these big hotels, and much more friendly attention, you know."

Delphine swishes a mirror behind Nora's head with the speed of a conjuror.

"Very nice," nods Nora, without really seeing.

"Pertwee, that's right. That's the name of the people. You'd like them. I've got their number in my address book, if you'd like it?"

While Nora fumbles in her bag for her purse, Delphine delves into her bag for her address book. "Yes, that's it – Pertwee. Shall I write it down for you?"

"Is it licensed?" asks Nora as she watches Delphine's cash register swallow up her hard-earned cash.

Delphine is apologetic. "I'm afraid not. But you're welcome to take in your own if you want to. We didn't bother. There's ever such a nice little pub down by the harbour, oldy-worldy, you know. We used to go down there after dinner."

"Is it easy to get to Brighton from there?"

"Oh, *yes*. Just along the coast road. Plenty of buses."

Just the job, thinks Nora as she pads her way home. Nice quiet place, good food, not far from Brighton. Pity about it not being licensed. Must try not to mention that to Len and Colin or they'll kick up a fuss and not go.

Being nearly lunchtime Nora decides to splash out for once and call in at Friddle's for some fish and chips. But when she gets home Len hasn't yet returned from The Mason and Magpie, where he has gone to replace any weight he may have lost that morning due to his exertions while cleaning and polishing his Ford Escort.

For once Nora isn't too annoyed. No time like the present,

she thinks. She'll seize this opportunity to take the first step towards that other important matter she has to deal with – the sale of her dad's old house.

She pops the fish and chips into the oven to keep warm and lifts the phone.

*****

Although Regal Chemicals plc, Fertiliser Division, is on Christmas Shutdown until the New Year for routine maintenance work to be carried out, Colin Stilwell, as a security officer there, has to go in. At the moment he is on afternoons, from two to ten, which means this morning he can join Len for a quick one before lunch at The Mason and Magpie.

Colin has more or less recovered from the shock of his failure to perform on Boxing Night. He hasn't yet ventured to try again, feeling perhaps a little rest from it would do no harm. Perhaps until next Friday, or the Friday after that, when his routine has returned to normal.

His son's loutish behaviour is his more immediate concern, but he thinks he may have cracked that problem. He has spent the morning in Boris's bedroom having a man-to-man talk with him while Elsie was busy vacuuming the living room carpet, trying to remove the trodden in cigar ash.

"You're twenty," Colin told him emphatically, as if Boris was unaware of the fact. "You've got to pull yourself together, act your age, not go haring off with a lot of teenage yobs, drinking and driving and God knows what-all else."

Boris, who is at least as tall as his father and a good three stone heavier, sat on his bed, his head on his chest, his eyes fixed on his enormous thighs. "Got to do something," he growled. "Entitled to drink like everybody else."

"Course you can drink. Course you can! A quiet drink never harmed anyone. But you can't drink and *drive*! What you need is to find yourself a nice little pub where you can have a quiet drink with your mates, near enough so you can *walk* home after."

"Only The Magpie round here," grunted Boris.

"Well, what's wrong with that? It's a pub, ain't it? Look, tell you what, you come down there with me this morning, see what you think. Can't do no harm. It's on me."

Boris wished his dad would piss off and leave him alone. He wanted to watch Sky Sports. But he knew he'd only keep on and on if he didn't go. Best to agree. If he played along for a bit his dad would soon forget all about it again.

Len's jaw drops when he sees Colin come into the pub with Boris in tow. Boris disconcerts Len at the best of times, and he certainly doesn't want to have to introduce him to his drinking cronies. The Mason and Magpie may be close to the Eastland Estate but it caters for a higher-class clientele, and charges accordingly. Many of the important people in the town foregather there and often hold serious discussions over their pints. Len is holding forth to several such people when he spots Colin and Boris comes in. Hastily he excuses himself and hustles them both to a table as far away from his cronies as possible.

"Boris thought he'd join us for once," Colin explains. "See what the beer's like here. Same again, Len?"

Colin buys the round. Boris perches himself on a round stool which disappears under his enormous behind. When Colin returns with the drinks, Len takes a draught from his tankard then loses no time in acquainting Colin with some disquieting news he has just picked up. "This place has been sold," he says. "New people coming in the New Year."

"Go on!" exclaims Colin.

Len goes into the whys and wherefores. He's annoyed with the present landlord for having kept it under his hat until the last minute. "Hope they don't start tarting the place up," he says, "trying to cash in on the estate."

"Doubt it, mate. They'd have to bring their prices down to do that. I'd say this place is a gold mine as it is."

"True," Len nods sagely.

"Pity old Jonesey is going, though. Best run pub in the town, this. Sort of place I wouldn't mind running when I retire."

Colin has mentioned this ambition to Len before. Len, who thinks he knows all there is to be known about pubs, has doubts about Colin's capacity in this direction. "Not easy running a pub these days," he says.

"Dunno so much. Pub's getting very popular. People not staying in so much watching telly and that."

"True," Len says again, "but that's cos of the food, not the drink. You've got to have good food in pubs. No good without it."

"I know that, mate, I know that." Warming to the subject, Colin shifts a bit closer to Len. "See, what I have in mind is running it as a *family*. I mean, Elsie's been in catering all her life, working in the canteen and that. Not much Els' don't know about catering." He gives his son a sidelong glance. "And what with Boris being out of a job and that, there'd be a job for him, helping out, working behind the bar. Just the job for you, eh Boris?"

"Pigs might fly," mutters Boris.

Len is just speculating as to what Mason and Magpie customers might think of Elsie's canteen catering when the pub door slams open and a callow-looking youth comes in.

Suddenly it is as if a thousand volts passes through Boris. "Hiya, Spikey!" he yells, leaping to his feet.

"Hiya, Borrie! Good to see ya, mate."

"Didn't know you drank with the nobs."

Heads turn. Len buries his head in his tankard. Colin gapes. Without a word to his dad Boris joins his pal and goes off with him to the bar.

Colin turns to Len confidentially. "Been a bit worried about him lately, as a matter of fact. Bike mad, he is. Wouldn't matter only he comes roaring back in the dead of night, drunk as a lord – well, you saw the other night."

Len remembers.

"Had a bit of an up-and-downer with him this morning. Told him straight, he's got to bloody pull himself together. He's twenty for God's sake! That's why I brought him here. If he wants a drink, I told him, he's got to have it in a decent place and be able to walk home afterwards, not drink and drive."

"What he needs is a job," says Len.

"Course it is. Course it is. But if he gets one it don't last more than a week." Colin pauses to wet his whistle. "And I'll tell you another thing," he resumes. "Elsie don't want him left alone in the house while we go on that holiday. She's scared he'll have them yobos in while we're away and duff the place up."

"You left him alone last year. He was all right then, wasn't he?"

"That was before he was in with this lot, before he had that bloody bike. Anyhow, Elsie's not having it this year. She says if the worst comes to the worst he'll have to come on holiday with us."

That gives Len a jerk. Nora won't go a bundle on that.

"I know, mate, I don't want it either."

"Couldn't he go somewhere on holiday by himself?" asks Len.

"That's what I said, but Elsie thinks he'd only get into more trouble, and she's probably right. End up in the bloody nick."

It is at this juncture that Len happens to notice the time. Nora will do her nut! He knocks back the remnants of his pint and rises hastily. "Sorry, Colin, got to go."

*****

The next morning Nora has Len drive her out to see her brother Cyril. This is why she made Len polish the car the previous day. Not that there was much point. By time they have driven down the narrow muddy lanes that lead to Cyril Bupp's market garden, the car is in a worse state than it was before.

But Nora is anxious to make a good impression on Cyril. She has some delicate negotiations to transact with him and wants to be in command of the situation. Although she would never admit it, she is aware that by and large her brother has done better in life than she has. He has a nice detached bungalow which she envies, if not its situation, and he does run his own business, a rather ramshackle one-man affair, it is true, but successful even so, despite Cyril's perpetual protestations of poverty.

Of course, he was lucky. He'd married Glennis Davey, who had brought with her the capital that enabled them to start the business. Nora often thinks marrying Len was the biggest mistake she'd ever made. He is lazy and has no ambition, and his salary as a clerk isn't worth mentioning. But then, it was Hobson's choice. Len was her only suitor to offer marriage.

But this morning she is full of confidence. She has already

worked out in detail her plan of campaign for persuading Cyril to agree to the sale of their dad's old house, so she feels able to apply her mind to the other currently important matter on her mind – the holiday.

She liked the sound of Mr Pertwee when she spoke to him on the telephone the day before. His voice reminded her of dear old Dr Cameron who used to be on the telly years ago. He'd assured her he had vacancies for her party in June at the moment, and promised to pop a brochure in the post for her right away. She hasn't yet mentioned any of this to Len, or anyone else. She wants to study it and check the prices first.

But Len interrupts her thoughts.

"By the way," he begins diffidently, "Colin said yesterday Elsie wants Boris to come with us on holiday." He has been delaying telling Nora but wants to get it off his chest while she is in a good mood.

"Oh, I'm not having that," she replies instantly. "If Elsie insists on him coming *we* shan't be going and that's the end of it."

"She's afraid if he's left alone in the house he'll get into trouble."

"I'm not surprised. Lazy good-for-nothing. Colin hasn't the first clue how to deal with him. I'd soon have him in order if he was mine."

Len can believe that.

"Trouble is he doesn't know what to do with himself," says Nora. "What he needs is a job."

"Trouble is, he can't hold on to it when he's got one."

"Trouble is, he don't want to."

"Um," says Len. "Anyhow, no point us going away if he's coming."

"I'm not having him spoiling our holiday." Nora is adamant. "Don't worry, I'll put a stop to it somehow."

They have arrived at the entrance to Cyril Bupp's market garden. The iron gate is rusty and screeches in agony as Nora opens it for Len to drive in. Autumn leaves still litter the drive. In the yard water butts lean, hose snakes at random, paint peels on the bungalow. The place is far from its normal pristine condition, and Nora wonders if all is well. In one way she is not upset by what she sees. It might even help her plans.

But Cyril emerges looking very much as usual, still wearing that disgusting trilby hat. He is very self-conscious about his bald head and is seldom seen without his hat, even indoors.

"Hello Cyril." Nora brushes her face against his, leaving a fine deposit of face powder on his unshaven face. "How are you?"

"Still lingerin'," replies Cyril. It is his stock answer. He shakes Len's hand limply without a word passing between them.

"Keeping fit then?" asks Nora as they traipse towards the bungalow.

"Getting a touch of the old rheumatics these days. Makes work harder."

Nora grunts sympathetically.

If the exterior isn't quite so tidy as usual, the kitchen is still as reassuringly chaotic. This is because it is the domain of Glennis, whose easy-go-lucky nature, as Nora calls it, seems to thrive amid the clutter around her.

"Come in! Come in!" cries Glennis in her bright Welsh voice. "Don't stand on ceremony."

The heat from the Aga and the lingering effluvium of the breakfast bacon knocks Nora back. At the table sit three of the Bupp's eight grandchildren. This is another irksome point with Nora. She is yet to become a grandmother, but now Gavin is married maybe she won't have to wait much longer.

"You small fry go and play in the shed," Glennis tells the children, when the greetings are over. "Y'grandpa wants to talk to y'Aunty Nora." When the children have gone she flicks the crumbs off the table like a French waiter and invites her visitors to sit down. "I'll just put the kettle on the hob," she adds.

Cyril pulls out his pipe and slowly fills it. "Yup," he says, "every year is getting a bit harder than the last."

"Never mind. You'll be getting the pension next year, then you'll be able to retire."

Cyril shakes his head. "Don't know about that. Can't really afford to retire."

"Get away with you!"

"Pension don't go far these days. Haven't been able to put much by either, what with the upkeep and that. That's why I think it's best if we don't sell Dad's house. Rent it out instead, so it brings in a steady income."

Nora hasn't been expecting the subject to come up this soon. She pulls herself up on her chair to do battle. "Wouldn't be worth it, Cyril. The rent would have to be split between us, don't forget. And the place would have to be done up from top to bottom before you could rent it. Then you can have a lot of trouble with tenants, wanting things done all the time, not paying the rent and that. You could be dead before you begin to make a profit."

"Ar." Cyril lights his pipe thoughtfully, sending billows of smoke into Nora's face.

"Much better to sell the house quick as we can, invest the money and use the interest to live on."

Cyril frowns at the stem of his pipe. "Ar, but I don't like the idea of selling Dad's house, Nora. You and me were born there. Best days of me life, with Mum and you. Don't seem right to sell it."

Sentimental old fool, thinks Nora.

"Sounds like a good idea to me," says Glennis as she washes four dirty mugs under the cold tap, ready for the tea. "Good to have a bit of extra capital behind us. Gain interest, see, for when we retire."

Nora feels encouraged; with Glennis as an ally she's almost home and dry.

But Cyril is still doubtful. "I dunno. I reckon it'd be better to sell this place and retire now. Then with the rent from Dad's house and me pension and that we'd have no worries."

"And nothing to do," adds Nora promptly. "Wouldn't suit you, Cyril, man like you, been active all your life. How long have you been here now?"

"Dunno. Thirty-odd year must be."

"There you are then. Does you credit this place. You belong here, spent best part of your working life on it. Don't want to see some upstarts coming in and ruining the place you've worked so hard to build up, do you?"

"Quite right," says Glennis.

Cyril blinks and frowns at the stem of his pipe.

"This place is part of you, Cyril," continues Nora. "You

should stay here until you're taken."

Cyril pulls at his right ear thoughtfully. "Ar, but I'm not getting any younger. And it ain't the same as it used to be in these parts. Bloody kids keep coming over and playing me up."

"What kids?"

"Kids from up on the farm," explains Glennis. "New people up there, see. Got a whole battalion of kids. Keep coming over stealing the produce."

"Little buggers," mutters Cyril, clenching his sizzling pipe between his teeth. "Keep coming over pinchin' me cabbages and that."

"It's the parents who send 'em over," says Glennis. "If they want a bit of veg or fruit for dinner, see, they send over the kids to get it."

"Got to put a stop to that," says Nora firmly.

"Easier said than done, Nora," moans Cyril. "Can't be everywhere at the same time. If I spot one at the cabbages, then there's another of 'em after the apples. And if I go after him, then there's another raiding the greenhouse for tomatoes."

"You need a security man!" laughs Glennis.

Cyril is not amused. "No laughing matter. It's not only what they pinch, it's the damage they do; costs time and money."

"Bit of a problem," agrees Nora. But little wheels and cogs start whirring busily in Nora's brain, as in a clock about to chime. "You know what I think, Cyril?"

"What's that?"

"I think you should stay here. Cut down on the outside work, cos of your back and that, and concentrate on the greenhouse side. Get another greenhouse and build it up."

"Can't afford no new greenhouse."

"Ah, but you can! If we sell Dad's house you could buy a really good one."

"Always wanted another greenhouse, haven't you, Cyril?" says Glennis as she dumps mugs of grey-green tea in front of her visitors. "You could grow vines then see, or melons. Lots of money to be made with melons."

"Quite right," says Nora, not knowing whether there is or not.

Cyril still tugs at his right ear. "Ar. But it costs a lot to employ people. There's the National Insurance and that."

"No problem, Cyril, cos we know just the bloke you need, don't we, Len?"

"Um," says Len, starting. All this time he has been staring meditatively at the mud splattered on his freshly polished shoes.

"Would you like a piece of my Christmas cake?" asks Glennis.

Nora wouldn't, but accepts. She wants to keep on the right side of Glennis. "I know just the bloke you need," she resumes, determined to keep the pot boiling. "Can't get a job, see. Wouldn't want much. Just needs something to do and a bit of cash to help out his Benefit. No need for Insurance and that."

"I've had blokes like him before," says Cyril. "Pinch more of the produce than them kids."

"This one won't. He's the son of an ex-policeman. Besides, his mum works in a canteen, so she can get any extras she wants buck-shee. And he's a big bloke, Cyril. Scare off them kids for you if anyone can."

If she's got Boris in mind, thinks Len, she must have gone mad.

Cyril changes to pulling his left earlobe and knocks out his pipe in his saucer.

Glennis deposits great slabs of Christmas cake in front of Nora and Len. The marzipan is the colour of mustard. "Seems like a good idea to me," she says. "Only one problem though."

"What's that?" challenges Nora.

"Nobody would want to buy that old house. Could take years to sell."

"Don't think so. Reckon it'll sell in no time; ideal for first-time buyers, youngsters just setting up home and that. Spruce it up a bit, give the front a lick of paint. Len's going to get on with it when the weather improves."

Len's leg jerks involuntarily. First he's heard about it.

"Seems like a good idea to me," says Glennis again when she finally sits down herself. "What d'you think, Cyril?"

Cyril glowers at his pipe and starts refilling it. "Well, have to think about it."

"Don't think too long, cos I want to get it all settled and that before I go on holiday in June."

"We'll ring and let you know," says Glennis.

Nora takes one look at the Christmas cake and decides it's time to go. But she has her trump card to play first. "Anyhow, we'll probably *have* to sell the house whether we like it or not, cos of the wording of the will."

"Eh?" Cyril looks up sharply.

"What it actually says is it's the *proceeds* from the house that's got to be divided between us, so it looks as though we don't have much choice. Got to sell it. Ought to find out if that's legally binding, I suppose."

Len wonders why didn't she tell them that in the first place.

Nora rises abruptly. "Got to go, things to do. By the way," she adds as she adjusts her scarf around her neck, "I'm going to get rid of all the old muck in Dad's house sometime soon. I'll let you know exactly when in case you want to come over and see if there's anything you'd like to keep. In the meantime you think about what I've said and let me know what you want to do soon as you can."

On the drive home Nora silently sucks a peppermint from a tin she keeps in the glove compartment, and unsolicited, pops one in Len's mouth.

"Well," she says eventually, "with any luck, that'll take care of Boris. Stop him having to come with us on holiday."

"Can't see Boris being much use to Cyril," says Len

"Don't know so much. Boris is all right. It's them mates of his that lead him astray. Can't get up to no mischief all on his own out there."

"Doubt if Cyril will be prepared to fork out the money, though."

"He will," says Nora confidently. "Glennis will see that he does."

That's true, thinks Len, and wonders why it is that women are always so quick to say it's men who rule the world.

*****

It is New Year's Eve, the 'Big Night' at the Sports and Social Club run for the benefit of its employees by Regal Chemicals plc, Fertiliser Division.

There is to be a cabaret, with a well-known comedian, a magician and a female vocalist. There will be dancing, raffles, balloons, then at midnight, after a special surprise item and Auld Lang Syne, the Chief Executive will wish all a Happy and Prosperous New Year. Music will be provided by a group calling themselves the Bunsen Burners, four young sparks from the Works Laboratory, and the compère of the proceedings is to be Jolly Johnnie Jackson, as he styles himself, from the Engineers' Department.

The Stilwells and the Scallys arrive early in order to nab their favourite corner table from which they can easily observe all the goings-on. Nora is wearing her second-best dress, her best being reserved for the Blooms. It is light grey, long-sleeved and high at the neck. With it she wears her dark blue beads. In contrast Elsie wears a garish multi-coloured dress, all flounces and frills, and looks like a Spanish dancer. Colin, whose fair hair and blue eyes are shown off to maximum effect by his best grey suit, looks handsome, and is looking forward to dancing with the girls. Len wears his navy blue Club blazer and besports a maroon bow tie. This is because he is helping out behind the bar, something he does on such occasions to earn himself a little pocket money and as many free drinks as he can consume.

"Good evening ladies and gentlemen…and others," booms the amplified voice of Jolly Johnnie Jackson, and the evening is underway.

Secure in Nora's handbag is the brochure duly sent to her with the compliments of Mr Pertwee of the Ocean View Private Hotel, Benthaven. She has carefully scrutinised the brochure and found it highly satisfactory, and looks forward to showing it to Elsie and Colin. She also looks forward to telling Colin about the job she has hopefully lined up for Boris at her brother Cyril's place.

Since Len is behind the bar, Colin has no choice but to buy the first round. While he is away Nora hands the brochure to Elsie for inspection. Best to do it before the place gets too rowdy and Elsie too drunk. It is a classy brochure. On the front is a stylish artist's impression of the facade of the hotel, with photos of the lounge, dining room and a typical bedroom and bathroom inside. On the back it says: 'Alec and Moira Pertwee Welcome

You to Our Comfortable Hotel.'

"Looks all right," concedes Elsie.

"Very well appointed," says Nora. "En-suite bathrooms, TV in the bedrooms and that. Good as any proper hotel, and a lot cheaper."

When Colin returns with the drinks he too inspects the brochure. "It'll do me," he says. He's not fussy about where he stays. His main concern in this holiday is to be near Brighton.

"Are we agreed then?" asks Nora. "Shall I go ahead and book it?"

"Don't forget we've got to make sure we can take the first two weeks of June off, first," Elsie reminds her.

"We must do that soon as we go back," agrees Nora.

Just then the Bunsen Burners start stumping out their music.

"Did Len tell you," shouts Colin to make himself heard, "we might have to take Boris with us?"

All Nora really hears is 'Boris', but that is enough. "I think I've got a job for him," she shouts back.

"A what?"

"A *job!*" She moves her chair closer to Colin, and bawling directly into his ear, acquaints him with her hopes of Boris working for her brother. "Good for him," she ends. "Good exercise, gardening. Get his weight down and that. Give him some responsibility."

She's got a bloody nerve, thinks Colin, taking it on herself to arrange all this. But it's not the time to pick a quarrel, being New Year's Eve and all. "Not sure it's a good idea to let Boris loose in greenhouses, Nora."

"Won't be working in the greenhouses. He'll be out in the open, working the cultivator. Should be good at it, being mechanically minded and that."

Colin hates to admit it, but she could be right.

"And another thing," shouts Nora, "he'd be in charge of security. Cyril's having trouble with the kids from the farm coming over pinchin' the produce. Part of his job would be to keep them out. You could probably give him a few tips on that."

Colin nods. That appeals to him, as Nora very well knows. "I'd have to inspect the premises first."

"No problem. Course, it would only be a part-time job, to

start with anyway. Cyril can't afford to pay him much, but I 'spect Glennis would give him a midday meal and that."

"Problem if it's only a part-time job. He'd lose his Security Benefit, wouldn't he?"

"Shouldn't think so. Wouldn't earn enough." A new thought strikes her. "Come to that, he could be entitled to a grant on some Government Training Scheme or other. Might be worth looking into."

She's got it all worked out, the cunning old cow. But Colin thinks it's worth a try. "What d'you think, Els'?"

"Sounds all right," answers Elsie, more concerned at the moment with dabbing powder on her shiny face.

"I'll put it to him," shouts Colin.

Abruptly, the Bunsen Burners cease their exertions.

"Just one thing," shouts Nora, forgetting to lower her voice. "He wouldn't be able to come on holiday with us if he took the job. June is Cyril's busiest time, but I 'spect Cyril would put him up for that couple of weeks for a small charge."

"Let's hope he takes the job then," says Colin.

The Sport and Social's smart ballroom is becoming crowded now. All the tables are taken. The hubbub grows.

"C'mon folks," booms Jolly Johnnie Jackson. "Let's be having you on the floor – how's that for an invitation you can't resist!"

The Bunsen Burners strike up again. Colin takes Elsie out on the dance floor, leaving Nora on her own. She doesn't mind; Len can't dance anyway. He can just about shuffle round in a slow waltz, and that's it. As he gyrates Elsie around the floor, Colin is keeping a sharp lookout for pretty girls with whom he may dance later. He's stopped worrying about his sexual prowess. He reckons if he's still got an eye for a shapely figure there can't be much the matter with him.

When Elsie and Colin return to the table they find Nora chatting to Elsie's friend Mavis. She is Elsie's bingo companion. They go together down the Trocadero Hall every Wednesday night. Nora never goes to bingo. She thinks it's a mug's game, but Elsie is often lucky, coming home with significant sums, which she blows with impulsive generosity on gifts for friends, including Nora.

Mavis is the supervisor of the army of cleaners, which invades the offices of Regal Chemicals every workday evening. Colin often sees her and stops for a chat when he's on his rounds checking security. Then she wears the standard green overall of her calling, but tonight he scarcely recognises her in a gaudy red dress, with enough jewellery about her person to open a stall in the market. Eye-catching though she is, it is her companion who captures his attention. She is a young woman of twenty odd, whose curvy figure is encased in a black low-cut dress, above which quiver the tops of two creamy breasts. Colin is quite unable to unrivet his eyes from them.

"This is Rachel," says Mavis. "She has just joined my girls."

He can't believe she's just a cleaner. She could be a model with that figure. "Welcome to the mad house," he says, taking her hand and squeezing it. Colin is inclined to make such ineffectual remarks when talking to girls, much to Elsie's aggravation.

Mavis and Rachel are selling raffle tickets in aid of the Save the Children Fund, Mavis doling out the tickets while Rachel takes the money.

Elsie immediately opens her handbag and hands over a fiver. Colin produces another one from his wallet. Nora, who can't allow herself to be seen to give less, parts with another.

"What about Len?" Mavis asks her.

"You'll have to see him," says Nora. "He's behind the bar." She's not going to dish out yet another fiver.

"Won't you ladies join us for a drink?" asks Colin.

"Can't stop," says Mavis. "Got to sell these tickets."

"Join us when you've finished then." Colin gives Rachel what he hopes is a seductive smile.

"We'll see," says Mavis.

The evening moves into full swing. The dance floor becomes crowded. Behind the bar Len is run off his feet. There is an unprecedented demand for the use of the toilet facilities. Then games are played amid shrieks of laughter until the intermission is announced during which the buffet opens and there is a scrimmage to reach the sumptuously laden tables.

A royal drum-roll and crash of cymbals by the Bunsen Burners' drummer heralds the commencement of the cabaret.

"And now folks...it's show time!" proclaims JJJ. "And what a line-up we have for you tonight! No...sorry, gents, no stripper, I'm afraid!"

The comedian, in a loud suit and straw boater, tells all the familiar jokes, eliciting ribald laughter from his audience. The magician conjures up endless lengths of pink ribbon, two live doves, and four rubber ducks from what appears to be an oversized cylinder from the middle of a toilet roll. Even though the doves persist in perching with their backs to the audience, he receives rapturous applause. Then the anorexic-looking female vocalist wails her way through several numbers, holding the microphone so close to her mouth that she seems in danger of breaking a tooth.

Another drum-roll and crash of cymbals brings the cabaret to a triumphant conclusion, and a further pause in the festivities follows to permit the Bunsen Burners to partake of their own refreshments.

Colin goes to the bar for further drinks, hoping that on the way he may bump into Rachel, literally if possible, but is disappointed. She is not to be seen, which is not surprising since she and Mavis are in the Ladies' Powder Room talking to Elsie, who has hurried there in order to perform a repair job on her eye make-up, ruined through laughing herself to tears at the comedian's jokes. Nora stays stolidly seated eating a pork pie, and for the moment on her own. She hasn't moved all evening. She has the reputation of having the most capacious bladder in the Fertiliser Division. Behind the bar Len works frantically and is getting dizzy trying to ensure he presses the right tabs on the newly installed cash register.

"No fiddling now," quips Colin over the bar in his policeman's voice as he waits to be served. "I've got me eye on you."

Everyone who knows them speculates as to what it is that makes the Scallys and the Stilwells such firm and long-lasting friends, but there is general agreement that alcohol has much to do with it. Even Nora can put away her gin and tonics pretty readily, although she normally confines this activity to Friday nights at the Sports and Social, when she and Elsie chat and drink while Len and Colin play snooker. Elsie's tipple is vodka, which she will drink anytime and anywhere. It quickly intoxicates her, causing her to become sentimental and maudling. Tonight is to prove no exception.

The Bunsen Burners strike up again, and the session leading up to midnight gets under way with more dancing. In the absence of Rachel, Colin is soon on the floor again with a young assistant from the Laboratory. Elsie's boss, the Canteen Manager, approaches Elsie on her way back from the powder room and invites her to dance with him.

He is a rotund, smooth-faced, middle-aged man, and although it has never occurred to Elsie before, he now reminds her forcibly of Brig, her erstwhile lover in Australia. But then, in her present state, even the Queen of Sheba is likely to remind her of Brig.

Oh Brig! Brig! She yearns as she dances, eyes fast shut, come and waft me away as you did for that lovely dirty weekend in Wagga Wagga! Remembering that portentous event brings a flood of tears to her eyes, ruining the repair job she's just done to her make-up.

It was after Wagga Wagga that she had returned home to Liverpool, near Sydney, to find Cliff had locked her out, bolted and barred the place against her, prohibited her entry, denied her access to her two lovely sons, had ensconced that *creature* in her place.

"I'm not having no bleedin' whore looking after my kids!" Cliff had yelled at her through the lavatory window.

She'd never been in that house from that day to this, never seen her sons again. It was the tragedy of her life, her 'Great Sorrow', from which she still hasn't, and is never likely, to recover.

The Canteen Manager, observing Elsie's anguish, stops dancing in alarm, staring in amazement as she scurries from the floor – back to the ladies' powder room.

But Elsie is not the only one to have been asked to dance by her boss. It is part of the evening's protocol that managers ask members of their staff to dance. So the Chief Accountant, Jim Broadbent, plucks up the courage to approach Nora. He has been putting it off, but being a man of iron will power, forces himself. Nora graciously accepts, but when she gets to her feet the gin begins to make itself felt. Dancing with Jim Broadbent is not easy for Nora at the best of times, he being so tall and lean and she so short and tubby. Jim is a stiff, rather sour individual who doesn't really care for all this kind of malarkey, and is aggrieved when Nora looks up at him, bright eyed and coy, and giggling uncontrollably.

For Colin, the effect of drinking is to make him more excited, causing him to perform extravagant antics on the dance floor and croon sonorously into his partner's ear during the smooches. In Len's case, drink is having a soporific effect, making it even more difficult for him to know what he's doing with the new cash register.

But now midnight is not far off and it is time for the raffle draw. JJJ booms out the results as he holds out his straw hat for the female vocalist to draw out the lucky numbers with her skinny fingers. Elsie has won third prize – a bottle of port and a plum pudding! But Elsie is still missing. Luckily, Nora has taken charge of all the raffle tickets, so she waddles up to collect the prize on Elsie's behalf.

Colin has now managed to persuade Mavis and Rachel to join them at their corner table, and Mavis, guessing where Elsie is, goes off to the powder room to impart the good news. She finds Elsie still weeping, sitting on a three-legged stool, which is provided for such contingencies, but when Mavis hands her the prize, it provides an instant cure. She insists on Mavis keeping the bottle of port, and after a further makeshift job on her face, returns in festive mood with Mavis to the ballroom, where Colin is busy chatting up Rachel.

Mavis immediately opens the port and pours them all a generous measure. Due the shortage of chairs, Colin has Rachel sit upon his knee. For him, life couldn't be better.

"Happy New Year!" they chant, for neither the first nor the last time this evening.

Another grand drum roll and JJJ announces it is time for the surprise item. The floor is cleared, the lights go down, and in a moment a weird wheezing noise is heard.

"Silence PLEASE!" booms JJJ, to quell the giggles and shuffles.

A spotlight comes up and picks out a stalwart Scotsman in

full regalia, blowing on his bagpipes. In solemn majesty and with measured steps he parades around the perimeter of the dance floor. It is an impressive sight, a deeply moving experience. Everyone is agape with wonderment.

"Old windbags!" cries a lone voice from the darkness.

As midnight approaches the evening crescendos to its 'Grand Climax'. Glasses are recharged. The female vocalist reappears to lead the community singing. Balloons cascade from above. A punch-up develops near the bar, scaring Len out of his wits, forcing Colin to off-load Rachel in order to eject the miscreants from the premises.

At three minutes to midnight, George Bollinger, the Chief Executive, arrives. The bar radio is switched on to relay the sonorous tones of Big Ben as it strikes the midnight hour. Tension mounts. Silence falls.

The hour strikes. Everyone cheers. Auld Lang Syne is sung. The Chief Executive wishes all health and prosperity in the year ahead – and leaves. Streamers stream. Balloons burst. Poppers pop. Pipes play. Hands clap. Feet stamp. Voices chant…

But it is not until after one, when the merrymaking finally peters out and the bar closes, that the Scallys and the Stilwells meander their way home. They all live less than a ten-minute walk away, but tonight it takes them twice that time.

The cold air has revived them slightly, except for Len, who is unrevivable. He drags along half-asleep, supported by Nora, whose own legs are feeling unusually weighty, a condition she attributes to the unaccustomed dancing. Elsie is still in festive mood, humming and crooning snatches of songs performed by the Bunsen Burners during the evening. She hasn't yet realised she has left the plum pudding she won in the raffle in the Ladies' Powder Room beside the three-legged stool. Colin is happily immersed in his own thoughts. He fancies he can still smell Rachel's pungent perfume and feel her warmth on his lap.

"I wonder," says Nora unexpectedly, "if by this time next year we'll be living in our new bungalow up in Webbley Park."

"You won't be able to come to this…this do if you're living up where…where the nobs hang out." Colin is having to be careful how he pronounces his words.

"Why ever not?" asks Nora pertly.

"Cos…cos…Len can't dink and dive."

Elsie hoots with laughter. It echoes down the silent road.

But Nora has that one already worked out. "Oh, yes we can – we can sleep at your place."

Chapter 3

After the joyous celebrations of its birth, the New Year is reluctant to stir into life. In the small Wiltshire town of Brockbury, the light is dim, the traffic sparse, and the shops deserted, apart from those buzzing with the New Year sales.

But the Fertiliser Division of Regal Chemicals plc is back in production, and the Scallys and the Stilwells are at their respective work places. Colin is in the gatehouse, raising and lowering the check-barrier. Elsie is in the canteen kitchen preparing the veg for the lunch-time rush, Len is in the Cashier's Office, feverishly coping with the backlog of payments received during the Christmas shutdown. Nora is in the Accounts Office sifting through the sheaves of invoices that have piled up during the holiday.

But Nora's mind is not entirely on her work. She is extremely anxious to send Mr Pertwee the deposit for their holiday. Their respective bosses know the Scallys and the Stilwells like to take the first two weeks of June off, and usually do, but formal approval has to be obtained first. Nora has already urged the others to obtain confirmation today if possible, but she is having trouble getting hold of the Accounts Manager to have her own dates approved, since he is in conference with the Chief Accountant and has been all the morning, so she has to wait.

Colin has been luckier. The Chief Security Officer just happened to look in at the gatehouse early that morning and Colin was able to pop the question.

"Okay, mate," said the Chief in his off-hand way. "Put it in the book."

Elsie too is lucky; the Canteen Manager, on his morning parade around the kitchen, recalls her quixotic behaviour when dancing with him on New Year's Eve, and in his caring way stops to have a word.

"Everything all right?" he asks benevolently.

Elsie, now all bright-eyed and bushy-tailed, asks him about

the holiday dates.

"Whenever you like," says the Canteen Manager expansively. "A holiday is just what you need. Have a nice time."

Len leaves it to the last minute to approach the Chief Cashier, who immediately calls a meeting to discuss the matter. The computerised holiday chart is consulted, and after protracted discussion, Len's dates are duly approved and entered on the chart.

But it isn't until last thing in the afternoon that Nora is able to pin down the Accounts Manager.

He looks at her superciliously. He can't abide this self-important little woman. As the clerical shop steward she's always bothering him. "Put it in writing," he tells her abruptly. "I'll let you know."

And Nora has to be content with that.

But when the phone rings in the evening shortly after she gets home Nora's flagging spirits are given a boost.

"Hi, Mum," says Gavin.

"Hello, dear. How are you?"

"Fine. Fine."

"And Georgina?"

"She's fine."

"That's good. Settling in nicely in your new flat?"

"Yes, It's great. Still a few things we need, but we're more or less straight. Actually Mum, we were wondering if you and Dad would like to come over on the thirty-first and see it. It's Georgie's birthday."

Nora is thrilled. "We'd love to, dear."

"We thought we'd also make it a sort of house-warming party. Marsha and Oliver are coming too."

She can't get used to Gavin calling his parents-in-law by their Christian names.

"Nothing very elaborate, of course," Gavin continues, "just a bite to eat and a bit of a natter."

"Oooh, lovely! We'll look forward to it, dear."

He's a good lad, she thinks as she puts down the phone. Doesn't forget his mum and dad now he's on the way up.

While she is by the phone Nora decides to ring Cyril. She

has heard nothing from him since her visit. She lifts the phone again.

It is Glennis who answers.

"Is Cyril there?"

"He's in the bath."

"Oh! Has he made up his mind yet about selling Dad's house, do you know?"

"Still can't make up his mind. You know what he is."

Nora sighs. "Well tell him I want to know by the end of the week, cos we're going to the house on Saturday to get rid of all the old muck and rubbish. So if there's anything he wants to keep he'd better come down then and have a look."

"Hold on." Nora hears Glennis pad away. "Cyril! It's Nora…"

Nora waits impatiently. She can hear them shouting to each other in the distance but can't make out what they are saying.

"He's says he'll come over," Glennis reports when she returns to the phone. "He says not to chuck anything away until he's had a chance to see it."

"Tell him to get there early then. We're going to make a day of it, so he'd better bring a hot drink and some sandwiches and that, cos the electric is turned off."

"Hold on."

Before Nora can stop her Glennis clanks down the phone again and is gone.

"He'll be there about ten," says Glennis on her return. "I'll give him a flask of soup and a pasty to bring with him."

"Oh, and tell him to come in his Land Rover, cos there's sure to be a lot of old stuff to take to the tip."

"Hold on…"

"Don't bother now," Nora intervenes hastily, thinking of the phone bill. "There's one other thing. Has he thought any more about what I suggested – taking on this chap I know part-time to help out?"

"Don't know that he has."

"Well, I'm hoping this chap will be there on Saturday, so he can talk to him, see what he thinks."

"I'll tell him."

"See him on Saturday about ten. And tell him I must have a

definite answer about selling Dad's house then. I've got to know where I stand. Try to make him see sense."

Glennis laughs. "There's hopeful!" and she puts down the phone.

Nora feels a bit discouraged, but at least she has fixed up for the clearing of Dad's house on Saturday, and now there's Georgina's birthday party to look forward to. She marks both events on the calendar.

*****

Gradually life settles down to its normal routine for the Scallys and the Stilwells. Len and Colin resume their weekly snooker sessions at the Sports and Social, and decide they'll enter this year's Snooker Doubles Tournament. Elsie and Mavis return to their Wednesday evening visits to Bingo. Len reverts to his nightly sojourns at The Mason and Magpie, while Nora, like the little piggy-wiggy, stays at home, doing her household chores before settling down to watch the soaps on telly.

And on Friday evenings, of course, they all meet up at the Sports and Social for a drink and a chat and a game of cards. By this time Nora has received official confirmation of her holiday dates and has lost no time in writing to Mr Pertwee, booking the holiday and enclosing the deposit.

"It's all fixed up," she tells Elsie and Colin at the Sports and Social. "All we got to do now is to sit back and wait until it's time to go."

"I hope this place is all you say it is," Elsie says dryly.

Nora bridles. "Well, you saw the brochure. Nothing wrong with it as I can see."

"Is it licensed?" asks Colin suddenly.

"'Spect so," says Nora smoothly. "Most places are these days."

Not anxious to dwell on that subject Nora proceeds to tell Elsie all about Gavin's invitation to Georgina's birthday party. "Can't wait to see the flat now they've got it all fixed up," she says. "They've spent a lot of money on it. Did it instead of spending it on a honeymoon, which I thought was *very* sensible of them."

Nora is always boring the pants off Elsie with tales of her wonderful Gavin, but tonight Elsie is able to make a bit of a comeback. "Had a letter from Andy yesterday. He's got a new job – with a butcher in Liverpool."

"Oh yes?" says Nora.

"Liverpool?" queries Len, on the ball for once. "I thought he was in Australia."

"Liverpool in Australia, you mutt," laughs Colin. "It's part of Sydney."

"Oh! Right!"

"Very good prospects Andy says," resumes Elsie. "Be a manager one day, I shouldn't wonder." And then she adds, "It don't seem possible that he'll be eighteen on the fourth of June. Shall have to be sure and phone him that day."

"We'll be on holiday then," Nora reminds her.

"Still phone him, can't I, from the hotel?"

"Course you can. No problem." Nora drinks up and gives Len a poke in the leg. "Come on, time we went. Got to make an early start in the morning on Dad's house. You coming to give a hand, Colin?"

"Might as well." He doesn't mind helping out on that sort of job. He reckons it'll give him a bit of exercise in the winter months when he can't get in the garden. Not only that, it'll get him out of the house while Elsie is frenetically running up costumes for the Brockbury Pantomime Society's production of Cinderella, which is due to open next week.

"See you about ten, then." Nora pauses and pretends to have a sudden thought. "Cyril is also coming over to lend a hand. I don't suppose Boris might be interested in coming too?"

"I don't suppose so, either," says Colin, grinning.

"Just thought it would be a chance for him to meet Cyril, see how they get on and that."

"Good idea," cuts in Elsie. "Get him from under my bloody feet."

"Well, I'll see how he feels," says Colin. "You never know, miracles do happen."

"Cyril's bringing his Land Rover to take all the old rubbish and that to the tip. Boris could give him a hand."

She's got it all worked out, Colin thinks, the crafty old so-and-so.

Chapter 4

The old terraced house down on the London Road where Nora's dad lived is the middle one of a row, the front doors of which open directly on to the pavement. These days most of the houses are brightly if gaudily painted, many with double-glazing, but the front door to Dad's house still retains what is left of its original dung-coloured paint, as do the windows and the rusty guttering above. Only the curtains look clean and trim, thanks to Nora who is fussy about such things.

Len's Escort pulls up outside promptly at nine. Both of them have come prepared for work. Nora is in a baggy blue romper suit and carries a holdall containing their refreshments for the day. Len is in his overalls with a duffle coat over them, and hopes none of his cronies from The Mason and Magpie are anywhere about to see him.

The house smells stale and damp when they go in.

"Disgusting old place," she says, sniffing. Even so, she feels a tug of nostalgia. The house contains many childhood memories, many of them happy. But the future tugs harder, in particular the prospect of Webbley Park.

"Let's start in the living room," she says, "go through all his old papers and that before the others arrive."

She knows her dad kept all his important papers in the left-hand drawer of the sideboard, amid a galaxy of other things. She tips the whole lot out on the table and starts sifting through them.

"Cold in here," complains Len, flapping his arms.

"Can't be helped. Gas and that's all off. You get on and sort out all the china in the sideboard. That'll help to warm you up."

He peers into the dim interior of the sideboard. "Where shall I put it all?"

"Put it on top of the sideboard for the minute. I'll look through it, see if there's anything worth keeping. And then go and get them dustbin bags we brought for putting the rubbish in."

With his woolly gloves still on, Len sets about his tasks

while Nora sifts through the clutter she's taken from the drawer. There is an abundance of old bills which, she is relieved to see, are all receipted. There are several old letters from people she's never heard of, a cancelled Post Office Savings book, a shoal of sepia photographs, Christmas and birthday cards, a half-consumed tube of Polo's, three toffees, two candle stubs and a box of matches, three expired insurance policies together with insurance books, a pen knife, a kitchen knife, a water pistol and a yo-yo.

And – a large buff envelope.

Nora pulls out the contents of the envelope. To her amazement, it contains three large old-style five-pound notes, which she hastily transfers to her handbag.

Earlier than expected Cyril arrives, his trilby hat firmly on his head, his pipe wavering even more between his teeth.

"Smells of mice in here," he says.

"You'd better look through this lot," she tells him.

Cyril pokes through the clutter on the table, picks out the photographs, studies them closely.

"That's Mum when she was young," says Nora, pointing.

"Well I dunno! Dear old Mum, God bless her!"

"And that's one of all of us on a day's outing at Weston. Remember riding on them donkeys?"

"Well, well, takes y'back, don't it?" Cyril's pipe wavers more than ever.

By the time they've looked through the rest of the photos Cyril has to wipe away tears from his eyes with the sleeve of his khaki work coat. Then something else takes his eye.

"Well I never! Me old water pistol! And me yo-yo! Well, well!" He dabs the yo-yo up and down.

"Well, this won't get the work done," says Nora briskly. "You go and have a good scout round the house and see if there's anything you want to hang on to. If there is, bring it in here so it won't get chucked out."

Still shaking his head Cyril wanders off, stuffing the photos, water pistol and yo-yo into his work coat pocket.

There is an almighty crash when half a dozen dinner plates slide through Len's gloved fingers. Nora is furious.

"Is there nothing you can do without making a muck of it?"

she scolds. "Get a dustpan and brush and clear it up."

Colin walks in just as Len is on his knees brushing up the pieces. "Really getting down to it now then mate?" he quips.

Nora is disappointed to see Colin is alone. "Boris not coming?" she asks.

"Still in bed. Says he might pop along later on his bike."

Some hopes, thinks Nora.

"Where do we start then?" Colin asks.

She takes him upstairs. One reason she wanted Boris to come was to help his dad lug all the heavy furniture down the stairs. Now Colin and poor old Cyril will have to do it between them. Len she knows would be more of a hindrance than a help.

Nora takes Colin into the back bedroom. It contains an iron bedstead, a rickety wardrobe and an ancient marble-topped washstand. Nora is appalled to think she slept in that room as a kid for so many years. Colin casts a critical eye over the room.

"I'll tell you one thing, Nora, I wouldn't issue this place with a fire certificate."

"Why ever not?"

"Just look at that wiring!" He points to the frayed flex from which a broken lampshade dangles. "Fire hazard if ever I saw one. Very nasty, electrical fires. Class E, if I remember rightly," he adds, struggling to recall his old security manual, "but also included in A, B, C and D as well."

Nora is impressed by this unexpected display of knowledge. She did well to have Colin come along. He knows all about that kind of thing. She must get him to repeat it to Cyril.

"And none of the windows fit or fasten," he goes on as they tramp from room to room. "High security risk these days. Must have windows that fasten."

In the front bedroom they catch up with Cyril, who is tugging at his ear as he stares at the heavy bedroom suite. Nora introduces them.

"How y'doing, mate?" asks Colin.

"Still lingerin'," replies Cyril.

Nora wants to get on. "Found anything you want to keep?" she asks him.

"Nice bedroom suite, that. Good solid oak."

"Never get it in your bungalow. You can't move for

furniture as it is."

Cyril looks sorrowful. "Get a good price for it, though."

Colin surveys the suite, pulls out the wardrobe and inspects the back. "Got the woodworm," he pronounces. "Won't get much for that."

"Can be treated," mutters Cyril.

Colin shakes his head. "Still won't get much for it. Best thing to do is get some second-hand dealer; see what he's prepared to give you. Same for the other stuff that's not too bad, which isn't much from what I've seen. Let's get all the better things together and put them in the back room downstairs and cart the rest off to the tip."

"Like to keep that," says Cyril, pointing to a decrepit commode, which Dad had used during his illness, and probably his dad before him.

Nora wouldn't touch it with a barge pole, never mind sit on it. "You're welcome. Take it down with the rest of the stuff."

"I'll give a hand," says Colin, stripping off his jumper.

Gradually work gets under way. Colin and Cyril manhandle the furniture, while downstairs Len, between fits of blowing on his hands, empties all the cupboards and drawers, arraying the contents for Nora to inspect.

Then he is detailed to light a fire in the front room with firewood and lumps of coal discovered by the outside toilet. "We can burn some of the rubbish," Nora says, "and have a bit of warmth to have our lunch by at the same time."

Len has a spot of trouble lighting the fire. The firewood is damp, so he uses a copy of the *News Chronicle*, which has been lining a kitchen drawer for the last half century, to draw the fire. He succeeds brilliantly in setting light to the newspaper but not the fire, causing a few moments of panic.

It is Cyril who comes to his rescue. He's had vast experience in dealing with recalcitrant fires, and he eventually manages to get it going, if somewhat sluggishly.

It is midday when Boris roars up on his motorbike. He lumbers in still wearing his helmet, and carrying a knapsack containing several tins of Heineken, two Cornish pasties and a copy of the *Sporting Life*. Nora is delighted to see him and loses no time in introducing him to Cyril. They eye each other suspiciously.

"Just in time to help us heave that wardrobe down the stairs," Colin tells his son.

While Cyril, Colin and Boris negotiate the wardrobe down the stairs, Nora wanders down the garden to inspect the tumbledown old shed at the bottom. But she can scarcely get inside it for an old sidecar, lying lopsided on its wheel. There is no sign of the motorbike to which it was once attached. Nora views it with dismay. She had no idea her dad still had it. It is another relic from her childhood. She has spent many holidays travelling in that sidecar. Whatever can I do with it? she wonders, and decides to consult Colin.

Boris pricks up his ears when he hears Nora telling his dad about the sidecar, and wants to go to the shed with them to look at it.

"Best thing if we chop it up and take it to the tip," advises Colin.

"Wouldn't mind having that," grunts Boris.

"We're not having that bloody thing cluttering up our place!" he cries.

"Wouldn't clutter up the place," mutters Boris. "Just do it up, see, and attach it to me bike. Could be useful." He's got some vague notion at the back of his mind about starting a window-cleaning business.

"You're welcome to it," says Nora.

Colin sighs. Keep him out of trouble for a bit, he thinks. Won't be able to belt along so fast with that thing attached to his bike. "Okay," he says. "But God help you if you just leave it lying around."

When all the furniture that Cyril wants to hang on to has been shifted downstairs into the back room and the first load of rubbish deposited into Cyril's Land Rover, Nora bangs on an old tin tray to summon her workers for lunch break. She is in her element and feels like a foreman.

They foregather before the fire in the front room. All except Boris, that is, who prefers to sit on the stairs with his cans of beer and *Sporting Life*. Len and Nora sit side by side on the sofa, Colin in the threadbare armchair, Cyril on his recently acquired commode.

"That's a nice old clock you've got there," says Colin, indicating a large timepiece standing on the mantelpiece. It is a gross black marble affair with pillars and topped by a fiery warrior on horseback. "That's an antique, that is. Could be worth something."

"Don't work," says Nora.

"Probably just needs cleaning. Reckon I could probably get it going for you." Colin has fancied himself as an expert on clocks ever since, more by luck than expertise, he managed to mend a cuckoo clock for his cousin.

"You can have it if you'd like it," says Nora in an unprecedented fit of generosity.

Colin can't believe his ears. "You mean – to keep?"

"Course. That's unless Cyril wants it."

Cyril shakes his head dolefully. "Ugly old thing."

"That's great! Thanks a lot."

Nora senses the time has come to take the bull by the horns. "So what have you decided, Cyril – do you want to keep the house or sell it?"

Cyril stares dismally at the pasty clutched between his hands. "Well...still reckon it's best to do it up and rent it. Provide a steady income for me old age, see, and still have the house to sell one day."

Nora is fully prepared for this answer. "Cost a bomb to do it up, Cyril."

"Don't see why. Just a lick of paint and that."

"Damn sight more than a lick of paint. Don't you agree, Colin?"

Colin is only too pleased to give his opinion. "Hell of a sight more. Place needs taking apart. Got to be re-wired for a start. All the windows and doors need renewing. And it probably hasn't got a damp course, so one would have to be put in. The actual structure looks sound enough. Don't know about the joists and that..." He gets to his feet and bounces up and down. The whole room shakes. "Seems all right," he comments as he sits down again. "But all them old lead pipes will have to be replaced with copper ones. And a lot of the ceilings need re-plastering. Then it needs decorating inside and out. And to do the job proper you ought to put in double glazing, central heating and that..." He scratches his head. "No, I reckon when all's said and done you won't get much change out of twenty thousand."

"Twenty thousand! That's ten thousand each!" It's sweet music to Nora's ears. "Couldn't possibly afford that!"

"Half each, Nora," mutters Cyril.

"Not even ten. Like I said, I need all my money for the move. No, if you're so dead keen on keeping this place you'll have to go it alone. You can buy my share of the value of it, if you like, and pay for all the renovations. Then it's yours and you'll get all the profit."

Cyril's pasty suddenly crumbles in his hand. "Couldn't afford to do that."

"Course, it could be a very good long-term investment," says Colin. "Might be able to get a mortgage, so it would pay for itself out of the rents."

"That's up to you, Cyril." Nora wipes tomato juice from around her mouth with a paper napkin. "But I need to know, cos if you don't want it I'm putting it on the market soon as I can."

Cyril lifts his hat and scratches the dead-white top of his head. "Suppose it'll have to go then," he mumbles.

Nora sits back in triumph. "That's settled that then! Now we'd best be getting on."

The better furniture having been stacked in the back room, Nora details Boris to help Cyril cart the rest to the tip, while Len and Colin are to clear the remaining bits and pieces from upstairs, ready for the next load. Nora burns a few suitable items on the fire, feeling it best to attend to that hazardous operation herself.

As they drive to the tip Cyril and Boris are both silent, each preoccupied with their own thoughts.

Cyril's hands are clenched tightly on the steering wheel, his pipe just as tightly between his teeth. He is still feeling a bit peeved about having to sell the house. It's all very well for Nora, but for him it represents the best years of his life.

Boris sits beside him staring glumly at a bag of onions on the floor of the cab and thinking his dad must be mad wanting him to work for this old git. On the other hand he's quite enjoying riding in the Land Rover. It's his kind of vehicle. He wouldn't mind driving a Land Rover himself.

"Me dad says you've got a job for me," he ventures after a while.

"Might have," replies Cyril cautiously. "Depends. You interested?"

Boris shrugs. "Something to do. Boring sitting home watching telly all the time."

"Don't you like watching telly then?"

"Sport's all right – and the horror movies and that."

Cyril brightens. "You like horror movies?"

"All right. Better than them soaps and all that stuff."

"Watch horror movies myself sometimes," says Cyril. "At night – when the wife's in bed."

"Yer?"

"Vampires are me favourite ones. Never tire of 'em. Dunno why, funny that."

Boris continues to contemplate the onions. "You seen Erotic Vampires?" he asks eventually.

Cyril screws up his eyes, trying to recall. "Don't think so. Good, is it?"

"Not bad."

"What is it – sexy and that?"

"Yer." Boris shifts his great weight a bit on the seat. "There's this female vampire, see, who goes round giving men love-bites. Makes 'em sex-crazy and that."

"Go on." Cyril glances at Boris, a twinkle in his eye. "Ain't seen nothing like that on the telly."

"It's a video. Borrow it if you like."

"Ain't got a video to see it on."

But he's thinking he might get one now he's coming into a bit of money. Brighten his life up a bit. Living has been pretty dull for him since he married Glennis and took up market gardening, not like before when he used to go up to London sometimes for a bit of excitement.

"You on this Internet thing?" he asks Boris suddenly.

"Nah. Dad ain't got a computer. He wants one, but Elsie won't let him spend the money."

"Cost a lot then, do they?"

"Yer."

Cyril looks disappointed. "What about them videos, they

cost much?"

"Dunno. I use me dad's. Don't cost much to hire the films, though."

"And you can hire horror films and that?"

"Yer."

Another silence. Cyril knocks out his pipe against the dashboard. "You know anything about gardening?"

"Used to do a bit on me dad's allotment, before he gave it up. Still do a bit in the back garden, in the summer, like."

They arrive at the tip. It is an exposed spot, a cruel wind cutting across it. 'USE THIS SKIP' says a crudely painted notice.

Boris gets a kick from hurling in all the old lumber. In fact, he's quite enjoying himself. Can't be a bad bloke, this old git, he thinks, if he likes horror movies and that.

Then a gust of wind whips off Cyril's hat. Boris lollops after it, and manages to retrieve it when it becomes trapped in the wire fencing.

"Thanks," says Cyril as Boris hands it back to him.

Not a bad lad, he thinks. Might be able to get on with him. Have things in common – horror films and that. If I buy myself a video, I could borrow the films from him or get him to hire some for me. Then Glennis needn't know.

"What about this job then?" asks Boris when they are on the way back from the tip.

"Have to think about it. Not the right time of year just now. Let you know soon."

When they arrive back at the house Colin and Len have already deposited another load of rubbish on the pavement for them to cart off to the tip, but before they can load it a stranger comes up, waving his arms like a madman.

"Hey mister, you know your chimney's on fire?"

Cyril's pipe drops from his mouth. Not for half a century has he moved so fast. He rushes into the house. "Chimley's on fire! Chimley's on fire!" he shouts.

Colin hurries out, stares up appalled. Sparks and billows of black smoke issue from the chimney. "Call the fire brigade!" he shouts to Nora. "Dial 999!"

"Can't," cries Nora from within. "There's no phone."

"No phone! Where's the nearest box?"

"Dunno."

"One outside the public toilets," advises the stranger.

"It's vandalised," shouts someone helpfully from the fast-gathering crowd.

"There's a phone in The Butcher's Arms," cries another.

"I'll go on me bike," says Boris, well acquainted with The Butcher's Arms.

"Good idea," says Colin.

Boris roars off down the road.

"Pub'll be shut," the onlooker shouts after him.

"There's a box outside the Fire Station. Try that!"

"We'd better try to dowse the fire," says Colin, hurrying indoors in a frantic but futile search for a bucket.

Then he discovers the water is turned off, and he has to grovel around for the stopcock. Once the water is turned on, Nora stands at the kitchen sink filling all the receptacles they can find while the others try to dowse the fire in the grate, which is now roaring magnificently. Colin uses the jug from the old washstand, Len a big vase that once housed an aspidistra, Cyril the bucket from his commode.

By the time the fire brigade arrives the smoke from the chimney has subsided. But the firemen ensure all is safe. Admonition and advice is given, notes made, forms signed. Nora is apologetic for not being able to make the firemen a cup of tea.

It is almost dark by the time the fire engine departs, so without lighting they are forced to call it a day. Colin makes a careful tour of the old house to ensure all is safe.

"Why don't we stop at The Mason and Magpie for a quick one?" he suggests, as they are about to depart, his throat as dry as the Gobi desert.

"Can't go there in me dirty overalls!" cries Len.

Colin grins at his friend. "I don't believe it! Never known you refuse a drink before, mate. History's been made!"

*****

Colin is back in form after his non-performance in bed on Boxing Night. It took him a fortnight to summon up the courage to try again, and then only because Elsie was desperate. But he was successful, and even on two further occasions.

At the moment Colin is on the two-till-ten shift at Regal Chemicals, which means it is part of his duties to make an evening patrol of the premises to ensure all is safe and well, and tonight he sets off from the gatehouse in a confident mood. He cuts a very impressive figure in his dark Security Officer's uniform, with his heavy black cape about his shoulders, his set of master keys in one hand and his flash lamp in the other.

Colin takes his work very seriously, checking thoroughly the perimeter fencing, locks and other safety devices on all the buildings, car and bicycle parks, toilets, and at the same time keeping a sharp eye out for forced entries, fire hazards, safety hazards, anyone acting suspiciously. It is a very responsible job.

But tonight he is not quite so thorough as usual. He can hardly wait to reach the office block where he knows Rachel is working. Ever since she sat on his lap at the New Year's Eve party he hasn't been able to get her out of his mind. He's seen her the last two evenings on his rounds and stopped briefly to bid her a cheery good evening and to say how much he enjoyed the party. But tonight he hopes to stop a bit longer, maybe buy her a coffee from the machine, chat her up a bit. Not that he's intending anything serious to develop. Colin was brought up by his maternal grandmother who instilled a strong sense of right and wrong into him, but he sees no harm in a bit of flirting. Keeps him young, he thinks.

As he approaches the office block his excitement mounts. As quickly as he can he passes through the Buying Department, the Traffic Office, the Personnel Department, the Accounts Office, checks the doors of the Strong Room and Cashier's Office, and then, with eager anticipation, ascends the stairs to the Sales Office.

It is a vast open-plan office, luxuriously carpeted, with rows of stylish desks each with its computer, and divided into sections by filing cabinets. When he enters he is surprised to find it apparently deserted. No sign of Rachel, or anyone else. He's been expecting to find her busy with the vacuum cleaner, or Mr Sheen and a duster. She must be having a tea break, he thinks, and decides to hang around for a while, and makes a display of checking the windows.

Then, suddenly, he comes upon her. She is bending over with her bottom in the air, emptying waste-paper baskets into a black plastic sack. In her green overall Rachel's sex appeal is radically diminished in comparison with the glamorous creature he'd fancied so much at the party. Even so, the sight of the erotic contour of her backside and the generous display of her brown-stocking legs as she bends over evokes an irresistible impulse.

He steals up on her and pinches her bottom. Rachel gives a terrifying, blood-curdling scream, making Colin jump back in alarm, but that's nothing compared with the way he staggers, like a punch-drunk boxer, when she turns to face him.

It isn't Rachel at all!

"Hey man! You jes gave me one hell of a fright!"

"Sorry, sorry!" gasps Colin. "I thought you were Rachel."

"Rachel!" The woman laughs, revealing a gleaming white set of teeth, like piano keys. "Hell, do I look like Rachel? You must be colour-blind man!"

"Well, from behind…" He stops in confusion, then adds words he's heard many a time in courtrooms. "Sorry, I don't know what came over me, I really don't."

"No sweat man. I's had many a worse shock than that!"

She continues to laugh, apparently finding it funny. Colin is relieved. Maybe his career hasn't come to a sudden unhappy end after all.

"Better sit down," says the woman. "I reckon we both need a drink."

"You're dead right," he says. "I'll get a couple of coffees from the machine."

She laughs again. "I mean a *real* drink man. Leave it to me." She goes to one of the desks, opens a deep bottom drawer and extracts two plastic beakers and a bottle of Bell's whisky. "Left over from Christmas," she says, winking.

Looking round to make sure there is no one about, Colin perches himself on the edge of a desk. He can't believe this is happening. By rights he should be reporting that whisky, not drinking it. But Christmas is only just over, after all.

"Cheers," he says.

"Bottoms up!" cries the woman with renewed laughter.

"What's happened to Rachel then?" he asks as his composure gradually returns.

"Transferred to the Works Lab. Don't ask me why. I've taken her place here."

"What's your name?" Colin asks, thinking the woman isn't all that bad a substitute for Rachel.

"Nerina."

"Nerina," he exclaims. "You're a gem!" And he means it. He reckons she could have made a hell of a fuss if she'd felt like it.

But as they sip their whisky and chat neither of them notice the shadowy figure that has crept up behind the filing cabinets.

It is the cleaners' supervisor, Elsie's bingo friend, Mavis.

*****

It is Saturday, 31st January, the day Len and Nora Scally are due to go to the new flat to celebrate Georgina's birthday.

In the morning, however, Nora has an appointment to meet Mr Hepplewhite, of Gravely and Hepplewhite, Estate Agents, at Dad's house for him to inspect the premises with a view to putting it on the market.

Sharp at nine thirty, Mr Hepplewhite rolls up in his vintage Jaguar and Nora is there to greet him. He is a freckle-faced young man with ginger hair and moustache to match. Nora doesn't altogether like the look of him, but he does his job thoroughly enough, measuring each room with the aid of some electronic gadget, making copious notes, crossing the road to survey the roof and to take photographs.

"Well," says Nora when he is done. "What do you think?"

Mr Hepplewhite strokes his moustache. "I take it you are hoping for a quick sale, Mrs…ahm…Scally?"

"Of course."

"Well, this type of property is what we regard as a 'First-time Buy' and should prove quite attractive to the lower end of the market. I think we might try forty-five thousand."

"Forty-five thousand!" echoes Nora. "Is that all?"

"Well, we might try, say, forty-eight. But I'm sure you must realise, Mrs…ahm…Scally, that the property is in a rather poor state of repair, so you could be expected to knock off two or three thousand from the asking price on that account."

Nora is disappointed and thinks she might try another agent.

"Of course," continues Mr Hepplewhite, reading her thoughts, "it might be worth your while giving the front a coat of paint. First impressions are awfully important, you know."

"I'll discuss it with my husband and let you know," says Nora.

When she arrives home Len is cleaning the car ready for the evening's big event. She takes him inside and tells him the news. Len, who is quite knowledgeable about property prices through having had endless discussions on the subject with his cronies at The Mason and Magpie, thinks forty-eight thousand is a reasonable price to ask.

"Course," he says, "depends how much it's going to cost to paint the front."

"That won't cost much," says Nora. "You can do it."

This gives Len a jolt. "I can't do it! Not this time of year. It's far too cold and wet."

"Soon as the weather improves a bit, then. Won't take long. 'Spect Colin will help you; he's a fast worker. Then we'll put it on the market and ask fifty-two thousand. And if Hepplewhite won't wear it we'll go to another agent."

*****

Gavin and Georgina's flat is on the top floor of a four-storey block of post-war flats. It is quite small, but Nora is astonished to find it fully furnished and looking like something out of *House and Gardens*. She is envious. Her own home looks tawdry and old-fashioned in comparison.

Shortly after Georgie has taken them on a tour of inspection of the flat, Marsha and Oliver Bloom arrive.

"Daddy!" cries Georgie. "I'm *so* delighted you've managed to come! I was afraid you might have been called away on one of your trips."

"My darling, I wouldn't miss this for the world," responds Oliver. "Happy birthday, Georgie!" He whips a huge bouquet of flowers from behind his back, Hollywood fashion. Oliver Bloom looks every inch a businessman, with his expensive suit, flash tie and spotless protruding cuffs.

"Happy birthday, darling," booms Marsha in her upper-crust voice, as she hands her daughter a bulky gift-wrapped present. Marsha is matronly, which is why she wears the rather shapeless kind of dress specifically designed for the 'fuller figure'.

Oliver turns his attention to the Scallys.

"Nora, my dear, how *are* you?" For Nora, he has a big hug and a warm wet kiss on the cheek. She wouldn't be human not to thrill to such an effusive greeting. "Great to see you again, old chap," he says to Len, pumping his hand. "Let me take your coat."

"Mummy!" cries Georgie, on opening her gift. "It's absolutely *gorgeous*!"

It is a cut-glass salad bowl, obviously expensive. Nora feels none too happy about the present she gave Georgie – a box of deluxe toilet soaps. Still, she consoles herself, there is also the bottle of Harvey's Bristol Cream Len has brought as a contribution to the evening's celebrations.

Refusing all offers of help, Georgie retires to the kitchen to attend to the meal while Gavin dispenses sherry to his guests with the aplomb of an experienced host, which makes Nora feel proud.

"And how are things with you two?" enquires Oliver, lounging back expansively on the settee. "Anything exciting happened?"

"No, not really," says Nora, pulling at her skirt. "Just busy working and that."

"I seem to remember at Christmas you were trying to decide where to go for your summer holiday. Any decisions yet?" Oliver is well aware that the subject of holidays is always a good opener.

"Oh yes! We're going to Brighton."

"Brighton!" exclaims Marsha.

"Well, not actually *in* Brighton," Nora adds hastily, thinking Marsha sounds scornful. "Just a bit further up the coast. A little place called Benthaven."

"I don't think I know it."

"Very select resort, I'm told. A friend highly recommended it."

"Really?" says Marsha. "Brighton, I always feel, is such a distinguished town."

"Used to be," corrects Oliver.

"Very historic, though," puts in Gavin, determined to make his contribution.

"Oh, *very*." Marsha warms to the subject. "I went to school near Brighton and came to know it quite well. Of course, I don't know what it is like these days."

"Pretty grotty, I should think," says Oliver.

He gets a cold look from Marsha. "You don't know that, Olly, we haven't been there for years. We must go sometime. It's the kind of town we might consider for when you retire."

"Brighton, and about a hundred other places on your short list," laughs Oliver, exposing an expensive set of pearly dentures.

Nora is alarmed. "You're retiring?" Just her luck if the Blooms retire to Brighton just as she's on the point of moving to Webbley Park to be near them.

"My dear, if only he would! I keep telling him all this globetrotting is awfully bad for him. He'll end up in Intensive Care if he's not careful."

"Nonsense! I'm only fifty-two, for God's sake, and as fit as a flea." But Oliver doesn't want to dwell on this thorny subject. He raises his sherry glass. "Anyway, here's to you both having a splendid holiday in – where did you say it was?"

"Benthaven," says Nora, dutifully raising her glass.

"Benthaven, then."

"What exactly *is* your job?" asks Len when the toast is over.

"My job? Oh, I'm just a general dogsbody." He makes a dismissive gesture. "My handle is Group Co-ordinator. I have to ensure all the Skyfly hotels all over the world conform to the specified standard."

"Coo!" gasps Nora.

"Sort of trouble-shooter?" Len suggests.

"You could say that. Plenty of trouble to shoot at too, I assure you, especially in the developing countries."

"Must be fascinating," says Gavin, who envies Oliver his glamorous job.

"And *very* exhausting," Marsha adds. "Very lonely for me

too, of course."

"Ready!" yells Georgina from the kitchen.

Gavin ushers his guests to the table and proceeds to uncork a bottle of Sainsbury's wine with an easy assurance that again overwhelms Nora with pride. She may have had only one child but she scarcely could have had a better one, with his dark good looks, slim figure and attractive charm.

Georgie comes in carrying an ovenproof dish and looking very red in the face.

"And what have you made for our delectation, dear?" asks her mother.

"Stuffed vegetable marrow, virtually fat free. Good for you." She places the dish in front of her father for him to serve.

"Really? How intriguing!"

While Oliver is serving the marrow Gavin pours the wine. When they are ready to eat Oliver raises his glass. "Here's to our birthday girl. Happy birthday, Georgie!"

"Happy birthday," chant the others.

"Quite delicious, dear," says Marsha after a first tentative mouthful of the stuffed vegetable marrow. "What is in it – apart from the marrow, I mean?"

"Oh, rice, tomato sauce and pieces of chicken. I hope you like it," she adds to Nora.

"Very nice," says Nora. "Isn't it, Len?"

"Um," says Len. He would be happier with fish and chips.

"I'll have to recommend it for the Skyfly menus," grins Oliver.

"Damn sight better for their guests than that muck they dish up," Georgie retorts. She irritably pushes back a stray strand of her blond bobbed hair.

"Just my little joke pet," he replies smoothly, reaching over to pat her hand. "It's *delicious*, it really is."

"I'll put on some music," says Gavin, jumping up.

"Don't let your food go cold," warns Georgie.

Gavin flicks on his CD player. Music obediently issues forth.

"That's Vivaldi," pronounces Marsha, who listens to Classic FM.

"Full marks!" cries Gavin. "The Four Seasons, actually,

Spring."

"I do so love Baroque music." Marsha turns to Nora. "So fresh and uncomplicated, don't you think?"

"Very nice," says Nora, who hasn't heard of Vivaldi, never mind the Baroque. She wisely turns the conversation to safer ground. "You must be finding it a bit lonely at home now Georgie's married and living away."

"I *do* miss Georgie, naturally. It is the evenings that are worst, especially when Olly's away on one of his jaunts. During the day I'm well occupied, of course. I am quite heavily involved with the church, as I believe you know, and I'm Chairperson of the Primary School Board of Governors, as well as being on several other committees. And then I have my golf. Do you play golf, Nora?"

Nora gulps. "No. No I don't."

"Splendid game, golf. Keeps one fit and alert, as I'm sure Georgie would agree." Marsha dabs her mouth with her napkin and glances at her daughter. "Speaking of the church, Georgie, I phoned the vicar of St Cuthbert's the other day and told him you would be around to see him shortly."

Georgina flushes. "Mummy, I do wish you wouldn't interfere! I'll go and see him when I'm good and ready!"

"You really must, dear. He sounds very sensible. We had quite an interesting chat on the phone, actually. He seems to hold with all the traditional moral values, I'm pleased to note. Not like the young clap-happy fellow we have in Webbley Park."

"I'll go when I can," Georgie answers shortly. "Now, who's going to finish up the marrow?"

Despite his protestations the marrow ends up on Len's plate. Georgie clears the dishes and returns to the kitchen for the dessert.

"Good job Georgie isn't coming with us on the QE2," grins Oliver while she is out of the room. "She wouldn't think much of the food they dish up. She'd die of starvation before she got back!"

"You're going on the QE2?" cries Nora.

"We're hoping to, yes," Marsha answers. "A cruise to the Caribbean. Oliver finds cruises restful after so much air travel."

"Don't you get seasick and that?"

"Good God, no!" exclaims Oliver. "Ideal holiday, if you ask me. Plenty to do if you want to, and if you don't, you can just lie back and do nothing."

"Sounds good," says Len, who fancies it might suit him.

Georgie returns with the dessert. "Witches Fluff," she announces. "Cranberry jelly, egg white and sugar. Virtually fat-free."

"Oh my!" exclaims Nora.

"Sounds delicious, dear," says Marsha.

Len would have preferred something hot, like spotted dick, but he quite enjoys the Witches Fluff and wouldn't have minded a second helping, but this time it goes to Oliver.

When the meal is over, the barrage of offers to help with the washing-up are resolutely turned down. It is to be stacked. Gavin excuses himself to go and make the coffee, but comes back instead with a bottle of champagne.

"What's all this then?" cries Oliver.

"Left over from the wedding," explains Gavin. "We thought we'd use it to celebrate Georgie's birthday, but as it happens we also have something else to celebrate, so we can use it for that as well."

"Something else?" queries Marsha.

"You've won the lottery?" grins Oliver.

"Much better than that," replies Gavin mysteriously.

When Oliver has dispensed generous measures of champagne all round Gavin stands up, glass in hand.

"I'm sorry you have to drink it from wine glasses instead of flutes," he begins, anxious for it to be known he knows what it should be.

"I'm sure it will taste just as good, dear," says Marsha.

"Anyway, as you know we asked you here to celebrate Georgie's birthday, but as I said, we have another reason for celebration, and…"

"Whatever can it be?" interrupts Nora excitedly.

Gavin smiles indulgently. "Parents and parents-in-law," he continues, as if addressing a meeting. "First of all, Georgie and I would like to thank each of you sincerely for having been such caring and loving parents to us throughout our childhoods and maturing years. I think I am safe in saying that if it hadn't been for you we wouldn't be where we are today!" A wry grin as he waits for the significance of his words to sink in. "We should also like to thank you for accepting our sudden decision to marry quickly with such understanding and for putting up with all the inconvenience that must have caused."

"Thank you, Gavin," says Marsha, feeling gratified.

Gavin permits himself another grin. "However, if you think your responsibilities are at an end and you can now just all sit back and enjoy yourselves, I'm afraid you're sadly mistaken. Why, you ask? Because, you see, there are soon to be more little feet running about for you to contend with. You are to be grandparents. Georgie is pregnant!"

"Oh my!" exclaims Nora, overcome. All the following congratulations, toasting and excited parley passes her by. She is to be a grandmother! She can't wait to tell Glennis.

But she does take notice when she hears Marsha ask, "And when is the happy event due to take place?"

"Oh, not until the beginning of August," says Georgie.

"What we are hoping to do," intervenes Gavin, "is for Georgie to finish at the hospital – temporarily, of course – shortly after Easter. Then in June I'm going to take her on holiday to Greece for some sun and air to build her up for the 'Big Event'."

"Great idea!" cries Oliver.

"Very thoughtful of you Gavin," says Marsha, "but don't you think it a little unwise for Georgie to fly all the way to Greece when she's seven months' pregnant?"

"Oh, I don't think that's a problem. Pregnant women fly all the time. Naturally, if we have any reason to think she may have problems we won't go. You may be sure of that."

"All the same dear, I would have thought it would have been wiser for her to stay in this country, go somewhere quiet, and not too far from home."

"You could come with us to Benthaven!" cries Nora. "We're going in June, aren't we, Len?"

"Um," says Len.

Gavin smiles benignly. "That's a super idea, Mum, but you know what the English weather is like. I want Georgie to get all the sun and air she can. It's the last decent holiday she's likely to get for a bit. Besides, it's all fixed up. We're booked for the first two weeks of June at a very nice hotel on the Greek Island of Thyros."

"I see," says Marsha, looking down her nose.

"More champagne?" asks Gavin smiling.

Nora only has a dim recollection of the remaining evening. She was only vaguely aware of all the speculation concerning the sex of the baby, and of Georgie's professional, but over-graphic, account of the process of pregnancy and childbirth. And when they leave she didn't even think to question Len's capacity to drive after all the drinking. She is going to be a grandmother!

"Do you realise," she says to Len on the way home, by this time having made a few calculations, "that Georgie must have conceived almost straight away after they were married?"

"Certainly didn't waste much time."

"I don't blame them, mind. Best to have children when you're young. That's where we went wrong, leaving it so late, only able to have the one."

"Couldn't afford 'em earlier."

"Things were different in them days. They're lucky, being able to have a nice home right at the start, thanks to that handsome cheque the Blooms gave them as a wedding present. They deserve it, mind. They make a lovely couple, don't you think?"

Len grunts. "Them Blooms must be rolling in money," he says.

"Oh yes! But such nice people. Don't give themselves a lot of airs and graces. I only hope they don't go and move as soon as we get to Webbley Park." Nora burps unexpectedly. "I can still taste that marrow." She opens the glove compartment and takes out her roll of peppermints. "I have to say I didn't think much of the food Georgie dished up."

"Bloody horrible if you ask me. Feel sorry for Gavin, having to put up with that sort of stuff."

"Oh, he'll soon put a stop to that," says Nora confidently. "He likes his food too much. He'll be the one wearing the trousers, don't you worry. Didn't you notice how he stood up to Marsha over taking Georgie to Greece? He wasn't going to be told what to do. Got the holiday all fixed up first."

Len doesn't answer.

Nora finishes gobbling her peppermint, then says, "Do you know what I'm going to do once we're in Webbley Park and settled down and that?"

"No, what?" Len isn't much interested.

"I'm going to take up golf."

Chapter 5

For once Colin is able to have a quiet evening at home on his own. Being Wednesday, Elsie has gone off to Bingo with Mavis, and Boris is out with his mates. It is an opportunity, he decides, to see if he can get that old clock Nora gave him to work.

He feels in a cheerful mood and whistles tunelessly as he spreads an old copy of the *Sun* over the kitchen table ready for the clock.

Then he braves the harsh February night in order to collect the clock and his tools from the shed at the bottom of the garden. On his return he places the clock on the newspaper and neatly lays out his tools beside it. And then, having supplied himself with a can of beer from the fridge, he sits down and contemplates the clock. He feels like a surgeon about to commence an operation.

But his eye is distracted by the photo of the topless model staring up at him from page three of the newspaper. It makes him think of Nerina. Her face does, that is. He doesn't know about the rest of her. Wouldn't mind knowing though, he thinks with a grin. Nerina has taken first place in his affections ever since he pinched her bum in mistake for Rachel's. He was lucky to get away with that, and wouldn't have done had she not been such a sport about it.

Resolutely he turns the clock around and opens the back. The interior is black with grime and looks as if it hasn't been opened in years. He gives the pendulum a few swings but each time it persists in coming to a standstill. Probably just needs cleaning, he thinks, and decides to take out the movement. After a struggle and a few choice words he succeeds in pulling it free of the case. He thrills with triumph.

But then something falls down inside the clock case. He stares at it in amazement. It appears to be a rolled up wad of paper, secured by an elastic band, which has partly perished and has become stuck to the paper.

"The old boy's love letters, I bet," Colin chuckles to himself.

But they are not love letters, they are five-pound notes – not those in circulation, but the more imposing, larger white ones of years gone by.

Colin is so dumbfounded he has to get another can of beer from the fridge. He takes a swig and stands staring at the notes. They remind him of his seventh birthday when a generous aunt gave him one such five-pound note. It was a lot of money then. He puts down the can and counts the fivers. Twenty of them – a hundred pounds!

It occurs to him there might be more bundles in the clock case, and sure enough, wedged in the top of it, he finds more. Six hundred pounds worth altogether, he reckons.

"Bloody hell!" he exclaims aloud, slumping back in his chair.

Then the phone rings.

"Gatehouse," says Colin, forgetting where he is.

"What? Who's that?"

"Sorry! Sorry! I mean, it's Colin – Colin Stilwell."

"Oh, it *is* you, Colin. This is Nora."

Nora! "Yes, sorry. I was dreaming."

"Are you all right?"

"Yes, fine. Elsie's at bingo I'm afraid."

"I know. It's you I want to talk to."

"Oh?" He feels a pang of guilt. Surely she hasn't found out about the money in the clock?

"Listen. My brother has hurt his arm."

"Your brother?"

"Yes – Cyril!"

"Oh, Cyril. Of course."

"Are you quite sure you're all right? You sound very strange."

"I'm fine. Just nodded off for a minute, that's all. Phone woke me up."

"Well listen. Cyril's hurt his arm as I say. Nothing serious, but he's got to rest it for a bit. Wants to know if Boris is still interested in going over and helping out."

"Dunno, but I reckon he might be. He's out at the moment.

When does Cyril want him?"

"Soon as possible. Before the weekend."

"Tell you what, I'll ask him when he comes in and give you a ring at work first thing in the morning."

"Lovely. Sorry to disturb you."

She rings off before Colin can say more. He's not sorry. He needs a bit of time to get over the shock of finding that money before he says anything to anyone. Beer seems inadequate so he collects the whisky bottle from the living room and pours himself a generous tot.

"The question is, who is the rightful owner?" he says aloud to himself as he sips the whisky. "Nora made me a gift of the clock so it could be said the money is mine. On the other hand, it was not her *intention* to make me a gift of the money, only the clock, in which case it could be said the money is hers. Then again, there is the principle of 'finders-keepers' in which case it's mine. Or, I suppose, it could even be regarded as treasure trove, in which case it could belong to the State." He realises his knowledge of the law on this subject is scanty. It never came up in his experience on the Force. But his conscience tells him he must tell Nora. He will tell her when he rings her in the morning, he decides.

The front door bangs.

My God, Elsie back already! He looks round for somewhere to hide the fivers. She mustn't know about them, not until he's had time to think about it a bit more. He opens the front of the washing machine and throws them in, and by the time Elsie comes in he has the clock movement in pieces, springs, wheels and cogs spread out on the newspaper.

He looks up innocently. "Hello, luv. Lucky tonight?"

She doesn't answer. She glares at the bits and pieces, plonks down her handbag and slams out again.

What's up with her? Colin wonders. Perhaps she's been drinking.

She has. Elsie won fifty pounds at bingo and has been treating Mavis to a small celebration at The Mason and Magpie on the way home. Elsie is often lucky, making small wins, some of which she spends on such celebrations, sending the rest to one of the charities whose appeals come flooding through the letterbox. But tonight it isn't so much the booze that is affecting her. She has a bone to pick with Colin; two, in fact.

She returns to the kitchen carrying several videocassettes, which she slams on the table.

Colin glances at them briefly and wonders what is going on. "What's all that?"

She glares at him, lips zipped up, eyes bulging.

"Come on, Els', what's it all about?"

"That tart!" she blurts out. "That's what it's all about."

"What tart?" He can only think of the blackcurrant flan they had for supper. Perhaps she thinks he has been raiding the fridge.

"That black tart in the Sales Office, that's what tart!"

Colin's face goes whiter than the cliffs of Dover. "You mean Nerina?" he asks nervously.

"Oh, so it's Nerina is it!" She picks up a cassette and hurls at him.

"Hey! Steady on!"

"You and her behind them cabinets."

"Whatcha mean? What cabinets?"

"You know. Lecherous bugger!"

"Don't be daft, Els'. Never laid a finger on her."

"Bloody sight more than a finger from what I've heard."

So that's it. Bloody Mavis opening her big mouth. "Then you heard wrong," he retorts. "I was on me rounds and we were only having a bit of a chat."

"Bloody liar!" She throws another cassette. "Funny sort of chat with that tart screaming all the time."

Colin becomes more alarmed. Mavis must have heard Nerina yelp when he pinched her bum. "She wasn't screaming. She only shouted out once – when she...er...hurt herself a bit, like."

"Oh yeh! Hurt herself doing what?"

Colin is not noted for his imagination. "Well, she sat down on one of the desks, see, and there was a drawing pin on it and it stuck into her, made her scream a bit. That's what drew my attention. That's how we got talking."

"Bloody liar!" Elsie hurls another cassette.

"For God's sake stop chucking them things about, they're from the video shop!"

"And that's another thing." She stops in the act of throwing a further cassette. "I'm not having this filth in my house!"

"What filth?"

"*This* filth." She shoves the cassette under Colin's nose. 'Erotic Vampires' reads the lurid label. "And this!" 'Monster in the Brothel' it reads.

Colin gapes. "Never seen 'em before in me life! Where the hell did you find 'em?"

"As if you didn't know."

"Els', I swear I've never seen 'em before in—" he stops abruptly. "It must be…"

Elsie suddenly becomes tearful. "I know you're a lecherous sod, but I didn't think you were a dirty old man."

"I'm not!" Colin is affronted. "It must be Boris who—"

"I've always let you have it," Elsie wails. "Every week regular, and twice a week on holiday. Aren't I good enough for you any more?" She bursts into floods of tears.

Colin feels a lurch of remorse. "Course you are. Course you are."

Out of the corner of his eye he is aware of the page three girl flaunting her breasts from the old newspaper on the table. Adroitly he shifts the clock case across her, and feeling the moment is ripe to make peace, goes up to Elsie to console her.

"Get away from me!"

"Aw, come on, luv. Honest, I know nothing about them videos. It's Boris, it's got to be, the bugger. Wait till I see him!"

He moves towards her but she backs away, fighting him off.

"Aw, come on, dry your eyes." He fishes in his pocket for a handkerchief but hasn't got one. The nearest thing to hand is a tea towel hanging by the sink. "Here, use this."

She snatches the towel, buries her face in it.

Colin waits. The worst is over, he thinks. When she re-emerges he should be able to put his arm around her, assure her of his innocence and his love, then in time all should be well.

But when she sees the black smudges she's made on the tea towel fire rekindles in Elsie's eyes.

"Now see what you've made me go and do! That was clean this morning!"

She opens the front of the washing machine and throws it in

savagely.

Colin panics. The fivers! He hopes to God she isn't going to start the machine there and then.

But at that moment a massive helmeted figure appears in the doorway. It's Boris, looking a bit like a monster himself.

"What's up?" he asks. He's not so insensitive he can't detect a hostile atmosphere.

"That's what's bloody well up!" screams Elsie, hurling 'Monster in the Brothel' at him.

Realising he's right, Boris quickly makes himself scarce.

"'Ere, I want a word with you!" Colin bawls after him.

But before he can follow Elsie explodes again. "I've had this place up to me bleedin' eyeballs," she hollers. "You, him, the bleedin' lot!"

"Now, come on, luv."

"I wish I'd never set eyes on the pair of you."

With one dramatic sweep of her arm Elsie whips the newspaper off the table, sending clock, beer, whisky, cogs, wheels, ratchets, nuts and bolts to the four corners of the kitchen.

"Why oh why did I ever leave Australia?" she wails, and slams out.

Tonight Colin sleeps on the settee. But safely tucked under his cushion is six hundred pounds worth of old Bank of England five-pound notes.

*****

Nora is vexed with the weather. It has been so atrocious that even she couldn't expect Len to get out on the ladder to paint the front of Dad's house. Until that is done she doesn't want to put it on the market, but with Easter already just around the corner, hopes of selling the house before she goes on holiday in June are becoming remote.

It takes an unexpected phone call from Gavin to distract her mind from this highly unsatisfactory state of affairs.

"Hello, Mum."

"Hello, dear. How's Georgie?"

"Fine, fine."

"No problems with the baby?"

"No, just a bit of morning sickness, that's all."

"Poor dear. Give her my love."

"I will. Listen, Mum, you've got a birthday coming up soon, haven't you?"

She is surprised by the question. "Yes, I suppose I must have. Why?"

Gavin hesitates. "Well, I hope you won't mind my suggesting it, but it occurred to us that it might be a good opportunity for you to invite Marsha and Oliver over to your place for a birthday tea or something. You did say at Christmas you'd invite them back."

This puts Nora on the spot. "Oh, I don't know about that, dear. I'd love them to come of course, but you know how small our rooms are. It's such a screw when we try to entertain. I was thinking we'd wait until we're in our new place, and then…"

"But it could be ages before you're able to move. No, don't worry about the house, Mum. They understand. They're just ordinary people, you know. I'm sure they'd appreciate being asked. They're always enquiring after you and Dad. They seem to have taken quite a fancy to you."

"Well, if you really think so dear…"

"Great! Now don't go making a lot of fuss. Just a birthday tea, a bit of ham salad, maybe, and a birthday cake to make it more of an occasion. I suggest you ask them for the Sunday nearest to your birthday, which happens to be Easter Sunday this year. We'll bring them over in the car."

"That would be lovely."

"We'll all look forward to it."

Nora is put into a bit of a tiz. She lies awake worrying about it all, about how shabby her home is, how small the rooms are compared with the Blooms' house. And they are both such big people. It's like inviting two elephants to tea in a doll's house. And then there is the question of food. Should she give them ham salad? She remembers that on the rare occasions her mother had people to tea she always gave them salmon salad. Perhaps that would be better. She would be happier giving them salmon salad.

As to a birthday cake, that poses a bigger problem. Nora's cooking is largely confined to fry-ups and the weekly roast. She has made the odd cake and pie, it is true, but knows better than to risk her hand at a birthday cake for the Blooms. I suppose I'll have to buy one, she thinks. That could be expensive.

But her little grey cells are ticking over nicely, and she falls asleep with a smile on her lips.

*****

After the traumas on the night of the clock mending, marital relations between Elsie and Colin are virtually back to normal. There was a protracted cooling off period during which neither spoke, apart from the odd abrupt necessary word.

It took a power cut to put things right. When the power came back on, the digital alarm clock on Elsie's bedside table ceaselessly flashed 1.37 at her, and since Elsie's many talents do not extend to things technical, she had no choice but to appeal to Colin to stop it. "Do you think you could possibly bring yourself to put this bloody thing right?" she snapped.

"You'll have to ask me nicely," grinned Colin.

Had she not felt so desperate about the flashing clock, she would probably have clobbered him, but Colin oddly underwent a metamorphosis before her very eyes. It was a bit like Beauty and the Beast. At one moment he appeared to her as some kind of loathsome fiend, and at the next, as a handsome smiling prince.

"Please," she said meekly, mesmerised by his lovely blue eyes.

The adjacent bed did the rest.

So when, at the Sports and Social the next Friday, Nora tells Elsie and Colin about how she's having the Blooms over to celebrate her birthday, she asks Elsie if she would mind making the cake for her, and Elsie, now being in a more amiable frame of mind, readily agrees.

"I'm quite happy to pay you for it, of course," says Nora.

"No need," says Elsie. "I'll make it your birthday present."

Which is exactly what Nora is hoping she would say.

"Do you want candles on it?" Elsie asks.

Nora doesn't much fancy having fifty-seven candles to blow out. "No, just put 'Happy Birthday' on it."

"Do we get invited to this birthday party?" asks Colin.

"I'd love you to come," lies Nora. "Trouble is, you know how small our rooms are. It'll be bad enough with six of us in our dining room as it is."

"What you mean is we're not good enough to meet your posh new in-laws," sniffs Elsie.

"No, it's not that at all," is the hasty reply. "I'd love you to meet them, but I thought it would be better to wait until we've moved, then we'll have a nice house-warming party and you'll be invited, of course."

"I'll keep you to that," says Elsie.

Feeling the conversation is becoming a bit tricky Nora changes the subject. "By the way, how's Boris enjoying working for Cyril?"

"All right," says Colin. "He don't say much about it."

"I bet he don't stick it long," says Elsie dryly. "You know what he is."

"He's stuck at doing up that old sidecar," Colin points out. "Down the shed working at it to all hours. Reckon you did him a good turn, Nora, when you gave him that."

Mention of the old sidecar reminds Nora about her gift to Colin. "Been meaning to ask you, managed to get that old clock working yet?"

Colin starts guiltily. He doesn't want to tell her the clock is also down the shed in a thousand pieces. Nor has he yet had the courage to tell her about the old fivers he found in it. They, too, are in the shed, well and truly hidden in an old paint pot with the lid hammered down.

"Haven't yet had much of a chance to take a proper look at it, Nora," he says, glancing at Elsie and hoping she won't let on about what happened in the kitchen.

But the young woman who has entered and gone to the bar has distracted Elsie's attention. It is Nerina, who's probably just popped in for a quick one after finishing work for the week. But Elsie doesn't want to risk Colin seeing her.

"Come on," she says to him curtly, getting to her feet. "We've got to go."

"Already?" Nora is surprised. It is not like Elsie to leave this early.

"Got to get on with them costumes for Kiss Me Kate. Got to get 'em finished before I start on that cake of yours."

Nora isn't going to stop her doing that, so she also gets to her feet. But she hasn't yet said all she wants to say. "Len's going to start painting the front of Dad's house on Good Friday, Colin. Any chance you could come and give him a helping hand?"

"Course I will, if I'm not working."

"Lovely! I shall be busy with the party and that, I 'spect, but Len will be along there about nine."

"If it don't rain," Len reminds her.

*****

But on Good Friday it does rain – hard. Even so, Len is not pleased. He would have preferred to have been out painting Dad's house with Colin rather than helping with the preparations for the birthday party, hoovering, dusting and polishing right through the house.

Nora herself spends the day in the kitchen, washing and ironing her best tablecloth and all the cushion covers, and making a batch of her little rock cakes to add to the spread to be laid before the Blooms.

On Easter Saturday morning Nora is down the market bright and early to buy the lettuce, tomatoes and spring onions for her salad, which she obtains from Cyril's stall. As usual Glennis is in charge of it, but to Nora's surprise, Boris is also there, off-loading the produce. He has had to drive Glennis in because of Cyril's bad arm.

"Are you enjoying your new job?" Nora asks him.

"All right," he grunts, and slopes off.

"How's your expectant daughter-in-law?" asks Glennis.

Nora swells with pride. "Oooh, lovely! She's getting a lot of morning sickness at the moment."

"Aw, God luv her."

"How's Cyril's arm?" asks Nora.

"Still painful, so he says. Making a big fuss about nothing, if you ask me, you know what men are."

Nora does.

When she arrives home Nora immediately phones the Stilwells. Her party is tomorrow and Elsie still hasn't come up with the birthday cake.

Colin answers. "She's down the Operatic," he tells her.

"Is the cake ready yet?"

"Well…it's made."

"Oh good. I'll send Len round for it."

"No good doing that yet, Nora. It's not iced."

"Not iced! But it'll never be ready in time!"

"Yes, it will. She'll be back soon. She's going to ice it this afternoon, let it set overnight, and then decorate it first thing in the morning. Don't worry, you'll have it in good time."

Nora is far from convinced. Once Elsie gets down the Operatic there's no saying how long she might be. "Tell her I *must* have it by lunchtime tomorrow."

"You will, don't worry."

Over their fish and chips Nora complains bitterly to Len about Elsie wasting her time and effort on making and altering costumes for the Operatic. "She lets them take advantage of her cos she's good with her needle and that. Too soft-hearted, that's Elsie's trouble. She ought to learn to say no to these people."

And not just the Operatic, thinks Len.

Early Saturday afternoon Nora phones again.

Colin answers.

"Has she iced it yet?"

"Not yet. She's had to make some last minute alterations to them costumes. She'll be finished soon."

"Let me talk to her," says Nora grimly.

"Shouldn't disturb her. She'll be through quicker if you don't. You'll have it soon, I'll let you know, don't fret."

But six o'clock arrives and there is no phone call. Nora can't stand it any longer. She's on the blower again.

"She's run out of icing sugar," says Colin. "She's just popped down the town to get some more."

Nora is aghast. "But the shops will be shut!"

"Tesco's is still open. She'll be back soon, then she'll get on with it right away."

Nora is furious. She knew in her bones things wouldn't run smoothly. Good job I made them rock cakes, she thinks.

But at eleven the phone rings.

"Thought you'd like to know the cake is iced," says Colin.

Thank God, thinks Nora. "I'll send Len round for it right away."

"Still got to be decorated. Elsie's going to do it first thing in the morning. We'll pop it round when it's done – about eleven, all being well."

It is the 'all being well' Nora doesn't like.

*****

Easter Sunday arrives. Bells peal out across the town. It is a bright, dry morning, ideal for painting Dad's house, but Len can't possibly start painting today. He is allowed his routine visit to The Mason and Magpie, mainly because Nora can't abide having him sitting around reading the newspaper. But she has instructed him to be home by eleven thirty sharp because she wants to have lunch early in order to re-lay the table ready for the birthday party.

But this consideration has to take a back seat when, at eleven o'clock, the promised cake still hasn't arrived.

Nora is back on the blower.

"Not quite ready yet," Colin tells her. "Gladys Savage has turned up."

"Who's Gladys Savage?" demands Nora.

"The leading lady in the show. One of her dresses has come apart at the seams, or summat."

"Can't that wait?"

"No, it's an emergency. Dress rehearsal is this afternoon, see. The show opens tomorrow."

A vexed tut from Nora. "How long will it take?"

"Dunno. Proving a bit tricky, judging by all the commotion coming from upstairs."

"I just can't be doing with all this, Colin," snaps Nora. "I think we'd best forget the whole thing. We'll have to manage without it, or buy one."

"Don't be like that, Nora! It's not Elsie's fault. Look, what's the latest time you need it by?"

She hesitates. She wants the cake if possible. "Well, I

suppose if it's here by three. But no later, mind."

"Oh, she'll do it well before then. Don't worry, you'll get it all right."

But Nora is taking no chances. Her rock cakes have turned out a bit too rocky and are scarcely a substitute for a birthday cake, anyway. So when Len comes back from The Mason and Magpie she sends him out again to try to buy some suitable kind of cake from the Spar grocers on the estate – if it's open on an Easter Sunday morning, that is.

It is open, but Len can only get a box of Mr Kipling cakes. Better than nothing, Nora decides.

Three o'clock arrives and there is still no sign of the birthday cake. Nora is livid. She had intended saving Elsie a piece of the cake for having made it, but now she intends giving her a piece of her mind instead.

At three thirty Gavin's Peugeot 106 draws up outside. Nora and Len hurry out to greet their guests. Marsha is prised out of the back seat by Gavin. But no Oliver follows.

"My dear, I'm most awfully sorry," says Marsha as she adjusts her clothing, "but Olly has been held up at Rio airport for two days by a wildcat strike, or something equally ridiculous, and he's just phoned to say he's at Heathrow and will be arriving home about six. Which mean, I'm afraid, that I'll have to leave by half past five. I'm so sorry. I hope you don't mind."

Nora doesn't. She is relieved in fact. She just wants to get the whole thing over and done with.

Marsha is ushered into the house while Gavin gathers up an armful of birthday gifts from the boot of the car. There is a bumper-sized box of chocolates from Marsha and Oliver, a book called *Cooking Your Way to Good Health* from Georgie, and a gorgeous bunch of flowers from Gavin himself, which brings his mother near to tears. It is years and years since anyone gave her flowers.

Nora decides to delay tea until four just in case the cake should arrive, so Marsha is taken into the sitting room where she sits in regal splendour in Len's armchair.

"What a cosy little room!" she exclaims. "And so neat and clean!"

Len is put to sit in the other armchair while Nora, Georgie

and Gavin sandwich themselves on the settee.

"I'm sorry Oliver couldn't come," says Nora.

"So is he, my dear, I do assure you. He sends his apologies, of course, and his felicitations for a very happy day."

"It must be a worry for you when he's held up like that."

"Oh, it happens all the time, you wouldn't believe. You would think in this day and age aircraft could keep to schedule, but there we are." Marsha turns to appraise her daughter. "So you've finally finished at the hospital, dear?"

"Yes, Mummy, for the time being."

"Not before time, judging by the size of you. How far gone are you – four months?"

"Fourteen weeks."

"Is that all? I would have believed you if you'd said twenty! Are you sure you're not having twins?"

"No, Mummy," replies Georgie, not amused. "It's only one."

"Really?" Marsha pauses to accept a chocolate Nora is pressing on her from her birthday box. "Then I should imagine it's going to be an awfully big baby. It's probably going to take after me!"

She rumbles with laughter at her own observation. The others dutifully laugh, except Georgie, who averts her head and stares at the picture of elephants hanging over the fireplace.

"What a lovely Easter Day it is!" exclaims Marsha, waving a hand at the sunlit window. "It flooded the church this morning. Did you manage to get there, Georgie?"

"No, I'm afraid not."

"Not on Easter Day, dear! Surely you could have found time today?"

"Well, I didn't." Georgie's speech is clipped.

"Actually," puts in Gavin smoothly, "she wasn't feeling too grand, were you, darling?"

"Really?" Marsha is immediately concerned. "Are you sure everything *is* all right? You seem to be having a lot of trouble. Shouldn't you see the doctor?"

"I'm fine, Mummy. No need for a lot of fuss."

"Well, when you *do* feel up to it, dear, do get along and see that nice vicar of yours. You're lucky to have him, you know, and I'm sure he'll be delighted to have you..." Marsha gabbles on.

The one advantage of having someone like Marsha to tea, thinks Nora, is that she does all the talking. Trouble is, Len is looking bored, sitting there staring at his clasped hands like a meditative monk, and looking in danger of falling asleep.

But Nora is keeping a sharp eye on the clock. She is giving Elsie until four to deliver the cake. If it doesn't arrive by then she will have to start tea and dish up Mr Kipling instead.

Four comes without the cake, so Nora says to Marsha, "If you are having to leave early I think we'd better have tea."

"How delightful, dear. I'm looking forward to it."

Nora goes off to the kitchen to put on the kettle and arrange the Mr Kiplings on a doilied plate, leaving Gavin to guide his mother-in-law into the dining room.

When he's helped Marsha to her feet, she hesitates. "I think, dear, I'd just like to go to the bathroom first."

"Of course," says Gavin. "I'll show you where it is." He ushers Marsha to the bottom of the stairs. "It's facing you at the top," he says, pointing.

Marsha must have been in the bathroom for about three minutes, because the kettle has boiled and Nora is making the tea when the heavy knock comes on the front door.

The cake! Just in time! Nora scurries to the door. Sure enough, there stands Elsie, looking wild eyed and still in her old trousers and jumper smeared with icing sugar.

In her hands is the birthday cake, with a pretty frill and 'Happy Birthday' carefully piped in pink on lemon icing.

"Happy birthday!" cries Elsie as she steps into the hall. "Hope it's in time."

"Just," says Nora shortly. "I'd given up on it."

"Couldn't get it done before. Had a hell of a job with them costumes and that."

"So Colin said."

"Well, I got it here as soon as I could," protests Elsie, not liking Nora's tone. "Even got Boris to drive me around in his sidecar. He's finished it. It's great! He thought you'd like to see. Look!" She opens the door wide for Nora to look.

Sure enough, parked next to Gavin's Peugeot is the

helmeted Boris astride his bike with the sidecar attached, which is now decked out in a bright two-toned colour scheme of yellow and green.

Nora goes a bit green herself. "Very nice," she says.

At that moment Marsha appears at the top of the stairs and commences her portly descent.

Elsie gapes at her.

Marsha gapes back when she sees Elsie standing in the hall looking like a demented gypsy.

Nora gapes at them both, feeling hot and bothered all of a sudden.

"Well, thank you very much for the cake," she says, hurriedly trying to manoeuvre Elsie out of the door. "Very good of you to bring it round. See you soon."

But Elsie doesn't move. She continues to gape as Marsha continues her descent of the stairs and returns to the living room without uttering a word.

Nora doesn't speak either. Nor does Elsie.

But for Elsie the world has suddenly taken on an unusually crimson hue.

"You bloody old snob!" she shrieks. "You might have introduced us!"

Nora becomes agitated. "Would have done," she hisses, "only there's no time now, she's got to get..."

But Elsie is in no mood for explanations.

Quivering like a Strongbow arrow she hurls down the cake on Len's freshly hoovered carpet and marches off to join the waiting Boris.

Chapter 6

As usual, with Easter out of the way, Nora starts counting the weeks to her holiday, but this year she doesn't do so with quite her usual enthusiasm. Elsie has announced she's not going on holiday, nor anywhere else, with that 'snobby old cow'. So far she has kept to it, not having seen Nora, phoned her, been shopping with her, or even attended the usual Friday night sessions at the Sports and Social.

It is at the Sports and Social Club that Nora tries to explain to Colin how it was she didn't introduce Elsie to Marsha. "There wasn't time," she tells him. "Marsha was in a hurry, see, cos she had to get home, cos Oliver was due back at half five and she didn't want him coming home to an empty house after a terrible journey with strikes and that."

"Not to worry, luv," says Colin airily. "Elsie'll soon come round. She's been a bit upsey-dupsy altogether lately." He should know! "I reckon it's this change of life business she's going through."

"She ought to go and see the doctor, then."

"I know. Getting her there is the trouble. You know what Elsie is."

The estrangement hasn't affected the relations between the two men, who have continued to assiduously work at their snooker. By some miracle they have just won their quarter-finals match in the Regal Chemicals Snooker Doubles Tournament, which has stoked up enough enthusiasm between them to set the town ablaze.

"Len was the Man of the Match!" Colin tells Nora, full of admiration for his mate's unprecedented performance.

"Oh yes?" Nora's not interested in Len's snooker abilities. Helps to keep him from under her feet, that's all she cares.

"Just luck," says Len modestly.

"That wasn't luck, mate, potting them long shots one after the other like that."

"Instinct then, cos I can't see them long shots all that well these days."

"You'll have to have some of them glasses like Dennis Taylor used to wear. Got to see right for the semi-final."

"You can't see proper?" Nora is quick to pick that up.

Len wishes he hadn't let it slip out. "It's nothing much. Can see all right otherwise."

"Eyes are very precious," Nora tells him. "You've only got one pair. Can't go down the market for more."

She loses no time in fixing Len up with an appointment to see the optician. Len is a bit of a coward when it comes to things of this nature, be it with a doctor, dentist or now with the optician. But he consoles himself that the optician can't be as bad as the dentist, not as undignified as lying on his back with his mouth agape and trying not to dribble while the dentist hangs hooks in his mouth and pokes around inside.

So when the day arrives, Len goes for his appointment in an equable frame of mind. He doesn't find reading the letters too bad, but can't make up his mind about the clarity of the little red and green circles, and is rather shaken by the plopping sensation of the glaucoma test.

But the real crunch comes when the optician starts peering into his eyeballs with his pencil torch.

"Have you had your blood pressure checked lately?" asks the optician.

Len jumps with alarm. "No – why?"

"Looks as though it could be up. Best have it checked next time you see your doctor."

He is appalled. He imagines himself dropping dead in the street, or even worse, during the snooker semi-final.

*****

He is tempted not to tell Nora about it, but fear as to what could be the matter drives him to do so.

"It's all that beer drinking," she tells him. "We'd better make an appointment for you to see the doctor."

But her concern isn't such that Nora can't let it wait until Len has painted the front of Dad's house, just in case the doctor should tell him he'll have to rest up. The weather is right now, and she is determined the house will be on the market before she goes on holiday.

To Nora's surprise the house painting goes ahead over the next two weekends without trouble. Colin does all the ladder work, Len's suspected high blood pressure now giving him a plausible excuse for only working from the ground. But the job gets done and it's the first heartening news Nora has had for some time. She loses no time in going down to see Mr Hepplewhite.

"Fifty thousand," she tells him. "That's what we'll ask. I'm prepared to come down to forty-eight thousand, but no further."

Mr Hepplewhite looks doubtful and fingers his ginger moustache thoughtfully. "It might be worth a try, Mrs...ahm...Scally. We'll do our best for you."

When she arrives home she immediately phones Cyril to tell him what she has done. He receives the news without comment. She is relieved. At least he seems to have come to terms with the selling of the house.

"How's your arm now?" she asks.

"Middlin'," says Cyril.

"What's that supposed to mean?"

"Still painful at times, like. Can't use it for heavy work and such."

"Boris still doing that, is he?"

"Ar."

"How's he getting on?"

"All right."

"You going to keep him on, then?"

"For the time being, any road."

"I should keep him permanent. You're not getting any younger, Cyril, and once the house is sold you'll have a nice little nest-egg, so you'll be able to afford him."

"Have to think about it."

This encourages Nora. At the rate Cyril thinks, the holiday should be well and truly over before he's made up his mind, and that means Boris is unlikely to be coming with them to Benthaven.

But Nora is still left with two problems – Elsie and her

continuing sulk, and Len's blood pressure. Where Elsie is concerned, Nora feels pretty sure she is unlikely to give up her holiday just because of this silly tiff, and if she does, she wouldn't be altogether sorry. It would be a change for Len and herself to go on their own. Nor is she too worried about Len's blood pressure. They can do things for that these days. So the next step, she decides, is to get Len to the doctor as soon as possible.

But before she can make the appointment she receives an unexpected phone call.

"Nora?"

"Yes?"

"It's Elsie."

"Oh yes." Nora decides to play it cool.

"I'm in trouble."

"Oh yes?"

"I'm all bunged up."

"Bunged up?"

"Constipated and that."

"Better see the doctor then."

A long pause, Nora can guess what's coming.

"Would you come with me?"

"If you want me to." Nora smiles to herself. Elsie is scared stiff of doctors. Then Nora has one of her famous brainwaves. "Tell you what," she continues, thawing just a little. "Len's got to see the doctor about his blood pressure. I'll make an appointment for both of you if you like."

"You'll come as well?"

"Course I will. Who's your doctor?"

"Barnabus."

"Same as Len. You can follow one another. I'll let you know when the appointment is."

Len is panic-stricken when he learns about the appointment. He reckons he's all right now. If he were going to drop dead surely it would have happened while he was painting Dad's house.

But Nora is adamant. "Got to be sure," she insists. She's not risking him being ill just as they are about to go on holiday.

On the evening of the appointment they pick up Elsie in

Len's Escort. Elsie comes scurrying down the garden path, looking more as if she's off to a disco than the doctor. She's done up in a black pencil skirt with black tights, and a rather fussy red and white top.

"Well, here we are again," says Nora, to break the ice.

Elsie doesn't answer. All the way to the surgery she sits bolt upright on the back seat of Len's Escort looking like a startled rabbit.

The patient's waiting room is full of waiting patients, patiently waiting. And a sickly lot they look too. I'm probably the only fit person here, Nora thinks smugly.

Elsie sits tensely, fidgeting with her hair, her handbag, her tights swishing as she keeps re-crossing her legs. Nora offers her a dog-eared copy of *House and Gardens* to read which she rejects with a jerk of her head. So Nora reads it herself, admiring all the photos of dream bathrooms and kitchens, the like of which she soon hopes to have herself in her new home.

Len stares gloomily at the large notice board on the opposite wall to which is pinned a collage of notices, pertaining to such assorted items as AIDS, Cancer Relief, Diabetes, Smoking, Arthritis, Ante-Natal Clinics, Post-Natal Clinics, Disseminated Sclerosis, and the Society of Breast-feeding Mothers, all with their respective help lines. And a daunting one about Alcoholism. Life will be over for Len if he's told to stop drinking.

After they have been waiting some twenty minutes Nora leans over and whispers in Elsie's ear. "While you're with the doctor you might as tell him about your other troubles."

"What other troubles?" snaps Elsie.

"Well, you know – your time of life, your nerves and that."

"Oh I couldn't!"

"Course you can! 'Spect it's that that's causing the other. Doctor's got to know if he's going to treat you proper."

Elsie tosses her head and buttons up her lips.

Nora sighs. Elsie's her own worst enemy.

At last the buzzer goes and the light comes up beside Dr Barnabus's name. It is Elsie's turn.

"Well, go on!" prods Nora. "Good luck."

Elsie looks panic-stricken. "Aren't you coming in with me?"

"Course not!"

"But you promised you'd..."

"I didn't mean I'd go *in* with you. Don't be such a baby! And tell him *everything*. Go on, you're keeping the doctor waiting!"

Clutching her handbag, Elsie teeters on her high heels to the waiting room door, then comes back looking frantic.

"What's his name?"

"Whose name?"

"The doctor's."

"Barnabus! Just call him doctor. Go on!"

When Elsie has finally gone Nora turns to Len. "You're next," she tells him.

"Um," says Len. As if he didn't know.

"Now remember there's nothing to worry about. 'Spect he'll just give you some pills and that, and tell you lay off the drink."

Len doesn't answer, but gazes moodily at a cuddly toy lying rejected in the middle of the waiting room floor. Nora selects another magazine from the pile, and flapping through the pages comes across an article on Brighton. "Well, fancy! Look, there's a photo of that onion-domed place. We must be sure we go to see it when we're there." Len's not too sure he'll be alive to have the chance.

Eventually Elsie comes tottering back, looking distracted and dishevelled.

"God Almighty!" she mutters as she slumps back on the bench beside Nora.

"How did you get on?"

Before Elsie can answer the buzzer goes again.

"That's you," Nora tells Len. "Off you go. Good luck!"

Len lumbers off to meet his fate.

"So what did he say?" Nora asks Elsie.

"He gave me a good going-over."

"It looks like it. You'd better zip up your skirt before you lose it."

Elsie hastily adjusts her skirt.

"Did you tell him about you know what?" asks Nora.

"Didn't have to. He told me. Says I've got to take it easy."

"Didn't I say? I was right. All that stuff you do for the

Operatic. It's too much for you. I reckon they've got a nerve expecting you to do it all the time. You've got to learn to say no, Elsie."

For the first time their eyes meet, and for a moment Nora is worried that the mention of the Operatic may remind Elsie about the birthday cake episode, and set her off again. But it doesn't. Instead, tears glisten, her tight mouth relaxes and quivers.

"Oh Nora!" she cries out, making heads turn. "I don't know what I'm doing half the time! I don't know if I'm coming or going."

"There, there," says Nora sympathetically. "It's just your time of life. Did he give you something for it?"

"Dunno," sobs Elsie. "Said he would – pills or summat."

"Tranquillisers, I 'spect, Valium and that. What about the constipation?"

"Bottle of something, he said. Don't ask me what."

"That'll be Lactulose." Nora speaks from experience. "That'll put you right. Cheer up! You've got a lovely holiday coming up soon. Look, there's an article all about Brighton here. Sounds lovely, and a photo of them…"

Nora is so engrossed in trying to interest Elsie in the glories of Brighton she doesn't notice Len come back, a fatuous grin on his face.

"How did it go?" she demands, when she does see him.

"Nothing wrong," he smirks. "Blood pressure's fine."

"Did he tell you to cut down on drinking?"

"No," lies Len.

"Well, you'd better just the same."

*****

All threats to the summer holiday have now been removed. Elsie has 'come round' and she and Nora are carrying on as if nothing ever happened. The alarm over Len's blood pressure has proved unfounded (Nora told Elsie that the optician should be struck off for having put the wind up Len like that), and Dad's house has been painted and is safely on the market. In her weekly progress calls to the agent Nora has been told several people have been to see the property, but so far there have been no takers.

"I suggest," Mr Hepplewhite said, "if you want to sell quickly, it might be as well to drop the price a little."

"No," responded Nora firmly. "We'll leave it as it is."

Even though these problems have been satisfactorily resolved and she feels she can confidently start counting the days to her holiday – currently twenty – Nora still has one little niggle at the back of her mind. Supposing there should be an offer to buy Dad's house while she is away? If Gavin hadn't been going to Greece at the same time she would have placed the matter confidently in his hands, but short of coming home herself to deal with it, the only other alternative is to let Cyril handle it. That doesn't appeal to her one little bit. But it is the only thing to do.

"Now listen," she says when she phones Cyril about it. "If they should offer the full price, accept right away, but if they haggle and offer less, then phone me in Benthaven and I'll tell you what to say. I don't trust that Hepplewhite man."

And that's about the best she can do.

In the Stilwell household, thanks to the doctor's medications, Elsie's motions and emotions are both more relaxed, and she turns her thoughts not so much to the holiday as to what to give her eldest son, Andy, in Australia for his eighteenth birthday in June. She wants it to be something very personal, something he will cherish and always remember her by. But her mind is blank and in the end she decides to leave it until she and Nora go on their pre-holiday shopping expedition to Bristol next Saturday in the hope of being inspired by something she sees in the big stores.

Colin is preoccupied by the number of break-ins that have been occurring recently on the estate, and is busy fitting new burglar-proof locks to the front and back doors, and to the windows. This he is doing in preference to redecorating the bedroom as he has promised Elsie he would. Elsie hasn't nagged him about it because she is still dithering about the colour of the wallpaper she wants.

Nor has Colin yet decided what to do about the old fivers he found in Nora's clock, which still languish in the old paint tin down in the shed. But his conscience is still bothering him. He really must tell Nora and offer to return them. Trouble is he's put it off so long now that it's going to be a bit tricky, and he can't risk upsetting Nora just before the holiday. It's best left until they come back.

For Boris, life has taken a bit of an up-turn. Fixing that old sidecar has boosted his morale and he is spending a lot of his time down the shed, trying his hand at bits of woodwork. Now he is also working three days a week for Cyril and quite enjoying it.

He finds working on his own in the open air much to his taste. At lunchtime, when the weather permits, he sits in the sun with his sandwiches, reading his *Sporting Life*, and quaffing his beer. Life is at its best, he feels, when he is alone. He has even made a friend of Tina, Cyril's little bitch, who has surprised her owner by giving birth to five puppies. Boris witnessed this event with fascination and has followed their progress with unexpected interest.

On the whole, he thinks, animals are to be preferred to people.

*****

The Saturday that Elsie and Nora decide to go together to Bristol on their pre-holiday shopping spree turns out to be the same day as Colin and Len are due to play their semi-final match in the Snooker Doubles Tournament at the Sports and Social.

This would be of no interest to Elsie and Nora if it didn't mean neither of the men would be available to collect them from the bus station, and therefore, much to Nora's annoyance, they will be forced to splash out on a taxi home.

The coach trip to Bristol proves pleasant. The sun is shining warmly and puts them in a holiday mood. Elsie is still trying to decide what to buy Andy as a birthday present.

"Why don't you just send him a cheque?" suggests Nora. "Then he can buy what he wants. Save the postage and that."

Elsie's not keen. "Got to be personal, something he'll remember me by when I'm dead and gone."

A gravestone then, thinks Nora. But the thought gives her an idea. "Why don't you send him a nice framed photo of yourself, autographed and that?"

"What, as I look now? Thanks a lot!"

"Well, 'spect you'll find something." Nora's not going to waste her time thinking of ideas if Elsie intends to disparage everything she suggests.

Apart from the gift for Andy, Elsie has a clear idea of what she wants to buy. Top of the list is a yellow bikini. It has to be yellow for some unfathomable reason. Then she wants new shoes, new sandals, two pairs of trousers, two sporty tops, high barrier suntan lotion and a pair of fancy sunglasses. She is also toying with the idea of buying herself a new holdall in place of the one she usually takes away with her, which is becoming a bit tatty.

Nora's list is very short; just a new dress to supplement her blue and grey for dinner in the evenings. She's determined not to spend more than she can help.

After their usual slap-up lunch in one of the department stores' restaurants, Elsie insists they look for Andy's gift first, but after she has dithered here and there for almost an hour without making up her mind, Nora gets fed up.

"Look," she says. "I'm not going to have time to find my dress at this rate. I suggest we split up – you do your shopping and I'll do mine."

"But I need your help!"

"No, you don't." Nora is firm. "I'll meet you in the cafe at half past four for a cup of tea. Don't be late, mind. We don't want to miss the coach."

Nora marches off, relieved to be free of Elsie for a bit, and makes straight for the ladieswear. But on the way she spots the babycare department and can't resist having a look round. It's a chance to buy something for her prospective grandchild, something within her budget, like a rattle. But she is so overwhelmed by all the lovely things on display that she comes away with several sets of baby clothes and a huge teddy bear.

All that is left of her spending money now is just enough to buy a pair of sunglasses. She'll have to manage with her blue and grey dresses, she tells herself sternly.

With time on her hands she wanders around the store window-shopping, gazing longingly at the bedroom and dining room suites, and other items she would love to have in her new home. She makes a note of all the prices in the little red notebook she always carries in her handbag.

She is early arriving at the cafe, and buys herself a cup of tea to drink while waiting for Elsie.

Four thirty comes but no Elsie. So does a quarter to five. Nora gets fidgety. She's not going to let Elsie make her miss the coach home. She'll give her five minutes more.

In fact she gives her ten, but no sign of Elsie. "That's it," she says aloud, getting to her feet resolutely.

But as she is leaving the cafe she meets Elsie, looking frazzled and laden like a donkey.

"Where *have* you been?" she demands roughly.

"I was bloody held up…"

"Oh, come on!"

"Must have a cup of tea first. I'm parched!"

"No time. We'll miss the coach."

"We can take a bus to the pick-up point, can't we?"

"In the rush hour? You've got a hope. Come *on*!"

Nora is right – there are long queues for the buses. They have to scurry through central Bristol to the pick-up point near the docks, Nora leading the way at the double, despite her stumpy legs and the monster teddy bear under her arms, Elsie dragging behind struggling for breath, sweaty hands hanging on to bags of shopping.

"Don't rush me," gasps Elsie. "They can bloody wait for us!"

"They won't!"

Again Nora is right. The coach is just moving off. They shout and wave shopping bags at it in vain.

"Now what the hell do we do?" cries Elsie.

"Only one thing we can do – get a train."

Nora is livid. Now she'll have to dip into the reserve cash she always carries with her for such emergencies.

They have an hour to wait when they reach Temple Meads Station, so they go to the buffet for Elsie to quench her thirst. Despite her annoyance with Elsie, Nora can't resist showing her all the lovely baby things she has bought.

Normally Elsie would have fallen hook line and sinker for

the big teddy bear, but the sight of the baby clothes strikes plumb in the centre of her mother's heart.

"Ooh they're gorgeous!" she drools, wondering misty-eyed if one day she'll have a grandchild to buy such things for. But if she does it will be born in Australia and she will probably never see it.

"What did you buy Andy in the end?" asks Nora, snatching back the baby clothes.

Elsie perks up. "A gold wristwatch. That's what held me up. Had to arrange to have it engraved and that."

"What did you have put on it?"

" 'With Love from Mum for Your Eighteenth Birthday.' You think that's all right?"

"Very nice," says Nora.

On the way home in the train Elsie shows Nora her new yellow bikini. Nora thinks it far too scanty and garish for a woman of Elsie's age and reckons she will look like a thin piece of bleached driftwood lying on the beach in that.

Elsie then dips into another plastic shopping bag and produces a bright red sunhat.

"This is for you," she says.

"Oooh lovely!"

Nora is not too keen on the colour but thanks her profusely. Because of her shortage of cash she hasn't bought anything for Elsie as she does normally. But Nora is nothing if not resourceful. She dips into one of her shopping bags.

"And these are for you," she says, producing the pink-rimmed sunglasses she bought for herself.

"Oh thanks very much." Elsie is disappointed. She has already bought herself sunglasses, a pair she much prefers – ornate, almost Dame Edna.

*****

When she eventually arrives home, over an hour late, footsore and weary, Nora is none too pleased to find Len asleep in the armchair, the telly entertaining itself.

"Weren't you worried where I'd got to?" she demands.

"Didn't realise it was so late."

"I worry about you when you're late."

Len has to listen patiently while she relates her tale of woe and exhibits her purchases for his approval. He nods his appreciation with restrained impatience. He has exciting news of his own to impart.

"Don't you want to know how *I* got on?" he asks at the first opportunity.

"Got on?"

"At the snooker match."

"Oh that. What happened?" she says absently.

"Which do you want first, the good news or the bad news?"

"Good news." She is carefully rewrapping the baby clothes.

"We won! We're through to the final!"

"You *won*?" Now she *is* interested. The Snooker Final is a prestigious affair, she knows that much.

"I made a break of forty-three," adds Len proudly.

"Oh very good." She doesn't know what that means. "That's thanks to them glasses I made you get, I 'spect. I must try to come to the final. When is it?"

"June the sixth."

Being preoccupied with the baby clothes it takes a moment for this to sink in. "The sixth of June?" she cries. "But we'll be on holiday then!"

"That's the bad news," says Len.

*****

It is Friday, 29th May, the eve of their departure for Benthaven. It is also the day Gavin and Georgina fly off to the Greek island of Thyros for their antenatal holiday, which means Nora is in a state of both excitement and apprehension.

The young couple called round the previous evening to make their farewells and wish Nora and Len a happy time on their own holiday. Nora was near to tears. She doubted if she'd ever see her beloved son again, and her expected grandchild never.

"Safest form of travel there is," Gavin assured her. "More likely to be killed crossing the road."

Since it is her last day at work before her own holiday Nora is unable to go to the airport to see them off, about which she is relieved in a way. To see them disappearing into the unknown after a lot of public kissing and goodbyes would have been altogether too much.

That evening the Scallys and the Stilwells meet up just as usual at the Sports and Social Club. They regard this as the first celebration of their holiday, a sort of sigh of relief at having been released from the yoke of work for two whole weeks. Tonight, however, since Colin is on the two-till-ten shift, he won't be joining them until he comes off duty.

Nora quickly acquaints Elsie with her anxiety about Gavin and Georgie travelling by plane. "Gavin says they will arrive in the dark," she tells her. "Don't know how they manage to land them big planes in the dark."

"Radar and that," says Len knowledgeably.

"Oh, they'll be all right," says Elsie airily. "Not far to Greece, not like flying to Australia and that. Gets boring, I can tell you, unless you get turbulence. I remember once…"

But Nora doesn't want to hear Elsie's flying experiences, so she quickly asks if she knows if Colin has yet asked Personnel about changing the date of the Snooker Final.

Elsie sniffs. "Supposed to be seeing them today. He'd better get it changed, cos I'm not breaking *my* holiday for a bleedin' snooker match. If they must play that stupid game they can come back on their own."

Nora's not so sure. "We ought to go as their wives. Cheer them on and that. Besides, no point in us being stuck in Benthaven with nothing to do."

"We can sit on the beach, can't we? If it rains we can go to that Regent Palace place you keep on about."

"Well, we'll see. Don't have to decide now. You all ready for the off in the morning?"

"Oh yes," lies Elsie. "Just a few last minute things to do." In truth, she still has to finish the new dress she is running up for herself, and hasn't even started to pack.

"We'll be round to collect you at nine sharp in the morning," Nora warns her. "Got to make an early start cos of the traffic and that."

"We'll be ready," promises Elsie.

"All being well," Nora continues, "we should get there about two. Mr Pertwee says he'll make us a nice cup of tea when we arrive, then we can have a bit of a rest and that before dinner."

Colin arrives, still wearing his Security Officer's uniform. "My God," he growls. "I need a bloody drink!"

Elsie looks at him sharply. "What's up with you?"

"You may well ask!"

Len half rises to go and get Colin a drink.

"It's all right, mate, I'll get 'em." Colin trudges off to the bar with the plod of a shire horse hauling a plough.

"Colin seems upset," observes Nora.

"Something to do with the bleedin' snooker match, I bet," says Elsie, who's been hearing too much about that recently.

When he returns from the bar with a double whisky for himself and Len he flops into a chair and takes a hefty swig.

"Out with it," snaps Elsie. "What's eating you?"

"Well…"

"Well – what?"

"Yes, don't keep us in suspenders," grins Len.

"Well," Colin repeats, "you know old Frank?"

"Old Frank?" queries Elsie. "Old Frank who?"

"Old Frank Pople – the Company chauffeur."

"Oh him. What about him?"

"Came into the gatehouse just before I left. Just got in from driving the bigwigs back from Head Office in London."

"Heard there was a big meeting," nods Nora. Being a shop steward, she likes to be thought in on these things.

"*So?*" persists Elsie.

"Well, on the way back he heard them saying they've been told the Plant has got to be shut down."

"What Plant?"

"*This* Plant, of course! The works, the whole caboodle."

"Bloody hell!"

"Rubbish!" declares Nora.

"Pretty sure about it. Frank said old Bollinger was nearly in tears about having to announce the redundancies."

"Don't believe it," says Nora. "Got to consult the unions before they can do that. I'd have heard."

"Only decided today. Telling the unions tomorrow, I 'spect."

"But why?" demands Elsie.

"He didn't say."

"Uneconomic," pronounces Len. "Not surprised."

"Don't take notice of what old Frank tells you," says Nora. "He's got a turnip where his brain ought to be."

"Just telling you what he said, that's all." Colin downs his whisky. "God, I need another of them."

This time Len does the honours.

"Fine way to start a holiday," moans Elsie.

"Shouldn't worry about it," says Nora. "No need to let it spoil the holiday."

Colin is indignant. "All very well for you, Nora. You and Len'll be retiring soon anyway. We got a fair way to go yet. Not easy getting another job at my age."

"You don't need to worry, Colin. Good security men are always in demand."

Colin shakes his head dolefully. "Dunno so much."

Nora shifts her weight from one buttock to the other. "Anyhow, it ain't happened yet, so cheer up, you're on holiday! Which reminds me, did you manage to get the Snooker Final postponed?"

"No, I didn't. Can't be changed. It's all fixed up, tickets been sold and that. Don't let it upset you, Nora. Len and I will come back on the Saturday and return to Benthaven on the Sunday."

"And what we supposed to do while you're away?" demands Elsie. "Build sandcastles?"

"*I* think," cuts in Nora authoritatively, "it is best if we all come back, spend the night at home and return on Sunday as Colin says. We can leave our things in Benthaven. I'm sure Mr Pertwee will see they're safe."

Len comes back with the fresh round of drinks.

"Well, here's to a happy holiday," says Nora, holding up her glass.

They all drink to that.

"Just think," says Elsie wistfully. "Two whole weeks with nothing to do! No work, no washing, no ironing…"

"No cooking," says Nora. "That's the best bit."
"No washing-up," says Len.
"And no job to come home to," adds Colin.

Chapter 7

The 'Great Day' dawns bright and clear.

Nora has already had her bath and is busy deodorising her body when the bedside alarm clatters at six. Len plunges across the bed to stop it, but knocks it to the floor where it clatters itself into silence. When Nora comes in from the bathroom in her dressing gown and shower cap Len is asleep again.

"Come on," she says, yanking back the bedclothes. "There's a lot to do."

When the cold penetrates his pyjamas the first thing Len sees upon opening his eyes is Nora stark naked apart from her shower cap. He quickly closes them again.

"It's half past six," she exaggerates. "We've got a lot to do before we leave."

Len manoeuvres his feet to the floor, fidgets them into his slippers and sits for a while, as is his custom, on the edge of the bed, elbows on knees, head in hands.

"Don't sit there all day," says Nora as she pulls on a clean pair of knickers. "Go and get your bath, and don't forget to put your shaving things and that into the toilet bag when you've finished."

Len shuffles off to the bathroom and sits himself on the lavatory. Not that he has much hope of going this time of the morning. No doubt the urge will assail him while they're belting down the motorway.

By the time Nora has finished dressing, done her hair, applied her make-up, made the bed, laid out Len's new blazer and slacks, gone down to the kitchen and laid out the breakfast things, it is time to listen to the weather forecast. The man promises a dry day, sunny in the morning but clouding in the afternoon, with temperatures in the low sixties. Just right, she thinks. She doesn't like it too hot, especially for travelling.

But it is the news she is most anxious to hear. While she spoons up her bran flakes she listens for any mention of air disasters. None is reported, so she feels safe in assuming Gavin and Georgie have arrived in Greece without mishap.

Satisfied about that, Nora consults the list she has made of things still to be done. Top of the list, ringed and underlined, is 'Ring Cyril'. She picks up the phone.

"Hello, Glennis? This is Nora. Is Cyril about?"

"He's doing his feet."

"Oh! Well, could he manage to come to the phone, only it's important and we're just off on our holiday?"

"I'll ask him. Hold on."

Eventually Cyril's dolorous tones reach her ear. "Hello, Nora."

"Sorry to bother you so early."

"S'all right."

"Now listen. The estate agent rang me at work yesterday. Someone's very interested in Dad's house and is going to look at it again. Mr Hepplewhite thinks he may well make an offer."

"Oh ar."

"If he does, the agent's going to phone you. Now I don't want you accepting any offers without consulting me."

"Right you are."

"Phone me at the hotel straight away. I gave you the number, didn't I?"

"Got it somewhere."

"If I happen to be out, leave a message with Mr Pertwee."

"Mr Percy?"

"Pertwee." She spells it for him. "I'll warn him you may be calling, and I'll phone you back soon as I can. Have you got all that?"

"Think so," says Cyril.

I hope to God he has, thinks Nora. As she puts down the phone Len comes trundling down the stairs all rigged out in his new blazer and slacks.

"My, you *do* look smart!" she exclaims, surveying him as an art lover might a Rembrandt.

"Blazer's a bit tight," he complains. He buttons it up to show how it strains across his beer belly.

"Leave it undone then."

"Trousers cut in the crotch too." He's not looking forward to driving all the way to Brighton with a cut crotch.

"Oh, they'll give a bit with time. Now go and get your breakfast – it's all ready. And don't sit reading the paper – time's getting on."

While Len is spooning up his bran flakes Nora packs the last-minute items in her holdall, then checks her handbag for handkerchief, compact, sunglasses, notebook and pencil, peppermint creams, cash, cheque book and National Savings book.

"Everything is ready for you to put in the car," she tells Len when she returns to the kitchen.

"Right," says Len, belching.

"I hope you won't do that at the hotel. I don't know what the Pertwees would think." She starts clearing the breakfast table while Len is still munching his toast and marmalade. "And you'd better just check the oil and that in the car."

"But it was only serviced a couple of days ago."

"Check it just the same. Can't be too careful. Costs a bomb if you break down on the motorway."

While Len sets about his jobs Nora does the washing-up, washes out the tea towel, cleans the sink, mops the floor and puts a note out for the milkman.

"If you want to go to the toilet," she says when Len returns, "you'd better go now, before I put Domestos down the pan."

Twenty minutes to nine, she notes with satisfaction. Just nice time. She consults her checklist. All that remains to be done now is for the gas, electricity and water to be turned off and the dustbin to be put out – all Len's jobs.

He has no trouble with the gas or electricity, but when it comes to the water Len has to rummage among the bushes in the front garden to find the stopcock.

"Don't dirty them nice trousers," warns Nora.

But it's not his trousers that get dirty, it's his cuffs.

"Now look what you've done! I told you to be careful."

But time permits for no more than a brisk rub with the clothes brush before attention has to be turned to the dustbin. Not being prepared to use dustbin bags because dogs are liable to tear them asunder, Nora always helps Len out with the dustbin in case he gets a hernia. But they have only lugged it halfway down the concrete path before she catches her leg on a straggling rose briar, drawing blood and snagging her tights.

"I told you to prune them roses! Now I'll have to go and change."

"Don't show much," grunts Len.

But Nora can't arrive in Benthaven with a bloody leg and snagged tights, so Len has to offload the luggage for Nora to retrieve another pair of tights from her case.

By time they are ready to go once more it is ten past nine. Nora takes a final look around the house to ensure everything is in order and wonders, as she always does, if she's ever likely to see her home again.

They are about to close the front door when the phone rings.

"Leave it," says Len.

"No. It might be Mr Hepplewhite."

But it isn't.

"Is that you Nora?"

"Yes?"

"It's Marsha – Marsha Bloom."

"Oh, hello, er...Marsha."

"I've just had a phone call from Georgie."

Nora starts with alarm. "From Georgie! I thought..."

"Just to let us know they have arrived safely."

"She rang all the way from Greece? Fancy!"

"They had an excellent flight and apparently she's none the worse for it."

"Oh good. I must say I've been a bit worried."

"They both send their love and hope you enjoy your holiday in Brighton. You're leaving today, I gather?"

"Just off. You only just caught us."

"Then I won't keep you, my dear. But there is just one thing. Do you think it might be a good idea if I had your number in Brighton? One doesn't anticipate trouble, but you never know."

Nora is only too happy to give her the number, but then Marsha starts rambling on, informing Nora how she's just come down to discover her cat Timmy has deposited the head and entrails of a rabbit on her back doorstep during the night. Consequently it is another fifteen minutes before Nora puts down the phone.

But Len's Ford Escort eventually moves away. Nora opens her handbag, and takes out her red notebook and pencil. She makes a note of the petrol, the mileage, and the time. 9.32.

*****

In the Stilwell household pandemonium reigns.

Like Nora, Elsie set her digital alarm clock to go off at six, but failed to realise she'd put it at p.m. instead of a.m.

It was Colin who woke first. Having spent the night at the snooker table, he'd leapt up in bed when he shot the cue ball straight into the eye of the Chief Executive.

As he rubbed his numb arm it dawned on him first that it was daylight, and second that they should have been up an hour ago. He bounced off the bed as if off a trampoline.

"Els'! For God's sake, wake up – it's twenty to eight!"

Bursting to go he dashes to the bathroom, only to find the door locked. Radio One blares from within.

"Boris! Get the hell out of there!" He hammers the door.

Elsie is roused, glares at the digital clock, shakes it, heaves herself out of bed, and stumbles down the stairs in her self-embroidered nightdress to put the kettle on. She can't function properly until she's had a cup of tea.

"You great lolloping lout!" Colin yells at Boris when he comes out of the bathroom. "Why didn't you wake us?"

"Didn't ask me to." Boris ambles off to his bedroom out of harms way.

Flailing his dead arm Colin rushes into the bathroom.

Elsie gropes her way back to the bedroom to dress while the water boils. She gets no further than her knickers and bra before the kettle starts screaming.

Colin relieves himself with his live arm, then decides to have a quick shower and nearly dies of shock when stone-cold water rains down on him. So he makes do with a lick and a promise and returns to the bedroom, shaving as he goes with his rechargeable shaver.

Elsie returns to the kitchen still in a state of undress to answer the call of the kettle. Feeling the nip of the morning air she grabs the nearest available covering to put round her shoulders which happens to be the tablecloth. Forgetting she has already put two tea bags into the pot, she adds two more.

In the bedroom Colin's rechargeable shaver has petered out, leaving one side of his face unshaved. He plugs in the shaver to recharge and goes to the wardrobe for clean underwear, but can only find pillowcases. Elsie's been shifting things round again. A frantic search reveals it to be in the dressing table drawer along with Elsie's frilly underwear.

Downstairs in the kitchen Elsie is also searching – for her tights, which she washed through last night and left hanging on the kitchen line, but which have inexplicably disappeared. She searches high and low, the tablecloth falling from her shoulders in the process.

Colin appears in the doorway in his underpants.

"You seen my jersey?" He is surprised to see Elsie now leaning against the sink sipping her tea.

"What jersey?"

"That brown one with the blue diagonal stripes."

She tries to work out which way is diagonal. "That's gone to Oxfam," she says as she passes Colin a mug of tea.

"Oxfam!"

"You never wear it."

"I keep it for holidays, don't I?" He takes one sip of the tea and makes a face like a gargoyle. "What the hell's this – liquid Christmas pudding?"

"You seen my tights?" demands Elsie as she resumes her search.

"What tights?"

"What tights do you think? Them tights I washed through last night. They were on the line."

"Sure you haven't sent them to Oxfam?"

"Don't you get sarky with me!"

The lugubrious figure of Boris appears in the doorway. Undaunted by the spectacle of his dad and stepmother supping tea in their underwear, he goes to the fridge and extracts a can of lager.

"What you think you're doing?" demands Colin.

"Thirsty," grunts Boris.

"You can't drink bloody beer this time of the morning, for

God's sake! Here, have this tea. That'll make your hair curl. And if you've got any sense you'll stay in your room out of the way until we've gone."

Boris lumbers off with the tea. He knows when he's not wanted, which is most of the time.

"Come on, Els', get moving. They'll be here at any moment."

"Got to find them bleedin' tights first." She recommences her search.

Colin picks up the tablecloth that dropped from Elsie's shoulders and points at the tights on the floor, thus revealed. "What's them then – seaweed?"

He picks up the tights, throws them at Elsie and marches out of the kitchen.

"Boris might have that jumper," bawls Elsie after him.

"What jumper?"

"That jumper with the blue stripes."

"Oh! Right."

Colin barges into his son's room. Boris is sprawled on the bed, earphones on, the mug of tea undrunk on the floor. Colin yanks off the earphones. "You got my jumper?"

"What jumper?"

"The one with the blue diagonal stripes."

"Dunno."

With his police-trained eye Colin makes a swift recce of the room and soon spots it on the floor beside the bedside table. In grabbing the jumper he jogs the table, which shakes the precarious pile of videos, which tumble on to the teacup on the floor, which spills its contents over the hairy green carpet tiles.

"*You* can bloody well clean that up," growls Colin. "Give you something to do."

When he returns to the bedroom Colin finds Elsie now without her bra, beavering away at a repair job on it.

"What the hell you doing now?"

"What's it look like?" seethes Elsie, needle between her gritted teeth.

There is a cheery toot-toot from a car outside.

"Christ Almighty, they're here!" cries Colin.

"Bugger 'em!" snaps Elsie.

Both scramble into clothes. Elsie slaps on make-up, dithering over which shoes to wear. Colin hauls out the suitcases and throws in everything in sight.

Outside, Nora's patience becomes exhausted. "Give 'em another toot," she tells Len.

Len toots.

"Bugger 'em!" cries Colin.

Elsie can't find the holdall she always takes with her on holiday for shopping and the beach. Colin is bothered about all the old fivers he found in Nora's clock, which are still in the old paint tin down in the shed. He doesn't want to risk Boris finding them while he's away, so thinks it best to take them with him.

Nora gets out of the car. "I'm going to jolly them up."

In the bedroom Elsie is going frantic looking for her holdall. She turns and glares at Colin. "You got it?" she demands roughly.

"Try Oxfam!"

Elsie hurls a hairbrush at him.

"Course I ain't got it. Don't waste time looking for that shabby old thing."

"But I need it!"

"Use a plastic bag or summat. I'll buy you a new one when we get there."

"I'll hold you to that," grinds Elsie.

The front door bell ding-dongs.

"Leave it," growls Colin.

But Elsie can't. With one shoe on and the other in her hand, she staggers down the stairs. Colin seizes the opportunity to take out his document wallet from its secret hiding place, which is a home-made contraption attached to the bottom of the bed. In the wallet he keeps all his important documents and his spare cash. But it is neither the cash nor the documents he wants. It is a money-belt in which he keeps his money while on holiday. This year, however, he intends to put the old fivers in it, that is, if he gets the chance to retrieve them from the shed.

Nora dongs again.

"Colin!" screams Elsie up the stairs. "I can't open the bleedin' front door! It's this new lock you've put on."

Sighing heavily, Colin stuffs the money-belt into his pocket and trails down the stairs, still in his bare feet.

"Coo-eee!" calls Nora through the letterbox.

"Wait!" yells Elsie.

"Anyone at home?" calls Nora.

Colin arrives and fiddles with the lock, eventually managing to open the door.

"What's going on?" asks Nora.

Colin mutters something incomprehensible and leaves Elsie to deal with Nora. It is an opportunity to get the fivers from the shed.

"We overslept," Elsie tells Nora tersely. "Won't be long."

"Got to get moving cos of the traffic and that."

"Five minutes," promises Elsie.

Sensing mayhem within the Stilwell house, Nora decides to wait in the car.

Undecided as to what to do next, Elsie eventually goes to the bathroom for a bit of a wash, but it's not until she's sloshed cold water all over her face that she realises she's already put on her make-up, and has to re-apply it.

Down in the shed Colin stuffs as many old fivers into his money-belt as it will take, then drops his trousers to fix the belt around his waist. The safest place for the fivers, he thinks. At night he'll have to take the belt off while Elsie is in the bath and hide it somewhere in the bedroom. Shouldn't be a problem.

Elsie, back in the bedroom, is furious to see the bed still unmade and littered with cases and clothes. She whips them off and pulls up the bedclothes, and as she does so catches sight of herself in the wardrobe mirror. Why the hell has she put on the dress she's just finished making to travel in Len's old car? She takes it off again and puts on her oldest trouser suit.

Colin returns from the shed, looking innocent.

"Where the hell have you been?" demands Elsie.

"Padlocking the shed."

"For God's sake finish packing them cases!"

More toots from without.

The two cases and three copious plastic bags are filled to overflowing. Colin bounces up and down on the top of the cases to get them shut, and having succeeded, suddenly realises his feet are still bare, and that he's packed all his socks.

"I wish I knew what happened to my holdall," moans Elsie as she starts searching for it yet again.

"Forget it," snaps Colin, feeling about inside the case for his socks. "I'll buy you another one, I told you."

After another fifteen minutes and as many toots they deem themselves as ready to leave as they ever will be, and go into Boris's room to make their farewells and administer a few final instructions.

Elsie goes crazy when she sees the sugary pool of dark tea on her carpet.

"I told you to clear that up!" yells Colin.

Elsie dashes off for the scrubbing brush and carpet cleaner, while Colin takes the opportunity to issue a series of dire warnings to his son about not killing himself through electrocution, gassing, drowning or bleeding to death, during their absence.

Prompted by further tootings from outside Colin at last gets round to heaving the luggage out to the waiting Escort.

"Are you aware, sir," he greets Len in his policeman's voice, "that it's an offence to keep honking like that?"

Not all the luggage will go in the boot, so Elsie's washing line has to be procured in order to secure the rest on the roof rack.

Elsie comes scurrying down the garden path and joins Nora in the back seat of the car. Colin sits next to Len in the front, road map on his knees.

And at last they are away.

Nora marks down the time in her red notebook. 10.47

"Straightforward enough," says Colin, studying the map. "M4, M25 and then M23."

"Don't want to risk the M25 this time of day," objects Nora. "Better go Salisbury way, on the A338 and that."

"Looks a bit complicated." Colin strokes his chin as he ponders the route. It is then that he realises one side of his face is shaven, and the other not.

"God Almighty!" he cries. "I've left me bleedin' shaver on charge!"

They turn back.

*****

"Look!" cries Nora as the Escort teeters down the precipitous road leading into Benthaven. "There's the sea!"

"Um," says Len, who is doing his utmost to prevent the car hurtling straight into it.

Elsie and Colin even fail to say that much. Both look as if they are under anaesthetic. Elsie lolls on the back seat, her head back, her eyes closed, her mouth open, her long legs permanently locked in an inverted 'V' position. Colin's rump has gone numb through sitting on the wallet in his back pocket and is trying to sit on his side to relieve it.

Nora, in her wisdom, had insisted on taking the scenic route, via Salisbury, with the result that they were delayed by several road works and took a few wrong turnings, notably one at Southampton which resulted in them going into the dock area of the town. But it did provide a glimpse of the QE2, or at least, of its funnel.

This proved too much for Nora.

"Marsha and Oliver are going on a cruise on that," she said excitedly. "To the Caribbean, would you believe!"

Elsie's lips tightened at the mention of the Blooms, and she remained silent for the rest of the journey.

But just before six they arrive safely at the little harbour which is the focal point of Benthaven, and half an hour later, and after several misdirections to Ensdale Terrace, which proves to be halfway back up the hill they have just descended, they pull up in the forecourt of the Ocean View Private Hotel.

At last they are here.

Nora is first out of the car. "Looks lovely!" she cries, surveying the hotel's granite grey fasade.

Len thinks it looks more like a penitentiary. The vestibule, however, proves bright enough, with white woodwork and pink and grey spotted wallpaper. There is a small reception desk, garlanded with posters and leaflets advertising the attractions of the area, and on the opposite wall, a payphone beneath a plastic cowl.

Nora tinkles the little bell on the desk. No response. She tinkles again with the same result. After a third unsuccessful tinkle she wanders through into what is clearly the dining room where she is accosted by a huge Alsatian dog who gives a basso profundo bark and sniffs under her armpits.

"Good dog," says Nora, backing off.

A short balding man appears from the kitchen. He is wearing an alpaca jacket, black trousers and a bow tie, and over them a plastic apron bearing the words 'Le Fruitier'.

"Aye?"

"Mr Pertwee?" Nora tries to emulate Marsha's authoritative tones.

"Aye."

"I'm Mrs Scally."

"Och aye! We were expecting you a wee while ago."

"It was the traffic and that," explains Nora, lapsing into her normal vernacular.

Mr Pertwee extends a warm welcome to the freshly arrived party, has them sign in and shows them up to their bedrooms. "Numbers six and seven," he announces as he hands over the keys. "Two double rooms with bath and toilet – and sea views."

"Oooh lovely!" exclaims Nora.

Mr Pertwee consults his watch. "You're just in time. Dinner will be served in half an hour."

The two rooms are a mirror image of one another, except that the wallpaper in Room Six is blue and gold, and in Room Seven green and gold. Nora plumps for Room Seven, that being her lucky number, and directs Len to bring up the cases.

The first thing Colin does is to look for the emergency exit. At the end of the corridor he sees a door marked 'PRIVATE. EMERGENCY EXIT ONLY'. He tries the door, finds it unlocked, so goes through. At the end of the corridor is another door with a green sign indicating it is the Emergency Exit. Beyond it is a fire escape. Satisfied, he turns back and as he goes notices little ceramic discs on the doors each side of the corridor. 'Mum and Dad's Room', 'Bathroom', 'Daphne's Room' they read. This must be the Pertwee's private quarters, he concludes.

When he arrives back at the bedroom Colin examines the lock on the bedroom door, but with this he is far from satisfied.

"Any half-witted villain could pick this lock," he complains to Elsie, who is frantically rummaging through a plastic bag in search of her Lactulose.

In view of the poor lock Colin decides he must secrete the document wallet containing all his cash and papers in a place where a thief is least likely to look. He decides on the wardrobe, and straps the wallet with the strong adhesive tape he brought against such a contingency to the underside of one of the shelves, right at the back. The old fivers from the clock, he decides, are best kept in the money belt around his middle during the day, but at night he will slip them into the wallet while Elsie's in the bathroom. He reminds himself firmly that once this holiday is over he must tell Nora about the fivers. He must own up, he thinks, there can be no two ways about it.

When Len returns to Room Seven with the cases he is surprised to find Nora standing on a chair. "You can see the sea ever so clearly," she tells him, pointing to the misty grey smudge above the recently erected flats on the opposite side of the road. "You have a look."

She dismounts for him to see, but Len's legs have had all the mounting they can take from lugging the cases up the stairs. "Can see it between the houses," he grunts.

A gong bongs from somewhere in the bowels of the hotel.

"That's for dinner," Nora declares. "Best not change, mustn't be late."

She just washes her hands, tidies her hair and exchanges her pink plastic necklace for her best pearls. Then she surveys Len. "You look very smart as you are. I'll just brush the scurf off your shoulders."

In the next room Elsie is already changing because the knees of her trousers have become baggy through her legs being bent so long in the car, and keeps everyone waiting while she struggles into the little black dress she ran up.

When they reach the dining room, which Elsie finds very claustrophobic due to the ceiling-high exotic plant casting its large leaves over a third of the room, several guests are already at their tables. By the net-curtained window, through which there is a ghostly view of the dustbins beyond, sit an impeccably dressed coloured family. At a corner table is a young couple, heavily engrossed in one another. Alone, at a table in the middle of the room, sits an old lady with a nut-brown face who, supplied with the appropriate headgear, could pass for an Indian squaw.

Nora beams and nods at all of them as she enters.

Mr Pertwee, now minus his apron, greets them warmly and ushers them to a table in the shade of the exotic plant.

"It's Lancashire hotpot tonight," he tells them proudly.

"Oooh lovely!" exclaims Nora.

Thank God it's not haggis, thinks Colin.

Len asks for his long-awaited pint.

Mr Pertwee splays his hands. "Och, I'm afraid we're not licensed."

"Not licensed!" Len's holiday is ruined before it has started.

"There's nae to stop ye bringing in y'own," Mr Pertwee adds hastily, "but I cannae sell y'so much as a wee dram."

"Bloody hell!" cries Colin.

"Never mind," says Nora brightly. "We'll bring our own for tomorrow night."

Len glowers. He can't wait until then. "Any pubs round here?" he demands.

"Och aye! There's The Fisherman's Float down by the harbour. Very popular. Live music on a Saturday night."

"Long way down to the harbour," Len objects.

"It's nae so far if y'take the short cut down the steps on the opposite side of the road."

"There you are then," says Nora. "We'll go down directly after dinner. Walk will do us good." When Mr Pertwee has gone to execute their orders Nora sits back in her chair and carefully arranges her paper napkin in her lap. "Well, here we are then," she announces. "Safe and sound. And very nice it is too. It is such a treat these days to find somewhere so quiet and old-fashioned. It's nice and clean too."

"And dry," adds Len.

Colin leans over and speaks confidentially to Nora. "You brought any valuables with you – cash and that?"

"Some," says Nora suspiciously. "Why?"

"Wouldn't leave 'em lying about in your room. Locks are nothing too special. You got shelves in your wardrobe?"

"Haven't had a chance to find out."

"Well, I've strapped mine under one the shelves with

adhesive tape. Thieves don't think of looking there."

"Haven't got no adhesive tape."

"Borrow mine, and another thing. You get all sorts of shady customers coming down from London to this neck of the woods, so don't carry your handbag when you go out."

"Got to have me handbag!" Nora is beginning to feel a bit uneasy.

"Put it in your holdall then, and keep a tight grip on it. You'd better do the same, Els'."

"If I had a holdall to put it in," says Elsie dryly. "You promised to buy me one – remember?"

"Give us a chance, we've only just got here! I'll buy you a really nice one when we go to Brighton."

A smartly dressed bald-headed man with horn-rimmed glasses comes into the room. He beams at the new guests as he passes. "Goood eeevening," he says, displaying a fine array of artificial dental work.

For once Nora is too taken aback to respond.

"Good evening," says Elsie instead, twitching a smile. She is beginning to recover and feeling more with it.

When the man has sat down Nora leans over to Elsie and whispers. "That man gave me quite a turn. I thought it was Oliver Bloom for a moment. He's the spitting image!"

"Looks like Sergeant Bilko to me," grins Colin.

Elsie stifles a snigger.

But the mention of Oliver leads Nora's thoughts in a new direction. "I wonder how Gavin and Georgie are getting on in Greece," she says wistfully.

"Having a bloody good time if they've got any sense," says Colin enviously. "Gavin's probably sampling the local plonk and Georgie's probably lying topless in the sun."

Elsie hoots with laughter. "What – in her condition?"

Nora is indignant. "She'd never do nothing like that! She's been too well brought up."

"Come off it, Nora," grins Colin," they're just the types who do that sort of thing when they're away."

"Not the Blooms," says Nora firmly. "They're very religious. Marsha's on the church council and that."

A buxom-looking girl with heavily made-up eyes and hair

like an upturned lavatory brush interrupts them. She's doing a balancing act with their bowls of soup.

"What kind of soup is it?" asks Nora.

"Fish soup," says the girl dourly.

"Oooh lovely!"

"Tell you what," says Colin when the girl has gone, "I wouldn't mind seeing *her* topless."

"Shut up," snaps Elsie. "Don't start."

"Colin's getting into his holiday mood early," Nora observes.

"Well, why not? That's what we've come for, ain't it? Got to make the most of it. Could be the last holiday we'll have."

"Last holiday? Why?"

"Cos if we're made redundant, Els' and I won't be able to afford it any more."

"You still worrying about that?"

"Could happen, Nora." Colin's geniality is beginning to evaporate.

"You'd soon get another job, I told you."

"Dunno so much."

"Well, I know what I'd do if I were you."

"What's that?" Colin takes interest. He's beginning to respect Nora's bright ideas.

"Sure to get redundancy money and that. I'd use it to set myself up as a private eye."

"Me? A private eye? Dunno about that."

"Why not? You'd be good at it."

Colin rubs the tip of his nose with the end of his soup spoon. "Very dicey though. Knew a bloke in the Force who did that. He went bust within the year."

"Just a suggestion."

"Wouldn't mind setting up me own business though," he continues musingly. "Be me own boss. Not police work though. Nice to do summat different."

By the time the girl returns with the Lancashire hotpot the thought of starting his own business has cheered Colin up no end. "You must be Daphne," he says as she gathers up the soup bowls.

She glances at him sharply. "Aye, that's reet."

"Mr Pertwee's daughter?"

"Aye."

"Oh, you're Mr Pertwee's daughter!" exclaims Nora, instantly revising her opinion of the girl. "Fancy!"

"Pretty name, Daphne," says Colin, firmly resisting the temptation to pinch her bum as she leans over to remove Len's soup bowl. "Pretty name for a pretty girl."

"I hope you're not going to make a bloody fool of yourself over that girl," says Elsie sourly, when the girl has gone.

"I only said she was pretty," Colin protests.

"Pretty! She's got eyes like a bloody cat!" rasps Elsie as she takes a first mouthful of the too hot hotpot, and burns her tongue.

"How did you know her name was Daphne?" asks Nora.

Colin grins mysteriously. "That's elementary, my dear Watson."

Len decides to move his chair before starting on his hotpot because a frond of the exotic plant persists in tickling his ear.

Colin notices his doleful countenance and grins. "Cheer up, mate! Could be worse. Here, have a nice glass of water."

*****

In the cold sea mist that now envelops Benthaven harbour The Fisherman's Float has an eerie Jamaica Inn feel about it, despite the string of fairy lights strung across its front in the forlorn hope of countering this effect.

But inside it is warm and cosy, and softly lit apart from the bar itself and the illuminated fish tank set into one of the exposed stone walls. The decor is all fishing – nets drooping from the corners, converted crab baskets for tables, a jungle of floats dangling from the ceiling.

Rather than drink and drive, the Scallys and the Stilwells have descended the four hundred or so steep steps from Ensdale Terrace to the harbour. The pub is already crowded when they enter, but are lucky enough to find seats when a party leaves.

"Oh, I like this," declares Nora as she parks herself on an antique settle. She's partial to a bit of atmosphere.

Colin volunteers to buy the first round. While he is waiting at the bar to be served he tries to decipher a sign over it painted in old German script. 'Dave and Dennis Welcome You to The Fisherman's Float', it seems to read.

"That's very friendly," he remarks to the burly macho-looking barman who eventually comes to serve him.

Colin's cheery smile suddenly changes into a gape of total disbelief. "You're Dave!" he gasps.

"Colin! Well I'll be damned!"

Big fists clench in a warm handshake across the bar.

"Just can't believe it!" Colin is overwhelmed. "How are you, mate?"

"Never better, and yourself?"

"Ditto, mate, ditto. Good Lord, it must be getting on for twenty years since I last saw you!"

"Seventeen years. That's when I left the Force."

"Is it really? Doing all right for yourself too, by the looks of it."

"Can't complain."

"You the 'Dave' up there?" Colin indicates the notice above their heads.

"That's right."

"Free house, is it? Yours?"

"In partnership with Dennis."

Colin is impressed, very impressed.

But there are people demanding to be served. "We must have a chat later," says Dave.

"Sure thing. Look forward to it."

Colin is full of it when he rejoins the others. "Used to be on the beat with him," he tells them. "Just can't believe it. Good bloke, Dave. Only an ordinary copper when I knew him. Now he's half-owner of this place. Shows what can be done with a bit of initiative. Reckon that's the sort of thing I'd like to do if I *am* made redundant – run a place like this."

"You couldn't run a raffle," snorts Elsie, who is pushing coins into a nearby fruit machine as fast as she can go.

"Why not? I'm not that daft."

"Huh!"

"Redundancy money wouldn't get you a place like this," says Len, after he's taken a fulsome draft of his pint.

"I know that. Means selling up, borrowing a bit from the bank, no doubt."

"Risky," says Nora. "Could lose everything."

"True," nods Len. "Pubs are pretty risky these days."

"Wouldn't say this place is doing too bad, anyhow." Colin glances round at the crowded bar.

"Can't go wrong with a pub like this, holiday resort, by the sea," Len agrees. "Depends where it is, on the area, competition and that."

"And who's running it," adds Elsie.

At that moment the pub door opens and a bald-headed man with glasses comes in.

"Hey," cries Colin. "Look who's just walked in – old Sergeant Bilko!"

Len and Nora turn to look, but Elsie is too intent on collecting her winnings from the fruit machine.

"Queer cove," says Colin. "Seems to be all on his own."

"Wish he didn't remind me so much of Oliver," says Nora.

"Reminds me of somebody too, but I can't think who."

"*Who* does?" asks Elsie, sitting herself on the settle beside Nora.

"That bloke from the hotel who looks like Sergeant Bilko."

"Oh him." Elsie picks up her vodka.

"Reckon he fancies you, Els'," grins Colin.

"Balls," says Elsie.

"Dunno so much. He was ogling you all through dinner."

"Happy holiday!" cries Nora, holding up her glass.

When they have once more drunk to that aspiration, Colin says, "So what are we going to do tomorrow?"

"Depends on the weather," says Nora. "If it's nice I vote we take a look round the town then go on the beach."

"Not much of a town to look round from what I've seen," says Colin. "Why don't we go to Brighton?"

"Sunday tomorrow. Shops'll be shut."

"Yes, best to wait till they're open," agrees Elsie.

"Most shops open on a Sunday now."

"Big shops don't."

"Some of 'em do."

"Best to wait and be sure, though," says Nora. "Besides, it'll be crowded tomorrow with trippers and that. Don't want to have to queue up to get in the Regent Palace."

"Don't forget you promised to buy me that holdall," Elsie reminds Colin. "I want a decent one, mind, not cheap rubbish."

"I promised, didn't I?" Colin's beginning to wish he hadn't.

"Got to try to get in some snooker practise before Saturday," Len reminds Colin.

"Too true, mate." He gazes around the bar. "I wonder if Dave's got a snooker table here. I'll have to ask him."

"I trust you two don't intend spending the bloody holiday playing snooker," snaps Elsie.

"Course not. Got to keep our hand in though, cos this time next week we'll be giving old Hodge and Cooney the thrashing of their lives."

"Won't be easy," says Len.

"With you in them new glasses mate, it'll be a doddle."

Elsie cranes her neck to see to the far end of the bar where an electronic organ stands ready for action, but unattended. The sight makes Elsie's fingers itch. "I thought there was supposed to be live music here tonight," she says to Nora as she turns back.

"That's what Mr Pertwee said."

"Perhaps it don't start till later," says Colin.

"Have to get a move on, it's gone nine already."

"I'll ask Dave what's happened." Colin gets to his feet. "Same again, everyone?"

"It's Len's shout," Elsie reminds him.

"You can do the next two, mate. I want to have a word with Dave." He collects the empties and hurries off to the bar.

"Organist hasn't turned up," Dave tells Colin. "Sleeping it off, no doubt, the bugger. Sorry, mate. I'll turn up the tape if you like."

"The wife is pretty good on the organ. Mind if she gives us a bit of a tune?"

"Feel free! Anything to cheer up the place a bit."

Elsie is only too happy to oblige. She downs her second vodka in one gulp and hurries off to the Ladies to relieve herself and refurbish her face.

But as she emerges, handbag under arm, who should be

standing close by but Sergeant Bilko, tankard of Guinness in hand.

"Goood eeevening once again," says he, beaming.

"Hello," says Elsie shortly.

"Down here for a holiday?"

"That's right."

"Weather looks good for you."

"Hope so." She tries to push past him but he's blocking her path.

"I hope you don't mind me saying so," he persists, "but I like your dress. I was admiring it at dinner. Did you make it yourself?"

Elsie looks down at herself, all confused and self-conscious. "Just something I ran up for me holiday."

"Indeeed!" He beams his approval. "Did you design it too?"

"Well…" She's not sure if it's the old come-on or if he's taking the micky. "Just did it out of me head, like."

He beams and nods. "Very striking! Very original! You have a lot of talent, dear lady."

Elsie blushes. "Thanks very much…"

"I know about these things. My brother is in the rag trade."

"Oh, I see. Well, I've got to go. I'm playing the organ for a bit of a singsong."

"You play the organ too! How talented you are! I love a singsong. Do you mind if I join in?"

"If you want to." She manages to push past him.

"My name is Billy Greenhorn," he says, following her. "You must call me Billy."

Elsie's organ playing, like her dressmaking, is quite spontaneous. She plays by ear whatever happens to come into her head, which is mostly old songs she heard her cousin trying to play when they were children. But she has a bright catchy style and in no time a crowd gathers round her.

Nora parks herself beside Elsie and joins in, only pausing from time to time to take a swig of her gin and tonic. Billy Greenhorn, his Guinness swaying to the rhythm, stands behind the organ beaming down at Elsie and keeps her well supplied with vodkas. Len, not into this kind of thing, goes to the bar with Colin, who introduces him to Dave.

"You got a snooker table here?" shouts Colin in order to make himself heard above the din.

"Pool table, in the other bar."

"No good, mate. We need a proper snooker table. We're playing in a Snooker Final doubles on Saturday."

"Go on?" says Dave. "Sorry mate, can't help."

Any snooker clubs round here we could go to?" shouts Len.

"Not round here. Have to go to Brighton. Plenty there."

"Have to see about it when we go to Brighton then," bawls Colin.

"*You were meant for me,*" chorus the revellers. "*I was meant for you...*"

"Tell me," Colin shouts at Dave. "You reckon small local free houses make a profit these days?"

"Eh?" He screws up his eyes as he tries to hear.

"Small local pubs! Do they make a profit?"

Dave shrugs. "Depends on the food."

"That's what I say," chimes in Len.

Dave moves off to attend to other customers.

The singing ceases for a moment while Elsie refortifies herself.

"Yes, good food is a must these days," resumes Dave, coming back to Colin and Len. "Dennis takes care of that side of things here. Worth his weight in gold is Dennis."

"The wife's a pretty good cook," says Colin. "Works in a canteen. Worked in restaurants too in her time."

"Dennis worked in a canteen before he was made redundant."

"Go on!"

"Used his redundancy money to take a course in catering, then got a bit of experience in hotels and restaurants before we set up in business together."

"Sensible fella." Colin is feeling hopeful.

"Need a lot of capital though to get started," says Len.

Dave grimaces. "Some. Trick is to start small. Build it up, sell it and get something better. We started with a small guest house."

"Guest house!" Colin exclaims. "We're staying at a guest house – well, he calls it a hotel, but that's what it is – the Ocean

View."

Dave nods. "I know it. Run by some Scottish git. Silly bugger refuses to have a licence. Got to have booze these days. Good food and drink, and a lot of hard work, and you're laughing."

"Couldn't agree more," says Colin devoutly. To his ears, this is much more like music than the din Elsie is now belting out again. He can just see himself as owner/manager of his own hotel, sitting in his office approving the menu for the day.

Dave moves off to serve another customer.

"Reckon I'm definitely going to have a shot at starting me own business if I'm made redundant," Colin shouts into Len's ear. "Nothing to it, really, matter of good business sense and plenty of hard work. Main thing is not to let yourself sit back."

"True," nods Len, although to him sitting back appears the more attractive option.

"*Maybe it's because I'm a Londoner*," chant the songsters.

The carousel intensifies; beer flows and so does the gin and vodka. To Elsie, Billy's beaming face begins to look like an unstable full moon. Nora can't sing for tittering. Colin and Len have drunk themselves into a drowsy silence.

Dave clangs the ship's bell hanging by the bar.

"TIME PLEASE!" he bellows.

*****

Roused by the bell, Colin and Len go in search of their spouses. Nora is still sitting in her chair by the organ, the expression on her face not unlike that of any one of the fish in the illuminated tank. But when she sees Len she lifts her arms dramatically for him to pull her to her feet. Colin finds Elsie flaked out over the organ. With some difficulty he hauls her up and leads her gently away, like a bereaved person from the grave of a beloved.

"My God!" he cries when they get outside. "How the hell are we to get these two back up them bloody steps?"

"Excooose me," says a voice at his elbow, "but I have my car. Pleasure to give you all a lift."

Colin views Billy with suspicion. He doesn't go for this

bastard at all, but it's no time to be choosy. "Thanks, mate, that would be helpful."

Putting his arm around Elsie's waist, he more or less carries her to the waiting car, which he doesn't fail to note is a Mercedes. Nora declines an offer of help from Len and sedately weaves her way to the car under what is left of her own steam. With the ladies safely deposited on the back seat and Len sandwiched between them, Colin sits himself in front with Billy.

"Your good lady is very gifted," says Billy as he drives off.

"I know," replies Colin shortly, "especially when it comes to vodka."

"*Very* musical; very exceptional technique and so quick with her feet. Is she a church organist?"

"Good God, no!"

"And very gifted with her neeeeedle."

"Bloody good cook too, if you want to know," grunts Colin, wondering just what this bugger's game is.

"Oooh, lovely car!" cries Nora, as the Merc glides effortlessly up the steep hill, which had so taxed Len's car earlier.

With her head lolling on Len's shoulder Elsie starts crooning. "*Ramona, I hear the mission bells above...*"

"Aw, shut up Els'," growls Colin.

Elsie stops to belch. "Manners."

"If there's one thing I detest more than a drunken man," pronounces Nora carefully, "it's a drunken woman."

When they enter the hotel they find two Alsatian dogs sitting at the bottom of the stairs like the lions at the foot of Nelson's column. Colin tries to manoeuvre Elsie past them, but they immediately sit up and growl, lifting their lips menacingly.

"Good dogs!" he cries to no avail. Then he remembers his police training. "Heel!" he commands sharply. "Heel!"

The dogs are unmoved.

"You have to give the password," says Billy Greenhorn. "Friend," he says to the dogs. "*Friend!*"

The dog's part to let him through but close ranks again before Colin can follow.

"Friend!" repeats Colin through clenched teeth. "Friend!"

It has no effect.

"They won't let you through until they've been told you are friends by Alec," explains Billy from the stairs. "He'll be in bed by now. I'll get him to come down."

"Thanks," grunts Colin.

"*For your friends are my friends and my friends are your friends...*" croons Elsie.

"My tum-tum feels a bit queasy," announces Nora. "Has anyone got a peppermint cream?"

"That's all we need," moans Colin. "You throwing up all over the place."

Elsie has become preoccupied with a castor oil plant standing in the corner, and is stroking its leaves. "*I think that I shall never see,*" she sings, "*a poem lovely as a tree...*"

"Give over, Els', for Pete's sake!"

Len, almost asleep on his feet, is startled back to life when Nora tinkles the little bell on the reception desk. "Hurry up, Mr Pertwee!" she calls.

"Ssssh!" hisses Colin. "You'll wake the whole place up!"

Elsie's attention is now focused on the dogs. She peers at them uncertainly. "We all pat the dog, we all pat the dog," she sings querulously, and steps forward to do just that.

"For Christ's sake don't touch 'em!" shouts Colin.

Mr Pertwee comes stumbling down the stairs in his dressing gown, what remains of his hair pointing skywards, as if he's had it spiked.

"Och, I'm so sorry, I dinnae introduce y'to the wee dogs. This is Boss, and this is Bess. Bess, these good people are *friends. Friends!*" He repeats the word as he points to each of his new guests in turn. "Boss," he says to the other dog, "these good people are *friends!*"

"Pleased to meet you," titters Nora.

The dogs look disappointed and slink away.

"They stand guard every evening in case some undesirable person should come in," Mr Pertwee explains. "Y'cannae be too careful these days."

"Too true, mate," agrees Colin, impressed for the second time that evening. When he gets his pub he must have a couple of dogs like that.

"Ex-police dogs, are they?" he asks.

"Och no! I trained them mysel'. A wee hobby, y'might say."

"Go on!"

Mr Pertwee gazes doubtfully at Elsie who is hanging on to Colin's shoulder. "Will y'be wanting early morning tea?" he asks.

"Might as well mate, not too early though. What time is breakfast?"

"From nine until ten."

"Let's say eight then."

"Aye. I hope y'all sleep well. Good neet to ye."

Mr Pertwee gathers his dressing gown about him and toils back up the stairs.

In Room Seven, Len is undressed and in bed while Nora is still dithering about, unable to decide whether to have a bath, a shower, a lick and promise, or not to bother at all. She decides on the lick and promise, and by time she has had it, cleaned her teeth and rolled up her hair, her head has cleared and she is almost back to normal.

"Well," she says as she clambers into bed, "have you enjoyed your first day?"

"Um," says Len, too knackered to decide whether he has or not.

"I enjoyed this evening very much. That's quite a nice pub. Elsie was good on the organ, wasn't she? It's such a pity she can't hold her drink better though. She makes such a disgusting exhibition of herself. I hate to think what Mr Pertwee must have thought."

Only heavy breathing from Len.

"You know what I fancy now? A nice cup of tea. Pity this place hasn't got tea-making facilities in the room."

Len is glad. If it had, he'd have had to get up to make it.

"I thought all hotels had it these days. Still, perhaps it's just as well. My tum is still a bit queasy from that Lancashire hotpot. Think I'd better have some Bisodol, just to be on the safe side."

"It's beside you on the table," mumbles Len. He has learned from experience.

"So it is!" She picks up the glass and stirs it round with her finger. "Well, I think we've done well coming here. It's a very nice place, even if it's a bit old fashioned and we can't make tea.

But Mr Pertwee seems very nice. I think we're going to have a lovely time." She drinks up the Bisodol and plonks the glass back on the bedside table. "Right. You can draw back the curtains now. And open the window. I want some of that nice sea air."

With a sigh Len heaves his feet to the floor.

*****

Next door, in Room Six, Elsie has collapsed on the bed, fully clad. Colin is now faced with the daunting prospect of having to undress her, but as he tries to do so her arms and legs flail about like one of those clockwork dolls.

"Keep still!" he hisses at her.

"*How much is that doggy in the window?*" croons Elsie tremulously.

"Belt up Els', for God's sake!"

Somehow he manages to get off the little black dress and her bra.

"Take me!" she cries suddenly as he's trying to haul down her knickers.

"Sssssh!"

"Take me!" she cries again, even louder.

Give him his due, Colin tries to oblige – but he can't.

Chapter 8

The next day being Sunday Benthaven slumbers on longer than usual, the peace being broken only by the screaming of gulls and the donging of the church bell summoning the faithful to Early Communion. But gradually there is a stirring of activity. Shutters are removed, menu boards appear, dog walkers roam the beach, and fishermen cast their lines from the end of the quay.

And the sun comes out.

It is nearly eleven when the Escort bumbles down the hill and comes to rest in the harbour car park. They have made the descent by car not only because clambering up and down all those steps has lost its appeal but also because of the need to transport all their beach gear – windbreak, mats, picnic lunch (supplied by Mr Pertwee at no extra charge), camera, binoculars, sun lotion, and other impedimenta, most of which is unlikely to be required.

"Three bloody quid!" moans Len as he Pays and Displays. "It's free at home on Sundays."

Their first task is to find a newsagent. They amble along the narrow main street, Colin and Len in front, Colin carrying the rolled-up windbreak over his shoulder, Len with the beach mats under his arm. Nora and Elsie follow a short way behind. Nora looks a bit like Sancho Panza in the new sunhat Elsie gave her. In accordance with Colin's advice her handbag is in her holdall along with the picnic lunch provided by Mr Pertwee. Elsie carries a Tesco's plastic bag containing everything but the kitchen sink.

They soon find a newsagent and Nora makes a beeline for the picture postcards. She likes to get that chore off hand as quickly as possible. Elsie also buys cards, mainly of the saucy variety, which she stuffs in her handbag and forgets all about. Len buys himself a *Mail on Sunday* to read on the beach, Colin a *Daltons Weekly*.

Then they wander back to the harbour area where, close to

The Fisherman's Float, stands a new stone-faced building housing three separate amenities, the Public Conveniences, the Tourist Information Bureau and the Harbour Cafe. After patronising the first they enter the second, where Nora helps herself to as many leaflets as she can manage to stuff into her holdall and Len enquires about snooker playing facilities in Brighton. Then they go into the third for coffee and for Nora to write her postcards.

The two men are content to sit and read while Nora carries out this task, but Elsie wanders about impatiently, inspecting the pottery and paintings by local artists, cuddly toys and other souvenirs offered for sale.

"There you are!" exclaims Colin suddenly. "That's just the sort of thing!"

"Mmmm?" murmurs Len, intent on his paper.

"'For sale,'" he reads from his *Dalton's Weekly*.

"'Superior private hotel in quiet south coast resort. Ten guestrooms, all with private facilities, plus private accommodation. Good class clientele. Phone... so and so.' Now that's exactly the sort of place I'd like to run."

Len looks up. "How much?"

"Don't say, but I've a good mind to phone and find out."

"Ten bedrooms? Cost a bomb."

"Couldn't afford that, I know, but it'd be interesting to know what they want for it. Give me some idea."

Elsie returns from her wanderings clutching a small teddy bear. "How much longer you going to be?" she asks Nora irritably.

"Nearly finished."

"What you got there?" demands Colin.

She holds up the bear for inspection. "Cute, ain't he?"

"What you want that for?"

"To put in the bedroom when you've decorated it – if you ever do."

Colin shakes his head in despair. He wishes she wouldn't squander her money on that sort of rubbish.

"There now!" cries Nora. "That's done!" She stuffs the postcards into her handbag. "Are we ready for the beach?"

"About time," grunts Elsie.

The beach proves to be mostly pebbles and shingle, and shelves steeply down to the water's edge, where tangles of scummy seaweed float about.

"Lovely little beach," proclaims Nora, "and not crowded."

"Looks polluted," says Elsie.

They find a vacant spot in the sun under the harbour wall, close to a lady so overweight she could qualify as a female version of the Michelin Man. Colin hammers home the poles of the windbreak between the pebbles with a large stone. But he isn't erecting it in order to break the wind since there is no wind to break. He erects it for reasons of modesty while they undress.

"Be like that then," says the fat lady to him, licking her candyfloss.

"For your own protection, luv," grins Colin. "You don't want a nasty shock from seeing things you shouldn't."

She wobbles with laughter. "Try me!" she cackles.

All except Len have come with their swimwear on under their clothes. Nora emerges in her navy-blue costume from which her limbs bulge like mottled sausages. Elsie is in her new yellow bikini, looking white and thin, and Colin in the smart red and white trunks he bought in an emergency the year they went to Weston-super-Mare, when his old trunks developed holes in unseemly places. Len doesn't go in for exposing himself on the beach, or anywhere else for that matter, his only concession being to remove his collar and tie, open the neck of his shirt, and turn his cuffs halfway up his forearms.

This ceremony accomplished, Nora sits herself on her beach mat, her back propped against the harbour wall, and immediately starts sifting through her shoal of tourist leaflets with a view to finding some interesting way to spend the afternoon. She's not keen on sitting on the beach all the time. She likes to get about a bit, see places, do things.

Len also props himself against the wall, bemoaning the fact that there are no deckchairs available for hire. He turns to the business section of his newspaper to see if there is any mention of the pending closure of the Fertiliser Division of Regal Chemicals.

Elsie dons her new sunglasses, stretches herself prone on her beach mat and stares into the blue void, imagining she is on

Bondi Beach with Cliff and her two boys listening to those great rollers crashing in. What a difference to this crummy beach! She must have been mad to have left, but then, finding herself alone after Cliff had kicked her out and Brig had deserted her for pastures new, and then with her sister Maureen agitating for help with their ailing mother, there was little else she could do but return home.

She mustn't forget to phone Andy on Tuesday for his eighteenth birthday, she reminds herself. She must phone about nine that evening if she is to catch him before he leaves for work at the butcher's shop on Wednesday morning.

Colin neither lies nor sits, but stands, languidly stretching his limbs and watching the beach ball bounce of a girl's buttocks as she stoically trudges over the pebbles to the sea. He is considering having a dip himself and this sight persuades him to do so. The problem is the money-belt, which he is still wearing beneath his trunks and bulges out a bit around the middle. It is supposed to be waterproof but he doesn't want to risk all those old fivers getting ruined. Nor can he risk leaving it behind with the others in case Elsie should take it into her head to look inside. In the end he decides it is best to keep the belt on and risk it.

"Think I'll take a dip," he announces. "Anyone else coming?"

"Not in that muck," says Elsie without stirring.

"Nora?"

But Nora, who has been known to take the occasional paddle should the water be warm enough, is too engrossed in her leaflets. There is no point in asking Len, so Colin stumbles and slides his way down the steep shelf of the beach to the water's edge on his own. He is not sorry to be alone for a while. He is feeling anxious. He has a lot on his mind – the redundancy rumour, buying a hotel, the fivers, not to mention his non-performance with Elsie last night.

But when he reaches the water the prospect of striking out and enjoying some exercise rapidly dispels his worries. As he bends over to take off his trainers, which he has kept on to descend the stony beach, it suddenly occurs to him that he could stuff the money-belt with the fivers into the toe of one of them.

He looks around. There is no one in the immediate vicinity, only a few teenagers playing with a beach ball in the sea a little further along. And he can't even see his companions sitting back against the harbour wall, due to the steep shelving of the beach.

So he stuffs the money-belt into one of the trainers, jamming a sock in afterwards to secure it. Should be safe enough, he thinks. Leaving the trainers well back from the water's edge to prevent them being claimed by the incoming tide, he wades into the sea until he is waist-deep, then strikes out manfully, rejoicing in the free movement of his body. He ought to do more swimming, he thinks, go to the smart new pool back home more regularly.

But he doesn't risk swimming too far out before surfacing. Shaking the water out of his eyes and hair he checks his trainers are still safe on the beach. Then, as he is about to dive under again, something light hits him plumb on the top of his head.

"Sorry!" calls a girl's voice from some distance away.

He looks round in surprise and sees a young woman wading towards him. It is the beach ball the youths are playing with that has hit him. He retrieves it and wades towards the girl until he is near enough to throw it to her.

"Och, it's you!" she exclaims. "I hope it dinnae hurt you."

At first he fails to recognise the face under the white bathing cap, but her Scottish voice and buxom bosom soon identify her to him as Daphne Pertwee. "Oh no, no, not at all!" he manages to answer.

"Thanks!" she calls, catching the ball. "Enjoy yoursel'."

He watches her as she wades back to her companions, his gaze lingering on her long, straight back and curving hips. He finds it hard to believe it is the same po-faced girl who served them at dinner the previous evening. He continues to watch as she rejoins her companions and their game recommences. He feels envious of their carefree pleasure, even tempted to swim closer in the hope the ball may come his way again or that he might even be drawn into the game. But he doesn't want to stray too far from his trainers, and instead swims a little closer to where he left them.

To his utter disbelief and amazement he can only see one of the shoes on the beach.

"God Almighty!"

He strikes out for the shore, alternately swimming and wading, the sea seemingly holding him back as if in some dreadful nightmare. When at last he staggers out of the water he grabs the trainer to see if it's the one containing the money-belt.

It isn't. He knew it wouldn't be.

He stares about in bewilderment. There is no one within at least fifty yards. Nor can the sea have washed it away in so short a time. He is completely baffled.

But not for long. Two Alsatian dogs are scooting along the beach in his direction. The leading one has something white in its mouth.

"Oi!"

Colin races towards the dogs as fast as his bare feet on the stony gravel will allow.

The dog with the shoe in its mouth, confronted by a man frantically waving his arms as if he's trying to halt the traffic on a motorway, stops dead, front legs pressed to the ground, behind in the air, eyes glinting.

"Drop it!" commands Colin.

The dog remains motionless.

Colin ventures a little closer.

The dog doesn't move, eyeing Colin warily.

"Good dog. Good dog. Give it us, then." He edges a little closer still.

He makes a sudden grab for the trainer, but the Alsatian is quicker, growling with delight as it dances out of reach.

"You bloody sod!"

The dog waits for Colin to try again, which he does, and with the same result, the dog circling him like a boxer. As this performance is repeated several times the other Alsatian bounds up, barking encouragement.

The dog eventually allows Colin to get a hold on the shoe, and a violent tug-of-war ensues.

"Let go, you bugger!" yells Colin.

There is no telling how long this pantomime may have continued had a shrill whistle not been heard coming from the direction of the sea.

The dog stops tugging, pricks up its ears.

Colin looks round.

Another whistle.

The dog gives a hefty tug, catching Colin unawares and, once again the sole possessor of the shoe, tears off in the direction of the bikini-clad figure emerging from the sea, its delighted companion following.

"Bess! You naughty dog!" scolds Daphne as the Alsatian bounds up to her. "Lie down!"

Bess grovels.

"Drop it!"

Bess drops it.

Colin comes limping up, gasping for breath.

"Och, I'm sorry about that."

"Its...its...all right," wheezes Colin.

Daphne picks up the trainer and hands it to him.

"Y'cannae trust the little devils for a moment. I hope she hasnae ruined it."

"It's fine! It's fine!" The sock is still in the trainer, so hopefully the money-belt is too. That's all Colin cares about.

She gives him a winning smile; without all that heavy make-up her face is very attractive, he thinks.

She seems about to return to her friends, but hesitates and turns back to Colin. "Mr...er...I'm afraid I've forgotten y'name."

"Stilwell – Colin Stilwell."

"Will y'nae do me a wee favour, Mr Stilwell?"

"Favour? Of course – if I can."

"Will y'nae mention this business to m'father? He'll rave at me if he hears about it. I should'nae have let the dogs roam. He does'nae know I come bathing when I take them out."

"Oh! I see. Well, not to worry, I won't breathe a word."

Another winning smile. "Thanks. You're a real spooort."

Colin's legs feel as if they're no longer strong enough to support him. "A p-pleasure," he stutters.

She smiles again, and orders the dogs to heel. "See you at dinner!" she calls over her shoulder as she goes.

For a second time Colin's gaze lingers on Daphne's departing figure. Now there's a girl and a half, he thinks. If only I were thirty years younger!

Feeling instead thirty years older, he removes the sock from the trainer to see if the money-belt is still in the toe.

It is.

*****

"Bramble Hall sounds nice," says Nora, who is still thumbing through her leaflets. "It's got an elephant sanctuary there. They look after sick and old retired elephants from all over the world. Fancy!"

There is no response to this information. Len is asleep, Elsie still on Bondi Beach.

"Only about three miles from here," continues Nora. "I suggest we pop over there this afternoon, make a nice little outing."

"I'm not bumbling round on a day like this looking at bloody elephants," grunts Elsie, who in other circumstances and in different mood would have wept buckets at the mere mention of such sick and aged animals.

Nora is about to make a tart reply to this effect when Colin trudges over the pebbles to rejoin them after his dip. "Well, did you enjoy it?" she asks him.

"Fantastic!" He towels himself vigorously. "Water's really warm."

"What was all that barking?"

Colin starts. "Oh, that Pertwee girl was down there walking them Alsatians." He is trying to sound casual.

"That must have made your day," murmurs Elsie.

"Got them dogs very well trained, I must say. It's amazing."

"Well, it's gone twelve," announces Nora, looking at her watch. "Time we had our lunch. You want to change first, Colin?"

"Might as well, I suppose." He closes the windbreak around himself. "Cabaret time," he says, winking at the fat lady.

"Can I have a ticket?" she banters.

"Cost you!"

"Thing is – is it worth seeing?"

"You pays y'money, luv, and you takes y'chance."

Colin wraps a towel about his middle and removes his

swimming trunks.

"Ole!" he cries as he flings the wet trunks over the side of the windbreak.

"Oooh la la!" The fat lady cheers raucously.

Nora is appalled. Since she has been associating with the Blooms she has begun to realise just how common the Stilwells really are. It really won't do for them ever to meet the Blooms. Once she has moved off the estate to Webbley Park she will try to gradually drop them. Make this our last holiday together, she thinks.

"Come on, wake up!" She gives Len a poke, just in time to save him from being decapitated by a scimitar wielded by an Arabian horseman.

"What time is it?" he mumbles.

"Gone twelve."

"Could do with a drink."

"Lunch first. Then we'll go to The Fisherman's Float."

Mr Pertwee's picnic lunch is not inspiring. Elsie takes the limp lettuce out of her tomato sandwich and buries it under the pebbles. Colin does likewise with his hard-boiled egg. A juicy piece of tomato falls from Len's sandwich on to his Daz-white shirt. Only Nora ploughs her way through it all, but even she balks at the cans of fizzy lemonade Mr Pertwee has provided.

"So," she says, dabbing her mouth with a napkin, "are we agreed we'll go to Bramble Hall this afternoon and see the elephants?"

"I told you," grunts Elsie. "I'm not wasting this sunshine gaping at bloody elephants."

"Too much sun's not good for you. You'll get skin cancer."

"Bugger that!"

Nora sighs audibly. "I do wish you wouldn't swear like that, Elsie. Not in public. People can hear."

"Bugger that!" says Elsie again.

"Don't much fancy driving a lot in this weather," says Len. "Be hot in the car, seats'll be all sticky and that."

"Too true, mate," agrees Colin. "Better leave that sort of jaunt until the weather's not so good."

"Could be like this for the whole fortnight," Nora responds.

"Wanna bet?" murmurs Elsie.

"Well," says Nora, knowing when she's outvoted. "Let's go and have a drink, and we'll see."

But even as she says the words the sun goes in and a chill wind skims across Elsie's naked midriff.

*****

At midday the atmosphere in The Fisherman's Float is much more sober than in the evenings. Everything is neat and freshly polished, and a slight odour of disinfectant pervades the air. Yachtsmen and windsurfers prop up the bar and fishermen discuss their catches, or the lack of them. Neatly dressed senior citizens tuck into Dennis's Sunday roasts.

Len eyes the latter enviously. "Ought to come here for our lunch," he says, "not have that stuff old Pertwee dishes out."

"You seen the prices?" retorts Nora.

Colin again insists on buying the first round and goes to the bar, taking his *Daltons Weekly* with him. He wants to obtain Dave's view on the advert in it offering a private hotel for sale. But it isn't Dave behind the bar; it's some elderly military-looking gentleman with a handlebar moustache.

"Dave not here?" asks Colin.

"Not today."

He is disappointed. "Will he be here tonight?"

"No, day off. Back tomorrow."

"Not to worry. I'll see him then. Used to know him years ago," Colin adds while the man draws off the beer. "We were both in the police, on the beat together. Met him again here quite by chance."

"Oh yes?" says the barman disinterestedly.

When he rejoins the others with the drinks, Colin finds Billy Greenhorn standing by the table, a glass of Guinness in his hand.

"Goood aafternooon," says Billy, beaming.

"Oh hello," replies Colin, shortly.

"I was just telling your good lady how much I enjoyed her beautiful music last night."

"Oh yes?"

"She is very talented, very gifted, very gifted indeed."

"So you said." He wonders what this geezer's game is.

"I've been asking her if she would honour us by playing again tonight."

"Dunno about that." Colin is not enthusiastic for a repeat of last night's performance. "Live music's only on Saturday nights."

"Dave wouldn't mind, I'm sure – very good for trade."

"Well, we'll see." Colin feels he owes the old boy something for his help with Elsie the night before.

Billy beams and nods his farewells, and wanders off down the bar.

"Bloody weirdo, that bloke," Colin says as he sits down. "Gives me the willies."

"Wish he didn't remind me of Oliver so much," says Nora, yet again.

"Got a feeling I've seen him before too. Never forget a face. But just can't place him."

"He used to be in show biz," says Elsie.

"Show biz? What, him?"

"So he said. Impresario or summat – talent-spotting and that. Said I could have quite a future playing the organ if I wanted to."

"Don't want to take notice of what he says, Els'. That's not the sort of talent-spotting he's into, I bet."

"You *would* say that," snaps Elsie, her dander rising. "You hate me playing the organ."

"Don't talk daft. Course I don't. All I'm saying is, you want to take what he says with a pinch of salt. He's bad news, Els', believe me."

"Balls," says Elsie.

"Never mind about him," cuts in Nora hastily. "The sun's gone in now, so shall we go and see the elephants after all this afternoon?"

"You and them bloody elephants!"

"It's too cold for the beach without the sun, so we might as well."

"For God's sake, let's go and be done with it!" cries Colin.

"Might be better to go to Brighton," Len puts in. "Find out about them snooker clubs."

"That's a thought, mate."

"What are we supposed to do while you two buggers go round looking for snooker clubs?" demands Elsie.

"Look round the shops. Buy that holdall you keep on about. I'll pay for it."

"It's Sunday, shops'll be shut."

"Not in Brighton they won't."

"Can't be sure," says Nora. She puts down her gin glass resolutely. "No, we'll go to Bramble Hall. We can go to Brighton tomorrow."

"The Voice has spoken," grins Colin, winking at Len.

"You've got tomato juice all down that shirt," Nora tells Len, "so we'd better go back to the hotel first so you can change it."

"And I've got to take this bloody bikini off," says Elsie. "It's cutting me in the crotch."

*****

But as Len's Escort grinds back up the hill to Ocean View it comes on to rain quite heavily.

"It's pissing down," moans Elsie. "I'm not bumbling around looking at elephants in this."

"Won't be much. It'll stop by time we've changed."

"Don't look like it to me," says Len hopefully.

When they reach their rooms at the Ocean View Nora also decides to change out of her swimming costume, and Len puts on a fresh shirt.

In the next room Elsie can't wait to change before having to visit the bathroom to answer an overwhelming call of nature.

Colin seizes the opportunity to remove the money-belt from around his middle and secretes it in the document wallet strapped under the wardrobe shelf. Best place for it, he decides. He'll just have to risk Elsie looking in the wallet.

While he is hanging around waiting for her, Colin has a bit of a brainwave. "Going down to make a phone call," he shouts to her.

"Who to?"

"This hotel for sale in *Daltons Weekly*. Find out the price."

"What for?"

"Just for interest. Give me some idea."

From behind the closed door Elsie mutters something inaudible but clearly not complimentary.

"Shan't be long," calls Colin.

When he reaches the foyer there is no one about. He goes to the payphone, and with the *Daltons Weekly* ready open at the relevant page, he taps out the number.

But the phone on the reception desk starts to chirp. Colin curses to himself. He's not going hear with that racket going on. He decides to hang up.

No sooner does he do so than the phone on the reception desk stops also. I'll try again, he thinks, and taps out his number once more.

The reception desk phone chirps again.

Bugger it, he thinks, I'll just have to put up with it.

Mr Pertwee emerges from the kitchen wiping pastry from his hands on his apron.

"Ocean View Hotel," he chants into the reception desk phone. "Good afternoon, how can I help you?"

"Good afternoon," says Colin into the payphone. "I'm calling about the private hotel advertised for sale in the *Daltons Weekly*."

"Och aye," says Mr Pertwee.

"Och aye," says the voice at the end of Colin's line. Suddenly realising what is happening Colin turns to stare at Mr Pertwee.

Mr Pertwee stares back in amazement. "Mr Stilwell!"

"It's you!" cries Colin. He hangs up and goes to the reception desk. "This your advert?"

"That's reet," replies Mr Pertwee, looking embarrassed.

"You mean *this* place is on the market?"

"That's reet," repeats Mr Pertwee, reluctantly. "I dinnae know y'were interested in buying a hotel."

"Well you wouldn't, would you? As a matter of fact, I was only ringing to find out the price."

Mr Pertwee splays his hands. "If I say, will y'nae promise to keep it to y'sel? I wouldnae want the other guests to know the hotel is up for sale."

"Course, mate, I understand. Mum's the word."

"Well then..." Mr Pertwee leans over the desk and mutters into Colin's ear.

Colin is thunderstruck. "*How* much!"

"Or near offer," whispers Mr Pertwee.

"That's more than a quarter of a million!"

"Sssh!"

"Sorry, mate, out of my league."

"Aye, thought it might be."

"Not worth that much, I shouldn't have thought. If you don't mind me asking, why are you selling – losing money, is it?"

"Och, it's nae that. I have been here nearly twenty years. I feel it's time for a change."

Colin nods. "Understand that, mate. Just how I'm feeling meself. What you thinking of doing then?"

Mr Pertwee appears reluctant to answer but leans even closer to Colin. "I intend to train dogs – guard dogs, y'ken."

"Go on! Good idea. Big demand these days. And you're bloody good at it too, judging by them two Alsatians of yours."

Mr Pertwee smiles appreciatively. "Y'too kind, Mr Stilwell."

"So good, in fact, you must have had experience before, surely?"

"Och aye! In the Army, before I came here."

"Well, I wish you all the best, mate."

"Thank you. But y'll nae tell a soul?"

"Course not. You can trust me."

But when he gets back to the bedroom he loses no time in telling Elsie who, now bedecked in bright pink trousers and an equally bright green top, is inspecting her face in the mirror for evidence of a suntan.

"How much!" she exclaims derisively. "Wouldn't give you tuppence for it."

"Dunno so much. Pretty big place, mind. Course, he says it's not losing money, but I bet it is. Needs a lot doing to it. Bringing up to date – license and that."

There is a sharp rap on the door.

"You two ready?" comes Nora's voice from the other side. "Time's getting on."

*****

When they emerge from the hotel it is raining harder than ever.

"No good going to see them elephants in this," says Colin.

Nora is reluctant to give in. "Probably clear up by time we get there."

"I'm not going," says Elsie, "so you can think again."

"Let's go to Brighton then," says Len. "Find out about them snooker clubs."

"What are *we* supposed to do?" demands Elsie. "Sun ourselves on Brighton Pier?"

"Could look round the shops and that."

"What! In the pouring rain? No thank you very much!"

"Tell you what," says Colin. "You could go to that pavilion place."

"What pavilion place?"

"You know – that place with the onions on top – the Royal Pavilion, that's it."

"You mean the Regent Palace," says Nora. "That's a good idea."

"Good as anywhere, I suppose," concedes Elsie.

"Brighton it is then," says Colin.

On the way he tells Nora and Len about the proposed sale of Ocean View.

"Can't think why he wants to sell a nice hotel like that just to train dogs," says Nora.

"Been there twenty years, he's fed up with it. Don't blame him. I'd like a change too. Reckon I could make a good job of running a place like that."

"Well you won't be," says Elsie.

"I know that. Pity though."

"What it needs is a bar," says Len.

"That, mate, and a lot more. A completely fresh approach – a new broom."

"What, to sweep out the bar with?" sneers Elsie.

"To sweep the whole lot out, Els'. Start again. Bring it up to date. I mean, you take the food. No one wants that Lancashire hotpot stuff these days."

"But that's what I like about it," objects Nora. "Good plain home cooking, none of this microwave muck."

"You might, Nora, but most people these days want modern foods, chips and that. Got to move with the times, give 'em what they want."

"For God's sake, shut up about it," says Elsie. "How could we buy that sort of place? Couldn't even buy it if the four of us clubbed together."

"Not saying we could. But it's a snip for someone with the cash and know-how."

"Well that ain't us."

"Stopped raining," says Nora, leaning forward and switching off the screen wipers.

"I'm not going to see them elephants now," says Elsie, "so you can forget it."

Nora bridles. "Not saying we should. Got to have enough time to see them. We'll do it proper, spend a whole day there."

Len doesn't like the sound of that.

"Hey!" cries Colin suddenly.

"What's the matter?" cries Nora, alarmed.

"That's a great idea of your, Els'."

"What is?"

"The four us clubbing together to buy that hotel."

"Don't start on that again!"

"No, listen! It makes sense. I mean, money aside, we've got all the know-how we need between us. You'd look after all the catering. Nora can deal with the financial side, reception and that, Len can keep the books and look after the bar."

"And you'll be the chambermaid, I suppose."

"I'm serious, Els'. I could be a sort of general dogsbody – look after security, keep the place in a state of repair, do the serving at table maybe. Fill in where needed. It's a fabulous idea!"

"And who's going to rob the bank to pay for it?"

"Reckon we *could* raise the money between us. Look, if the Plant closes down as old Frank says, then our redundancy pay should come to quite a bit. And the sale of our house and Len's house should come to say, a hundred thousand, and Nora should get a bit more from the sale of her dad's house. Still have to borrow some, I know, but with the hotel as security we'd get it all right. What do you reckon, Len?"

Len purses his lips. "A bit dicey. Vital to have enough capital to start."

"It's bloody lunacy," snaps Elsie. "Forget it."

"You're the brainy one, Nora. What do you think?"

For once Nora is undecided. She rather fancies the idea of being a receptionist, but she is not prepared to give up her current plans. "We're moving to Webbley Park, remember? Besides, we don't want to be stuck down here just as Georgie and Gavin are having their first baby. Want to be on hand, to help out and that."

"Course you do," agrees Elsie. "Take no notice of the silly sod."

"Well," sighs Colin, downcast, "it was just a thought. All the same, if I'm made redundant I *am* going to do something different. Be me own boss. Do something worthwhile for a change."

"I've already told you what to do," says Nora. "Start your own detective agency. That's what you know about."

Elsie snorts. "Don't encourage him, for God's sake. He'll think he's Sherlock Holmes next and start learning to play the fiddle."

By this time they are entering Brighton and they start looking for somewhere to park. But they can find no vacant space along the front, which is lined from end to end with cars and coaches, so they have to search further inland, ending up on the fifth level of a multi-storey car park a good half mile from the front.

But it does have the merit of being not too far from the Royal Pavilion. A watery sun has managed to break through by this time and once they are in the grounds Colin loses no time in bringing his camera into use, taking photos of the others posing before the Pavilion and ensuring he gets in the incongruous cupolas, which are looking particularly dramatic against the stormy sky. Unfortunately, he has to stand so far back to get them in his subjects are reduced to the size of ants. Then he has a passer-by take one of all four of them.

"Reckon I'm going to get meself one of them camcorders,"

he says when this ritual is over.

"No, you're not," says Elsie.

"Don't see why not. Getting cheaper all the time."

"Shut up about it. You men coming in with us or what?"

He eyes the long queue waiting for admission. "No time if we're going to find a snooker club. Poor old Len won't be happy until we have, will you, mate?"

"Important to practise if we're to win on Saturday," nods Len.

"Too true," says Colin.

"Bloody snooker," moans Elsie.

"So where are we going to meet?" asks Nora.

"Back at the car probably best."

"Thought you were going to buy me that holdall?" says Elsie.

"Thought *you* said the shops'll be shut! We'll come back tomorrow and get it, promise."

So the two men wander off in search of a snooker club while the ladies join the queue to view the interior of the Royal Pavilion.

Once inside Elsie is disappointed. She finds the dark red décor throughout claustrophobic.

"Like being in hell," she comments. "No wonder he went mad." But when they reach the vast kitchen she is more approving, and wishes the kitchen at Regal Chemical was as big.

Nora is fascinated by the fine display of old cooking utensils, and is impressed by the magnificent silver tableware, which she thinks makes Marsha's look pretty paltry.

But for Elsie the grand climax of the tour is the King's bedchamber, a huge if depressing room, which dwarfs the enormous four-poster bed it houses.

"Now that's what I call a king-sized bed," she comments to Nora. "I bet he had a bloody good time in that!"

I could too, Elsie thinks. Not with Colin – with Cliff. He was a king among men if ever there was one. If *only* she was still with him! But it's no good crying over spilt milk. At least she's had two wonderful sons by him, which reminds her once again not to forget to ring Andy on Tuesday.

With the aid of the street plan of Brighton supplied to Len

by the Benthaven Information Centre, the two men manage to locate a couple of snooker clubs, but find them both shut.

"Course, it's Sunday," moans Colin. "We should have known."

"Some open on Sundays, surely," says Len.

"Well, these aren't. Now what do we do?"

It is only half past four. They have an hour to kill before meeting up with the ladies at the car park.

"Suppose we ought to go back to the Pavilion and join Elsie and Nora," says Colin without enthusiasm.

"Might not find 'em in all that crowd," Len answers.

"Why don't we just go and have a quiet drink somewhere?"

"Now you're talking! But the pubs won't be open, either, this time of the afternoon, will they?"

"Some bound to be open all day in a resort like this."

"True. Let's go and see if we can find one."

In this quest they are more successful and find a small pub in a quiet street leading down to the front. It is poky, gloomy and almost empty.

"Long time since we had a quiet chat," says Colin, when Len returns from the bar with the first round. "Lately we seem either to be busy with the snooker cues or have the women with us. No disrespect to them, of course. Cheers, mate!"

"Cheers," responds Len.

Colin savours his first sip. "Not bad stuff."

"Tasted better."

"Tell me, what d'you *really* think of this hotel idea of mine, then?"

"No good without enough capital."

"I know. Realise that. But if we could raise it, would you be game for us joining forces, running the place between us?"

Len purses his lips. He quite fancies running the bar, keeping the accounts and that. So long as he's not expected to do a lot of physical work. "Well...suppose so. Trouble is, it's no good if Nora and Elsie are against it."

Colin nods. "All too true, mate, all too true. All got to be dead keen and pull our weight or we're in trouble right off. Cooperation is the name of the game in that sort of caper. Pity. Course, if we do lose our jobs they could change their minds."

"Not Nora," says Len.

"You never know, funny creatures, women. Old Elsie can be dead against something one minute and all for it the next. Granted Nora's different. She knows what she wants all right, and goes for it."

Len often wishes she didn't.

But mentioning Nora reminds Colin about the old fivers and seizes the chance to obtain his friend's views on it.

"Not easy to know how women will react to things," he says. "You take a bloke I know at work. Some old lady – an aunt of his or someone – made him a present of an antique desk. He decided to do it up and that, and found a secret compartment in it containing a lot of them old fivers – you know, the big old white ones?"

"Not legal currency now, though," nods Len.

"I know that. But the point is, he's hung on to them for quite a while now, not knowing if he ought to give 'em back to the old girl or keep 'em. Asked me what I thought was the right thing to do. Tricky point, mind. Who is the rightful owner? Do they belong to the old lady, or is it a matter of finders keepers? Or could it be regarded as treasure trove and be the property of the State?"

As he takes a quaff of his beer Len stares into his tankard as if it's a crystal ball. "I'd say the fairest way would be to split 'em fifty-fifty. No point in dragging in the State."

Colin starts. He hasn't thought of that! "Reckon you're right, mate. That's the fairest way. Trouble is, he says he's left it so long now he don't know how the old girl would take it. Never know with women, see, and he don't want to upset her. Supposing it was Nora, what do you reckon she'd say?"

"She'd do her nut," answers Len without hesitation.

"That's the trouble," nods Colin. "Hard to know what's the right thing to do." But he's beginning to think that in the interest of peaceful relations it's best not to tell Nora about the fivers.

At that moment a whole crowd of youths come tumbling through the door, laughing and shouting noisily. One goes straight to the jukebox. Strident music issues forth.

"Bloody hell!" exclaims Colin. "No peace for the wicked. Drink up, mate, let's get out of here."

*****

Len is well and truly puffed by the time he has climbed the five flights of steps to the level where his car is parked.

"Why is it", he complains between gasps, "that the bloody lifts never work in these multi-storey places?"

"It's deliberate," grins Colin. "They do it to help blokes like you to keep your weight down."

When Len has regained his breath they go in search of the car.

"We're early," continues Colin, consulting his watch. "Women won't be here for another ten minutes or so."

"That's if they're on time."

Suddenly Colin stops, putting a restraining arm on Len. "'Ello, 'ello, 'ello," he says in his policeman's voice. "What have we here?"

Two youths are sitting on the bonnet of Len's Escort, munching crisps and gulping Coke. One has carroty hair, the other is a good imitation of a bulldog.

Len's mouth drops like a drawbridge.

"Leave this to me, mate," whispers Colin as they move forward slowly. "It's the oldest trick in the book."

"This your car?" asks the carroty one.

"What the bloody hell d'you think you're doing?" roars Colin. "Get off there! Go on – hop it!"

"Now there's gratitude for you," says the youth. "After we've been protecting your car so nicely and all."

"Yeah," says the other youth. "Real friendly."

"I'm warning you," growls Colin. "I'm a police officer."

"And I'm Adolf Hitler," responds the bulldog.

Colin feigns surprise. "Well now – fancy! Didn't recognise you without your 'tache."

"Right comedian we have here, Pug," sneers the carroty one.

"Yeah. Right bellyful of laughs."

"If you're not off there in two seconds flat," warns Colin, "I'm placing you under arrest."

Pug opens his mouth and lets a crisp float into it like a snowflake.

Colin sees his chance and darts forward, but in a flash the carroty youth flicks open a knife.

Colin stops dead.

"There now," says the youth amiably. "Thought you'd see sense. No need for unpleasantness when we're doing you a service. Lot of yobos round here, see, ready to knock off a nice little vintage car like this. Right, Pug?"

"Right, Jasper."

"Then again there's them who enjoy scratching their initials in the bodywork..." He makes a savage slashing movement with the knife a millimetre above the surface of the bonnet. "Very nasty. Don't want that sort of aggro, not when you can be protected for just eighty quid, know what I mean?"

Never before has Len been known to reach for his wallet so fast. Colin instantly restrains him.

"Ain't got eighty quid," he says.

"Hear that, Pug? These poor gents have come all the way to Brighton for a nice little holiday without their spending money. Sad that."

"Sad," says Pug.

"What you might call a pity."

"Pity," echoes Pug.

Jasper's face takes on a savage look as he again threatens the bonnet of the car with his knife.

"Hang on," says Colin hastily. "There may be a way round the problem."

Jasper leers. "Usually is, if you think about it."

"But I'll have to consult with me friend first – in private."

The youths look suspicious and exchange glances.

"What about?" demands Pug.

"If you want the money, just wait."

Colin leads Len a short distance from the car before they have time to stop him.

"Listen," he whispers to Len, at the same time keeping an eye on the youths. "I'm going to jump 'em."

"Let's pay," pleads Len, quivering as if on a vibrator.

"Not bloody likely! Listen carefully. I'm going to tell 'em our wives are down on the road waiting for us, and if they want their money they'll have to let me go down and ask 'em if they've got the cash. They won't let you come with me, of course, so you'll have to stay here."

"You can't leave me here with them!" cries Len.

"Ssssh! Don't worry; I know what I'm doing. Now what I want you to do when I go down is to just stand still and count slowly to yourself up to twenty. Then I want you to do something to attract their attention."

"D-do w-what?"

"Anything. Something unexpected."

Len couldn't look more scared if he'd been told to jump in a river. "B-but what?"

"Well, start singing or something."

"I can't sing!"

"Do a little dance then. Jig about, strip off, anything to distract 'em for a few seconds. I'll do the rest. Got it?"

Len's got it, but doesn't want it.

"Come on. Don't worry."

They return to the youths.

"My friend thinks his missus might have eighty quid," says Colin, "but she's waiting for us down in the street with my missus, cos she's an invalid in a wheelchair and the poor old luv can't get up here due to the lift being out of action and that. So how would it be if my friend stays here while I go down and get the cash?"

The youths glance at each other again.

"He *goes*, you *stay*," says Jasper.

"Ah, well, not quite so easy as that. My mate here's got a dicky heart, see, nearly killed you having to climb all them steps just now, didn't it, Len?"

"Um," gulps Len, feeling it might have been a blessed release if it had.

"Could finish him off having to climb 'em all again so soon. Don't want that, do we? Not in your interests at all."

The youths mutter between themselves.

"Course, we can always wait till the wife comes up to find out what's keeping us," adds Colin helpfully.

"All right," says Jasper. "You go. But no funny business or your mate's a dead duck."

"Not worth it for a measly eighty quid, chum. I know when

I'm licked."

With a beatific smile Colin turns and walks casually towards the stairs.

Len stands petrified. He hears the door to the stairs clang behind Colin. He's on his own, deserted by his best mate. He starts counting, one...two...three...

What can he do to distract these two thugs? He hasn't a clue. Eleven...twelve...thirteen... If only Nora was with him, she'd know what to do. Fifteen...sixteen...seventeen... Perhaps he could pretend to drop dead. No, that would be tempting providence. The youths are staring at him, knife at the ready. Eighteen...nineteen...twenty!

In desperation Len starts to hum, swaying slowly from side to side as he does so. He undoes his blazer, and being unable to think of anything better to do, starts unbuckling his trouser belt.

"Oi!" cries Pug. "What's your bleedin' game?"

Len unzips his trouser front, starts trying to waggle his hips like a hula dancer to encourage his trousers to fall.

Jasper sits up and takes notice, flick-knife poised menacingly.

Come on, Colin!

Colin comes. With a blood-curdling roar he leaps from behind a pillar and flings himself at the youths like a tiger at its prey. He slides across the bonnet of the car, sending the youths crashing to the ground on the far side. The knife skates away harmlessly.

The youths, not knowing what's hit them, flee for their lives just as Nora and Elsie hove into view. They both stare transfixed at Len with his trousers around his ankles.

"Now there's a pretty sight!" grins Colin.

Chapter 9

At the Ocean View that evening Colin and Len are the heroes of the hour.

As soon as he heard about the valiant way they had foiled the two thugs, Mr Pertwee instantly forgave them for being back late for dinner. He even went further when told Colin had hurt his back and had been to the hospital to have it checked – happily it was nothing worse than a strain – and generously presented them with a bottle of his best Scotch.

"Strictly for medical purposes, y'ken," he told them with a wink.

At dinner Nora soon supplies the other guests with all the details, emphasising the incredible presence of mind shown by Len during his part in the incident. Elsie suddenly becomes the loving wife, solicitous of Colin's back and bestowing adoring glances upon him. Billy Greenhorn, alone at his table, nods and beams as Nora expounds. The coloured family by the window listens with suitable tuts and exclamations of "Deary me!" Even the young loving couple momentarily divert their attention from one another to hear the lurid details. And when Daphne comes in to serve the main course, Nora recounts the whole event all over again for her benefit, causing the roast chicken on the tray she is holding to get cold.

While the Stilwells and the Scallys are still sampling their sherry trifle, Billy Greenhorn pauses at their table on his way out of the dining room.

"Shall we be enjoying your beautiful music again tonight at The Fisherman's Float?" he enquires of Elsie.

"Not tonight, mate," Colin, answers for her. "No way, not with me back and that."

"We're all going to have an early night," adds Nora.

"It has made us all feel a bit dithery."

"Of course. Of course." Billy looks suitably sorrowful. "Another time, perhaps. I shall look forward to it."

"I wish I could remember where I've seen that bugger's mug before," says Colin as Billy wends his way from the room.

Dinner over, the four of them go through to the lounge for coffee. The lady with the nut-brown face, whose name they soon discover to be Miss Dibble, is in there watching the telly. The sound is quickly turned down so that she can be told all about it.

"How *awful*!" she exclaims in her aristocratic voice, which sounds odd coming from someone who looks as if she should be smoking a pipe of peace. She turns and looks at Colin with great respect. "How terribly brave of you!"

"Couldn't have done it without me old mate here," he answers modestly. "He was brilliant!"

Nora puffs up with pride. "I always knew he had hidden talents," she says.

"And he wasn't afraid to show 'em!" laughs Colin.

Len grins sheepishly as all eyes turn upon him.

If Miss Dibble was shocked by this innuendo she doesn't show it. "We live in such *dreadful* times," she observes. "It is most gratifying to learn that for once these beastly fellows were foiled. I *do* hope the police manage to catch them."

"Didn't bother to tell the police," says Colin. "No point – they've probably hopped it back to London by this time. Still, I reckon they won't try it again in a hurry."

Daphne comes in with the coffee. Colin watches her as she pours it out, imagining the gorgeous figure he'd seen on the beach that morning, which must still be lurking under that unbecoming black dress she is now wearing. He finds it hard to believe it's the same girl, she looks so bored and dour. But when their eyes meet she smiles and, although he can't be sure, she seems to give him a saucy wink.

His stomach churns, and it's not due to the roast chicken. She fancies me! he thinks. Or was the wink just because of their collusion over the dog escapade on the beach?

When the subject of the car park incident has been well and truly exhausted they all settle back to sip their coffee and watch the television, partaking of Mr Pertwee's Scotch as they do so.

Len soon begins to feel drowsy. "What's wrong with Britain's water?" he hears a voice-over ask on the telly, but he's not awake to learn the answer.

Nora, not being particularly interested in Britain's water, is imagining herself back at work relating Len's exploit to her colleagues. Elsie is thinking that perhaps Colin isn't the old woman she's always thought, and resolves to try to be more loving and considerate towards him. Colin himself is fantasising over Daphne Pertwee. He has a vision of seeing her in bed without her bikini. He should be so lucky!

Yet when she comes back into the lounge to collect the coffee cups Daphne smiles at him again and looks at him significantly, as if trying to tell him something. Then to his surprise, just as she's about to leave the lounge with the coffee cups, she comes over to him.

"If y'should be wanting the loo," she whispers into his ear, "there's one through the kitchen. Save y'going all the way upstairs with y'poor back."

"Oh! That's very kind! Very thoughtful, I'm sure. Thank you."

She smiles again, and as she turns to leave gives him another meaningful look. I must be imagining it, thinks Colin. She must just be wanting to save me climbing them stairs with me bad back. What other reason could there be? He's no idea, but he's bloody well going to find out if there is one.

So after a decent interval he tells Elsie he's just going to the loo, and leaves the lounge, his hand pressed against his painful back.

In the kitchen the Pertwees are busy clearing up after dinner. When she sees him Daphne comes over.

"I'll just show y'where it is," she says as she leads him towards a glass-panelled door at the far end of the kitchen. "Down there on the right."

As she holds the door open for him she gives a conspiratorial wink and as he passes through, presses a tightly folded piece of paper into his hand.

Colin's heart pounds like a ship's engine. There can be no doubting *that* wink! She *must* be up to something – but what? Surely it can't be an invitation to a secret assignation? But what else could it be?

Once safely inside the loo he opens up the piece of paper.

It turns out to be a leaflet. It reads:

THE BLACK SPOT
Benthaven's Premier Nite Club
*** Mon 1st June BANK HOLIDAY SPECIAL ***
**** MISS WET T-SHIRT COMPETITION ****

Tuesday 2nd June GOLDEN OLDIES NITE
Wednesday 3rd June PARTY BONANZA NITE
Thursday 4th June T-SHIRT AND SHORTS NITE
Friday 5th June LUCKY DIP NITE
Saturday 6th June CHEAP BEER NITE

Each side of the Bank Holiday item is a thick cross, drawn with a red felt-tipped pen. And on the back of the leaflet are scrawled the words 'BE THERE!'

*****

It isn't so much Colin's aching back that keeps him awake, it's the prospect of seeing Daphne in a wet T-shirt, and the puzzle as to how he can possibly work it so he's there to see her.

But work it, he must. He's heard about these wet T-shirt competitions, but had no idea they still took place, and certainly not in somewhere like Benthaven. He's a bit shocked, he has to admit. I bet her dad doesn't know she's into this kind of thing, he thinks. And why should she want him to 'be there'? He can't believe she really fancies him like that. Perhaps she's trying to reward him for not telling her dad about the dog escapade. But whatever it is, he fully intends to go and find out. Somehow he must make it.

But how?

One thing is certain, he realises – to go alone is out of the question. The Stilwells and the Scallys always go everywhere together on holiday, except for the odd occasion when they go in pairs, like yesterday afternoon. But he can't imagine Len coming with him to a place like this.

Despite the painkillers the hospital gave him, Colin twists and turns until the first glint of sunshine penetrates the curtains.

But he is still no closer to solving the problem. In desperation he gets up and goes to the bathroom. There he takes another look at the leaflet, hoping if he stares at it long enough he might be given some kind of miraculous inspiration.

Oddly enough, he is.

He can't believe it! He is amazed at his own ingenuity. But *dare* he? It is a brilliant idea, but dangerous. If it misfired he'd be in dead trouble.

And another thing, he thinks, as he takes his place again beside the snoring Elsie, he'd need an accomplice. Who? Not Len, for sure. He'd never be party to such a deception, and not Daphne herself. The less she comes into it, the better. And certainly not old Pertwee. What about that Greenhorn bloke, he seems the only other possibility? No, he wouldn't trust that bugger anyway.

I'm not going to manage to get there, he thinks gloomily. It's just not on. A great pity, but there it is.

Then, just as he is dozing off, a name drops into his head, unbidden but certainly not unwelcome.

Dave! Old Dave down at The Fisherman's Float!

*****

At breakfast the next morning Colin is inundated by kind enquiries about his back. He has to be cautious how he answers. He mustn't give the impression he is fit enough to trail off looking at orphan elephants; on the other hand he must profess to be fit enough to go to The Black Spot in the evening.

"It's feeling a bit easier," he tells them, which is somewhere near the truth.

'The sun is out again," announces Nora, "so we might as well spend the morning on the beach. See how you are at lunchtime and decide about the afternoon then."

That suits Colin perfectly. "And we'll have lunch at The Fisherman's Float. No more of old Pertwee's picnics."

No one disagrees with that.

So Len's Escort weaves its way down the hill to the harbour car park, and they take up the same positions under the harbour wall that they occupied yesterday. The fat lady is there, sucking a Mr Whippy ice cream.

"Hello, luv," says Colin. "Been here all night?"

"Waiting for a repeat performance," she banters.

Colin grins. "Sorry, it's me day off."

Nora opens her holdall and sifts through her leaflets once again. Colin is a bit alarmed. What if there is a copy of The Black Spot leaflet among them? That could bugger things up for him.

Len rolls up his sleeves to half-mast and loosens his tie, then scans the business section of his newspaper again for any mention of redundancies at Regal Chemicals.

Elsie anoints herself with suntan lotion and stretches herself flat on her beach mat, her mind immediately flitting back to Australia. If only she was still living there! Perhaps, she thinks, if we *are* made redundant we could afford to go there for a holiday, see my two boys. The thought lifts her spirits. She might do that anyway. Save up for it. Give up these tedious holidays with the Scallys.

Because of the pain in his back, Colin doesn't bother to strip down to his swimming trunks and decides just to take off his shirt. At least today, he thinks, the old fivers are safely tucked away under the wardrobe shelf.

The fat lady cheers as he pulls off his shirt. "Thought it was your day off?"

"It's only a *half* day," he quips.

He gingerly sits himself down with his back against the harbour wall and once more opens his *Daltons Weekly* to see if there are any other small hotels for sale. But he is unable to concentrate, his mind being on what he wants to say to Dave when they go to The Fisherman's Float. He also keeps a sharp eye out for Daphne, hoping he'll see her again in her bikini. But she fails to appear, and the morning drags on as if it's never going to end.

When the church clock eventually chimes twelve, Colin immediately struggles to his feet. "Must get to The Fisherman's Float early," he says. "It's Bank Holiday, could get crowded."

No one's going to argue with that.

Colin is relieved to see Dave is back on duty behind the bar. "Make up your minds what you want to eat," he tells the others, indicating the board on which the copious lunch menu is chalked in neat but curly writing, "and I'll go and do the ordering."

"I'm just having a jacket potato with cheese," announces Nora. "It's roast beef tonight at the hotel. I don't want to spoil me appetite for that."

Despite the promise of roast beef Len elects to have the steak and kidney pie, Elsie the lasagne, and Colin good old plaice and chips, all served with side salad.

"*Uncooked* cheese on my jacket potato, mind," Nora warns Colin as he hurries off to the bar to do the ordering.

"Tell me," Colin says to Dave while he draws off the pints, "what do you know about The Black Spot?"

Dave stops and looks at Colin in surprise. "Black Spot? Well, it's a sort of glorified disco, mate, up on the hill. Why?"

"I've been invited to go there tonight."

He shows Dave the leaflet.

"Wet T-Shirt Competition?" Dave laughs. "Your good ladies not taking part in that, surely?"

"Course not! But I've been invited to go and see it."

"You haven't changed much, Colin!"

"It's not like that at all!" Colin sounds affronted. "The thing is this girl up at the Ocean View – a nice kid – asked me to go, and I don't like to let her down."

"Course not," grins Dave.

"Thing is, it's not the sort of show I can take the others to. But I've had an idea." He leans over the bar. "I need you to help me, mate."

Dave looks suspicious. "How?"

In a low tone Colin explains what he wants him to do.

Dave's eyes widen in amazement. "Taking a bit of a risk, aren't you?"

"I know, but it's the only way. Feel I ought to go, see, cos the girl feels she wants someone older there to keep an eye her, make sure she's okay. Can't be too careful in a place like that."

"Reckon it's you who'll need to be careful," replies Dave. "They'll have you for breakfast, them youngsters. That place has got a bit of a reputation."

"All the more reason for keeping an eye on her. Look, you going to help me or not?"

Dave sighs. "Okay, mate, just for old times' sake."

"You're a pal."

When he joins the others with the drinks, Elsie looks at him suspiciously. "You've been a hell of a time," she snaps. "What was all that about?"

"Nothing much, just chatting to him about another hotel I've seen in *Daltons Weekly*."

"Oh my God, you're not still harping on that!" Elsie's already forgotten her resolve to be more loving towards him.

"No, no, just a matter of interest."

"Did you tell him about what happened last night?" asks Nora.

"Last night? Oh, you mean the car park caper. No, didn't think of it, to be honest."

"Should have thought that would have been the first thing you'd have told him, him having been a copper and that." Nora takes a sip of her gin and tonic. "How *is* your back now, by the way?"

Colin answers carefully. "Well, fair, y'know. Fair."

"Up to going to see the elephants this afternoon?"

"Oh, I don't think so, Nora. Not quite yet. The rest on the beach did it good this morning, but it's still painful at times. Still needs a bit more rest."

Elsie has noticed her arms are getting red with the sun and is delving into her Tesco's bag for her sun lotion. "I can't stick this bloody plastic bag any longer," she complains. "I thought you were going to get me that holdall in Brighton this afternoon?"

"Oh, I don't think I'm quite ready for a lot of walking, Els'. Besides, it's Bank Holiday – the big shops will be closed."

"Not here they won't."

"Tomorrow, Els', I promise. Sure to be open then."

"Well, what *do* you want to do?" says Nora.

"Best to go back on the beach. Reckon if I take it easy this afternoon it'll be pretty well all right by tonight."

"Looks as though it might rain again," objects Nora.

"Well, if it does, I think I'll rest up on the bed for a bit," Colin answers. "But don't let me spoil your fun. You three can go off – go and see them elephants."

"Oh, we're not going without you," says Nora promptly.

Dave comes up to their table with the meals, a broad smile on his face.

"Colin didn't tell you about what happened last night, then?" says Nora, as he distributes the oval-shaped plates.

"No. What was that?"

"You tell him, Colin."

So Colin has to wade through the whole story again. Dave listens with increasing surprise and an equally increasing grin.

"That was bloody quick thinking, mate," he comments at the end. "A bit dicey though, wasn't it?"

"Well, have to take a chance sometimes, don't you? Can't always let these buggers get away with it?"

"All the same, you'll have to take it easy for a bit."

"It's getting easier all the time, Dave. I reckon by tonight it'll be gone." He looks at Dave significantly.

"Yes, well don't overdo it. I tell you what, though," he adds. "You folk enjoy a bit of a sing-song, don't you, judging by what went on on Saturday night?"

"Course we do," agrees Nora.

"You ought to go up The Black Spot tonight. It's Golden Oldies night tonight."

"Black Spot?" she queries, not liking the sound of the name. "What sort of place is that?"

"Well, it's a sort of nightclub-cum-disco. Mostly youngsters hang out there, but they also have nights for older people. Golden Oldies, they call it. From what I gather it's a sort of cabaret with community singing – all the old songs and that."

"Sounds all right," says Nora.

"And it's on tonight. They have Golden Oldies every Bank Holiday."

"Sounds great," says Colin, trying to sound casual. "Whereabouts is this place?"

"Up on the hill, just above your hotel. Turn right at the end of Ensdale Terrace, you can't miss it. It's all lit up, only about half a mile."

"What time does it start?" asks Elsie, who's feeling a bit of excitement wouldn't come amiss.

Dave scratches his head. "Show starts about nine, I think. Should be okay if you get there about then."

"We'll think about it," says Colin. "Thanks, Dave."

"Hope you enjoy it." He gives Colin a broad grin and returns to the bar.

"Well, what d'you think?" Colin asks, keeping his fingers crossed.

"Nine's a bit late," says Nora.

"That's cos it's a nightclub, I 'spect. Still we can always lie in tomorrow morning, and rest up a bit this afternoon."

"But what about your back?"

"Shouldn't hurt that. Only got to sit there and sing. Nice to have a bit of a sing-song."

"Since when have you been so keen on singing?" asks Elsie suspiciously.

*****

During dinner that evening Daphne is conspicuous by her absence. Mr Pertwee himself is serving, and Colin informs him they will be late in.

"Will it be after eleven thirty?" asks Mr Pertwee.

Colin hesitates. He doesn't want to tell him where they are going. "Not sure, could be after midnight."

"Och, then you'll be needing a front door key."

When he returns with their Black Forest gateaux he also brings the key. "Be sure to let me have it back in the morning, it's the only spare I have. Guests forget to leave them behind, y'ken."

"No problem, mate," says Colin, pocketing the key.

"And if y'll be as quiet as possible, so as not to disturb the other guests?" Mr Pertwee doesn't want a repeat of Saturday night's fiasco.

"What about the dogs?" asks Nora.

"Och, they know you now. They'll nae make a fuss."

For their first 'Big Evening' of the holiday Nora puts on her navy-blue dress and her pearls, and Elsie her Spanish dancer-style dress, which she hasn't worn since the New Year's party at the Sports and Social. Len wears his new blazer with his red-spotted bow tie. Colin, who forgot to pack his best suit in the rush when they left home, wears his jumper with the blue diagonal stripes.

"You'll have to go easy on the drink tonight," Nora warns Len. "It's Bank Holiday, so the police will be on the watch out. Still, it won't hurt you to lay off for once."

What with a lot of singing to endure and little in the way of alcoholic solace Len reckons he's in for a pretty grim evening.

"Oooh, what a lovely old building!" exclaims Nora as they pull into the car park of The Black Spot.

It is all leaded panes and trailing ivy. Although it is still not dark, the building is lit with enough fairy lights to decorate a forest of Christmas trees. Over the entrance is an incongruous enormous black spot painted on a yellow background.

Once inside the heavily Victorian entrance hall, they are accosted by an equally heavy-looking gentleman in evening dress, who issues them with temporary membership.

"That'll be eighty pounds," he says, holding out his hand.

"Eighty pounds!" cries Nora. "That's twenty pounds each!" Working in accounts has made her good at mental arithmetic.

"Includes entrance," says the man in a take-it-or-leave-it manner.

"Even so I'm not paying-"

"My treat," cuts in Colin hastily. He's not going to let Nora turn tail having got this far. "I feel generous tonight. The evening's on me."

That should shut her up, he thinks.

And it does.

"What time does the show start?" asks Elsie.

"Show?" The man looks doubtful, his eyes swivelling to Nora. "Straight on, through the double doors."

As they approach the doors they hear the thud of pop music coming from the other side. Nearby, an unstable suit of armour vibrates in sympathy.

Inside it is like the bottommost depths of hell. Flashing coloured lights, mostly purple and green, punctuate the darkness giving intermittent glimpses of figures convoluting tortuously on the floor. At the far end, bathed in a red glow, are demonic creatures leaping about, twanging guitars.

A bunny girl, smelling like a perfumery, greets them and ushers them to a free table, where they grope their way into plush but hard seats. The noise is deafening.

So is the silence when the music stops and the roar of applause is over. Dim lights come up, revealing a small hall with crimson satin wall covering, and a quite small dance floor, surrounded by heavy dark tables, red seating and gilt fittings.

Nora doesn't like the look of it at all. She thinks it looks like a brothel, or rather, what she imagines a brothel to look like.

Another bunny girl quickly comes up to take their orders for drinks.

"My treat!" cries Colin, hoping to curry favour.

They all order their usual.

"I thought you said it was Golden Oldies night," says Elsie accusingly to Colin, having caught him looking at the bunny's fishnet tights.

"You heard what Dave said – hope he hasn't got it wrong."

"So do I," says Nora.

"'Spect it doesn't start till later." Colin takes a furtive glance round to see if he can spot Daphne, but can't see her anywhere.

But at that moment the lights go down again and bedlam is resumed.

Nora fumbles in her handbag for her earplugs. Len wishes he had some too. Elsie is beginning to feel very irritable and she puts on her long-suffering look. Colin is on tenterhooks in case she demands to leave there and then.

But the bunny girl comes to the rescue by returning with the drinks, which prove very expensive. Colin's glad he had the foresight to bring most of his reserve cash with him. It had better prove worthwhile, he thinks.

"This isn't a nightclub, it's a bloody discotheque," growls Elsie.

"Dave said it was a Golden Oldies tonight," he protests defensively.

"Don't you try telling me all these kids have come to hear Golden Oldies!"

"Course not," agrees Nora. "Obviously Dave got it wrong. Might as well go when we've finished our drink."

"What, after I've paid all that money to come in!" Colin sounds desperate. "Look, let's hang on a bit longer and see what happens." He looks round for Daphne again, but there is no sign of her. Nor of any wet T-shirts.

"Goood eevening," says a familiar voice in Elsie's ear.

"Oh hello, Mr...er..."

"Greenhorn," he finishes. "But please call me Billy."

That's all I need, thinks Colin, bloody Sergeant Bilko shoving his nose in. But on second thoughts, he thinks, maybe he'll make Elsie more prepared to stay on. "Didn't expect to see you here, mate," he says. "You on your own?"

Billy beams and nods.

"Come and join us then. Draw up a pew. What'll you have?"

"Allow me to buy the next round," says Billy as he sits down.

"That's very civil. Ta."

Billy pulls the bushy tail of a passing bunny. "Same again for these good people. Pint of Guinness for me."

Randy old bugger, thinks Colin. He's here for the wet T-shirts too, I bet.

"Have you come to hear the Golden Oldies?" asks Nora, finishing off her first gin and tonic.

Billy looks bewildered. "No Golden Oldies tonight, dear lady, they're on Tuesdays."

"There you are!" cries Elsie. "Bloody Dave's up the creek without his paddle."

"No point in staying then," says Nora.

"Can't go yet, Billy here has just bought us a round of drinks," Colin reminds her. "Besides, it might improve later. This is supposed to be a nightclub, so there ought to be a cabaret or summat."

"No cabaret." Billy shakes his head. "Competition night tonight."

Elsie pricks up her ears. "Competition? Talent competition, you mean?" She thinks she might have a go.

Billy beams. "In a manner of speaking, dear lady."

I've had it, thinks Colin.

But he is saved in the nick of time, not by the bell, but by the lead guitarist grabbing the microphone and booming out a torrent of words, the only decipherable ones to the uninitiated being 'Smoochie Time'.

The psychedelia recommences, albeit at a more tolerable

and less frantic level.

"Do you mind," says Billy to Colin, "if I ask your good lady for this dance?"

Colin is only too glad. "Course not, mate. Feel free."

With old-fashioned courtesy Billy pulls back Elsie's chair and escorts her to the floor, where, amid the smooching teenagers, they shuffle sedately around.

What with the mood music and soft lights, and two vodkas safely inside her, Elsie is beginning to feel more harmonious in her soul. And the old boy isn't a bad dancer at that. Her holiday is starting to take off, she feels.

"I did so enjoy your organ playing the other night," murmurs Billy presently.

"Thanks," says Elsie.

"And your dress! Is this another of your own creations?"

"As a matter of fact, it is."

"Very fetching, very Spanish. It becomes you!"

"Thanks," says Elsie.

"You must have Spanish blood in your veins."

"No," says Elsie.

Billy beams at her. "Even more remarkable! You are really very talented, dear lady."

"Thanks," says Elsie again.

Once more she wonders what the old boy's game can be, and still can't decide if it's the old come-on or if he's taking the piss.

"You really should take up the organ professionally," he continues, squeezing her waist.

"What me? Don't talk daft!"

"I mean it, dear lady. I know about these things. I used to be in the music business."

"So you said."

"I was a talent-spotter at one time. I have made many discoveries – Branny Buncombe for one."

"Oh yes?" She's never heard of him.

"And Harry Cooper, the trombone player, Charlie Hobbs, Pete Maclean, and the singer Helena Bracebridge. You may have heard of her."

"Fancy I've seen her on the telly."

Billy looks startled and misses a step in his dancing. "She's not on the telly, dear lady! She's an opera singer, a prima donna, or was until she unhappily got run over."

"Oh yes?" Elsie's beginning to get bored with all this.

"I am retired now, of course, but I still have many friends in the business. I could help, put you in touch with someone."

Elsie is beginning to wonder if he does mean it. "Oh, I'm just a hick player. Just play by ear. Can't read music and that."

Billy dismisses the objection with a shake of his head. "Not important."

"But I only know the old stuff. I can't play all this modern pop."

"Plenty can do that. Not many can play the oldies – not like you. You have the style. The old folk would love it. Brings back the good old days. You'd get more work than you could cope with, up and down the country, pubs, clubs, resorts, hotels, Radio Two! Blackpool Tower even, one day."

The mention of Blackpool Tower rouses Elsie's interest. She's been there, and she's still got some of her mum's old seventy-eights of Reginald Dixon.

"Are you kidding or do you really mean it?" she asks.

"Of course I mean it, dear lady."

"Well, I dunno. Have to think about it."

Billy beams, and pulls her closer to him.

*****

Back at the table Nora is taking two Paracetamols with her second G and T. "This din is giving me a terrible head," she complains. "It's nothing like I was expecting. We'd have done better to go to The Fisherman's Float and got Elsie to play the organ."

"Don't keep on, Nora," growls Colin. "I wasn't to know, was I?"

"You should have checked, not taken Dave's word for it."

Colin remains silent. He's beginning to wish he hadn't started it all. I'm a bloody fool, he tells himself. Shouldn't have taken notice of that girl. Probably just trying make a mug of me, the bitch. Might as well go when Elsie comes off the floor before more damage is done.

"Hi!" says a voice at his elbow.

Colin's heart leaps. He looks round, and who should be standing there but Daphne, Mr Pertwee's lynx-eyed daughter, wearing a blood red T-shirt with 'BRISTOL ROVERS' emblazoned across the front. "Hello!" he cries. "Where did you spring from?"

"Och, we've just arrived. We're sitting behind you." She points vaguely. "How's y'poor wee back?"

"It's improving all the time," grins Colin.

"Enough to give me this dance?"

"Let's find out."

Daphne grabs his hand and pulls him towards the floor.

Nora looks down her nose. "Now there's a fine thing, I must say. Here we are, supposed to be his guests and he hasn't even the good manners to ask us if we'll excuse him! I mean, fancy leaving us on our own in a place like this! When he comes back we're going, whether he likes it or not."

On the floor Daphne is clinging to Colin, arms around his neck, her face against his chest. He can feel her soft breasts pressed against his stomach. It improves his back no end.

"I'm glad you managed to make it," she murmurs after a while.

"So am I. Glad you asked me."

"I was afraid your friends would'nae want to come."

"They wouldn't have done if they'd known about the Competition. I let them think it's Golden Oldies night."

"Och, y'naughty boy! Won't y'be in trouble when they find out?"

"No doubt. They already want to leave. I may still not have the pleasure of seeing you in your wet T-shirt."

Daphne raises her head to look at him. "I'm afraid y'won't anyway. I was going to take part but m'grandfather's here."

"Your grandfather!"

"Aye. M'father sends him to spy on me when I go out."

"What's he do that for?"

"To keep an eye on me. He's scared I'll get into trouble."

He could be right, thinks Colin.

"Father's a miserable old sod. Doesnae trust me an inch. He

thinks he can rule m'life even though I'm over eighteen now."

"Then tell him to go to hell."

"Och, it's not worth it, he'd make m'life a misery. But you go and see the show just the same. You'll enjoy it – nothing disgusting about it, just a bit of fun."

"Well, if you're not in it I'm not bothered. Only came because you asked me. I'm enjoying just dancing with you more in fact."

"Och, you're such a wee sweet man!"

She smiles and presses herself against him and Colin's blood pressure shoots up like a rocket. But all too soon the smooch comes to an end.

"Come on," says Daphne. "I want you to meet my friends. I've been telling them all about your heroic exploits."

"Well, I ought to be getting back to—"

"Och, come *on*!"

*****

Back at the table Elsie and Nora are having a disputation. Elsie and Billy have returned from the dance floor to be greeted by glowering looks from Nora.

"Can we leave now, please?" says Nora in a long-suffering voice. "This noise has given me a splitting head."

But Elsie doesn't want to leave. "I'm just beginning to enjoy meself," she objects. "I'm not leaving yet."

Nora sniffs. "That's all very well. You two want to learn some manners, you know, leaving me and Len alone here like a couple of lemons while you go off dancing and Colin flirts with that girl."

"What girl?"

"That girl from the hotel – Daphne, or whatever she calls herself."

"*She's* here?"

"Didn't you see them canoodling together on the dance floor?"

"Well, bugger 'em!" At this moment Elsie's mind is on her 'Golden Future' as an organist. Colin can go to hell as far as she's concerned.

"I suggest you go and root him out before he makes a complete fool of himself," continues Nora, "and then let's get out of this horrid place."

"I'm not ready yet, I've got to talk to Mr Green...er...berg. And I need another bloody drink."

"Same again?" asks Billy.

"Don't *you* get 'em," Elsie tells him. She points a finger at Len. "It's *his* turn."

"No it's not," cuts in Nora. "We're leaving."

"That's right," snarls Elsie, eyes aflame. "Bugger off as soon as it's your turn to dib out."

Nora becomes prim. "It's not that, as well you know. I told you, I've a splitting headache. I can't bear it in this hellhole a moment longer."

"You can wait a *few* minutes, can't you? Go and have a dance or summat while I talk to Mr Green...er...baum."

"*Dance*? With that lot? Never!" Nora is quite adamant.

Elsie bridles. "Oh, I *see*! Not good enough for you, I suppose. Not Webbley Park enough."

"That settles it! We're going."

"Good riddance!"

"Come along, Len."

"But how will they get back to the hotel?" protests Len, not willing to leave his old mate in the lurch.

"Since Colin is so flush with money all of a sudden, I'm sure he can run to a taxi."

"I shall be honoured to give you and your good hubby a lift back to the hotel," says Billy, who has been surveying this exchange with bland surprise.

"That's all right then," says Nora, gathering up her bits and pieces. "That settles that!"

"Right," says Elsie.

"Right," says Nora.

She scrambles to her feet and turns to go.

Then she falters, and turns back.

"You sure you won't come?"

"Go to hell!" snaps Elsie.

Nora turns again abruptly and hauls Len after her towards the exit.

"Now who's got bad manners?" yells Elsie after them. "Walking out after Colin paid all that money to come in!"

Nora stops dead, then stumps back to the table.

"So that's it!" She delves in her bag and rashly plonks several ten-pound notes on the table under Elsie's nose.

"Never let it be said we wasted Colin's money!"

Elsie grabs the notes and flings them after Nora's departing figure. "I don't want y'bleedin' money!"

Heads turn. Billy nearly drops his Guinness. Len scurries around trying to retrieve the precious notes before chasing after Nora to the exit.

*****

"This is Cheryl," Daphne says to Colin as she introduces him to her four friends, who are lolling around a table on which stands a half-empty bottle of whisky with glasses to match.

"Hi," says Cheryl, raising a thin, white arm to half-mast.

"And this is the brave chap I was telling you about – Mr Stilwell."

"Call me Colin," says Colin.

"And this is Carlos. He's from Spain."

"Hi," says Carlos. Heavy lids lift slightly from over dark Mediterranean eyes.

"And Dodo and Alice."

No response from Dodo and Alice, who are kissing in a languid sort of way.

"Pleased to meet you," says Colin.

"Have a drink?" invites Daphne. "You look as if you need it."

Colin does.

"Well, I ought to be getting back to me friends really..."

"Och, go on. Just one. Have a seat."

"But isn't that your seat?"

"Never mind." She pours him a generous whisky. "Go on, sit doon!"

Colin sits. He wonders if he should drink that whisky on top of the two pints of beer he's already consumed.

Cheryl extends her thin, white arm. "Pour me another while

you're about it, Daph. If I'm going to be dowsed in water I need it to keep out the cold."

"Pour it yoursel'," says Daphne sourly.

To Colin's amazement and alarm Daphne plonks herself on his lap and wraps her arm around his shoulder. He hopes to God Elsie isn't watching.

"Are you going to see the show?" Cheryl asks him.

"The show? Oh that! No, me friends are getting fidgety. They want to leave."

"Och, they can wait a wee while," says Daphne. "It'll be starting very soon."

Colin glances over at the table, expecting to see Len and Nora sitting like a couple of dummies, but instead he sees Elsie sitting there talking to Billy Greenhorn. She seems well occupied, he thinks.

"Well, all right then. Just for a few minutes."

"You look like the kind of fella who might enjoy it," says Cheryl, eyeing him over her whisky. "Go with Carlos, if you want company. You're going to see it, aren't you, sweetie?"

"Ah si!" His trim moustache lifts at the ends as he grins leeringly at the prospect.

"No, he's coming with me," says Daphne, running her fingers through Colin's hair.

It suddenly occurs to Colin that the reason Daphne was so anxious for him to be there is because, unlike her friends, she doesn't seem to have a partner.

"Such a pity you can't take part, Daph," says Cheryl. "Sure you won't change your mind and give Colin a thrill?"

"Och, I darenae, not with m'grandfather here."

This grandfather of Daphne's is beginning to make Colin a bit uneasy, and he glances round to see if he can spot anyone around who might fit the part. He's visualising some old Scot in a kilt who could storm up at any moment and bash him silly for seducing his granddaughter. Luckily, he can see no such person.

"You going in for it, Alice?" asks Cheryl.

Alice is still drooling over Dodo, her arms wound round him like the tentacles of an octopus.

"Alice!" shouts Cheryl.

"What?"

"You going to take part?"

"What in?"

"The show, you berk. Show off y'boobs to Dodo?"

Alice looks adoringly into Dodo's sallow face. "Shall I?" she giggles.

"Ah boobs," intones Dodo, his close-set eyes apparently focused on an invisible crystal ball. "The two blessed mounds of Venus!"

They're bloody stoned, the pair of 'em, thinks Colin. Perhaps old Pertwee is wise to have her grandad keep an eye on Daphne.

"You don't know your female anatomy," Cheryl informs Dodo, "and you call yourself a poet!"

"This show, what is it exactly?" asks Carlos, suddenly showing more interest.

"Don't you know? You haven't been around, have you?"

"Not have in Spain, I think."

"I bet they do!" Cheryl snuggles closer to Carlos and dabs her finger on the end of his nose while she speaks. "Well, sweetie, they put on a tape and the girls have to dance to it while they're drenched in water by some guy with a hose. Then at the end, out of the girls who haven't chickened out – if there are any – the one who danced the best is judged the winner. At least, that's how they do it in this dump. Compris?"

"Ah si," nods Carlos gravely.

"But surely they don't hold it in here?" asks Colin, imagining the dance floor flooded with water.

"God, no! They hold it in what they call the Outhouse."

"It's a converted cowshed," explains Daphne, refuelling his glass with whisky. "This place used to be a farm."

"Oh, I see." Colin suddenly wonders if the police keep an eye on the goings-on here. Just his luck if they should decide to raid it tonight!

The relative peace is shattered when a youth with a face like Jesus but dressed more like Satan grabs the microphone.

"Friends, the Midnight Hour has struck! The moment you have all been waiting for is nigh, so will all the brave girls willing to take part in our Miss Wet T-shirt Competition please go now to the Ladies Cloakroom, where you will each receive one of our complementary T-shirts. Don't be timid, girls! Give the lads a treat. Your turn will come next week when we hold our Mr Wet Y-Fronts Competition! The big prize tonight is a magnum of champagne, with a bottle of gin each for the two runners-up. So on with the show! May the best girl win!"

A blend of applause, catcalls, whistles and stamping greets this announcement.

"You'd better be there rooting for me, Carlos sweetie," says Cheryl, leaning over and tweaking his black moustache, "because I intend winning that champagne."

"Ah, si!" A man of few words, Carlos.

"You too, Daph. Since you're too scared of your grandpappy to take part yourself the least you can do is come and shout for me. And see your lovely new man does too." Cheryl blows Colin a kiss. "Come on, Alice, let's go and get into our armour."

She prises Alice off Dodo and leads her away giggling to the Ladies Cloakroom.

"Bloody bitch!" mutters Daphne.

"Who?" asks Colin in surprise.

"Cheryl."

"Why?"

"Och, dinnae ask me!" She leaps off Colin's lap. "But she'll nae make a ninny o' me!"

"Where you going?" asks Colin, also leaping up.

"To do battle!"

"But I thought—"

"You go to the Outhouse with Carlos, but be sure y'shout for *me*. See y'later for the champagne!"

"I really ought to be going..." he calls after her.

But too late. Daphne has gone.

*****

"This is definitely the last holiday we're having with the Stilwells," announces Nora as they are driving back to the Ocean View Hotel. "They never did have very good taste, but really, that place tonight takes the biscuit."

"Colin wasn't to know," says Len, feeling compelled to

defend his old mate.

"No, but he was only too keen to stay, wasn't he? So was Elsie once that Greenberg man came on the scene. What Colin should have done was to turn round and walk out as soon as he saw the sort of place it was."

"But he'd just paid a lot of money to go in!"

"He should have demanded it back. No, there is no excusing him. Having been a policeman and that you'd have thought he would have known better. This has spoilt the holiday for me, I can tell you, and it's only the second full day." She tugs at the seat belt, which is cutting her across the throat. "No, if I thought there was any hope of getting back our deposit I'd pack up and go home tomorrow."

That would suit Len. So far, it hasn't been his idea of a holiday either. And he's missing his cronies at The Mason and Magpie something chronic.

The church clock strikes midnight as Len drives his Escort into the Ocean View forecourt. Suddenly it is bathed in a brilliant white light.

"Now what's happened?" demands Nora, shielding her eyes with her hand.

"It's a security light," says Len. "Infra-red or summat. It'll go out when we've gone in."

"Then let's get in as quick as we can. All these security gadgets are more nuisance than they're worth, and do precious little good as far as I can see."

But when they reach the front door they find it locked.

"Course, it's gone eleven," says Nora. "We'll have to use that key Mr Pertwee gave us."

"Colin's got it," groans Len. "We'll have to go all the way back for it."

"That we won't! Ring the door bell."

"But it's after midnight!"

"Can't be helped. I'm not going back grovelling to Colin for the key. Go on, ring!"

But Len doesn't fancy having to haul poor Mr Pertwee from his bed again. "There might be a window open or summat," he says and wanders along the front of the hotel in the hope of finding one.

"Don't be ridiculous! Ring the bell!"

Nora snorts impatiently and presses the doorbell herself.

Somewhere inside the bell rings. Bess and Boss launch into a duet of barking.

Len prises at one of the windows to see if he can open it.

A mighty clanging breaks out. He leaps back in alarm.

Nora is livid. "Now look what you've gone and done!"

"But I only just touched it!"

"I said not to!"

"Let's get out of here!" Len heads for the car at the double.

"Where you going?"

"The police'll be coming!" He knows through Colin that these security systems can be linked to the police station.

"Rubbish! Come back here!"

Hotel lights go on. Dogs bark. Heads poke out of windows.

"What's going on?" demands a voice from somewhere up aloft.

"Turn off that bloody row!" shouts another voice.

"Pertwee's going to be hopping mad," quakes Len.

"It's his own fault," rasps Nora, keeping her finger on the bell. "He should have enough pass keys to go round."

The light in the foyer comes on. A convoluted figure can be seen through the crinkly plate glass front door.

"Who's there?" demands the figure.

"It's Mrs Scally! Open up, we can't get in!"

"Wait!"

They wait.

The alarm stops. The figure mysteriously grovels on the floor behind the door.

"What's he doing now?" asks Nora.

"Dunno," says Len.

"Hurry up!" she shouts through the door.

"Will y'nae take y'finger off the bell?" the figure shouts back.

"Put out that light!" yells the voice from aloft.

At last the door opens and there stands Mr Pertwee in a Noel Coward dressing gown, holding a rifle like a sentry. Nora scarcely recognises him with his sparse hair standing on end and his toothless mouth crumpled.

"Friends," Mr P. growls to Bess and Boss, who slink away disappointed. "Dinnae I give y'a path key?" asks the toothless Mr P. grumpily.

"Our friends have got it. We left early. We weren't stopping in that disgusting hole."

"Y'dinnae have to thet off the alarm."

"Sorry," says Len hastily. "Thought there might be a window open. Didn't want to disturb you and that."

Mr Pertwee mutters something, and stands aside for them to enter. "Next thime, will y'nae make sure y'have the key?" he adds, again grovelling on the floor.

"There won't be a next time," states Nora firmly. "We won't be going to that place again."

"Then I'll bid y'good neet."

Having ensured all is safely locked and barred once more Mr Pertwee toils wearily back up the stairs, the rifle under his arm as if he's off to a shoot.

*****

Elsie is in the Ballroom at the top of Blackpool Tower 'playing' Golden Oldies to an enthralled audience, who sing, clap, cheer and keep calling for more. She is so carried away by this fantasy that she is oblivious of the exodus to the Outhouse taking place around her. Nor does she notice Colin come up.

"What's happened to Len and Nora?" he demands.

Elsie descends from the Blackpool Tower with a bump. "Gone," she snaps.

"Gone? Gone where?"

"Back to the hotel, where d'you think? Thanks to you going off with that bloody cow and leaving them alone."

"Daphne came up and asked me to dance!" Colin boldly matches Elsie's belligerent tone. "Couldn't very well say no – could I?"

"Oh *no*, not to *her*."

"Anyhow, you can talk – going off with old Bilko like that."

Elsie draws herself up. "That was different."

"Whatcha mean? What's different about it?"

"Cos he says he could help me earn a lot of money playing

the organ. Become famous and that."

"Don't talk daft! The bugger's winding you up."

"No he ain't. He says he can put me in touch with someone in London who can get me started."

"What, playing them old-time ditties you churn out? Don't you believe it, Els'. I told you, that bugger's bad news."

"What do you know about it? He says I've got a rare talent. Not many left that can play the Golden Oldies like I can. He says I can make a fortune playing 'em for the old folk to sing to, in clubs and that."

"And you fell for it!"

"Oh, go to hell," says Elsie, knocking back the remains of her fourth vodka.

"Anyhow, you coming to see the show?" Colin asks hopefully. It would solve his dilemma.

"No, I'm bloody not."

"Aw, come on, Els'. It's only a bit of fun."

"Huh!"

"Well, *I'm* going."

"That's it, go and get yourself an eyeful."

"It's not that. As a matter of fact, Daphne asked me to. She wants someone to shout for her. Come on, you come and shout too."

"Oh, piss off!"

"All right, if that's how you feel." Colin marches off, a look of righteous indignation on his face.

Elsie glowers at her empty glass. The bloody sod. How can she ever hope to be a success with him jeering all the time?

Billy Greenhorn materialises at her elbow. He has just come back from the Gents where he has been disposing of the consequences of a superfluity of Guinness.

"Another?" he asks, taking the glass from Elsie's hand.

"Why not?"

"Lovely eeevening we're having," he observes as he sits down after he has accosted a bunny girl with the order.

"Oh, great."

"You look tired, dear lady."

"I'm all right." Elsie turns to him and speaks sharply. "Look, are you winding me up about this organ playing, or what?"

Billy looks taken aback. "But of course not! You are very gifted. You could go far."

"Only it's very important to me, see. There's a rumour at work that we're all going to be made redundant, so it could be a way of making money."

Billy beams his appreciation of the situation, and then pulls out his wallet. "I will give you my card. It is, of course, out of date, since I am retired, but my name is still respected in the business. I am writing on the back the name and number of someone you can contact in London."

Elsie takes the card and promptly bursts into tears. "Oh, Mr Greenbum, how can I thank you enough?" she cries.

"Call me Beely," says Billy, producing a pristine handkerchief from the breast pocket of his jacket and presenting it to Elsie, who does a mop-up job on her face.

A sour-faced bunny arrives with the fresh drinks. She's pretty pissed off with having her tail pulled, but when Billy presents her with a twenty and tells her to keep the change her official bunny smile is swiftly restored.

"I feel awful," wails Elsie, upon whom the vodka is starting to have its desired effect. "How could I have ever doubted you?"

"Only natural, dear lady. Come, drink up, and then perhaps we can have another little dance?"

"Oh, I can't dance now. My legs have gone to jelly."

"Then shall we go and see the show?"

"No, no, I couldn't! I'm all of a do-da now. Think I'd better get back to the hotel and go to bed."

"Of course, dear lady. Just finish your drink and we'll go."

"Oh, I didn't mean for you to take me."

"It would be a great honour."

"But I don't you want to spoil your evening."

"I'd much rather see you safely back," says Billy. "But what about your good hubby? Shall I find him for you?"

"Oh, sod him! He can find his own way back."

Billy's face registers bland surprise.

Elsie finishes off her fifth vodka. "I'm ready, Mr Greenbum, if you are?"

Billy beams but doesn't answer.

*****

"Quite frankly," says Nora as she is preparing for bed, "I am disappointed in this hotel. I don't know what Delphine was thinking of in recommending it."

Len pauses in hauling on his pyjama trousers. "You can't beat a good three-star hotel, with a proper bar and ballroom and that."

"Trouble is they cost so much."

"Cheaper if you go on a package holiday."

"True." Nora pauses in the act of rubbing cream into the flab of her face. "Course, it's even cheaper if you go abroad, to countries like Spain and that. I suppose, once we've settled into our new home, we really ought to think about going abroad for our holidays."

"Weather's more reliable too."

"Well, perhaps next year if we can afford it. I'm not going with Elsie and Colin, though. Their behaviour tonight was disgusting. Did you see the way Elsie flung that money at me? And Colin, leaving us to chase after that Pertwee girl? They're just the sort of people who get us Brits a bad reputation abroad."

Len climbs into bed without answering. It was only last night, he thinks, that Colin was a hero and could do no wrong.

At last ready for bed, Nora goes through her pillow pummelling routine. "What would be nice," she says, "would be if we went abroad with Gavin and Georgie and the baby, when it's old enough. We could go to Greece. Gavin will know the ropes a bit." She climbs into bed. "Don't forget the curtains," she adds.

With an inward sigh Len heaves himself out of bed and pads to the window.

"Don't let anyone see you," she warns. "We don't want people in them flats opposite complaining. There's been enough trouble for one night as it is."

She snaps off the bedside lamp, leaving Len to fumble with the curtains in the pitch dark.

"Course," she goes on, "the trouble with going abroad is the travelling, going in them planes, delays at the airports, strikes and that. Look how Oliver is always being held up for days on end at airports."

"Um," says Len, groping his way back into bed.

"I must say I shall be relieved when Gavin and Georgie are safely back. Can't help worrying about them."

Nora adjusts her hairnet and settles herself down.

"Well, today has been a bit of a disappointment. I suppose now Elsie will be sulking for the rest of the holiday. If we hadn't just got here I'd be inclined to cut it short and go home now."

"Um," Len murmurs again, the blessed hand of sleep already caressing him.

But a sharp knocking on the door soon puts an end to that. Nora jerks upright.

"Now who can that be? If it's Elsie I'm going to give her a piece of my mind. Who is it?" she calls out.

"Mr Perthwee."

"Who?"

"Perthwee!"

"What do you want?"

"There was a thelephone methage for ye."

Len is all set to spring into action, but for once, Nora restrains him.

"*I'd* better go." She gets out of bed and dons her dressing gown. "Wait a minute!" she calls.

When she opens the door Mr Pertwee is standing there in his Noel Coward dressing gown, but minus the rifle.

"I forgot to thay there was a thelephone methage for you earlier from a Mr Papp."

What with his accent and absent teeth Nora finds it difficult to gather what he is saying.

"Papp? You mean Bupp."

"Aye- Pupp."

"What did he say?"

"He thed to be sure to wing him early in the morning."

"Did he say what about?"

"He dinnae, only it was urgent."

Nora thanks Mr Pertwee, and closes the door in a state of great excitement.

"You know what that means, don't you?" she says to Len as

she removes her dressing gown. "Somebody wants to buy Dad's house. I told you it wouldn't take long to sell."

As she snaps off the light again she suddenly realises that the curtains are drawn back and she has been exposed to public view. But for once she's not concerned.

"It's settled one thing, anyhow," she says. "We go home tomorrow."

*****

Back in the Outhouse at The Black Spot the Miss Wet T-shirt Competition is in full swing – in more senses than one.

About a dozen girls jive, rock, twist or shimmy doggedly while a perpetual shower of water is sprayed over them from two hoses manned by a couple of youths. The girls shriek. The crowd roars and whistles. Taped pop music blares.

Many of the girls dropped out at the first dowsing, including Daphne's friend, Alice. But Daphne and Cheryl dance doggedly on, their complementary T-shirts clinging revealingly to their bodies.

Colin can't take his eyes off Daphne, shouting out her name at the top of his voice. Her body is absolutely gorgeous, he thinks. What wouldn't he give for a night with her!

Carlos, the dark handsome Spaniard, stands next to him, cheering Cheryl on with equal gusto. Dodo the poet, however, is not present, having unexpectedly been inspired at the last moment to compose some muse.

More girls drop out, but both Cheryl and Daphne forge on. The excitement mounts. Only five girls left, now four as another contestant chickens out. But Cheryl and Daphne are still there.

"Keep it up, Daph!" bawls Colin.

"Ole!" cries Carlos. "Up Cheryl! Up Cheryl!" Then he lapses into incomprehensible Spanish.

The music ceases suddenly.

A split second of silence, then an almighty cheering and stamping of feet breaks out.

"Has to be Daphne," Colin shouts at Carlos.

"Is Cheryl," insists Carlos.

"Bet you a tenner it's Daphne!" cries Colin.

"Is *Cheryl*!"

Midge and Max Watchett, the adjudicators, step up to the four bedraggled girls to proclaim the winner, raising her right arm like a victorious boxer's. It is Cheryl! Daphne has come third.

Cheers and boos greet this decision.

"Ole!" cries Carlos.

"They're mad!" shouts Colin. "It was obviously Daphne."

Carlos, beside himself, dashes up to Cheryl and enfolds her soaking wet body in his arms.

Colin ventures up to Daphne, who looks inconsolable.

"You were great," he assures her. "You should have won."

"Och, who cares?"

Colin fights off the temptation to follow Carlos's example by taking Daphne in his arms. "Well, at least you were third," he consoles her.

"Aye. Thanks for rooting for me. You were greet. You're a good spoort. You must come and join the celebration."

"Oh, I dunno about that."

"Och, come on!"

He would like to, but he's not exactly top of the charts with Elsie as it is. Well, he decides, in for a penny, in for a pound.

"Oh, what the hell," he grins.

*****

Despite being in a mild state of inebriation Billy Greenhorn is driving his Merc with ease and confidence back down the hill to the Ocean View. Elsie, in a much greater state of inebriation, is sitting beside him humming snatches of 'A Nightingale Sang in Berkeley Square'. She is feeling euphoric again. The glamour of fame seems just around the corner. Before long she will be rich, have a posh house in London; be wearing sequinned clothes like Liberace, playing the organ all over the world to clamouring crowds, being asked to play in the Royal Variety Performance at the London Palladium. Dame Elsie Stilwell even. Who knows?

"Tell me, dear lady, where did you learn to play so beautifully?" asks Billy out of the darkness.

Elsie returns from her time travels. "Me, learn? Didn't

really. Just picked it up."

"Indeed!"

"Mum had an old piano and used to sing the old songs. I used to pick 'em out on the piano while she sang."

"You have a very natural musical talent, dear lady."

"Suppose I have. Comes easy to me."

"Is your good hubby musical too?"

"*Him*? God no!" Mention of Colin produces a spurt of venom from Elsie. "Sex!" she proclaims suddenly. "That's all he thinks of. Sex and bloody snooker! Living with him ain't easy, Mr Greenbum, I tell you. It's like a little fairy trying to live with a crocodile."

The thought reduces Elsie to tears, and Billy, having previously supplied her with his handkerchief, has to feel for the glove compartment to find her a tissue.

"Are you married, Mr Greenbum?" she snivels as she mops up.

"My good lady has passed over."

"Oh dear. How sad. You must be very lonely."

"Not when I'm with you."

Elsie glances at him surreptitiously and is swept overboard by a mighty wave of compassion. He seems a tragic figure, sitting at the wheel of his smart car, in his expensive jacket and horn-rimmed glasses, and with that perpetual bland smile on his face.

"I'll do you proud on the organ, Mr Greenbum," she promises. "I'll think of you every time I play."

"Call me Beely," says Billy.

"Beely," repeats Elsie obediently.

He beams at her in approval and brings the Merc to a quiet standstill in the forecourt of the Ocean View Hotel.

Up come the security lights. Elsie blinks. For a moment she thinks she's in the limelight on stage.

"I will just go and unlock the front door," says Billy as he helps her from the car.

Elsie tries to focus her eyes upon his back as he approaches the front door. But she thinks her eyes must be deceiving her, since he has apparently fallen to his knees and seems to be praying to the door rather than opening it.

"Are you all right, Mr Greenbum?" she coos.

"Quite all right, dear lady. I am unlocking the door. The lock is at ground level, a very silly arrangement."

He opens the door. Bess and Boss come padding up, but Billy quickly dismisses them with the password.

Elsie peers doubtfully at the stairs, vaguely recalling the trouble she had with them before, and is likely to have again.

"Shall I see you to your room?" asks Billy.

"Oh, you *are* so kind!"

As they begin the ascent, with Billy supporting her by the elbow, Elsie starts singing again all about the 'Nightingale in Berkeley Square'.

"We mustn't wake all the good people," whispers Billy.

"Sssh!" titters Elsie.

After a tortuous ascent of two flights of stairs they finally come to rest outside bedroom Number Six. Elsie peers into her handbag. "No key," she says blankly.

"Has your good hubby got it?"

"Dunno." She titters again.

"Perhaps it's on the key board in reception. Stay here, dear lady, I'll go and ascertain."

"You're the kindest man I've ever known, Mr Greenbum. What would I do without you?"

"Call me Beely," says Billy.

"Beely," repeats Elsie.

He leaves her leaning against the door, and when he returns with the key she is still there, starry-eyed, crooning to herself.

"Allow me to open the door for you, dear lady."

"Oh, you are so very kind. I've never known no one so kind as you. You are my guardian angel."

She props herself against the doorframe while Billy unlocks the door and pushes it wide open.

"Well..." says Billy, lingering.

"Well..." says Elsie.

"Thank you for your delightful company this eevening," says Billy.

"You're welcome," says Elsie.

She feels like a young woman on her first date, can't decide whether or not to invite him in. The trouble is, she doesn't really fancy being made love to by her guardian angel. It's those false teeth. At the moment she'd much rather dream about the London Palladium.

To her surprise Billy takes her hand and kisses it.

"Good night, dear lady," he says, pressing the door key into her hand. "I hope hubby finds his way back safely."

"Sod him," says Elsie.

Billy wanders off rather unsteadily down the corridor.

Furious with Colin, fed up with Nora, confused by Billy and totally befuddled by vodka, Elsie shuts the door and flops fully clothed on to the bed, and dreams of nothing.

*****

The victory celebration of the Miss Wet T-shirt Competition is well under way at The Black Spot. The champagne is flowing. The participants, now dry and re-perfumed, are back in their own gear, Daphne again sitting on Colin's knee, and the victorious Cheryl on Carlos's.

The dowsing suffered by Alice, brief though it was, has brought her back to life, and she clings adoringly to Dodo, upon whom the composition of his poem seems to have had a cathartic effect, since he is now passionately reciting it from the back of the beer mat upon which he wrote it.

"…And there upon the concrete her glistening body lies," he concludes triumphantly. "The streaming water is her tomb, and her T-shirt is her makeshift shroud." He looks up for approval.

"Super," says Alice.

"Bullshit," says Cheryl.

"Que?" says Carlos.

"Don't get it," says Colin.

"More champagne?" says Daphne.

"Please," says Cheryl.

Daphne pours the champagne without bothering to get up from Colin's lap, perching herself on the edge of his knees and leaning forward. Colin is not yet so far gone that he fails to appreciate the erotic thrill this affords him.

"You coming up to London with us in the summer, Daph?" asks Alice.

"Och, I doot it."

"Go on, it'll be a whirl."

Cheryl laughs scornfully. "If Daph comes she'll have to bring her Grandpappy too."

"He didn't stop her from wetting her T-shirt," Alice points out. "Can't be that bad an old buffer."

Daphne glances round to see if she can see him. "He must have gone before it started. Anyway, it's m'father who's the trouble. He'll nae let me come to London."

"Tell him to sod off," says Alice.

"Well, here's to boobs!" cries Cheryl, raising her glass. "God bless 'em!"

"Ah si, boobs!" cries Carlos.

Colin is appalled at the way that word is used so openly these days. It seems such an ugly word for what he considers to be one of God's most sublime creations.

"Is hot," says Carlos suddenly.

"What's hot?" asks Alice.

"Champagne."

"It's not iced, if that's what you mean. What you expect – a silver ice bucket?"

"You're a waiter, aren't you, sweetie?" says Cheryl. "So naturally you expect things to be done in the proper way."

"Must have ice," nods Carlos.

At that point the musicians, who during the competition have been resting on their instruments and preventing the onslaught of dehydration, suddenly spring into action.

"Let's dance," says Daphne to Colin, jumping up from his lap and holding out her hands.

My God, the energy these youngsters have! "Better not," he parries. "Have to go and find me wife."

"Och, come *on*!"

"No, really! I *must* go." He looks round anxiously for Elsie, but can't see her anywhere.

"Wael, if you really must. Thanks for coming, anyway. I hope y'dinnae get into too much trouble."

"It's been worth it," grins Colin.

"Will y'nae come for the Mr Wet Y-fronts next week?"

He jolts. "Oh, dunno about that. Doubt it. Will if I can."

"Och, you're a greet spooort." She gives him a big warm hug and kisses his cheek. "Good neet then. See you back at the hotel." As she turns away she seems to wink at him suggestively, just as she had done when she'd first given him that leaflet about The Black Spot.

Now what did that mean? he wonders as he reels away in search of Elsie. Does she mean she'll see me at breakfast the next morning, or was it a veiled invitation to visit her room later tonight – or more accurately – during the wee small hours, which are already advancing swiftly? No, she couldn't possibly mean that. Forget it.

When he reaches the table where Elsie and Billy have been sitting he finds it vacant. He slumps down on a chair with a big sigh of relief. The excitement, beer, gin and champagne are all taking their toll. But where is Elsie?

He peers at the figures still jiggling about on the floor as animatedly as ever. There are far fewer now, a lot having left after the competition, but he can't see Elsie and Billy among them. Perhaps they've gone to the toilet, he thinks. He'd better wait a bit.

A bunny comes up to take an order but he dismisses her with a curt shake of his head. He's had enough for one night. He glances at his watch. Nearly two!

He's almost asleep when the dance ends, but still no sign of Elsie or Billy. He begins to feel concerned. Perhaps that bugger has abducted her! He drags himself to his feet.

"Excuse me," he says to a pimply youth at the next table who is snogging a girl in a shiny lime-green dress. "Do you know what happened to the couple who were sitting here?"

The youth looks up malevolently. "What couple?"

"A tall, thin lady with a bloke who looks like Sergeant Bilko."

The youth looks vacant. "Sergeant *who*?"

"A bloke with a bald head and glasses then."

"Oh them," chimes in the girl. "They've left."

"Yeah, that's right," says the youth. "Pissed off."

"You mean, gone out? Left the club?"

"Course, *ages* ago," says the girl.

Colin tries to pull his swirling thoughts together. Either that bastard has taken Elsie back to the hotel without him or they're having it off in the back of his bloody Merc. He'd better go and find out.

When the cold night air hits him, Colin's senses reel even more. He meanders up and down the cars remaining in the car park, looking for the Merc, muttering incoherent threats against Billy.

No Merc. So they must have gone back to the hotel without him. "I'll kill the bugger," he mutters.

But how is he to get back himself? No hope of getting a taxi at this hour, and anyway, he's skint after all the money he's spent on the admission fee, drinks and the tenner he lost to Carlos in that stupid bet. He'll have to walk. Not a bad thing. It will clear his head a bit. He's not too sure of the way, but he reckons if he follows the road downhill he can't go far wrong.

As he blunders along the dark streets his mind flits back and forth from dark thoughts of what he intends to do to Billy Greenhorn when he gets hold of him, to the incredible spectacle of the T-shirt Competition and Daphne's apparent...well...*lust* for him. He can think of no other explanation for it. And that wink! Is she expecting him to go to her room?

I'm getting too old for this sort of caper, he tells himself as he pauses to rest a moment against a lamp-post. His back, which he'd forgotten all about at The Black Spot, is aching again with a vengeance. His advancing years are making life more of an ordeal.

He stumbles on until he comes to a cross-roads. Now which way is it – right, left or straight on? Straight on, he decides, still downhill. It's easier walking downhill.

The church clock intones two thirty. The road is deserted, only the occasional streetlight still burning. The silhouette of rooftops against the heavy sky looks menacing. Suddenly he feels lonely, even a bit frightened. Stupid for an ex-cop to feel frightened, he scolds himself. If a roving police car should hove into view perhaps they'd give him a lift to the hotel, him having been a policeman and that. On the other hand they might haul him off to the nick for being drunk or acting suspiciously.

The street continues down, down, down. This can't be right, but he can't face the uphill walk back to the cross-roads. So he limps on, his mind on a merry-go-round of thoughts about The Black Spot, T-shirts, Daphne, Elsie, Len, Nora, snooker, holdalls, Dave, The Black Spot, breasts, Daphne, until he becomes totally bemused.

The road begins to slope even more steeply downwards, which is agony on his back, but then it levels out and comes to a sudden end. He stops abruptly. The shock pulls him round a bit. Another step and he'd have been in the water!

Slowly it dawns on him where he is – Benthaven Harbour. And there on the quayside stands the slumbering hulk of The Fisherman's Float to prove it. He's come too far. He groans. Now he has to climb all those bloody steps back up to the Ocean View.

The prospect daunts him. He feels like dossing down like a tramp for the rest of the night on one of the benches. Or, he realises, he could knock up old Dave and beg a bed. But his old mate wouldn't go a bundle on that. No, nothing for it, he decides, got to face them steps. Take me time, rest on the way. Don't really matter if it takes me until morning.

But it only takes until three thirty, according to the church clock. The hotel is once more in darkness and quietly sleeping when the security lights come on as he stumbles up to the front door of the Ocean View.

Being familiar with such devices the security lights cause him no concern, but he panics when he finds the hotel front door is locked.

"Bloody hell!" he exclaims.

He pummels madly on the door, the only effect of which is to conjure up a snarling Boss and Bess on the other side.

"Open up!" he roars.

Unfortunately the dogs haven't been trained to carry out this instruction, and there is no one else around.

"Bloody Pertwee," Colin mutters. "I warned him we'd be late back."

Then he remembers – the key!

"Stupid sod," he scolds himself as he dives his hand in his pocket. To his relief he finds it and peers around for the lock on the door.

But he can't find it. No bloody lock!

Muttering savagely, he peers all round the push-plate of the door, but no keyhole. He shakes the door violently, but even this doesn't produce one. The dogs set up a fresh chorus of barking. The hotel slumbers on.

But Colin hasn't been a policeman without learning something about breaking and entering. He reckons that with the aid of his all-purpose penknife he might be able to slip a catch on a window.

So following Len's route earlier he tries the first window to hand.

Off goes the alarm.

Hotel lights come on. Voices shout. Mr Pertwee, again looking like Noel Coward off to a shoot, comes down. Again he grovels at ground level to open up.

"I gave y'the key," he snarls through the door.

"What's the good of a key if there's no bloody keyhole?" Colin snarls back.

"It's at the boffam."

"Boffam?"

"At the boffam of the door!" cries the toothless Mr P.

"That's a bloody stupid place to put a keyhole! Who'd think of looking down there? You should have told me."

Mr Pertwee mutters something to the effect that after a lifetime of trying shop doors on the beat Colin should have known, then marches back up the stairs.

But Colin's problems aren't over by a long chalk. He still has to face Elsie. When he finally arrives outside the bedroom door, he stops and listens. All is silent. He tries the handle, but the door doesn't give. He taps gently.

"Elsie?" he calls softly. "You there, Elsie?"

No response. That can mean she's not in there, or in there but dead to the world, or just dead, or in there tucked up with Billy Greenhorn, or tucked up with Billy Greenhorn in Billy Greenhorn's own room.

Remembering he left the bedroom key down in reception, he totters back downstairs to see if it is still there. It isn't. She's obviously come back then. She *must* be in the room if she's got the key.

Colin hauls himself back up the stairs to the bedroom and

again taps gently on the door.

"Elsie? Els'? It's me! Open up!"

No answer.

He taps a bit louder. "Els'! Come on, let me in."

No answer.

Losing his cool, he thumps the door. "Elsie, for Chrissake let me in!"

"Piss off!"

Colin is stunned. "Don't be daft! Come on, let me in!"

"Piss off!"

"You've got that bleedin' Bilko bloke in there with you, is that it?"

"Piss off!" yells Elsie yet again. "Go and sleep with that big-titted sow of yours. And good riddance!"

He is about to heave his shoulder against the door in true cop fashion when the door opposite opens and Miss Dibble, looking even more like a pensioned off Minnehaha with her grey hair in pigtails, pokes her head out.

"If you don't mind," she says sourly, "people are trying to sleep. We've had quite enough disturbance for one night."

"Sorry, sorry," mutters Colin.

She slams the door in his face.

Colin, mentally concussed and confused, leans against the corridor wall. He can't believe all this is happening.

But Elsie hasn't finished yet. "She's welcome to you, you lecherous toad!" she yells. "I wish her joy."

"Belt up, Els', for God's sake," he hisses through the door. "People are complaining."

"Go on, go to her, you randy bugger!"

In the next room Nora sits bolt upright in bed and listens. "Elsie and Colin are at it," she says to the snoring Len. "I'm not surprised. They're so common!"

Elsie rants on until in desperation Colin gives the bedroom door a vicious kick.

"All right!" he bellows. "I'll *go* to her!"

He kicks the door again, knocking over a pedestal of artificial dahlias in the process, and stumps off up the corridor.

*****

If that's what she wants, he thinks, that's what I'll bloody do!

Brave thoughts indeed. Doing it is another matter. But the very thought of snuggling up to Daphne in bed gives his courage a brisk stir.

"I'll bloody do it," he tells himself again. "She was inviting me when she winked like that. Couldn't have made it plainer."

I can't, I don't know where her room is, he suddenly realises. He feels a strong sense of relief. It lets him off the hook. Can't go barging into all the bedrooms looking for her.

But then it comes to him with a horrible jolt that he *does* know where her bedroom is. Hadn't he seen it when he was sussing out the emergency exit the day they arrived? 'Daphne's Room' it had said on that little enamel disc, plain as a pikestaff. That was how he'd learned her name.

He breaks out in a sweat. Will he? Won't he? He feels ripped in half. Well, Elsie only has herself to blame. Told him to do it clear enough, didn't she? And what's he supposed to do if she's locked him out – sleep at the foot of the bedroom door like a guard dog?

Besides, sleeping with a girl like Daphne is not to be sneezed at, not at his time of life. Probably never get a chance like this again. In for a penny, in for a pound, he thinks.

He approaches the door marked 'PRIVATE, EMERGENCY EXIT ONLY' with trepidation, half hoping it is locked. But it isn't. He goes through and steals down the corridor like a thief, peering at the enamel discs on the doors. There it is! 'Daphne's Room.' No doubt about it. Right opposite the door marked 'Mum and Dad's Room' where Mr Pertwee must be asleep, his rifle by his side. That thought brings him no comfort.

He gives a gentle tap on Daphne's door. Possible she's not yet back from The Black Spot.

He taps again, a little louder.

"It's open," calls a voice softly.

He slips in; the room is in darkness.

"Och, so you've finally decided to come," says the voice.

"Yes, of course," whispers Colin, surprised at her brusque tone. "Got lost on the way back, that's why I've been so long."

There are some sudden sharps movements and the bedside light clicks on. And there lies Daphne, just withdrawing her shapely bare arm from the lamp.

"Och, it's *you*!"

"Of course it's me! Who did you think it was?"

"Carlos."

"Carlos!" Colin is dumbfounded. "But I thought he was with that blonde piece…"

"Och No! He's my fella really. That bitch Cheryl is trying to take him from me."

To Colin it had looked as if Cheryl had succeeded. "But when you said 'See you later'," he protests, "I thought you meant me to—"

"I dinnae mean that! God no! I just wanted Carlos to think I did – to make him jealous."

Colin is beginning to get the picture. His legs weaken and his blood boils. "You've been making a bloody monkey out of me!" he raves. "Using me to make him jealous!"

"Ssssh! M'father will hear!"

"Don't bloody care if he does!"

"Look, I'm sorry. I shouldnae have done it, I know. Let me explain."

She hoists herself up slightly in the bed, and allows the sheet to slip from over one breast.

My God, she's naked!

"Sit doon," she says, patting the bed beside her.

"I..." The words dry up in Colin's mouth.

"Y'see," she resumes when he has sat and she has recovered the breast. "I'm stark staring crazy aboot the guy. I'll let y'in to a wee secret if y'promise y'll nae tell m'father."

"Depends," says Colin suspiciously.

"We're supposed to be secretly engaged, y'ken? Carlos is going back to Spain and I was going with him. We were going to be married, that is, until that bitch got her claws into him. He was hooked, dropped me like a burning cinder. I wasnae having that. Y'dinnae blame me?"

"Suppose not."

"So the other neet, after y'fooled those two thugs, I thought if he saw me with a handsome, real strong, virile man like you, it might make him jealous and make him come back to me." She pauses to lean forward and look deeply into his eyes, putting her hand on his thigh. "No one could have been more perfect than you."

She squeezes his leg. Colin swallows hard. The sheet has slipped from over her breasts but he can't bring himself to take advantage of it.

"Och, I know I shouldnae have done it, but I was desperate. When y'madly in love y'do anything, don't you?"

"I...I suppose so," gulps Colin.

"I was going to tell y'tonight when we were smooching, but I hadnae the heart. Y'seemed to be enjoying it so much. Och, I'm sorry, I truly am! You're a super wee man. I dinnae mean to hurt you. Say y'forgive me?"

She puts her arm around his neck and draws his head towards her to plant a gentle kiss on his cheek.

"And y'll nae tell m'father aboot any of this?"

"No no, course not." The less Colin has to do with Mr Pertwee at the moment, the better.

Daphne gently releases his head and lies back again, pulling the sheet back over her.

"Y'may nae believe it," she says, "but m'father is a reet tyrant. He's very strict and old fashioned, doesnae trust me an inch. Willnae trust me out of his sight without sending m'grandfather to spy on me."

"Yes, I know. But your grandfather wasn't exactly doing his job tonight, was he?"

"Och, that's because m'grandfather's a wee sweet man. He enjoys a bit of fun himsel', so he doesnae tell on me. It's m'father that's the trouble. I've just got to get away from him and lead m'own life. That's why I want to go to Spain with Carlos. Y'dinnae blame me, do you?"

"No, not really." Colin is beginning to feel avuncular. "Providing you really *are* over eighteen and truly in love."

"I'm nearly nineteen, and I couldnae be more in love."

"But I dunno about this Carlos bloke. He seemed pretty stuck on Cheryl to me."

"Och, that's just a flash in the pan. I'll get him in the end without doot."

She will too, he thinks.

"Look," Daphne goes on. "I dinnae want to drive you away, but Carlos might still come up tonight."

"You mean he lives here, works here?"

"Och no. He's a waiter at the Craxton. He's got one of m'father's spare front door keys and lets himsel' in. He comes a couple of times a week – or did before that cow got her talons into him."

"I'd better go then," says Colin, getting to his feet.

Daphne clasps his hands in hers. "I'm sorry to disappoint you. I dinnae mean to hurt you. I hope y'understand." She takes his hands to her lips and kisses them. "Now off y'go."

With trance-like obedience Colin goes to the door, then turns to take one last look at her. As she blows him a kiss the sheet slips again. It is a sight Colin is to keep locked in the vaults of his heart forever.

He reels blindly down the corridor until he's back outside his own bedroom door. He feels as if he's on a roller coaster, one moment ecstatic, then overwhelmed by concern for her, then furious with himself for having been such a bloody fool.

But what does he do now? He's not going to risk trying to knock up Elsie again, that's for sure. He can only think of one thing he *can* do. Tired, aching and despairing, he trails downstairs to the lounge and flops on to the sofa.

His mind is blank in seconds. He is unaware of Bess climbing up and planting herself across him like a duvet.

Chapter Ten

At seven the next morning Nora is already up, bathed, dressed, beautified and off down to the foyer with a cache of silver coins to feed into the payphone.

"Glennis?"

"Yes. Is that you, Nora?"

"Yes. Is Cyril about?"

"He's washing his feet."

"Again! At *this* hour?"

"He washes them every morning."

"He wanted me to call him urgently. Can he come to the phone?"

"Hold on."

Pause.

"Hello, Nora."

"Hello, Cyril. What's happening about the house? Do they want it?"

"They made an offer."

"How much?"

"Forty thousand."

"Forty thousand! That's no good. You didn't agree. I hope?"

"Said I'd ask you."

Nora exhales with relief. "Do you think they might be persuaded to up their offer a bit?"

"Dunno."

"Well, we're not knocking off that much, that's for sure. I'd better have a think about it."

"Okey-dokey. Only don't think too long."

"What you mean?"

"They want an answer by tomorrow and to settle the whole thing by the weekend, like."

"Why? What's the hurry?"

"Getting married or summat. Off on their honeymoon."

"Oh, I see."

"Dunno why they're bothering. Been living together the last ten years it seems."

Nora's not interested in their marital affairs. "Look," she says. "I've decided to come home today, I'll think about it on the way."

"Right."

"If they should ring again during the day, tell 'em I'll be in touch tomorrow morning."

"Right."

"And I'll ring you again as soon as we get home."

"Right. Safe journey, Nora."

"Let's hope so."

Back in the bedroom Nora tells Len all about it.

"Make a counter-offer," he suggests. "Always worth losing a bit to get a quick sale."

"True," she admits. But it goes against the grain. "I'm not knocking off much, though. Forty-eight is the lowest I'm prepared to go."

"Have to be more than that if you really want to sell it to 'em."

"Well, we'll see. Let's pack everything first and put it in the car, then we'll be ready to leave as soon as we've had breakfast."

*****

It wouldn't be accurate to say Elsie wakes up this morning in a black mood. Violent purple is nearer the mark. Once she has sufficiently come round to notice Colin's pyjamas are still neatly folded on his pillow, just as the chambermaid left them, the events of the night pierce into her brain like a dagger through a curtain.

He must have slept with that bitch after all!

As she jerks herself up from the bed she realises she is still wearing her flouncy Spanish-style dress. Now, it's looking like a lot of ravelled bunting. She hauls it off savagely and makes a beeline for the toilet.

As she sits there, head in hands, the face of beaming Billy presents itself to her. She groans. She'd forgotten about him. Of course, he'd brought her back. She remembers him opening the door for her.

My God, had she...?

No, she hadn't, at least, she didn't think she had. No, she couldn't have done, she was still fully clothed when she woke up. Unless she'd been too far gone to undress. Surely she hadn't! Not with that old fool, and certainly not in her Spanish-style dress. But it is all extremely hazy.

But what was all that crap he'd dished out about her becoming famous playing the organ at Blackpool Tower and that? And she'd believed him! Swallowed it whole, like a whale swallowing a herring. She must have been bloody drunk to have done that. Yet she doesn't remember drinking all that much. She reckons he must have deliberately given her doubles.

But what does she do now? she wonders as she flushes the lavatory. She feels terrible. Her brain is grinding round like a cement mixer, her head is thumping, her mouth feels as if it's been given a thorough sandpapering. Before she can even hope to think clearly she'll have to have a shower, a cold one – well lukewarm anyway – and then coffee, strong and black.

The shower cools her brain somewhat as well as her body and she begins to think more rationally. It's Tuesday, she decides. For some reason Tuesday seems significant to her, but she hasn't a clue why it should be. Well, it'll probably come to her later.

Elsie hauls on her jeans and a top, roughly combs through her hair, applies a bit of powder and lipstick to her face. My God, she thinks as she stares at herself in the mirror, I look like a bloody witch! Oh, what the hell! Who cares?

As she makes her way down to the dining room she wonders if Billy what's-his-name will be in there. She's going to feel a right berk if he is. But he isn't. The dining room is empty apart from Miss Dibble who is sitting at her usual table, partaking of a kipper.

And Len and Nora.

Suddenly Elsie remembers the tiff she had with Nora at The Black Spot, and her anger sharply rekindles. She takes her seat with them without so much as a word.

Nora is sitting there like a judge in session, spooning up a bowl of Rice Krispies. Len is contemplating a glass of orange juice.

There is an icy silence.

"Got back all right last night then?" says Nora eventually in a clipped tone.

"Looks like it, don't it?" snaps Elsie. She sits on her chair, her head back, her eyes closed as if she's about to receive a blessing from the Pope.

Mrs Pertwee, po-faced but with her plastic hairdo looking untouched by human hand, comes in from the kitchen. She has a lightly boiled egg for Nora, who doesn't like travelling on too heavy a meal, and a full English breakfast for Len, who does. He thinks it's likely to be the only square meal he'll get for a bit.

"We're having to return home today to attend to some important business," Nora informs Mrs Pertwee. "If we can't come back do we get a refund on our deposit?"

"I'm afraid not," says Mrs Pertwee stiffly.

"I see. In that case we shall certainly return if we can, although we can't say exactly when."

"As you wish." Mrs Pertwee glances at her watch, and then at Elsie. "It's gone ten. I'm afraid you're too late if you're wanting breakfast."

"Don't want no breakfast. Just a coffee – black."

"I see. Very well."

Mrs Pertwee marches off and another silence descends. Nora snaps, crackles and pops. Len concentrates on his full English breakfast. Elsie still sits with her eyes shut.

"By the way," says Nora at last. "Cyril phoned last night while we were at that awful place."

"Oh yes?" Elsie is disinterested.

"I've just rang him back. He says we've got a buyer for Dad's house."

"Oh yes?"

"So me and Len are going home this morning to deal with it."

"Oh yes?" Cold disdain oozes from Elsie.

"Like I said, we'll be coming back if all goes well. Can't say exactly when."

"Don't bother," growls Elsie. Two ominous fiery patches

appear on her cheeks.

"Where's Colin?" Len asks her, ill advisedly.

She snorts. "With *her*, no doubt."

"Her? Who?"

"Who d'you think!"

"Oh!" Wisely, Len concentrates on his breakfast.

A vacuum cleaner whines into action in the lounge. It sounds quite loud in the dining room because all the doors have now been wedged open to facilitate cleaning activities.

"You would think," declares Nora, getting to her feet, "that they would wait until breakfast has finished before making a din like that. My ears are still singing from the terrible racket in that place last night. I wouldn't be at all surprised if it hasn't done them permanent damage. I'm extremely sensitive to sound, you know."

She marches over to the dining room door to remove the wedge, and as she does so Colin lurches from the lounge, bleary-eyed and rubbing his neck.

"Ah, there you are!" she cries. "We wondered what had happened to you. What ever's wrong? You look terrible."

"So would you if you'd spent the night on that bleedin' sofa."

"Elsie's in the dining room. She's in one of her moods. You'd better come and make your peace."

"Not if she's in one of her moods."

"You'd better. She's mad about last night. And I don't blame her, leaving us and going off with that girl. It was a disgusting way to behave."

"Yes, I know. Sorry about that."

Nora pronounces absolution. "Well, never mind. Come and have a nice strong cup of coffee, you look as if you need it."

"Certainly do."

Their arrival at the table coincides with Mrs Pertwee coming back with the coffee for Elsie.

"Perhaps you would kindly bring another cup for Mr Stilwell," Nora asks her brightly.

Mrs Pertwee glares at her and marches off again.

Thank God it's not Daphne on duty this morning, thinks Colin, as he gingerly lowers himself on his chair.

"That Mrs Pertwee is very dour," observes Nora, "but I don't think she's a Scot."

"Moira is a Scottish name," Len points out.

"I know, but she don't speak like one." Nora gives Colin the benefit of her attention. "And how's your back this morning, still troublesome?"

"A bit."

"Serves you right, dancing and giddying about like that. You're not young no more, you know."

Colin scowls but doesn't answer.

"I think it's time I gave both of you a piece of my mind," Nora continues. "Your behaviour last night was absolutely appalling. Len and I were most embarrassed, weren't we, Len?"

"Um," says Len.

"And what was all that carry on in the night? It woke me up."

"Mind y'own bleedin' business!" snaps Elsie.

Upon which request Miss Dibble loudly clears her throat, throws her screwed-up napkin on to the dissected skeleton of her kipper, and marches out.

"There you are! You've gone and upset her. That's what I mean. You must be more careful about your language in public. I think it's high time you *both* pull yourselves together and try and behave in a more civilised manner."

"She's right, Els'," agrees Colin. "We've both made bloody fools of ourselves what with one thing and another. I admit I made a bloody fool of meself with that girl. It won't happen again, I promise you. Look, let's start afresh and bury the hatchet."

"Yes – right in her bloody neck!" Elsie boils over. "Led you on, did she? Forced you into watching her exposing herself? Glued your eyes on her tits with superglue, I suppose? Put you on a lead and led you into her bedroom."

"I didn't spend the night with her!"

"Ha!"

"Gospel truth, Els'. I spent it on that sofa in the lounge."

"Oh, sod off. You stink of sweat."

"So would you if you'd had a bloody great Alsatian on top of you all night!"

"That's enough!" cuts in Nora. "Now listen. I strongly advise you spend the time while we're away getting yourselves sorted out. Then when we come..."

"You're going away?" interrupts Colin. "Where to?"

"Home, of course! We've got a buyer for Dad's house."

"But we've got to go back on Saturday for the Snooker Final! Can't it wait till then?"

"No, it can't!"

"Surely you could do it by phone?"

"Can't deal with an important matter like that by phone. We've been made an offer, but it's far too low. I've got to make 'em up it a bit."

"And what are we supposed to do?" demands Elsie. "Build sandcastles?"

"As I was just trying to say, you could try spending the time sorting out your personal problems, so that when we get back we can make a fresh start to our holiday. Why don't you have a day out together for once? You could take Elsie to Brighton, Colin, buy her that holdall she keeps on about."

"And how we supposed to get there?" demands Elsie.

"Won't hurt you to go on a bus for once, will it?"

"It's a good idea, Els'," says Colin. "What d'you say?"

He puts his hand on her arm but she flings it off, and averts her head just in time to see Billy Greenhorn come in to the dining room, looking as spruce as ever.

"Goood morning!" he beams.

Elsie just about manages a smirk. Colin scowls. Nora nods curtly. Len looks up from his breakfast with fried egg around his mouth.

"Let's get the hell out of here," mutters Elsie savagely.

*****

After Len and Nora have departed for home in a cloud of exhaust smoke, Elsie and Colin toil up to their room in a silence pregnant with hostility.

"Going to have a bath," grunts Colin, pulling his jumper with the blue diagonal stripes over his head.

"Hope you drown in it," mutters Elsie.

In the privacy of the bathroom Colin sighs deeply with relief. Well, it could have been worse. She'll soon come round, he thinks. I'll treat her like a VIP today, give her a slap-up lunch, buy her that holdall and that.

Nora's quite right, he tells himself, as he flops into the bath. I've made a bloody idiot of meself. Should have known better. It's got to stop. It's over mate, you're past it. Got to act your age, be responsible, settle down. What you've got to think carefully about is what you're going to do if you're made redundant, not about bloody girls.

All the same he can't help feeling chuffed that his audacious plan worked. He *did* get to The Black Spot, he *did* see the Wet T-Shirt Competition – and more! The sight of Daphne in bed was something else!

When he eventually emerges from the bathroom, feeling fresh and full of new resolve, he finds Elsie savagely brushing at his jeans.

"Covered in bloody dog hairs," she mutters.

"What you expect? I told you, I spent the night on the sofa with that dog."

"Ha!"

"It's the truth, Els'! She don't want me. She's in love with some Spanish bloke called Carlos. She was just using me to make him jealous."

"Balls," says Elsie. She takes his jeans to the window and opens it.

"All right, I did let her make a bloody fool of..." He stops in alarm as he sees Elsie hold his jeans out of the window. "Hey! Don't do that!"

She gives the jeans a venomous shake, and Colin's loose change goes raining down like pennies from heaven on Billy's Merc, parked below. But Elsie shakes the jeans so viciously she loses hold of them and they float down as well.

"Christ Almighty!" cries Colin. "Me wallet's in them jeans!"

As yet only dressed as far as his boxer shorts, Colin charges from the bedroom and down the stairs two at a time, passing a startled Mr Pertwee on the way.

He discovers the jeans straddled across the Merc's bonnet,

the coins flung far and wide. He's relieved to find his wallet is still in the hip pocket so, retrieving what coins he can see, he scampers back into the hotel as fast as he can, only to be accosted by an irate Mr Pertwee, waiting for him in the foyer.

"I'd like a wee word," says Mr Pertwee, now fully dentured and wearing his 'Le Fruitier' apron. He hustles Colin into the lounge and closes the door. Colin is seized by panic. Has he found out about his nocturnal visit to Daphne's room?

"I have been receiving complaints," continues Mr P. in an urgent whisper, "aboot the disturbances in the neet, aboot the alarm, and aboot the raised voices and foul language in the wee small hours. And *noo*, I find y'running aboot half naked in the...!"

"Me wallet was in them trousers mate, I had to..."

"It has to stop," interrupts Mr P., raising his hand. "I cannae tolerate such behaviour. If y'cause more trouble I'll have to ask y'to leave. Do I make m'sel' clear?"

"Fair do, mate, fair do. Point taken. No more trouble, I promise."

Mr Pertwee looks relieved and splays his hands. "I hope not. I dinnae like having unpleasantness with m'guests, especially with a courageous gentleman like y'goodsel', but I cannae have m'regular guests upset, y'ken?"

"Course not, mate. I understand. Say no more."

Colin tries to push past him, but Mr P. hasn't finished.

"And y'would pass a wee word to y'friends as well? I dinnae want to make too much of a fuss."

"Will do. No problem."

"Then we'll say nae more aboot it."

Mr Pertwee pokes his head round the lounge door to ensure none of his valued guests are about, then signals Colin to make haste back to his room.

Colin sighs with relief as he lumbers up the stairs, thankful it wasn't about Daphne after all.

"We've got to cool it, Els'," he tells Elsie after he's given her the gist of Mr Pertwee's complaints.

"Bugger him," says Elsie. She is sitting on the bed, her emotions still kaleidoscopic.

"No good being like that. He's got a point, mind." He

hurriedly pulls on his clothes then sits on the bed beside her and puts his arm round her waist. "Look, let's forget it, eh? Kiss and make up? Start afresh? Let's go to Brighton like Nora said. I'll treat you to a slap-up meal, and I'll buy you that holdall. What you say?"

Elsie doesn't say anything. She flings off his arm, gets to her feet and starts undressing again.

Colin looks at her in surprise. "What you doing now?"

"Can't go to the Royal Hotel dressed like this."

"Royal Hotel!"

Elsie pauses, her jeans around her ankles, and looks at him challengingly. "A slap-up meal you said, or don't you think I'm worthy of the Royal Hotel?"

It's not Elsie's worth he is worried about, it's his dwindling cash supply. "No, no. That's great. Royal Hotel it is."

Before Elsie can answer there is a sharp rapping on the bedroom door.

"Now what?" grunts Colin, going to answer it.

Mr Pertwee again. "Is Mrs Scally aboot?" he asks.

"Mrs Scally? Gone home, mate. Urgent business."

"Gone home!" Mr Pertwee tuts. "She dinnae say!"

"Told your wife. She'll be back in a day or two. Why, what's the problem?"

"There's a phone call for her – very urgent the lady said."

"*Very* urgent?"

"Aye."

"Who is it?"

"She dinnae say, only it's very urgent."

"So you said! Well, you'd better tell her to ring her at home tonight when she gets there."

"Aye." But Mr Pertwee seems reluctant. "Well, perhaps it would be best if you were to have a wee word with her?"

Colin sighs. "Perhaps my wife will..." He glances at Elsie who is still down to the bare essentials. Got to keep Mr P. happy, he thinks. "Oh all right, I'll talk to her."

"Most kind."

Mr Pertwee hurries Colin down to reception to the waiting phone.

"Hello?" says Colin.

"Hello, Nora, this is Marsha Bloom."

"It isn't Nora. She's not here."

"I asked to speak to Nora Scally. It's most urgent."

"Well you can't. I told you, she's not here. She's gone home."

"Gone home? Then to whom am I speaking?"

"I'm Colin Stilwell. We're friends of hers."

"Oh yes, I believe Nora has mentioned you. She's back home, did you say?"

"Not yet. She only left here about half an hour ago."

"What time will she get there?"

"Well, judging by the time it took us to get here, not until about six."

"Not until six!"

"Well, you could try about five, I suppose."

"Drat it!" says Marsha, and puts down the phone.

Chapter 11

In the event, Elsie changed her mind about lunching at the Royal Hotel. The Bumperline mini-bus dropped them close to the Marine Life Centre in Brighton, so she couldn't resist paying it a visit then and there.

Determined to give Elsie a good day, Colin is happy to go along with it, even though he is pretty bored himself. But it proves to his advantage because by the time Elsie has 'ooohed' and 'aaahed' her way around the aquatic attractions her mood has mellowed, and she emerges no longer yearning for the Royal Hotel, but falls for a 'Fresh Dressed Brighton Crab' lunch instead, which she has noticed advertised on a chalkboard outside a quaint side-street pub.

Colin, mindful of his rapidly diminishing stock of cash, is relieved, and although the meal proves both expensive and indigestible, he reckons it's a good deal cheaper than the Royal Hotel.

The pub's interior proves intimate and softly lit, so softly, in fact, that they could each do with a Davy lamp to see what they are eating. But for Elsie it has the effect of mellowing her mood still further and with the aid of a couple of vodkas and the bottle of wine, on which Colin recklessly splashes out, she becomes both winsome and talkative, cooing to him about Billy Greenhorn's big ideas for her as an organist, and making stars sparkle before her eyes once again.

"Says I could be the Winifred Atwell of the organ," she tells him dreamily.

Colin knows he has to deal with this one cautiously. "Shouldn't take too much notice of what he says, Els'," he advises.

"But he's been a what'sit – an impresario in Tin Pan Alley and that. Gave me his card, he did."

"Maybe, thirty years ago. Times have changed."

But Elsie is well on the way to Planet Fame.

"Still keeps in touch though. I reckon he wouldn't say I could be playing in America, Australia and that one day if he didn't honestly think so."

Believe that and you'll believe anything, thinks Colin. "I dunno. There's something about the bloke I just don't trust."

"He's all *right*," insists Elsie. "A gentleman. He could have taken advantage of me last night, but he didn't. He just kissed me hand and went off to his room."

"Kissed your hand!"

"What's wrong with that?" Elsie becomes defensive.

"Nothing, nothing! He's a queer cove, that's all. Okay, so you play the organ pretty well. Fine for pubs and that. But you're not going to make America or Australia, nor the Blackpool Tower, even. Forget it, Els'."

But luckily, the mention of Australia has sent Elsie's thoughts spinning off to a different planet.

"I remember!" she cries suddenly, upsetting her wine glass in her excitement.

"Remember? Remember what?"

"What I've got to remember to do today."

"What's that?"

"Ring Andy in Australia. Got to phone him tonight. It's his birthday tomorrow."

"You'd better make sure you don't get bloody plastered then, hadn't you?" grins Colin.

The stars in Elsie's eyes turn to tears. "Oh Andy, you'll be eighteen tomorrow and I'll not be with you! Eighteen years! It seems only yesterday I brought you into the world. It was a terrible day, thunder and lightning..."

Colin has heard various versions of that story many times before, but he looks at her with genuine concern. He knows how she grieves over her past, and he's afraid it might spoil their day out together, which so far he thinks is going pretty well.

"Cheer up, luv," he says, handing her a paper napkin to dry her eyes. "At least you can *talk* to him tonight."

Elsie mops up and blows her nose. "Must ring about ten, catch him before he goes to work in the morning."

"We'd better have a quiet evening at the hotel then," he says, getting to his feet. "Come on, let's go and buy that famous holdall."

*****

Elsie has set her heart on buying a yellow holdall to match her bikini, but after visiting just about every appropriate shop in the town the quest proves fruitless, and by the time they find themselves in Hambledon's, one of Brighton's leading department stores, Colin is getting a tiny bit fed up.

"You're never going to find a yellow one, Els'," he says. "Can't you manage with a different colour?"

Luckily, Elsie is smitten with some gay red and white striped ones on display at a 'Greatly Reduced Price', and to Colin's relief, she eventually decides on one of those.

But, as Colin has feared, the shopping expedition doesn't end there. Few could be unaware of the huge notices rainbowed across the ceiling proclaiming a 'Summer Sale' is in progress, and certainly not Elsie.

"I think I'll see if I can find meself a new trouser suit," she says to Colin's dismay.

They trail down to the Ladies Fashions on the first floor, where Elsie rummages among the endless racks of trouser suits, while Colin, who feels highly embarrassed at having to loiter about among ladies wear, tries to look invisible. "Hurry up, Els', for Pete's sake," he keeps muttering.

Elsie selects three suits to try on and takes them to the fitting rooms, where a shop assistant accosts her, gives her a numbered token and directs her to a cubicle.

"You come with me," says Elsie to Colin.

"Sorry," cuts in the shop assistant. "No one else allowed with you in the cubicle."

"Why ever not?" demands Colin. "I'm her husband for God's sake!"

"Security rules, sir, you know how it is these days."

"Course. Should have realised. Security bloke meself." He turns to Elsie. "Better let me take care of your new holdall and your handbag. Put it in the holdall."

Elsie goes off to the cubicle, laden with the trouser suits. The shop girl twitches Colin a brassy smile, and he moves further away, dumps the holdall down beside him, and prepares himself for a long, boring wait. Look at it as your penance for last night, he tells himself. Pity Nora had to go home. He and Len could have been practising their snooker now while the two women did all this shopping.

Elsie emerges from time to time in different trouser suit and asks Colin for his opinion.

"Very nice," he says to each of them in turn. "Suits you."

"Which do think is best?" Elsie asks when displaying the third trouser suit.

"That one," says Colin firmly, hoping to prevent further procrastination.

"Dunno so much," says Elsie. "Think I preferred the first one. Felt happier in it."

"That suited you too."

"Not my colour, though, no, on second thoughts, the second one. Red is my colour, don't you think?" she asks the sales girl.

"Suited you," agrees the girl with an air of indifference.

"Go with your new red holdall too," says Colin helpfully.

"No." Elsie is decisive. "I'll take the first. I felt *right* in it. That's what matters."

She marches back to the cubicle. Colin sighs. He feels a real 'nana standing there with women inspecting racks of knickers and bras all around him.

Then some sort of sales promotion that seems to be going on a short distance away attracts his attention. A well-dressed young man is demonstrating something and women are gathering around him. Curious, he moves a bit closer. The man appears to be offering a free piece of jewellery with every bottle of a new stain remover.

"Just what you've been praying for, ladies," he is saying. "Absolute magic! Removes any stain instantly. Doesn't leave a rim around where it has been used. And guaranteed not to rot or weaken the fabric. What more can you ask? Well, you *can* ask more, because we are giving away with every purchase a very attractive brooch absolutely free as part of our initial promotion! It may not be the Kohinoor but I'm sure you'll agree it's very pretty and useful. What about you, madam, will you be the first to...?"

Colin listens with fascination. He is amazed how people are

taken in by this kind of thing. Elsie would be, that's for sure. He'll have to steer her away from it when she's ready.

"Colin!"

Colin turns to see Elsie, back in her own clothes and handing the trouser suit she's decided to buy to the shop assistant.

"Ready?" he asks.

"Where's me holdall?"

"Down there." He points.

"Where?"

"Down there! On the floor."

"I can't see it."

With a impatient sigh Colin comes back to show her.

"Down *there*!" He points.

"It ain't."

Colin looks himself. His face goes bloodless.

No holdall.

"Christ Almighty!" He looks round desperately, knocking clothing stands awry, peering underneath them. He turns on the shop assistant. "You saw me put it down there, didn't you?"

She nods.

"So where is it now?"

"Search me!"

Declining that invitation Colin turns back to Elsie. "You must have taken it into the cubicle with you!"

"No, I bloody didn't!"

He pushes past the sales girl and dashes to the cubicles, pushing aside curtains, making half-naked women scream, but no holdall.

His eyes are several shades brighter blue with panic when he returns. He's completely mystified.

"Somebody must have bloody nicked it!" he cries.

"My handbag!" wails Elsie.

His eyes sweep the store frenziedly. Everything appears normal. People mooching about with bags of shopping, women fingering garments, the well-dressed man still peddling his stain remover. Colin's policeman's training begins to take over. "Can't have got far," he muses. He focuses his eyes more sharply. That red and white holdall should be easy enough to spot.

And it is – in the hand of a redheaded woman dressed in black who is hurrying towards the lift.

"Oi!" he yells.

It is a fruitless call, since the woman is too far away to hear.

"Wait *here*!" he shouts at Elsie as he dashes off in hot pursuit. "I'll be back!"

He reaches the lift just as the doors close, the woman in it. It is going down. He flies to the stairs, leaps down them two at a time.

But the lift has reached the ground floor and has disgorged its passengers. Colin reclimbs a few steps so he can scan over the crowds to see if he can spot the redhead with the holdall.

He does, just leaving through the front entrance. Off he goes, pushing his way through the shoppers shouting, "Stop thief!" at the top of his voice.

Outside the store he stops, looks agitatedly in both directions. There she is, just boarding a double-decker bus! Heedless of his aching back, his fatigued condition after a sleepless night and indigestion induced by the rich crab lunch, Colin moves like an Olympic runner and manages to hurl himself on board the bus just as the doors hiss shut.

"All the way, mate," he gasps to the driver-conductor, glancing along the lower deck for the woman.

He can't see her, so he climbs to the upper deck, and there she is, about halfway down, the red and white striped holdall beside her on the seat.

"Got you, my beauty," he mutters to himself, sitting a few seats behind her. He feels a tremendous surge of satisfaction. He hasn't felt so pleased with himself for many a day.

He won't cause a fuss by apprehending her on the bus, he decides. Wait until she gets off. He hasn't a clue where he is going, but that is the least of his worries. He's going to stay with her, come what may.

The bus stops and starts through the traffic-choked streets, out to the suburbs, along seemingly endless roads of shops and houses, and still the woman sits on. Colin looks at her abundant red hair. It's too abundant, he thinks. Probably a wig, or possibly a disguise. She could be a professional shoplifter.

At last the woman gets up and makes for the stairs. Colin glances at her casually as she passes him. She is older than he thought. Her haggard face is heavily made up. She is wearing a black mini-skirt, with black tights and a low-cut black top. A right common piece, he thinks. She probably lives on some estate on the outskirts of the town.

He rises and follows her down the bus stairs. The bus stops. She alights. He follows. She walks rapidly away, the red and white striped holdall in her hand. He waits until the bus has moved on, and then follows.

He keeps behind her until she turns into a side street, then quickly catches up with her and places a heavy hand on her shoulder.

"This is a citizen's arrest," he proclaims. "I am arresting you on the suspicion that the holdall you are carrying is stolen property."

The woman turns. "You what?"

"I have good reason to believe that holdall is stolen property, the property of my wife, in fact."

"Yeah?" An evil-looking leer appears on her face.

She turns and starts to walk on.

Colin quickly blocks her path. "I'm afraid I must ask you to accompany me to the police station."

"Sod off!"

She tries to push past him, but she can't.

"This is a serious matter," says Colin. "You must come with me."

"You must be insane, duckie. I jest bought it at Hambledon's."

"You didn't buy it, you stole it. That holdall contains my wife's handbag."

"No, it don't."

"Yes, it does."

"No, it *don't!*"

"All right, then I suggest you open it and prove it."

"*You* open it."

She shoves the holdall into his hands.

Taken by surprise, Colin hesitates. "Right. I will!"

He places the holdall on a garden wall, unzips it and opens it up. Inside are several of Hambledon's smart plastic bags, but no handbag.

"Satisfied?"

Colin is staggered, flabbergasted, dumbfounded and generally knocked about "I-I-I..." he stammers.

The woman pulls open one of the plastic bags and displays the contents under his nose. "Frilly knickers, dearie. All paid for. There's the bill."

"I-I'm s-so s-sorry! I really thought. You see..."

"You should be more careful, going round accosting people like that."

"I wasn't accosting you, I was...."

"Not much! Clamping y'hand on me shoulder, putting the fear of God into me, blocking me path."

"I didn't mean to..."

"You're the one who ought to be arrested, duckie, not me. Could have been a rapist, couldn't you? Shakes a woman up something chronic, I can tell you. Ought to report it to the police."

Colin is thoroughly alarmed now. He could be in dead trouble. Placate her, he thinks feverishly. Grovel. "Sorry, sorry, didn't mean to scare you, honest. That holdall is exactly the same as the one my wife just bought. Look, I can see you're pretty shaken. Let me buy you a drink – a brandy or something."

"No pubs round here, handsome."

"Oh! Well..."

The woman's attitude seems to change. The harshness goes out of her face, and her voice. "Oh, what the hell. You meant well. You're the one who needs the drink by the look of you. I live only a couple of doors along. Come up and have a quick snifter."

"Oh, no, no, no!" cries Colin, amazed by the offer. "I couldn't after what I..."

"Come on, we both need it."

"Well, I ought to be..."

"Five minutes. Just to get over the shock."

Colin doesn't like to say no. After all, she could have landed him in deep trouble, and he finds himself following her up the steps of a large but tawdry terraced house.

"My name is Carlotta," says the woman as they climb the stairs to her top floor flat. "What's yours, handsome?"

"Colin."

"Nice name. I know lots of Colins."

When Carlotta opens the front door, a slovenly looking old woman emerges from the kitchen.

"I shall be busy for a bit, Greta," Carlotta tells her in an indifferent tone.

The old woman stares at Colin disinterestedly, and returns to the kitchen without speaking.

"That's my maid," explains Carlotta casually.

The room into which she takes him staggers Colin. It is small but the Royal Hotel itself couldn't be more sumptuously furnished, long lush sofa, deep armchairs, a huge cocktail cabinet and a television the size of a chest of drawers. But fussy looped curtains cut out most of the light, making the room overwhelmingly claustrophobic.

"Take a pew," says Carlotta, going to the cocktail cabinet. "Brandy?"

"Please." Colin sinks into the voluptuous sofa.

"So your wife had her bag nicked?" she says as she hands him the brandy. "Shame."

"Yes..." Anxious that she should understand how it was he mistook Carlotta's holdall for Elsie's, Colin goes into a long-winded explanation about what happened in Hambledon's. While he is doing so, Carlotta sits herself beside him on the sofa, her mini-skirt becoming even more mini as it rides up when she crosses her legs, her bony knee showing white through her black tights. She lights a cigarette and adopts the posture of a twenties flapper as she slowly exhales a stream of evil-smelling smoke.

"Don't fret yourself about it, dear," she says as Colin finishes. "Easy mistake to make. No harm done. But this *is* my holdall. I bought it because they were going cheap. Thought it might come in handy when I go to the Bahamas next week."

The Bahamas! A maid! All this posh furniture! The woman must be loaded. Perhaps she's won the Lottery, he thinks.

"Like another?" asks Carlotta, taking the empty glass from him.

"No, thanks all the same. Look, I really must be going."

"Oh, do you *have* to?"

It is the second time in little more than twelve hours that a woman has made such a plea to him. He's not sure what is going on, but it's all rather worrying.

But not as worrying as when Carlotta begins to pull affectionately with her long fingernails at his jumper with the blue diagonal stripes.

"I-I'm afraid I must. The wife is…"

Her hand travels downwards. "Mmmm, a real hunk of a man, aren't you? Fancy a quickie?"

Before he knows what's happening, she's on her feet, the mini-skirt around her ankles, hauling down her tights.

"Should be a hundred, but seventy quid to you, handsome, for a quickie. Up front, if you don't mind. Put it on the mantelpiece."

God Almighty, she a bloody prostitute!

Had she bitten him he couldn't have shot to his feet more quickly. "S-sorry! Gotta go!"

He's out of the door, helter-skelter down the stairs, and out into the fresh air at a meteoric speed.

*****

Around the time Colin is making his sharp exit from Carlotta's flat, Nora is thankfully putting the key in her front door. She and Len have made better time on their return journey than they did going, thanks partly to Nora deciding to risk the motorways rather than losing their way on the scenic route.

Nora is pleased. She wanted to be home in time to have a word with Mr Hepplewhite before the estate agent's office closed.

But she has to phone Cyril first. "Tell me everything Mr Hepplewhite said," she asks him.

"Told you this morning," answers Cyril. "He said if we'd accept forty thousand they could be interested."

"Sure he said *forty* thousand?"

"That's what he said." Cyril's never sounded more positive.

"What else did he say?"

"Only that they wanted a quick answer, cos they're getting

married and that on Saturday."

"Mr Hepplewhite didn't say if he thought they might increase the offer a bit?"

"No."

"Right. I'm going to ring him now, arrange to meet these people tomorrow, see if I can talk 'em into upping their offer. You want to be there?"

"No," says Cyril.

But Mr Hepplewhite is engaged with a client when she phones. "Shall I ask him to call you back?" asks the girl in the office.

"Yes. Tonight, mind. It's very important."

Nora is vexed about having to wait. "I bet he doesn't bother to phone," she says to Len over the pot of tea he has made. "These people never do. I'll give him till five."

At ten to five, Mr Hepplewhite hasn't phoned so Nora is on the blower again, with better luck.

"John Hepplewhite."

"Ah, there you are. It's Mrs Scally."

"Oh, Mrs...ahm...Scally. I was about to phone you."

"So I believe."

"Sorry to keep you. Quite frankly, it's been one of those days. What can I do for you?"

Nora informs him she is not prepared to accept the offer, but might consider knocking off a thousand. "I'd like to talk to these people myself, Mr Hepplewhite. Could you arrange for me to meet them tomorrow morning?"

"Ahm..." Mr Hepplewhite doesn't go for that idea. "Quite frankly, Mrs Scally, I don't think it would do any good. In fact, I know it wouldn't. The gap is too wide. Perhaps – and I say *perhaps* – if you were to reduce the price by say, three thousand initially, then they might – and I say *might* – be prepared to meet you halfway at forty-five thousand."

"Five thousand off!" Had Nora been given to swooning she would certainly have done so now. "Mr Hepplewhite, I have come home from my holiday specially to negotiate with these people. Perhaps if I spoke to them personally I could get them to up…"

"That wouldn't do any good, Mrs...ahm...Scally, I do assure

you." Mr Hepplewhite's voice has gone cold. "Quite frankly, your property is only one of many they are looking at."

Nora purses her lips. "Well, I'm prepared to knock off two thousand but no more, if they are prepared to settle the matter quickly. Perhaps you would tell them that and let me know what they say."

"Certainly, Mrs Scally, but I doubt very much if they will be interested, quite frankly." No one could be more frank than Mr Hepplewhite.

"I am anxious to resume my interrupted holiday, so please give it your immediate attention."

"Of course. Leave it to me. Good afternoon."

"Good afternoon, Mr Hepplewhite."

"Really," says Nora, when she returns to the kitchen where Len is preparing spaghetti bolognese for their supper. "You'd think that Mr Hepplewhite was working for *them*, not us. If this deal falls through I'm going to change the agent when we get back. Your toast is burning, by the way."

Len hastily withdraws his toast from under the grill. "You know," he says, "I don't reckon these agents are worth what they cost. Might do better to advertise it ourselves."

"That's occurred to me too," says Nora, to whom no such thought has in fact occurred.

*****

In the women's wear department of Hambledon's Brighton store, Elsie is obediently waiting for Colin to return from his chase after her stolen holdall. The floor manageress has appeared on the scene, put the hand-wringing Elsie to sit on a rickety chair and provided her with a cup of tea from the coffee shop on the fourth floor, while the shop assistant discreetly unwraps the trouser suit for which her customer is no longer in a position to pay.

Curious shoppers gather round, sympathising and tutting. The store's Security Chief arrives, surveys the scene of the crime, questions Elsie, takes down her particulars and mutters into his mobile, moving people along.

Elsie explains to him between bouts of anguish and gulps of

tea how her husband has taken off in pursuit of the thief and instructed her to remain where she is until he returns.

"Can you describe the suspect?" asks the Security Chief.

"Didn't see him meself," snivels Elsie. "Me husband is very sharp eyed. He used to be a policeman."

"So did I," comments the Security Chief, as if that was no big deal.

"Me handbag was in it," wails Elsie. "What am I to do without me handbag?"

The Security Chief has her list the contents of her bag, and she bursts into tears again when she remembers it contains a photo of her two sons. "It's the last photo I have of them," she cries. "Me eldest is eighteen tomorrow, and I've got to phone him at ten tonight so I catch him before he goes to work in the morning."

The Security Chief fails to follow this line of reasoning and thinks the poor soul is probably rambling. "I'll go and re-run the CCTV," he says. "See if it caught anything."

Elsie sits on. People, bored by the inactivity, move off. The stores clock clicks away another minute.

"I hope he's all right," moans Elsie. "He's such a brave man."

The motherly floor manageress thinks Elsie is probably in a state of shock, and supplies a woolly cardigan from the Oddments Clearance counter to put around her shoulders, whispering to the shop assistant to make sure the poor dear doesn't make off with it when she leaves – if she ever does.

The Security Chief returns and reports the only thing the CCTV has picked up is some sort of madman rushing from the stores.

"That's him!" cries Elsie. "That's my Colin!"

"That was timed forty-five minutes ago," observes the Security Chief. "He's taking his time."

"Supposing he never returns!"

"He will, with or without the suspect. I should sit tight for a bit."

A bleep from his mobile diverts the attention of the Security Chief, and he wanders off muttering into it.

Elsie sits on. The store is gradually emptying of shoppers.

The hands of the clock point to five twenty.

"We'll be closing soon," says the sales girl. "You'll have to leave shortly."

"I can't! Not without my Colin."

"Well you can't stay here."

"But I've got no money!"

"You'll have to wait for him outside. Don't suppose he'll be long."

The Security Chief wanders back. "Hubby not returned yet? Taking his time, I must say."

"I dunno what to do," weeps Elsie. "I've got no money."

"Oh, he'll turn up. Daresay he's caught the suspect and taken him straight to the nick. Save us a job if he has."

A disembodied voice announces the store is closing in five minutes.

"You'll have to leave now," the sales person tells Elsie during a sudden burst of pre-closing-time activity.

"I'm not leaving without my Colin!" Elsie is sounding defiant.

"Got to, luv," says the Security Chief. "Come on, finish your tea and I'll escort you to the front entrance."

"It's not good enough! I demand to see the manager."

"No chance. He'll have gone home long ago."

"Oh, whatever's happened to him?" cries Elsie in another burst of desperation. "What am I to do?"

"Shush now," says the Security Chief, leading her gently towards the stairs. "He'll turn up. Hasn't lost his memory, has he?"

"No, but supposing he's been kidnapped – murdered!"

"Doubt it. He's an ex-cop. He can look after himself."

Impatient employees are holding the automatic doors at the entrance open while the dregs of the customers saunter out. The Security Chief brings Elsie to a standstill just outside.

"Now you wait here, luv. He can't fail to see you. He'll be along shortly."

"But what if he isn't? What am I to do? Can't you stay here with me?"

"Work to do. Got to make sure there's none of the sods still lurking inside. Search the toilets. You'd be surprised what they get up to."

"But I can't just stand here for ever!"

"No. I suggest you wait a while – an hour say. If he doesn't turn up, best thing is to go to the nick, tell 'em the tale. They'll see you right."

"Don't know where the bloody nick is, do I?"

"Not far. That way, second on the right, first left. Can't miss it. Sorry, got to go. Good luck."

Worried and furious, Elsie stands outside the store, alone and penniless. The automatic doors close and lock behind her. Blinds come down on the store's windows. People scurry past, bent on getting home. The rush-hour traffic roars by.

Elsie stands. Nearly an hour passes and still no Colin. She feels rooted to the spot. She feels peculiar. She doesn't know what to do with her arms without her handbag to cling on to. Her face must be a dried-up delta of mascara rivulets and she can't do anything about it.

Sod the bugger! She thinks, anger getting the upper hand. I'm not standing round here like a trollop any longer. I'm going to the bloody police station; they can get me back to the hotel. Where did that bloke say it was? First right, second left? That's it.

She strides out in the direction indicated by the Security Chief with all the determination of a Grenadier Guard. First right, second left. The road leads gradually upwards. She marches on. No police station. Onward and upward she goes. Feeling utterly exhausted she comes to a stop, not outside the nick, but outside a dismal-looking church. Her head aches, her feet ache, it feels as if that crab she had at lunchtime has got its claws into the lining of her stomach. She feels like a waif, unwanted and forgotten.

If only Nora were here! She'd know what to do. Probably have half Brighton out looking for Colin by now. But she's not so concerned about Colin as she is about getting back to the hotel to ring Andy. She must make that phone call at all costs. But all she can think of doing is going into the church and offering a prayer and resting her aching feet. Not a bad idea at that. Maybe the vicar would lend her the fare back to Benthaven. But the church is locked and there is no sign of the vicar.

He'll be in the vicarage having his tea, no doubt. Then, as she is gazing about looking for the vicarage, she spots a newsagents on the opposite side of the road. It is still open. Perhaps they'd lend her enough money to get back to Benthaven. Then again, perhaps they wouldn't. They didn't know her from Adam – well Eve, that is. She could try leaving her earrings with them as a security. Elsie hates asking for money. She much prefers spending it, but this is an emergency.

As these desperate measures are going through her mind, a young lad rides up to the shop and goes in, leaving his bicycle outside. Elsie has one of those impulses that have been so significant in shaping her destiny. Without further thought, she hurries across the road, jumps on the bike, and peddles off down the hill.

It is many moons since Elsie rode a bicycle. It feels like the first time, and probably is on a man's sporting bike, with her bum high in the air and her nose almost scraping the ground. She wobbles and weaves, but rapidly gains speed as she careers wildly down the hill, her weary legs pistoning like a steam locomotive.

But all she's intent on doing is getting back to the hotel. Nothing is going to stop her phoning Andy at ten. And at the rate she is going she'll be in Benthaven in no time – if her legs will stand up to it, that is.

At the bottom of the hill she can see traffic lights, green at the moment, thank God! A heavy goods vehicle comes alongside her. The lights turn to orange, then to red. The HGV is beside her, hemming her in.

Elsie plies the brakes, wavers, skids, panics, loses control, ploughs straight into the traffic light – and blacks out.

*****

When the phone rings, Nora and Len are doing the washing-up after their tin of spaghetti bolognese on burnt toast.

"Ah!" declares Nora. "That'll be Mr Hepplewhite. He must have decided to talk to them people tonight. Doesn't want to risk losing a deal. You see what a little firm handling can do?"

But it isn't Mr Hepplewhite.

"Nora?"
"Yes?"
"It's Marsha – Marsha Bloom."
"Oh! Hello...er...Marsha."

"I phoned you at your hotel this morning and a person informed me you were on your way home. All is well, I trust?"

"Oh yes. We had to…"

"Splendid. Now listen. There's absolutely no call for alarm, but I've had a phone call from Gavin. Apparently Georgie has been taken into hospital over there."

"What!" Nora has to lean against the wall for support.

"It would appear there is some complication with her pregnancy."

"Oh dear, oh Lor'! Whatever's the trouble?"

"According to Gavin there's nothing to worry about but he doesn't seem to know exactly what the trouble is – you know what men are."

"And them in foreign parts!" cries Nora. "I knew they shouldn't have gone!"

"I agree with you entirely, Nora. I told them so, didn't I? But there is no telling young people these days. Anyhow, I've decided to go over there myself and find out exactly what's what."

"You're going to Greece? On your own?"

"I most certainly am, although I did wonder if perhaps you would care to come with me."

"*Me?*" Nora's in need of treatment for shock. 'Me, *fly* with you to Greece?"

"I would much value your company, my dear. Oliver is in Singapore at the moment so he can't come, and Greece is scarcely the place for a woman to be on her own. But if you feel unable to at such short notice, I shall understand perfectly, of course."

Nora hasn't been in such a dither for many a day. What about the selling of the house? What about her holiday? What about the cost? But her first grandchild must have priority. Besides, Marsha's word is her command.

"Well, if you really want me to," she says weakly. "But I don't know no Greek nor nothing."

"Neither do I, but we'll manage. Now listen very carefully. I'll attend to booking the flights and all that, and I'll do all the paying. It's easier that way. We can settle up when we get back. You have a passport, I take it?"

"Er...no." Nora feels relieved. She's off the hook.

"No matter. Greece is in the EU. We'll get you one first thing in the morning."

Then Nora remembers. "Yes, I have! I got it when I went to Denmark."

"How long ago was that?"

"Er...about six years ago."

"And it was a full ten-year passport?"

"Yes...well, I think so."

"That's all right then, but you'd better check it. I'll phone you back with the details. In the meantime I suggest you pack a bag, just light things for two or three days. It will be hot there, no doubt."

"Oh dear," cries Nora, not knowing what to worry about first. "I do hope Georgie's going to be all right."

"I shall make quite sure she is," declares Marsha grimly. She is about to put down the phone, but then says, "Oh, there's just one further thing. Do you think Len would be good enough to drive us to the station when we go?"

"Oh, I 'spect so." The least of Nora's worries.

"Splendid. It will save a lot of fuss with taxis. Don't forget about your passport. I will call you back later when I have the details. God bless."

Nora totters back to the kitchen and dumps the news on Len like a load of washing. She is in such a state that he has to take off his kitchen gloves and make her a fresh pot of tea.

"Why do these things have to happen?" she wails. "And right in the middle of our holiday!"

"Sod's law," says Len.

"And with this business of Dad's house to deal with! I suppose I shall have to leave it for you to look after."

Len is only too thankful he isn't expected to go to Greece as well. He won't be sorry to be on his own for a bit – he'll look forward to it, in fact. With any luck he should be able to spend a little time at The Mason and Magpie.

But one thing is bothering him. "Will you be back by Saturday?" he asks.

"How do *I* know? Depends what's wrong. Why?"

"It's the Snooker Final."

"Oh, that. Can't be bothered with all that now."

*****

Colin doesn't pause for breath after leaving Carlotta's apartment until he comes to a solid-looking war memorial, beneath which is a bench with an aged gentleman sitting on it, leaning on his stick.

He slumps down beside the old boy, puffed, distraught, furious with himself. Bloody idiot! Should have realised she was a pro. Written all over her. I must be getting senile. God only knows what I'll be like when I'm as old as this old boy.

When he's regained his breath he looks at his watch.

Ten to six!

Elsie!

He hasn't a clue where he is, but he got here by bus, so presumably he can get one back. "Excuse me," he says to the old man. "Can you tell me how often the buses run back into Brighton?"

The old gentleman jerks back from his memories. "Buses? Wouldn't be sure, sir. Every hour I think."

Every hour! It could be seven before he gets back to Hambledon's. Elsie will have gone berserk! "Any taxis round here?"

"Taxis? Oh, I doubt it, sir. Not in these parts."

"Well, what about a phone box?" persists Colin. "So I can ring for one."

The old chap raises a gnarled finger to scratch his ear. "Used to be one five hundred yards or so down the road on the left. Doubt if it's working, though. Vandals, see."

Colin thanks him and sets off at as brisk a pace as his back will allow, chastising himself all the time for having been such a bloody fool. He is really worried about Elsie now, so worried in fact that he fails to recognise the two youths who pass by him in the opposite direction.

But they recognise him.

"Is that who I think it was?" asks one of the other.

"Yeah."

"Shall we…?"

"Why not? Bugger asked for it,"

The youths turn round, hurry back past Colin and turn into a passageway between the houses some fifty yards ahead. When Colin draws level with the passageway he hears such a commotion that he instinctively looks to see what is going on. The two youths are going at it hammer and tongs and shouting abuse at each other at the tops of their voices. Colin's policeman's instinct is too strong to be resisted.

"Oi!" he yells, charging down the passageway. He grabs the youths by the scruff of their necks and hauls them apart. Only then does he recognise them. He gapes. It's the thugs from the car park incident, Jasper and Pug.

"Well, well, so we meet again," says Jasper.

"Nice to have a little reunion," says Pug.

"And a chance to finish a little unfinished business," says Jasper.

Before Colin can recover they set about him, punching and kicking him, hurling him to the ground.

As he falls he hits his head against a van, parked in the passageway.

Colin, too, blacks out.

Chapter 12

Wednesday dawns grimly, and nowhere more so than over the small Wiltshire town of Brockbury, where gales from the northwest blow harshly down the silent streets and squalls of driving rain beat against curtained windows.

But Nora is already up, scurrying about feverishly preparing for her 'Maiden Flight'. She is in a dither as to what to wear, in a dither about what she should eat (if anything) prior to flying, in a dither because having left her holdall at the Ocean View she hasn't a suitable sized case to take, in a dither because if she doesn't stop dithering she and Len are going to be late collecting Marsha at six thirty to take her with them to the station.

As promised, Marsha phoned back the previous evening with the travel details. The flight is due to leave Heathrow at 14.30 hours, which means they have to catch a train from Brockbury at 07.22 so as to be sure of being at the airport an hour before take off to check in.

By six, by some miracle, Nora is as ready as she thinks she's ever likely to be. She has decided against breakfast, there's no time for it anyway, but yields to Len's pleading to at least have a cup of tea. She drinks it standing up, and takes advantage of this momentary lull in activity to issue him with his final instructions.

"Whatever you do," she tells him, "don't go chasing off to The Mason and Magpie before Hepplewhite has phoned. And don't forget we're not dropping the price by more than two thousand, so if they don't agree the sale is off. And you'd better phone Cyril and tell him what's happened. Say I've left *you* in charge of the negotiations. Oh, and I suppose you'd better phone Colin and Elsie in Benthaven, tell them what's happened. Goodness knows if we'll ever be able to get back there. Say we'll let them know what we shall be doing as soon as we can."

"What about the Snooker Final on Saturday?" asks Len.

"That's your affair. You and Colin will have sort that out

between you." She takes a final sip of tea and plonks down the cup. "Come along, we mustn't keep Marsha waiting."

It has just gone six-thirty when Len's Escort draws up outside the Blooms' house in Webbley Park. Marsha is already at the gate, cowering under her umbrella, a large suitcase on the ground beside her. Len sandwiches the case into the boot while Marsha sandwiches herself into the back seat of the car.

"Heard anything more about Georgie?" asks Nora as soon as they drive off.

"I phoned Gavin last night after I phoned you and he says her condition is unchanged."

"That's good news at least."

Marsha sniffs. "That we shall see. I am extremely dissatisfied with the whole situation, Nora. I've instructed Gavin not to allow Georgie to undergo any form of surgery before we arrive and know exactly what the trouble is. I don't want her poked about by some ham-fisted Greek. If an operation should prove necessary I shall have her flown home, whatever the cost."

Nora hopes she won't be expected to contribute to that. This trip is going to make a big enough hole in her moving money as it is. They arrive at the station by ten to seven, and Nora tells Len not to wait to see them off. "Better get home cos Hepplewhite might ring early."

Having no desire to stand around waiting for them to go, Len refrains from commenting that at that hour he doubts if Mr Hepplewhite has yet vacated his own comfy bed, never mind given any thought to his day's work.

Nora finds it embarrassing to make her farewells with Marsha standing there. She is not normally given to kissing, considering it unhygienic, but since she feels she should demonstrate their affection before Marsha, and mindful that she may never see Len's dear old face again, she kisses him full on the lips. "Do look after yourself," she tells him. "There's plenty of food in the fridge and plenty of tins in the cupboard. Don't have a lot of fry-ups, but if you do have one, then don't forget to put out the air-freshener before you start and open all the windows afterwards."

She gives him a pathetic little wave as he drives off. It will be the first time they have been parted since her ill-fated trip to

Denmark, and she feels an unexpected tug of affection for him.

It is donkey's years since Nora has travelled by train, apart from that unscheduled return from Bristol with Elsie after their shopping expedition. And she has never travelled first class at all, so as she enters the smart carriage her anxieties are momentarily forgotten as she is quite overcome by its luxurious ambience.

"This is very nice, I must say," she observes as she settles herself in her seat opposite Marsha. "*Very* comfy."

"At least it's better than driving down that awful motorway," says Marsha, carefully arranging her clothes about her. "I am always trying to persuade Oliver to travel to Heathrow by train, but he insists it's quicker by car, which no doubt it is at the speed he drives."

"Must be very worrying for you with him travelling so much and that."

Marsha pulls out the copy of *The Times* she bought at the station. "One never becomes completely resigned to it, my dear. It is always there, at the back of one's mind. One is always half expecting to learn news of some disaster. It is not so bad during the day. I have my golf, of course, and my work for the church and various other committees. It is at night that it's the worst – alone in that big house, especially now that Georgie has left home. It can be really unnerving at times, I can tell you."

"Suppose it can." Nora can appreciate that.

Marsha spreads the newspaper out on the table between them and turns to the crossword. "Do you do crosswords, my dear?"

"Er...no. Not very often."

"I find it passes the time better than anything when travelling."

"Well, we don't travel all that much, only for holidays and that."

"Then you should count yourself fortunate. Travelling is a vastly overrated pastime in my opinion. I envy you, Nora, I must say."

"Envy me?" Nora is amazed.

"Being able to lead a normal home life I mean, having Len for company the whole time."

"You said something at Christmas about Oliver retiring soon. Then you'll have him."

"Oh, he'll never retire – not until he's forced to. He keeps promising to think about it, but that is as far as it goes." Marsha opens her handbag and takes out a small silver pen.

"Course, you can understand it," says Nora, "him having such an important job and that. He must find it very interesting."

The corners of Marsha's mouth tighten. "I very much doubt if it's the interest that holds him. It's the perks he gets he's not anxious to relinquish."

Nora wonders what kind of 'perks' she is referring to.

But she doesn't need to ask. With sudden resolution Marsha lays aside her silver pen and leans forward confidentially, her stomach pressing against the edge of the table. "I haven't mentioned this to a single soul before, Nora, so please don't let it go any further."

"Course not," promises Nora, feeling proud to be taken into Marsha's confidence.

Marsha glances round the carriage to ensure there is no one within earshot. "Oliver, I'm afraid, is a womaniser." It is scarcely more than a hiss.

Nora is astounded. "What – Oliver? I don't believe it!"

"I'm afraid it is all too true," nods Marsha sadly.

"But he's such a perfect gentleman!"

"So he leads everyone to believe, although 'charmer' would be the more appropriate word. Of course, when he's home he behaves like a gentleman. He likes to give the impression that we're a devoted couple. He comes to church with me on Sundays, even reads the lesson on occasions, affords me every attention. But when he's away abroad..."

Marsha's face crumples. She reaches in her handbag for a tissue.

"But how can you be sure? I mean, when he's away how do you know what he…"

"Oh, there's no doubt about it. You'd been amazed how things get back to me. He has no idea I know, of course."

"Well, I wouldn't put up with it," declares Nora stoutly.

"It's easy to say that, my dear, but what can one do? I scarcely relish the scandal of a divorce at my age. And there's

Georgie and now the baby to consider. No, I've endured it this far and I shall have to go on doing so until I finally manage to talk him into retiring." She dabs her eyes with the tissue, then gives her nose a hefty blow. "I'm so sorry to burden you with it, but it is a relief to tell someone, since now you are part of the family, so to speak."

Part of the family! Nora is exultant. Whatever lies ahead, Marsha has made her day. "I still can't believe it of Oliver," she says.

"Well, there you are." Marsha blows her nose again and pulls herself upright. "One never knows what people are really like. But you won't breathe a word, will you?"

"Course not."

"But one thing I can say, I do derive considerable comfort from my faith. I doubt if I could have endured all these years without it. My one regret is that Georgie seems so determined to have nothing to do with the church now she's grown up."

But she is interrupted by a voice somewhere in the carriage roof inviting passengers to the restaurant car for the first breakfast sitting.

"I'm famished," says Marsha, struggling to get out of her seat. "Come, let us go for breakfast."

*****

When Elsie comes round she thinks she is in hospital having a baby. The plain walls and hard bed, her aching head and body, all seem to testify to that. Furthermore, not far off, she can hear women groaning and is aware of people scurrying to and fro, and noises that sound like the rattle of trolleys.

Elsie carefully raises her head. It feels twice its size and three times its weight. She is indeed in hospital, although she's not so sure about the baby part of it.

An eagle-eyed nurse has spotted her slight movement, and comes up to her. "Had a good sleep then?" she asks cheerfully.

"Where am I?"

"In hospital, dear."

That's not what Elsie meant. She meant whereabouts, what town, but can't be bothered to pursue it.

"You're a bit of a Jane Doe, aren't you?" continues the nurse, taking Elsie's pulse. "No ID on you when they brought you in. What's your name?"

"Name?"

"Your *name*, dear, your handle. What people call you?"

"Erm...dunno."

"Don't know? Try to think, there's a luv."

Elsie's face contorts with the effort. "Dunno. No idea."

The nurse looks at her sharply. "You mean, you *really* can't remember?"

Panic assails Elsie. "What's happened? Where am I? What am I doing here?"

"I'll call the doctor." The nurse lets Elsie's wrist drop like a stone and bustles off.

Elsie struggles to remember what happened to her but her mind is blank. Who is she? Where is she? What the hell has happened? And she has this nagging feeling that there is something vitally urgent she must do, but hasn't a clue what it is. All she knows is that she's got to get out and do it.

She struggles to get out of the bed, but can't, falling back exhausted, half in, half out.

"Nurse! Nurse!" cries a patient in alarm.

Elsie is half aware of being put back to bed, then the next thing she knows a man in a white coat is standing over her. He looks like a schoolboy. "What's happened to me?" she cries. "Am I dying?"

"You'll live," says the schoolboy, smiling brightly. "You had a slight altercation with a traffic signal – and I'm afraid the traffic signal won. Nothing too serious. No bones broken. A few bruises and a mild concussion."

"Gotta go!" cries Elsie, again struggling to get out of bed. "Something I must do. It's urgent!"

"Oh?" The doctor restrains her gently. "And what may that be?"

"Dunno!"

"Not much point in going then, is there? Much better let us keep an eye on you. I gather you can't remember your name?"

Elsie shakes her head, and immediately wishes she hadn't.

"Well, is there anything you *can* remember? What you were

doing before the accident, where you live? No? Well, you're wearing a wedding ring, so presumably you're married. Can you remember your husband's name?"

"No!" Elsie stares at him wild-eyed.

"Not to worry. It'll all come back I expect." He grins impishly. "And when it does you'll probably wish it hadn't."

The doctor withdraws a little way and mutters to the nurse, "A mild amnesia, I suspect. What she needs is rest. Give her another sedative."

"Cliff!" cries Elsie suddenly.

The doctor turns. "Sorry?"

"His name is Cliff!"

"Whose name?"

"My husband's!"

"Oh! Splendid. Cliff who?"

"Dunno!"

"Not to worry. It's a start."

*****

When Colin comes round he thinks it is Nerina, the cleaner at Regal Chemicals, who is bending over him. She has the same black, round face, brown eyes and flashing white teeth. But it's not Nerina, it's a nurse.

"Where the hell am I?" he demands.

"Sssh!" she hisses. "You're in hospital, nothing to worry about. Go back to sleep."

"Elsie!" he cries. "I've got to find Elsie!"

"Now, now. We'll see about it later. Go back to sleep."

"But…"

The next time Colin wakes the ward is all babble and bustle, and a schoolboy in a white coat is standing over him. "Not to worry, old chap, a few bruises that's all. Might have a bit of a head. Memory okay?"

"Memory?"

"Know your name, do you?"

"Course I do!"

"Jolly good. What you need is rest."

"But me wife! I've got to let her know…"

"Not to worry about that, old chap. Someone will be along shortly to deal with that for you. Police want to see you, too."

When he wakes again Colin sees a pert young woman in a white coat standing beside him, clipboard in hand. She pulls up a chair, and takes down his particulars.

"Gotta get hold of me wife," he keeps repeating.

"Tell me what happened," says the young woman. Colin tells how he chased after the red-haired woman whom he thought had stolen Elsie's holdall, discovered he was wrong, and describes how the two thugs mugged him, but carefully omits to mention his visit to Carlotta's flat.

The young woman listens gravely, chewing the cap of her ballpoint. When he's finished she says, "Well, I doubt if your wife is still waiting at Hambledon's."

"Course she bloody ain't!"

"In which case she probably went to the police for help. They most likely would have seen she got safely back to this hotel in Benthaven and told her to stay put and wait for your return."

"For which she's still bloody waiting!" fumes Colin.

She mulls it over, gnawing her pen cap. "Best thing if I phone the hotel for you, inform your wife what has happened."

"Can't I phone her meself?"

"You have to rest."

"Can't rest, can I, till I know Elsie's all right?"

To his surprise she seems to understand. "I'll see what the doctor says."

Eventually a telephone is brought, and after a bit of a do obtaining the Ocean View's number, he gets through to Mr Pertwee.

"Mr Stilwell! Y'dinnae tell me y'wouldnae be into dinner last neet." Mr P. sound doesn't sound too pleased.

"Because I was bloody mugged that's why!" shouts Colin. "I'm in hospital!"

"Och, dearie dear! How terrible! We live in dreadful times, Mr Stilwell. The Devil stalks the Earth."

"Never mind the Devil, I want to talk to me wife."

"But she dinnae attend dinner last neet either, nor breakfast this morning."

"What!" Colin is mortified. "She could still be asleep. Go and knock on her door. I'll hold."

"Aye."

Colin holds until Mr Pertwee eventually returns.

"Are y'still there, Mr Stilwell?"

"Course I am!"

"She's nae there."

"She's not! You sure?"

"Och aye. The chambermaid was there doing the room. The bed has nae been slept in."

"I knew it!" cries Colin, slamming down the phone. "She's in trouble. I've gotta get out of here."

Just as he is struggling to get out of bed the doctor makes a timely return, with a police constable in tow. "You're not going anywhere," he says with his schoolboy grin. "This officer wants to quiz you about last night."

"Never mind about all that. What about me wife? She hasn't arrived back at the hotel."

"All in good time, sir," says the constable. "But first I must make my report on last night's incident."

"That's all you blokes do these days – make reports," growls Colin. "You're like a lot of bloody vintage cars."

Once again Colin has his particulars taken down, and once more he omits the bit about his visit to Carlotta's flat.

"Did you have a wallet or cash upon your person, sir, when the incident occurred?" asks the policeman.

"Course I did!" Colin stops and pales. "You don't mean they…"

"Afraid so, sir. None was discovered upon your person."

"No ID at all," adds the doctor. "You were a bit of a John Doe. Odd that, we had a Jane Doe too last night. Night of the dodos you might say!" Rare sense of humour, this doctor.

"The buggers," mutters Colin. "I'll get 'em yet."

He's even more furious when he recalls that nearly all of the cash he'd brought from home was in his wallet, having taken it from under the wardrobe shelf to pay for the kiss-and-make-up outing.

"Would there have been any credit cards and such in your wallet, sir?"

"Course there would. But never mind that now – what about me wife?"

"It would appear she is missing, sir."

"No appearances about it mate, she *is* missing! What you doing about it, that's what I want to know?"

"Suppose we'll have to look into it," sighs the policeman. He takes down Elsie's particulars, and then folds his notebook. "We'll be in touch, sir," he says, and departs.

When he returns sometime later Colin is sitting up and being presented with boiled cod in parsley sauce.

"Well?" demands Colin, pushing aside the food.

"No luck as yet, sir, I'm afraid. No person answering your wife's description has been arrested for loitering outside Hambledon's, nor has such a person been reported as having had an accident."

"Thank God for that! You're quite sure, I suppose?"

"Oh, absolutely, sir. Only two accidents were reported last evening. One was a poor old soul who ran into a traffic signal on her bicycle and gave herself concussion with resulting amnesia. Can't remember a thing – only that her husband's name was Cliff. That isn't your name is it, sir?"

"No. Nor was Elsie on a bicycle. What was the other accident?"

The police officer permits himself a wry grin. "Ah well, sir, that was a young couple snogging in the back of a Fiat Uno. Left the handbrake off, didn't they? Car ran down an incline in the car park straight into the public convenience. Shaken up, that's all. But it didn't do the Fiat much good. Toilets still working, though."

"And that's all the accidents there were?"

"All reported, sir. Tuesday's a quiet night for accidents."

"What about rapes and murders?"

"None, sir, I'm afraid."

Colin is relieved, but still worried. What could have happened to her? "And muggings?" he asks. "Was anyone mugged last night?"

"Only your good self, sir," the officer reminds him. "Tuesday's a quiet night for muggings too."

"Where the hell has she got to then?" cries Colin.

"Probably a simple explanation, sir. Shouldn't worry unduly. Perhaps she decided to walk all the way back to Benthaven and hasn't got there yet. You'll probably find her there safe and sound when you're discharged from here."

"If I ever am," growls Colin.

*****

Marsha and Nora have arrived safely at Heathrow.

"We want Terminal Two," announces Marsha, the veteran traveller.

She marches off. Her case has wheels attached to it and she trails it behind her like a little dog. Nora has to lug hers, changing it from one hand to the other every few yards, and she's thankful when she can put it down on the moving walkway. The walkway fascinates her. They could do with one of those down Brockbury High Street.

Eventually they emerge at Terminal Two.

"Oh my!" cries Nora. She has seen Heathrow on the telly before now but is unprepared for the crowds, lights, signs and shops that confront her.

Marsha glances at the clock. It is midday.

"Just in nice time," she observes.

She quickly spots the Olympic Airways desk and collects the tickets, and then they both join the queue at the check-in for Athens. Nora's spirits drop and drop. She feels unreal. It's as if a semi-transparent shroud has descended over her. Marsha attends to most of the business, Nora standing beside her, her spirits sinking still lower as she watches her case slide away. She feels half of her has disappeared with it.

"We've got nearly an hour to kill now," says Marsha. "We might as well go and have some lunch."

"I thought we ate on the plane," protests Nora.

"Plastic food, my dear. We'll lunch at one of the restaurants. Come along."

She leads Nora to an expensive-looking restaurant, all glass and glitter. Marsha, now truly back on form after her unprecedented outburst on the train, orders herself a sirloin steak the size of a cowpat, with all the trimmings. Nora has fish, but scarcely touches it.

"Is it not to your taste?" asks Marsha.

"It's not that. I'm just not hungry."

"I should try to eat a bit more. Olly always says it's best to fly on a full stomach, then if you're in for a bumpy ride you've something to be sick on."

Nora does her best to oblige, but can't go beyond a few more mouthfuls for fear of being sick before she even gets airborne.

After the meal Marsha orders coffee and two large brandies. For once, Nora is quite unable to face alcohol, so Marsha drinks both the brandies herself.

Then Marsha produces some travel pills from her copious handbag. "Have one of these if you're nervous, my dear. It'll settle your stomach and calm you down."

Nora is only too happy to accept that, and swallows the pill tremblingly with a sip of coffee.

Much too soon for Nora, after a last-minute visit to the toilets, they are on their way to the plane. Marsha leads the way through to Passport Control and the security checks. Nora is scarcely aware of this procedure, being more conscious of the glinting eyes of evil-looking officials boring into her. She feels as if at any moment she will be apprehended and frog-marched to the nearest Gulag.

Instead, she suddenly finds herself aboard the aircraft where a smartly tailored hostess welcomes her like a long-lost friend and smiles at her reassuringly.

"Would you like the window seat?" asks Marsha.

"No, thank you." The less Nora sees of the outside world, the better. But she can't help being aware of the wind buffeting the plane and the rain slashing against the windows. "We're not taking off in this awful weather, are we?" she asks Marsha nervously.

"Oh yes, nothing to worry about. We'll be above it all soon. You'll see."

The doors are closed. The engines wheeze into life. The aircraft is pulled from its moorings and trundles innocuously towards the runway, while the hostess stands at the front of the cabin performing antics intended to convey how to don the life jackets should there be an emergency, none of which Nora comprehends.

The aircraft settles itself on the main runway and halts. A tense pause. The engines whine to an excruciating pitch. The aircraft shudders. Then, as if someone had given it an almighty kick up the backside, it shoots off along the runway.

Nora grips the arms of her seat, shuts her eyes, prays fervently for the first time since her honeymoon night, trying to think about Len, Gavin, Georgie, the baby, Cyril, Mr Hepplewhite, Elsie, Colin, anything except what is happening.

"Look!" cries Marsha suddenly. "You can see Olly's hotel – over there – the one that looks like a tombstone."

"Very nice," says Nora, her eyes still firmly shut.

"You missed it," complains Marsha, when the world is blotted out as the plane enters the mist of the cloud. She settles herself back in her seat. "You know," she continues, "if *only* Gavin had told us he was taking Georgie to Greece, Olly could have arranged for them to have stayed at the Athens Skyfly Hotel and saved us a three-hour trip by boat to this silly island."

"By boat!" Nora involuntarily opens her eyes – wide.

"Thyros is an island, my dear, the most ridiculous place possible for Gavin to have taken Georgie in her condition."

The higher the plane goes the lower Nora's spirits sink. She is never going to survive it all.

But then, suddenly, the aircraft bursts through into brilliant sunshine. Below them is a sea of fleecy cloud.

"Good afternoon, ladies and gentlemen. This is your Captain speaking…"

*****

In the Brighton hospital, Colin has just been informed that he is fit enough to leave, and that in view of his impecunious state, arrangements have been made for him to be taken back to Benthaven in the outpatients' ambulance. So at four thirty, feeling relieved he's at last on the move, he sets off along with a number of sad-looking patients who are being returned home after treatment.

What he hasn't been told is that the ambulance is visiting

other places first, meandering all around the outskirts and dropping off patients on the way, making Colin seethe with frustration. As a result it is getting on for six before he arrives at Ocean View.

Colin's hopes of finding Elsie has arrived back at the hotel are dashed as soon as he sees the bedroom key is still on the keyboard in the foyer, where he'd left it the previous morning. Now what? he wonders. What the hell can have happened to her?

While he is still standing forlornly in the foyer, Mr Pertwee puts in an appearance.

"Och, Mr Stilwell! You're back!"

"Looks like it, don't it?"

Mr Pertwee stares with concern at Colin's patched-up face. "What a dreadful thing to have happened! And y'poor wee wife missing too! I'm so sorry."

"She's not back, then?"

"Och, no, I'm afraid not. But try not to worry. I'm sure there must be a simple explanation."

"I'd like to know what it is then," says Colin acidly. "She's been missing twenty-four hours now, mate. I dunno what sort of simple explanation there can be for that."

Mr Pertwee splays his hands and looks sorrowful. "I dinnae know what to say. If there's anything I can do?"

"Nothing we can do, not now, not till the morning at any rate."

Colin takes the bedroom key from the keyboard and limps to the stairs.

"Och, Mr Stilwell, y'friend phoned." Mr P. calls after him.

Colin stops. "Friend? You mean Len?"

"Aye – Mr Scally. A wee while ago."

"What did he want?"

"He dinnae say. He wants you to phone him."

"Yes, all right."

Colin wearily climbs the stairs to the bedroom. He looks at the untouched bed. He gazes around the room, so unnaturally neat and tidy, as left by the chambermaid. He wanders into the bathroom. Elsie's yellow bikini hangs over the shower curtain rail, where she put it after washing it through before they left for

Brighton the previous morning. It is bone dry.

He sits on the edge of the bed, bent forward, hands clasped together, arms on his knees. Never before has he had such a chastening experience. Never before has he felt so wretched, so utterly alone.

Restlessly, he gets up and wanders to the window and looks down at the forecourt below in the futile hope that he might see Elsie arriving back. Not a chance mate, he tells himself. Got to face up to it, something awful *must* have happened to her.

He turns back, feeling desolate and alone. No Len to commiserate with him. No Nora to tell him what to do. But at least he can talk to Len on the phone. He might as well do that now.

But the thugs have taken all his money, including his loose change, so he'll have to take what cash is left from the wallet he strapped under the wardrobe shelf. Thank God he at least had the good sense to do that.

He goes to the wardrobe and extracts the contents of the wallet. To his dismay he finds there are only two ten-pound notes left. The thugs must have got away with at least a hundred pounds, he reckons, because although he spent a lot that night at The Black Spot and in Brighton yesterday, he should have had quite a bit left. And they got away with his credit cards as well, which means all that he has to use is this twenty quid!

He's still got all these old fivers, of course. Bloody useless things! They seem to be haunting him. He wishes now he'd given them straight back to Nora and been done with it.

Feeling more despondent than ever, Colin puts one of the ten-pound notes back in the wallet under the wardrobe shelf and pockets the other. He'll have to get old Pertwee to change it so he has coins to phone Len. He leaves the bedroom and wearily makes his way down to the foyer.

Mr Pertwee is only too willing to oblige Colin with the change, so he goes to the payphone to ring his old mate.

*****

Len is in the bath when the phone rings. He is not normally given to taking baths at seven in the evening, but he's decided to have his Wednesday bath early, before going to The Mason and Magpie, so he can watch the sport on the telly as long as he likes when he gets back and then just tumble into bed.

He's enjoying his day of freedom. He phoned Cyril as soon as he got back from taking Nora and Marsha to the station, and just before lunch Mr Hepplewhite rang to say his clients weren't interested in the revised price of Dad's house and the sale was off. So he was able to make haste to The Mason and Magpie where he treated himself to a slap-up lunch.

He is actually enjoying his wallow in the bath and his first impulse is to ignore the phone. If it's Colin he can phone him back when he's dry and dressed. But it could be Nora phoning from Greece to say she's arrived safely, so he hauls himself out of the bath, wraps a towel about him and hustles down to answer it.

"That you, Len?"

"Hello, Colin. How's things?"

"Bloody awful, mate. I'm in dead trouble. Elsie's missing."

"*Missing?*"

Colin pours out his tale of woe to the astonished Len. "I'm at me wit's end, mate, I can tell you. I'm worried out of me mind about Elsie, me head is like a football, me body feels as if it's been on the rack, and I've only got twenty bloody quid in me pocket. I just don't know what to do with meself."

Len is overwhelmed by compassion for his friend. "Not much you can do. Just got to stay put, I reckon, and try not to worry."

"Easier said than done, mate. I feel so bloody useless, kicking around in this hole. I tell you one thing- when she does turn up, *if* she does, you won't see my arse for dust out of this place."

"You won't get far on twenty quid," Len points out.

"True. Well, I'll have to borrow a bit somehow. I dunno, I can't believe all this is happening. If only you were here, mate. Being here on me own doing nothing is sheer hell, I can tell you."

"I'll come down," offers Len rashly.

"Oh, no, no, you can't…"

"Yes, I can. I'm on me own too. Nora's gone to Greece."

"Gone to Greece?"

"That's what I phoned to tell you. Georgie's been taken to hospital. Some problem with the baby."

"Go on!"

"So Nora's gone with Georgie's mum to find out just how serious it all is."

"Bloody hell! Sorry to hear that. Never rains but it pours, does it? Well, you can't come back here with that sort of worry on your plate."

"Actually, there's nothing much I can do here. Nora can't possibly be back before Friday, so I could come down – bring you some cash and that – and be back in plenty of time."

"Couldn't put you to all that trouble, mate."

"No trouble. Nothing else to do."

Colin wavers. "Well, if you're quite sure...?"

"Course I am!"

"But supposing Nora rings you from Greece or summat?"

"She won't worry. She'll think I'm at The Mason and Magpie."

"Well, it'd be great to see you, mate. I'm in a right state, I can tell you. Thanks, you're a pal."

"That's what pals are for, ain't it? Help out in times of trouble?"

"Too true, too true. So when you coming?"

"Might as well come tonight."

The payphone starts agitating for more money.

"Don't put more in," shouts Len. "I'll leave right away. See you soon as I can..."

He is all of a quiver when he puts down the phone. He's done it now! What's Nora going to say? Well, she'll understand when she knows Elsie is missing and Colin's all on his own and in a bit of a state.

He looks at the hall clock. Quarter past seven. He could be in Benthaven well before midnight if he gets a move on.

He hurries back up the stairs to get dressed.

Chapter 13

At the Skyfly Hotel in far-flung Singapore Oliver Bloom has also had one hell of a day.

It started with him having to fire both the manager and under-manager for colluding in cooking the books. "If I want the books cooked," he'd yelled at them, "I'll get the chef to do it!"

As a result he had to supervise the everyday running of the hotel himself and also seek replacements for the fired managers. There being no time to advertise the posts in the normal way, Oliver was forced to seek the assistance of a catering agency, who sent him a wild variety of applicants, none of whom proved suitable, either because they didn't know the first thing about managing a hotel or because they lacked the necessary personality. Personality is everything in Oliver's view.

It is the Company Policy to employ British subjects for managerial posts wherever possible, but he was sent only one such applicant, a fiery-looking Welshman. He had plenty of personality but he also had a luxuriant white beard. Oliver considered a black beard would lend a certain dignity to a manager, but a white one could have an undesirable Father Christmas effect. Even so, although the Welshman flatly refused either to shave it off or to dye it, he had no choice but to give him the manager's job. For the post of under-manager he engaged a rather smarmy Arab, whom he chose simply because an Arab and a Welshman seemed unlikely to collude in cooking the books.

Nor did Oliver's problems end there. In the three days he's been there the hotel has played host to a summit meeting of political leaders during which the air conditioning broke down, and a guest has shot himself. As a result the place has been swarming not only with tiresome politicians but also with workmen and police.

So to console himself for having to suffer these tribulations, and despite feeling decidedly under the weather himself – a condition he's been afflicted with now for more than a week but hasn't had the time nor the courage to do anything about – Oliver has just taken the new head receptionist to his bed. Oliver is rather partial to receptionists. They tend to be a bit more intelligent, and a lot more attractive, than chambermaids.

Oliver attributes his enviable ability to seduce women to his own exuberant personality, being aware that his bald head, heavy glasses and Bilko grin are not in themselves enough to do the trick. Not that tonight he is feeling all that exuberant, what with the exhausting day and this persistent feeling in his body that someone has pulled out the plug and his innards are gradually draining out of him.

Akita, the new head receptionist, is of indeterminate race, mostly Asian he suspects, but whatever her origins she's bloody good in bed, much more so than her predecessor, Rosemary, the previous head receptionist, whom he'd found somewhat phlegmatic, and chattered too much.

Even so, he'd been rather fond of Rosemary, and was sorry when he learned she'd been forced to leave suddenly due to ill health.

"Tell me about yourself," says Oliver as he pours the champagne after their first bout of lovemaking.

"Wael..." begins Akita in a slow American drawl, "I was born in Rangoon. Ma momma is Burmese and ma daddy a Texan. I have four sisters and three brothers. I went to school in the States and..."

Oliver leans back on his pillows and lights himself a small cigar while the girl drawls on. He finds most girls are happy to talk about themselves after making love, and he always lends half an ear to what they are saying. Much of it bores the pants off him, or would do, were he wearing any, but considering himself a student of human behaviour, he occasionally picks up something of interest to him. And, of course, these lulls in activity give him a chance to regain his strength ready for the next bout of lovemaking.

"Incidentally," drawls Akita, "have you heard about Rosemary?"

"Rosemary?" Oliver is startled by the question.

"Ma predecessor."

"I know. What about her?"

"She died yesterday."

Oliver, who considers himself unstunnable, is stunned. The girl only left a few weeks back.

"She's *dead*? I hadn't heard! Are you *certain*?"

"Sure, it's all over the hotel."

"Why the hell wasn't I informed?" His business mind clicks on instantly. Since she didn't die in the hotel, at least he won't be concerned with all the arrangements, but he'll have to extend the hotel's sympathies. "I'll send a message of condolence to her family," he reflects aloud. "Better arrange for flowers too." He pauses as a thought strikes him. "I wonder if her body will be flown home. I'll have to find out in the morning."

"She was only thirty-two," says Akita, not interested in his ruminations.

"I know. Poor kid. Nice little thing, so sudden. I knew she was ill, of course, that's why she left, but I'd no idea it was so serious. What was it – cancer?"

"AIDS."

"AIDS!" Oliver sits bolt upright. The cigar drops from his mouth right on to Akita's bare bosom.

"OW!"

Showers of sparks and ash scatter over the bed. The cigar rolls to the floor. Champagne soaks into the sheet.

"Sorry about that," says Oliver, wiping ash from her bosom with his finger once order is restored. "It was the shock, you know. It's not too bad a burn, is it?"

"Nothing another drop of bubbly won't cure." Akita smiles alluringly, and holds out her glass.

Oliver pours the champagne with an unsteady hand. He is thoroughly shaken. He is desperately trying to remember when he last took Rosemary to bed.

"And can I have one of your cigars, Olly?" asks Akita.

*****

It took Len nearly an hour before he was ready to leave for Benthaven, which for him was pretty good going, seeing as he had to dress, repack his bag, take the cash he'd promised to lend

Colin from the secret hoard Nora keeps in the cupboard under the sink, ensure the electricity and gas are turned off, and get the car filled with petrol at the local garage.

But now, just after eight, he is off, feeling exhilarated and amazed by his own daring. He can't recall having had such an adventure before, never undertaking to drive such a long distance without Nora at his side issuing orders and giving directions.

When he reaches Newbury he decides to take the short cut through Basingstoke rather than go all round the M25 and M23. He reckons at this time of night there will be less traffic than on the motorways.

And he is right. He makes good time past Basingstoke to Alton, and even finds his way on to the B road without taking a wrong turning. But by now he is beginning to feel a bit peckish, not to mention thirsty. He's left home without bothering with a meal, so he feels justified in stopping briefly at the first pub that hoves into view.

It turns out to be a village pub, crowded, with all the tables occupied, but he manages to find a stool to sit on, and perches his pint and chicken sandwich on the edge of a table where a number of farmers are sitting arguing avidly over BSE and its effect on the price of beef.

They take no notice of him as he quietly sips his pint and munches his sandwich. He finds himself thinking about Nora, wondering if she has safely arrived in Greece. And about Georgie and the baby, hoping nothing too serious is amiss. If she were to lose her first grandchild, Nora would be in a terrible state. Let's hope it doesn't come to that, he muses.

The repeated click of balls on the pool table in the adjoining bar reminds him about the Snooker Final on Saturday evening in which he and Colin are taking part – supposed to be, that is. At the moment it's looking increasingly unlikely, what with this trouble in Greece, Elsie missing and Colin up the wall with worry. Tomorrow is Thursday. If they are going to have to cancel or postpone the match, then they'll have to let the Sports and Social know first thing in the morning. They'll have to decide tonight what is the best thing to do.

Not finding the pub's atmosphere very congenial, Len

decides not to linger, so finishes his sandwich and drinks up. The sooner he gets to Benthaven now, the better.

By now it is almost dark and it has come on to rain heavily again, lightning flashing on the horizon. He doesn't like lightning, not that he's afraid of it, but hates its suddenness, especially when driving. Tonight though it adds to the drama, stimulates him, makes him feel a man.

But he is no more than ten miles down the B road when a 'ROAD CLOSED' sign looming up in his headlights confronts him. Beside it is a yellow 'DIVERSION' sign with an arrow pointing to the left, down a narrow lane.

That wasn't there the first time they came, he's sure. Well, he's come too far to return to the motorway now, so he turns into the narrow lane and proceeds cautiously as it meanders this way and that between high hedges and overhanging trees. The rain is slashing down now, the lightning more vivid and persistent. It is as if he's in some dramatic Victorian melodrama. He's half expecting some spectre to materialise in the lane before him.

Imagine his shock when it does!

The figure is a ghostly white, waving its arms at him demonically. He slams on the brakes, his heart leaping into his mouth. The apparition moves towards him and opens the car door.

"Oh sir! Please help me! Please help me, sir, for the love of God!"

Len gapes. It is a woman, clad only in a sopping wet nightdress. "W-what's wrong?" he stammers.

"It's me man, sir, he's got the drink in him. He's turned me out of the house."

"Turned you out!"

Before he knows what's happening the woman has climbed into the passenger seat, and is oozing water all over his carefully preserved upholstery.

"I shall have to go back in the house for some clothes, sir," the woman hisses, "but he'm so raving I fear he'll do me mischief. He'm so violent, see, with the drink in him he could even murder me."

"Murder you!"

"Just a little ways along the road, sir. If you would just come with me while I get some clothes. He won't harm me if you are there."

"B-b-b-but…"

"It'll only take a couple of minutes. Oh please, sir, *please* help me!" A cold, wet hand grips Len's thigh. "I can pay you for your time. We'm not poor – we'm farmers."

It's not the money, nor the woman's pitiful condition, nor even the prospect of being a 'knight in shining armour' that prompts Len to agree – it's years of obeying female demands. Besides, what choice has he with the woman already firmly ensconced in his car?

When they reach the farmhouse it is ablaze with lights. The front door stands open.

"I'll wait here," says Len.

"Oh no, sir. You must come in! He won't harm me if he sees you."

It's not just you I'm worried about, he thinks.

They hurry through the driving rain into the house. At the foot of the stairs the woman stops to listen. All is silent.

"He may have passed out, the Lord be praised," she whispers. "You go up first, and I'll follow."

"Me go up there?"

"Oh yes, sir. He'll be in the bedroom, like as not."

Len leads the way up the lino-clad stairs, gingerly stepping over a pair of discarded wellies. On the landing they pause to listen again. Noises and grunts come from behind a closed door.

"Ah, he'm in the bathroom, being sick, I 'spect. You wait here while I go and get dressed. If he comes out, push he back in and shut the door."

The woman disappears into the bedroom.

Len stands. His instinct is to flee for his life while the going is good, but his legs feel rooted to the spot. Growls, grunts and groans continue to come from behind the bathroom door, followed by the flushing of the cistern. Len tries to think of something he could do should the man emerge. Letting down his trousers again as he had done in the Brighton car park doesn't seem an appropriate option on this occasion. If only Colin were here!

His worst fears are soon realised. The bathroom door opens

and a half-naked giant of a man, red of face and hairy of chest, lurches out. He stops in amazement when he sees Len, and passes a massive arm across his eyes in the hope that it will make this apparition disappear. Pink elephants he could have understood.

"Who the bleedin' hell are you?" he roars.

Never let it be said again that Len lacks imagination. He draws himself up to his full height and emulates Colin's authoritative tones. "I'm a police officer," he says.

"Bleedin' fu-fu-fuzz!"

"I must warn you I'm here to protect your wife. If you so much as lay a finger on me – or your wife – I shall arrest you on…um…a serious charge."

The man props himself against the wall, scowling at Len, his mouth working with rage.

"Fu-fu-fuzz off!" he yells, blundering towards Len with a Frankenstein gait, tree-trunk arms raised belligerently.

Len may not be noted for being fleet of foot, but the man is less fleet, and Len manages to dodge him as the man stumbles forward. Len seizes his chance and dashes into the bedroom, where he is just in time to see the woman pulling on her knickers.

"He's coming! He's coming!" he yells. He slams the door and leans against it, shaking with terror.

From the landing comes an almighty thud which sends the floorboards dancing. The woman pauses to listen. All is silent.

"There! He'm passed out now, sir. He'll be no trouble now."

But Len is taking no chances and keeps all his weight against the bedroom door, and his eyes firmly shut.

"If you don't mind, sir," she says when she has finished dressing, "I'll just pop a few extra things into my zip-bag to take with me."

"Hurry up, then." It is still silent on the landing and Len wants to be away while the going is good.

"I was wondering, sir," continues the woman as she tosses various items of apparel into a bag, "being the good Christian gentleman that you are, if you would mind giving me a lift as far as Fendleton, to my mother's place. I wouldn't ask it of you, sir, but for it being such a rough night for walking seven miles."

"Well...all right," says Len ungraciously. "But hurry. I've got to get to Brighton."

"If you'll just let me pass then, sir, I'll just go to the bathroom to answer a call of nature and collect a few toiletries, and then I'll be ready."

Len opens the door a crack and peers out. Sure enough the man is sprawled out on the landing.

"He'll be there till cockcrow now, sir," observes the woman as she steps over him to reach the bathroom.

When they are safely back in the car Len relaxes a little. Once he has disposed of this woman, he can be on his way.

"I'll not go back to him," says the woman, clutching her bag. "Not this time. You don't blame me, do you, sir?"

"No, I don't," says Len with feeling.

"I am an honest Christian woman, and I'm aware of my duties as a wife. As the good Lord could tell you, I've always let him have his way without complaint, if you follow my meaning. And I've endured ten long years of being knocked about and suffering other unmentionable indignities. But now, marriage vows or no marriage vows, I say enough is enough. I'm sure you'd agree, sir?"

"Um," says Len.

The rain, which has eased a little while they were in the house, now comes on again with renewed ferocity. Lightning flashes. Thunder vibrates the car.

Suddenly, there is a loud bang.

Good God, he's shooting at us! panics Len. The car swerves violently, but by some miracle he manages to avoid running into the bank and brings the car to a halt in a field gateway.

"Trouble, sir?" enquires the woman.

Len heaves himself from the car without answering. The night is pitch black, and he has to grope his way around the car to look for the trouble. A vivid flash of lightning soon reveals it.

His front nearside tyre is as flat as a pancake.

"Bloody hell!" cries Len, who reserves strong language for just such occasions. What is he to do now? Never in his whole life has he felt so miserable and helpless.

*****

Gavin, bless his heart, is waiting on the quayside on Thyros to greet his mother and mother-in-law when they arrive – if they ever do. He has been waiting an hour already and is beginning to wonder if anything is amiss, but having experienced the unreliability of Greek sailings himself, he knows it is far more likely that the caique bringing them from Skiathos is late.

Gavin is annoyed that Marsha decided to come to Thyros. He hasn't bargained for her chasing over in a wild panic and dragging his own mum with her. It is complicating the situation for him no end. If it had occurred to him they might come charging over he wouldn't have phoned in the first place. But Gavin is confident he can cope. He has to, for Georgie's sake.

It is knocking on for ten, Greek time, before the caique, which is little more than a clapped-out fishing boat, rounds the headland, and well past ten before it finally docks. But there on the deck, looking befuddled and bedraggled are Marsha and Nora, waiting to disembark.

For Nora the trip has been a nightmare. Once she settled down she quite enjoyed the flight to Athens and even partook of some of the meal the hostess brought her, but the bus trip from Athens to Piraeus, and skimming over the water at an alarming rate in the Flying Dolphin hydrofoil to the island of Skiathos, and particularly this final leg of the journey from Skiathos in the swaying caique, has been an endurance test she would never have survived had the indomitable Marsha not been with her to lead her through it.

"Hello, Mum."

"Gavin!" Nora throws her arms around his narrow waist and hugs him to her like a hot water bottle.

"What about Georgie?" demands Marsha, viewing this display of affection with distaste.

Gavin extricates himself from his mother. "Still the same, I'm afraid."

"The baby hasn't arrived?"

"Not yet."

"But Georgie's all right?"

"Yes. It's just a question of waiting."

"But you said on the phone there were complications."

"As far as I could gather they said there could be problems with the birth, yes."

"What sort of problems?"

"Quite honestly, I don't know. The doctor tried to explain, but his English was very poor."

"Then we'll go straight to the hospital and find out." Marsha is decisive.

"I don't think that's a good idea," says Gavin hastily. "They've promised to let me know if there is any change. Besides, I doubt if they'll allow us at in this time of night."

"We'll see about that!"

"No, it would be a waste of time," persists Gavin. "The doctor is sure to be off duty, and Georgie will no doubt be asleep."

Marsha hesitates. "I suppose these people do know what they're doing?"

"Of course they do. Georgie is quite impressed by them, actually. She's in very capable hands, I assure you. As I said on the phone, there was no need for you to have come all this way."

"If she has to be operated upon it's not going to be by some ham-fisted Greek."

"I doubt very much if it will come to that."

"You sound very unconcerned about it all I must say, Gavin."

"Only because there's absolutely nothing to worry about, even if the baby should be premature. It is not a big problem these days. Come on, I'll take you to your lodgings. It's not far."

Gavin seizes their baggage and marches off with it purposefully, the two ladies trailing after him.

"Don't we need a taxi?" asks Marsha.

"Oh no, it's only a couple of hundred yards along the front here."

Marsha glances doubtfully along the waterfront. Although Thyros is a small remote island, the front is glittering with lights and thronged with people. Music issues from the tavernas, a smell of cooking pervades the warm still air.

"I trust you've found us a reasonable hotel?" she says.

"Well, actually I couldn't get you into a hotel at such short notice – the tour operators make block bookings, that's the trouble. But I've managed to find you a room in a nice little taverna."

"A taverna!"

"It's quite pleasant. The room has a sea view."

Marsha sniffs. "I'm not bothered about the view. It's a bath I need. I feel as if I've been dipped in treacle."

"There isn't a bath, I'm afraid."

"No bath!"

"But there is a shower," Gavin adds hastily. "Few places have baths over here."

"That I can believe! Well, if it's the best you can do, I suppose we shall have to manage."

"We're here." Gavin comes to a halt before a taverna, where people are sitting at tables outside, eating, drinking and talking animatedly. From within comes the twang of strange sounding music, the like of which Nora hasn't heard since the last Eurovision Song Contest.

Gavin hurries his wards through the crowded bar and up dark twisty stairs to their room. It is clean and tidy – but small. A vast double bed occupies most of it.

Marsha glowers at it. "Couldn't you have found us single beds – or are they also in short supply over here?"

"It would appear they are," answers Gavin evenly.

She sweeps her eyes around the rest of the room with distaste and goes to inspect the bathroom. It is little more than an alcove.

"This place is primitive," she comments on her return. "Surely there must be somewhere better than this?"

"It was the best I could find in the time." Gavin smiles broadly at his mother-in-law. He's damned if he's going to apologise for the crummy room. She shouldn't have come belting over, interfering. "Now what about food?" he continues. "Do you want something to eat? They'll still be serving downstairs if you do."

"Eat down there? Certainly not!"

"Or we could go out somewhere if you'd rather."

"Gavin, all I want to do is get to bed. We've been travelling since six this morning."

"What about you, Mum? What about a nice cup of tea?"

There's nothing Nora would like more, that or a nice mug of Horlicks, but she too has had enough for one day.

"Not tonight, dear. I'll just get to bed."

"Then I'll leave you to it," says Gavin. He glances at the bed. "I hope you sleep well."

"So do I," replies Marsha tartly, "but I doubt it. I'd take a sleeping pill but I daren't in case there's a call from the hospital in the night."

"Oh, I don't think that's very likely."

"Well, if there is, I expect you to let us know immediately, not leave it until the morning."

"Of course, but I'm sure it won't be necessary." Gavin sidles his way towards the door. "All being well, then, I'll call for you in the morning at ten and take you straight to the hospital to see Georgie. Don't worry, everything's fine. Sleep well."

When Gavin has left, after he has given his mother a reassuring hug and pecked Marsha on the cheek, Nora flops on the bed in despair.

"Oh dear, oh Lor'!" she wails. "This is terrible!"

"There is something going on I don't understand," says Marsha, with conviction. "I shan't be satisfied until I've seen Georgie." She unzips her case viciously. "But we've no choice but to leave it until the morning, so we might as well get to bed. I'll sleep on the left, if that's all right with you, Nora."

"Wherever you like." She's past caring.

"I *must* have a shower first, though." Marsha goes to the bathroom and looks in with disgust. The shower looks as if it's the one the animals used in the Ark. The washbasin is about the size of a chamber pot, and the lavatory would be more at home in a museum. "Honestly, I've been in some places in my time, but this takes the biscuit!"

She comes back into the bedroom and begins to undress. Nora, feeling embarrassed, busies herself with unpacking her few belongings, but she can't help watching with horrid fascination as Marsha takes off her corset. Released from its straightjacket, her figure billows.

Marsha wobbles her way into the bathroom and shuts the door. Nora sighs, relieved to be on her own for a bit.

She decides to take advantage of Marsha's absence to

undress. She hasn't undressed in front of anyone except Len since she was a child. But she hasn't got far before Marsha re-emerges with a face like thunder.

"I can't see how one turns that damned thing on," she growls. "See if you can do it, Nora."

Together they go into the bathroom. Nora stands in the shower and looks for a knob or something to turn, but can't find one. Nothing they do will produce a drip of water.

"I dunno how it works," wails Nora. "We haven't got a shower at home."

"I wonder..." begins Marsha, and marches back into the bedroom to inspect a notice hanging on the back of the bedroom door. "Ah, I thought so! They charge extra for showers. One has to go down and pay first, and then they come up and switch it on! Well, I'm not doing that!"

Shouldn't think so, dressed as you are, thinks Nora.

"This is altogether too much!" rants Marsha. "I'm sure Gavin could have done better for us if he'd tried." She stumps back into the bathroom and slams the door.

Nora shrivels up to nothing. It's not Gavin's fault, she tells herself. I'm sure he did his best. Her misery is complete. For two drachmas she'd cry her eyes out, if only she could.

Before long Marsha comes out of the bathroom, now clad in yellow lacy nightie, and heaves her bulk on to the bed without a word.

Nora's turn to use the bathroom; she also makes do with a lick and a promise, mostly promise. When she returns, Marsha is humped on the bed, so without Len to do it for her, Nora goes to the window to pull back the curtains and open the window.

"Don't open it, if you don't mind," snaps Marsha. "The air gets very cold at night in these places. And leave the curtains closed. The lights are glaring straight into my eyes."

If she hadn't been so deadbeat Nora would have rebelled at that. As it is she buttons her lips and flops into bed beside the mountain range formed by Marsha's body.

The room is stifling. From downstairs, twanging music and raucous singing permeate the floorboards. Outside people gabble in strange tongues. Beside her Marsha keeps shifting erratically.

Nora's spirits are at zero. She imagines Len at home, safely tucked up in their bed. Oh, if only she were there, warming her feet on his!

*****

Except that Len isn't tucked up in bed. He is attempting to change the front nearside wheel of his Escort in a dark Hampshire lane, with the rain pouring down and a farmer's wife shining a fast failing torch anywhere but at the source of the trouble.

He's never changed a wheel before, but he reckons it to be within his ability. So far he's managed to jack up the car after a couple of attempts, and is now faced with removing the hubcap, which refuses to budge as much as he tugs at it. He fancies he's seen mechanics knock them off with a spanner, and by adopting this method succeeds in removing it and sending it clattering off down the lane.

The woman abandons her post and chases after it.

"It is truly a blessing, sir," she gasps when she returns with the hubcap, "that you are a gentleman so useful with his hands."

"Um," says Len.

Next he has to unscrew the four nuts holding the wheel in place. Although not over-endowed with muscle power he manages to remove three of them fairly easily, but the fourth remains obstinate.

"I am praying for your success, sir," says the woman, as Len struggles and strains. "The Lord be with you."

Suddenly the nut relents and Len sinks to his knees in the mud. But so far so good. The worst is over. All he has to do now is to remove the wheel and fit the spare.

The torch is now reduced to a glimmer.

"Give it a shake," he tells the woman.

With the return of a little light Len sets about removing the wheel. Should be easy enough, he thinks, but to his surprise it won't budge. Now what's the matter?

"God give you strength, sir!" cries the woman.

Len grips the wheel with both hands, shakes and pulls.

The wheel comes away. So does the jack. Len topples on his back. The car sinks on its axle. The torch goes out.

"Sod it!" he cries with commendable restraint.

When he has recovered a bit Len tries lifting the car in the hope the woman can replace the jack, but his muscle power won't run to that.

"I am a farmer's wife, sir, and as such I am blessed with more strength than most of my sex. Allow me to try."

He lets her, but she can't raise it either.

Len looks round in despair; he'll have to get help.

"Is there a phone near here?" he asks.

"Ah no, sir. It's all farmland hereabouts. There is a hotel a little way up the lane."

"How far?"

"Half mile or so."

"Well, I'll have to walk there and phone for help. I won't be longer than I can help. You stay in the car."

"Oh, I couldn't stay here by myself! These are evil times, sir. I wouldn't feel safe. There could be rapists lurking."

With a sigh Len agrees to her coming, and they set off, the woman clutching her bag with one hand and clinging to his arm with the other. To his surprise he finds himself limping. His ankle is hurting like hell. He must have wrenched it when he fell over.

They haven't gone far before the headlights of an approaching car illuminate the lane. Len's hopes rise. He sticks his thumb out like a hobo, but the car roars by, showering them with mud and rain.

"We live in uncharitable times, sir," observes the woman. "There are no Good Samaritans any more, saving your good self. But fear not, they will answer to the Lord."

They trudge on. The rain slashes down.

"You appear to be limping, sir," says the woman presently. "You have done yourself a mischief."

"Um," says Len. "Is it much further?"

"We shall come upon it any minute, I am sure."

But another twenty minutes pass before the woman halts before a narrow eerie-looking lane.

"Here we are, sir. This is it."

"What – down *there*?"

"It's a country hotel, the Fendleton Manor Country Hotel.

Open to non-residents."

Great relief for Len. "Thank you. I should be able to get help there. But it will take a while, no doubt, so I'm afraid you'd better walk to your mother's after all."

"Oh, I couldn't leave you in this plight, sir! Of course I couldn't, seeing as how it was in doing your Christian duty helping me that this misfortune befell you."

"Don't worry about me, I'll be…"

"No, I insist. I shall not rest until I see you safely back on the road. Come along, sir, this way."

Len allows himself to be led like a child down the muddy track lined with dripping rhododendron bushes. He is too weary now to protest. He just wants to get out of the incessant rain and off his ankle, which is becoming more and more painful with every step.

"It'll not be far now, sir. Lean on me and take the weight off your poor ankle."

"I can manage, thank you."

"My name is Alice Potts, sir," says the woman presently. "May I enquire as to yours?"

"Scally," grunts Len. "Len Scally."

"Oh, a very dignified name, as well befits you, sir."

The lane winds on and on, but at last the welcoming lights of the hotel come into view.

"Here we are at last, Mr Scally, the Lord be praised."

The entrance hall is baronial, but deserted. Len limps to the reception desk and tinks the bell.

The night porter appears, and eyes the rain-sodden couple suspiciously, uncertain whether to be obsequious or churlish. "Can I help you?"

"My car has broken down just up the road, I was wondering if I could…"

"Have a room for the night?" finishes the night porter. "Certainly, sir."

"No!" cries Len hastily. "I just want to phone a garage to get them to come out to it."

"Payphone over there," says the porter less civilly. "But you'll not get a garage to come out this time of night. You can try if you like."

"Surely there's some sort of all-night service!"

The porter tweaks his walrus moustache. "Not hereabouts, sir. Are you a member of the AA or RAC?"

"'Fraid not," says Len forlornly.

"Ah well, sir, in that case you're in dead trouble. They *might*, of course, still come out, but it would cost you."

Len's hand involuntarily flies to his wallet.

"Might I make a suggestion, sir?" continues the porter, sensing the long-term possibility of a tip.

"What's that?"

"If I may say so, you both look all in. I know of an excellent garage in the village, which will be happy to attend to your car first thing in the morning at a very reasonable cost. Might I suggest you stay here the night and in the morning, with your permission, I'll contact the garage just before I go off duty. Then by the time you have partaken of a leisurely breakfast your car will be ready for you to continue your journey."

"But I've got to get to Brighton *tonight*!"

"It would be unwise for you to drive further tonight, Mr Scally," cuts in the woman quickly. "Not with your agonising ankle. You need to rest it, sir."

"Quite right," confirms the night porter. "And as it happens one of our best rooms is vacant due to a cancellation by an old couple who'd booked it but refused to sleep in it when they discovered it was Room Thirteen. You're not superstitious are you, sir?"

"We'll take it," says Alice Potts instantly. "Rest assured you have nothing to fear from me, Mr Scally, I am a God-fearing woman. And I shall pay my share, as the Good Lord is my witness."

Len, more accustomed to obeying than getting his own way, gives in. He's exhausted. He can't face having to hobble all the way back to the car and hang about for the AA or RAC. Even a night with Alice seems less daunting.

The night porter hands Len the key. "Room Thirteen, then. First floor. Turn right when you leave the lift. Would you like some refreshments sent up, sir – tea, coffee, sandwiches?"

"Um, yes, I suppose so." Might as well go the whole hog, thinks Len.

"You need something stronger than that, sir," cuts in the woman. "Something to keep out the cold after your long wet walk, and to soothe your poor ankle."

"I'm afraid the bar is closed, madam, but leave it with me, I'll see what I can do." The porter winks broadly.

Clutching her bag, the woman leads Len to the lift.

"Very helpful, wasn't he, Mr Scally sir?" she says as the lift grinds slowly upwards. "Very helpful indeed. No doubt he'll be expecting a handsome tip when we leave."

"No doubt," groans Len.

The room is large but rather gloomy. The sight of the huge four-poster bed with its looping drapes appalls Len. Otherwise the room seems comfortable and inviting enough.

"I hope you don't mind my sharing the room with you, Mr Scally," says Alice Potts as she removes her wet coat, "but I felt I couldn't face the walk all the way to Fendleton on my own in such inclement weather. I'm sure such a sympathetic gentleman as yourself appreciates that."

"Um."

"As I have already said, I am happy to share the cost of the room with you, seeing as how you so bravely came to my rescue in my hour of need."

"Very kind," mutters Len as he divests himself of his rain-soaked coat.

"I am very grateful to you, Mr Scally, so it's only fair we should go Dutch."

Len slumps with relief into one of the comfortable chairs, only too thankful to think that at least his car problem is taken off his hands. He's even past caring all that much about this damned woman – and the expense.

"I know you to be an honourable gentleman," she goes on, "so I have no need to remind you that I'm a respectable married woman, and a devout Christian, and as such not given to adulterous behaviour."

"Don't worry," grunts Len. "I can sleep perfectly well in this chair."

"Oh, there's no need for that, sir. On no! You're done in. You need your rest. And you must have your ankle up. I am happy to share that handsome bed with you if you are prepared to keep yourself to yourself, if you gather my meaning?"

Len suddenly realises. "But my pyjamas and that are still in the car!"

"Not to worry, Mr Scally. I'm sure you must be wearing underwear, and spotless it is, I have no doubt. We can place a pillow between us so as to avoid any unintentional bodily contact in our sleep."

"Um," says Len doubtfully.

"And now," continues the woman, opening her zip-bag and extracting her nightdress and toiletries, "I should be obliged if you would refrain from looking in my direction while I undress and prepare to take a bath."

Len nods, but thinks it pretty pointless since he's already seen her virtually naked at the farmhouse and isn't likely to be seduced by her jumbo-sized body, anyway.

"Mr Scally, perhaps you would kindly close your eyes while I make my way to the bathroom."

He can scarcely comply before she sweeps past him and he watches her bare back disappear into the bathroom. When she has shut the door he slumps in despair. He can't believe he's landed himself in this predicament. He shouldn't have agreed to the woman staying the night, that was his mistake, but he hadn't the heart to send her out into that terrible night on her own. Well, feeling dog-tired and being such a heavy sleeper, he'll probably know little about it. Always supposing his ankle doesn't keep him awake, that is.

He rolls up his sodden mud-stained trouser leg and takes off his shoe and sock to examine his ankle. It is swollen and painful to touch. Supposing it's no better in the morning and he can't drive? Well, sufficient unto the day...

There is a tap on the door.

With one shoe on and one shoe off Len hobbles to the door to answer it. It is the night porter, carrying a tray containing food covered by a napkin and a bottle of Johnnie Walker with two glasses.

"Here we are, sir. It's the best I could do."

"Thanks."

"That'll be thirty-five pounds in all, sir." The porter tweaks his moustache. "I'm afraid I had to slip the barman a few quid to supply the bottle, if you follow my meaning?"

Len does, all too well, and hands over four tenners from Nora's emergency supply intended for Colin.

"Oh! Thank you very much, sir!" beams the porter, pocketing the lot. "Now if you will just let me have the keys, I'll deal with the matter of your car first thing in the morning."

Len hands over the keys.

"Thank you, sir. Good night, sir. I hope you sleep well – and your good lady."

Len takes the tray to the table beside his chair and pours himself a stiff Johnnie Walker. Well, the situation could be worse, he consoles himself, as the drink begins to get to the root of the problem. The car is being taken care of for him, the woman, thank God, is clearly not expecting him to prove his virility, or rather his lack of it, and hopefully by the morning his ankle will be rested enough for him to be able to drive on to Brighton.

The bathroom door opens and Alice Potts emerges, looking fresh and demure in her clean nightdress, which, to his horror, Len sees is a shortie.

"I am feeling more human now," she declares. "Water is one of God's greatest blessings, Mr Scally. It has the power to refresh not only the body but also the soul. Cleanliness is next to Godliness, as my dear mother is fond of saying." She clambers into the four-poster with no trace of embarrassment. "What a noble bed, Mr Scally! We should be afforded a reposeful night in this, God willing. Now is that the refreshments I spy over there?"

"Um," says Len. "What would you like?"

"I do not normally indulge in the demon drink – you have seen for yourself the evil it has wrought on my man – but in view of our unhappy experience I am sure the good Lord would approve of my partaking of a little to stave off the possible onset of a chill."

"Would you like water with it? He didn't bring any soda I'm afraid."

"Just as it is, thank you. And one of those sandwiches would be welcome."

Now the whisky is doing its job Len is beginning to feel

more charitable towards her and hobbles over to the bed with the sandwich and the drink. It's almost like being with Nora.

"Goodness, Mr Scally, your trousers are soaking wet! I should get them off if I were you."

"I haven't got me pyjamas!" protests Len.

"And your shirt too! You're soaked to the skin! I should get it all off – you don't want to catch your death."

"But..."

"There's no need to feel embarrassed in front of me, Mr Scally. There are some large, dry, warm towels in the bathroom. I suggest you wrap yourself in those and make yourself cosy."

"Perhaps you're right," mumbles Len.

He knocks back the remainder of his whisky and limps into the bathroom to undress, emerging presently swathed in two large bath towels and looking like Nero.

He is startled to find Alice Potts out of bed and pouring herself another whisky. "A nightcap, Mr Scally," she explains, "and one for you, to ensure we have a good night's rest. We are, after all, having to sleep under somewhat unfamiliar conditions."

Amen to that, thinks Len.

Alice returns to the bed with her drink and another sandwich. Len sinks back in his chair and takes a sandwich. Chicken! The second he's had this evening.

"You no doubt noticed the brevity of my night attire," says Alice. "I apologise for it, but as you know I had to make a hasty selection of clothing to take when we left, and this happened to be the first nightie to hand."

Len carefully adjusts the towel over his plump white knees, but says nothing.

"Normally I would not buy such a nightdress," she continues, "but I bought it for my honeymoon night in Bognor Regis. I might as well have worn a sack for all he noticed. Blotto, he was, Mr Scally, on our wedding night. In fact, if you will pardon me for mentioning such an intimate matter, it was a week before our marriage was consummated. Naturally, as a good Christian woman, I was unsullied at the time, so his brutality came as a terrible shock. With the drink in him, he is no more than an animal. I notice you wear a wedding ring, Mr Scally."

"Um," says Len, his mouth full of chicken.

"And happily married, I have no doubt. I wish I could say the same. As God is my witness, I have tried to do my duty by him, but tonight I said, 'Enough is enough.' I expect you have noticed the bruises on my thigh..." She sticks her leg out of the bed to show him. "There is a limit to what one should endure, don't you agree, Mr Scally?"

Len nods vaguely. He is beginning to feel drowsy.

"You have a very noble head, Mr Scally, do you know that? Very patrician. Appropriate for this majestic bed..."

As her voice drones on Len drifts off. From somewhere in the upper atmosphere, or so it seems, he fancies he can hear singing; but it isn't a heavenly choir, it's Alice Potts, singing a hymn in a loud, clear voice.

"That was 'Abide With Me'. Number four in the New Mission Praise," she tells him when she has finished. "Do you sing, Mr Scally?"

He makes a noise roughly indicating the negative.

"Singing is very therapeutic. It expands the chest. I sing in the church choir on Sundays, except when it's Early Communion. And sometimes I sing at funerals. Do you know 'The Old Rugged Cross', Mr Scally?"

Alice Potts starts singing again. As he again hovers on the brink of slumber Len begins to feel some sympathy for the woman's violent husband, and reckons he's well rid of her. He is also vaguely aware of her refilling her glass, and saying, "Do you want topping up, Mr Scally?"

Then he drops into blessed oblivion, but not for long.

"Mr Scally! Mr Scally, sir!"

Len wakes with a start. "What's the matter? What's up?"

"Are you proposing to take a bath, sir, or perhaps a shower, before retiring?"

"Um..no. I had one before I left home." Two baths within a few hours is altogether too much for Len.

"Then I'll just visit the toilet once more before settling down for the night. Perhaps while I am away you would care to jump into bed and save yourself the embarrassment of having to do so in my presence."

But as she gets out of bed her legs sag under her. She

giggles girlishly.

"Oooh, sir, I do believe the drink has got to me! As I have already mentioned, I am not accustomed to partaking of the demon drink. I do so strictly for medical purposes only, you understand."

When Alice Potts, far less purposefully than on the previous occasion, has found her way to the bathroom and shut the door, Len rouses himself. He is tempted to stay in the chair, but for the sake of his ankle he decides he *will* lie on the bed, but *on* it, not *in* it.

He gathers his towels closely about him, limps to the bed and carefully sandwiches himself between the bedspread and the blanket. He hears the cistern flush in the bathroom. I'll pretend to be already asleep, he thinks. With any luck she'll let me be.

Alice Potts emerges from the bathroom singing, 'Now the Day is Over'. "I'm glad you've taken my advice," she says, seeing Len. "You have nothing to fear from me, I assure you. I am educated in the word of the Lord, Mr Scally, and fear His Retribution."

Len pretends to snore, being careful not to overdo it.

"And speaking of the good Lord," she continues, feeling her way to her side of the bed, "before settling down to rest I will just give a few words of thanks to Him for delivering me into your capable hands. But for His Divine Providence, sir, it may well have been a rapist who came along instead of your good self."

She drops to her knees beside the bed and clasps her hands in fervent prayer.

"Oh Lord, thank you for sending Mr Scally to me in my hour of need, for preserving me from the brutalities of my husband, for sparing me from the lusts of rapists, from the demon drink and from all the evil and sin sent by the Devil to tempt a simple God-fearing woman. Amen."

She's raving mad, thinks Len, still simulating gentle snores. He couldn't have blamed her husband if he'd murdered her, not just knocked her about.

Suddenly he feels his leg being shaken.

"Mr Scally! Mr Scally, sir! Wake up, Mr Scally!"

She continues to shake his leg agitatedly.

Len feigns waking up. "Whassa matter?"

"The demon drink has gone to my legs. I am quite unable to rise from my prayers!"

He pretends to fall asleep again, but the agitation persists.

"Mr Scally! You must come to my rescue yet again, or I shall perish with cold in this scanty attire!"

Obedient to the last, Len rolls off the bed to go to her assistance, clutching his towel closely about him.

"If you could just lift me from under the armpits, sir."

He endeavours to do as instructed, but her weight is too much for him in his present condition. He needs a hoist to get her into this high four-poster.

"Heave, sir!"

Len heaves, half raising her. Alice Potts grabs at the bedclothes but subsides again in a fit of giggles.

"Oh, Mr Scally, this is no use! Perhaps if you were to give me a push – from under the buttocks, if you have no objection?"

Len doesn't care where he pushes so long as he can get the bloody woman on to the bed. He places his hands under her ample buttocks, and pushes upwards.

"That's the way, sir! Push!"

Alice Potts scrabbles with the bedclothes to haul herself up, Len pushing valiantly from behind. But his hands slip on the nightie, which he has purposely tried to keep over her posterior, and she flops on to the floor on her back, Len landing on top of her and losing his makeshift toga in the process.

"Oh, Mr Scally! You naughty, naughty man!"

Whether it is due to exhaustion, the whisky, a deep-seated desire to forget, or a combination of all three, Len is destined never to remember what happened next.

Chapter 14

And so Wednesday ends with Nora and Marsha in bed together in a stuffy room in Thyros, Len in bed with a farmer's wife in deepest Hampshire, Elsie heavily sedated in a Brighton hospital, and Colin pacing the bedroom floorboards of Room Six at the Ocean View in Benthaven.

The first to surface as the sun comes up on Thursday is Elsie. It is daylight but the ward is quiet. Patients snore and splutter, and there is neither a nurse nor a doctor in sight.

Elsie has slept most of the time since her bicycling accident on Tuesday night. She feels decidedly peculiar as her brain begins to get a purchase on consciousness. She's not at all sure where she is nor what she is doing there, but still has the feeling that there is something vitally important she has to do, even though she hasn't the remotest idea what it is.

But there is something even more immediate she *does* know she must do, and that is go to the toilet. She clambers out of bed and wanders dazedly down the ward.

"Hey! Where you going, luv?" A nurse comes running after her.

"I'm looking for the lav," says Elsie.

"In there." The nurse puts a restraining hand on her arm. "Are you supposed to be up?"

"Dunno. Why not?"

The nurse looks at her suspiciously. "What's your name, dear?"

"Elsie."

"Elsie who?"

"Elsie..." She screws up her face in an effort to remember. "...Brannigan."

"Elsie Brannigan?" The nurse frowns. "Don't think we've got an Elsie Brannigan on the register. What you in for, luv?"

"Dunno." Elsie wriggles and crosses her legs like a child. "Look, I wanna go bad."

"Well, you might as well now you're up. But don't be too long, you'll get cold. Haven't you a dressing gown?"

"Dunno," Elsie says again, and goes into the toilet and slams the door.

When she comes out the nurse is waiting for her, holding a dressing gown. "You'd better put this on. Are you the patient suffering from amnesia?"

"Amnesia?"

"Loss of memory, dear."

"Can't remember."

The nurse grins. "That figures. We've got you down as Jane Doe. You say your name is Elsie Brannigan?"

"Think so."

"Aren't you sure?"

"Look," cries Elsie suddenly. "I've got to get out of here! There's something urgent I've got to do."

"Oh? What's that?"

"I...can't remember! But it's important. I've got to get home!"

"You remember where you live now, then?"

"Liverpool."

"Liverpool! You *are* a long way from home."

"Why? Where am I then?"

"In hospital."

"I know that," growls Elsie, "but *where's* the bloody hospital?"

"Sssh! You'll wake the other patients! Come into the office. We'll put all this down before you forget again."

The nurse leads Elsie to the office like a geriatric and sits her down. "Like some coffee?"

"Just tell me where I am," demands Elsie.

The nurse pours the coffee just the same. "You're in Brighton."

"Brighton?" Elsie cudgels her brains. She's heard of it dimly – somewhere the other side of Melbourne, she thinks, but one hell of a way from Sydney. "What am I doing here?" she asks blankly.

"We're hoping you can tell us that." The nurse hands her the coffee.

"I mean, why am I in hospital? Did I fall down a bloody manhole, or what?"

"You ran into a traffic signal on a bike and knocked yourself out. Hence the amnesia."

"What, a motorbike?" She has some vague recollection of having some kind of association with motorbikes.

"No, dear, a push-bike."

Elsie is incredulous. "But I haven't got a push-bike!"

"It wasn't yours. It seems you stole it from a newspaper boy."

Elsie gapes. "Don't be daft! I don't go round pinching bloody bikes! You've got your knickers in a twist. You want to be more careful."

The nurse looks alarmed and consults her register. "No, it must be you. You're the only amnesia case at the moment. Look, let's get down what you *do* remember. What did you say you name was?"

"I told you – Elsie Brannigan."

"You're sure?"

"Course. Look in me handbag if you don't believe me."

"That's the problem. You didn't have a handbag when you were brought in."

"No handbag! Course I got a handbag!"

"Well, the police say no handbag or other means of identification was found at the scene of the accident – it says so here."

"Then it must have been pinched."

"Possible, I suppose. Drink your coffee, luv, and let's get down what details you do remember. Where did you say you come from?"

"I told you – Liverpool! You talk about *my* memory!"

"Do you remember the address?"

Elsie screws up her eyes. "Ahm...421 Rockfall Way West, yes that's it."

"Postcode?"

"Dunno."

"Never mind. Remember your husband's name?"

"Cliff."

"Cliff Brannigan?"

"Course!"

"Phone number?"

"Can't remember."

"No problem. We'll get the Liverpool police to call round and tell your husband what has happened."

Elsie becomes restive again. "That's no bloody good. I've got to get there meself – it's urgent!"

"But *what* is?"

"I dunno. But I'm telling you I've just got to get there. It's an emergency!"

The nurse gets to her feet. "You're in no fit state to go anywhere, dear, except back to bed, and that's where you're going now. When the day staff come on I'll ask them to have the doctor see you as soon as possible."

In the normal way Elsie would never have allowed herself to be led back to bed like a horse to a stable, but she's still feeling very woosey and not sorry to lie down again. In moments she is asleep.

*****

Colin, after having paced the bedroom at the Ocean View well into the wee small hours, finally flopped on to the bed fully clothed and, spread-eagled like a badly drawn X on a ballot paper, slept heavily until awakened at seven thirty by a gentle tap on the bedroom door.

He starts up. "That you, Elsie?"

"No, it's Daphne," comes the answer.

Daphne! "Come on in, it's unlocked."

Daphne enters carrying an early morning cup of tea. She is on breakfast duty this morning and looks sombre in her black working outfit. "Och, y'poor wee face!" she cries when she sees his plasters. "M'father told me y'ran into those thugs again."

"Took me by surprise this time. Didn't stand a chance."

"And y'wife missing too! Has she nae turned up?"

"No, she bloody hasn't." Colin hauls himself up and sits on the edge of the bed, running his fingers through his hair in despair. "I just don't understand it," he keeps repeating. "I can't think what could have happened to her."

Daphne stands, cup in hand, looking down at him with compassion. "Och, I'm so sorry! Is there nae I can do?"

"Nothing no one can do. Just got to sit it out."

"Drink y'tea," she advises, offering the cup.

"Bugger the tea!"

"Och, come on! Have a wee drop." She presses the cup into his hands and sits beside him on the bed. "Tell me all aboot it."

Colin pours out his tale of woe for Daphne. This morning her gorgeous body seems to have lost its magnetic pull. It could be that of a tailor's dummy. But even talking to a tailor's dummy does seem to calm him a bit. "I reckon the best thing I can do this morning is go back to Hambledon's," he says. "Try to find out what happened to her after I left. Follow it up from there."

"Aye, that seems sensible. But why do y'nae ring the police first? They may have some news."

"I doubt it." He sips the tea thoughtfully. "But I suppose it's worth a try."

"Y'better have a wash and shave first," she advises. "Y'look like a wounded hedgehog."

He fingers his patched chin and grins.

"And then go and have y'breakfast."

"Oh, I can't be bothered with…"

"You *must*." Daphne studies him with concern. "Y'must eat, y'ken."

He looks at her and smiles sadly. "Suppose so."

She takes his cup and gets to her feet. "Breakfast in half an hour," she says firmly as she leaves the room. "Be there!"

Colin has to force himself to get on. When he eventually makes it to the bathroom he removes the patches from his face and is relieved to find his grazes have almost healed. But the bruises look horrible and he runs the shaver over them very gingerly. It could have been much worse he consoles himself. The loss of his wallet is the bigger problem. Thank God Len is on his way with some cash.

Suddenly he remembers Len said he was hoping to arrive last night, and wonders if he's in bed and asleep in the next room. The thought brightens him, and he goes and knocks on the door of Room Seven.

No answer. Poor old sod's probably dog-tired after his

journey, he thinks with a wry grin. Won't disturb him now.

So he goes downstairs to phone the police. He's feeling a bit more human and in control of himself after his shave and shower and change of clothes.

No, the police inform him, they have nothing to report about his missing wife. There have been no more accidents reported during the night, nor have there been any further muggings, rapes or murders.

"What are you going to do about it?" demands Colin.

"We are circulating her description, sir," the gruff voice at the other end tells him. "The boys are keeping out a sharp eye. We'll inform you of any possible sightings. Not to worry, sir. Early days yet."

Just about what he thought they would say.

While he's by the phone he decides to ring home. Just as well to let Boris know about Elsie. Not that Boris is likely to be interested or concerned.

"'Ullo," comes Boris's sepulchral tones over the line.

"Boris?"

"Yer?"

"It's y'dad."

"Yer."

"Listen, Elsie isn't with you by any chance, is she?"

"Nah. Ain't she with you?"

"She's gone missing."

"Go on!" Even Boris is surprised.

"Completely vanished! I'm worried sick." Colin gives him a rough picture of what happened. "Look," he goes on, "today's not one of your working days, is it?"

"Nah."

"Well, don't go out. Don't go buggering off on that bike of yours. And if she should turn up or phone you call me straight back, got that?"

"Yer."

"Everything all right with you?"

"Yer."

"Good. I'll let you know of any developments, so stay put."

Colin is thankful to find the dining room empty when he goes in. He helps himself to a bowl of cereal and sits down at their usual table. It feels weird, no Elsie to nag him, no Nora planning everything, no Len to joke with. He's got to carry the burden of Elsie's disappearance entirely on his own. Thank God Len is here, or at least on his way. It'll help to have someone to share it with.

Daphne comes in to take his order. "Any news?" she asks immediately.

"No..." He growls out the word.

"At least it's not bad news. Try not to worry. Ready if I bring y'breakfast?"

"Oh, these cornflakes are enough."

"Y'must *eat*. I'm bringing y'the works. And black coffee."

"But I've got to get the bus to Brighton."

She looks at her watch. "You've missed the first. The next is ten, so you've plenty of time." She marches out before he can protest further.

He watches her go. She's trying to mother me, he thinks, trying to make up for making a monkey of me the other night.

Miss Dibble comes into the dining room looking prim, but she does manage to twitch him a frosty greeting. Suddenly he realises he hasn't seen Billy Greenhorn lately, not since that night at The Black Spot, in fact. But then, he hasn't been around much himself to see him. A sudden horrifying thought thuds into his head. Could Elsie have gone off with Billy Greenhorn? No, surely not! Don't be daft! Elsie was with him at Hambledon's when she disappeared.

Even so, he'll ask Daphne when she returns with his breakfast if she's seen Billy around. But when she does return, Daphne gets in first with a bright idea of her own.

"I've been thinking," she says. "I'm taking the van into Brighton to get provisions when the breakfasts are finished. Would y'nae like to come with me? Save you waiting aboot for buses."

"That would be great. Sure you don't mind?"

"Of course I dinnae. Enjoy y'breakfast."

She smiles at him and turns back to the kitchen. Again Colin's eyes follow her. Her desire to help does seem to be genuine. She's not really a bad kid, he thinks.

Then she turns back. "Och, and one further thing. Will y'nae bring an item of y'wife's clothing when we go?"

"Whatever for?"

"Boss always comes with me. M'father thinks he might be able to pick up her scent. Personally I have m'doots, but it might be worth a try."

*****

The sun smiles benignly on England this Thursday morning, but over the Greek island of Thyros it is already glowering harshly.

As yet, in the Taverna Efstathiou, Nora and Marsha are both unaware of the growing heat. They are still heavily asleep, both having failed to drop off until the early hours when the room had sufficiently cooled. So it takes a pretty sharp rat-tat-tat on the door to rouse them.

At least, it arouses Nora, who thinks it is a machine-gun. She was in the thralls of a nightmare in which she was pinned down by a dead body in a steamy swamp after having been shot at by a horde of guerrilla fighters.

She wakes up drenched in sweat. Apart from it being Marsha's arm clamped across her bosom and not a dead body, she might well be in the jungle.

The rat-tat-tat is repeated.

"Who is it?" she croaks.

"It's me, Mum – Gavin."

"Wait a minute!"

Marsha is only just beginning to come round, making a faint moaning sound, so Nora heaves Marsha's arm to one side, throws her coat over her nightdress and totters to the door.

"It's come, Mum!"

"What's come?" She's not out of the jungle yet.

"The baby! A bonny baby boy!"

"Well fancy!"

"You're a grandma!"

Overcome, Nora hugs her son in ecstasy, the clammy heat forgotten. "Oh, congratulations, luv! Many, many, many congratulations! And everything's all right?"

"Perfect. No problems at all."

"You hear that, Marsha? It's a boy!"

But Marsha is still out, sprawled face down and moaning like a boxer on the deck. Gavin shakes her gently by the shoulder, and Nora takes the opportunity to throw open the shutters and let in some fresh air. Normally she would have exclaimed at the magnificent sea view, but today it passes her by.

Once she is fully awake and has roundly berated Gavin for not letting them know when the call came, Marsha is all beams and delight. "I am *so* relieved there were no complications," she booms. "Being premature is worrying enough as it is without other troubles. What does the little mite weigh, may I ask?"

"Er...three and a half kilos."

Marsha looks confounded. "What's that in English?"

Gavin produces his Personal Organiser from his pocket and makes a rapid conversion. "Roughly seven and a half pounds."

"Seven and a half pounds! A premature baby? Never!"

Gavin starts guiltily. "Well, perhaps I've got it wrong," he says hastily.

"I should think you have! Is he in an incubator?"

"Er...no."

"Then surely he should be, if he's so premature?"

"Well, you see—"

"This proves what I've said all along. These people are simply not competent. We must get to this so-called hospital without delay and find out what's going on."

"I assure you everything is—"

"Go and wait downstairs, Gavin, while we get ready."

"But what about breakfast?" he protests. "There's no great hurry. Everything's fine."

Having missed dinner last night Marsha relents. "Very well, but we must be quick about it."

But 'quick' is a word not known to these Greek waiters, either in English or their native tongue, and breakfast proves a drawn-out affair. But it's not so much because of the waiters or the breakfast, which only consists of rolls, jam and coffee, that it lasts so long. It is because of the barrage of questions Gavin has to counter about the colour of the baby's eyes and hair and other personal details, which he valiantly succeeds in doing – until the million-dollar question from Nora.

"What are you going to call him?" she asks.

"Georgie wants to call him Kevin," says Gavin, "but I think it sounds too much like Gavin. I'd rather give him a strong name like Garth."

"Garth!" Marsha splutters over her coffee. "Isn't that rather a common name, dear? Garth Scally sounds ridiculous. It should be a longer name – like Sebastian. Sebastian Scally sounds more impressive, don't you think?"

"I'd rather it was something simpler – like Peter," says Nora, "or just John."

"Jonathan is better than John. I think Jonathan Scally sounds quite well, or Simon, or even Archibald..."

"Oh, not *Archibald*!" retaliates Nora. "A nice easy name is best, like James or Frank, or…"

"It should be a saint's name, of course," continues Marsha, not listening. "I rather like the sound of Jonathon Scally, but I'm not sure if there's a St Jonathon."

"There's a St John."

"I know that, Nora. But Jonathon is just that little bit more…"

"I'll just go and phone for a cab while you finish your breakfast," says Gavin, cutting into this debate at the first opportunity. "Then we can go straight off."

There is no argument about that. The cab arrives, the ladies are ushered into it and Gavin instructs the driver to drive them to the hospital.

"Is it far?" asks Nora as the cab heads out of town and up into the olive tree-strewn hills behind it.

"Oh, no, about a mile. It's quite pleasant, actually. I think you'll like it. Not IKA, of course."

"Not *what*?" demands Marsha.

"IKA – the Greek version of the National Health. It's not quite so efficient as ours, so we decided to go private."

"Very sensible." At least Marsha approves of that.

The hospital turns out to be a smooth white building perched on the hillside amid the olive trees, with a panoramic view over the sea. It is quiet, cool and clean. Not even Marsha can fault it.

Gavin leads his guests down a dim, sanitised corridor and

into a small private room where Georgie is sitting up in bed, glasses perched on the end of her nose, reading a book on child psychology.

"Georgie darling!" effuses Marsha, enveloping her daughter in her bosom and dislodging her glasses.

"Hello, Mother." Georgie's tone is cool.

"I've been so worried. Are you all right?"

"I'm fine."

"Really and truly?"

"Really and truly."

"Did you have a terrible time?"

"No, not really. A bit protracted, that's all."

"And the baby's all right?"

"Fine. Look for yourself!"

Georgie points to the cot beside the bed. In it lies the baby, snug and sleeping peacefully, only his pink, beatific face to be seen. But this is enough for Nora.

"Oh my, oh my!" she cries. "Fancy!"

Marsha's face dissolves into a wreath of smiles. "Oh bless the little mite! He's lovely, dear! Congratulations!"

"Yes, congratulations!" repeats Nora, her face as pink as the baby's.

"But shouldn't he be in an incubator?" asks Marsha.

"He was, for the first couple of hours, just for observation," says Georgie.

"Only two hours? If he's nearly six weeks premature, he should be there for days, not hours, I should have thought."

"Well, he wasn't," Georgie sounds short. "Don't fuss, Mother. He's fine. He's absolutely normal."

"I don't understand," mutters Marsha. "What was the trouble, then? Why the urgent calls?"

"Oh, they thought at first it was going to be a breech birth, that's all. But he rectified his position himself and everything went perfectly."

Marsha frowns heavily. "But I *still* don't understand. Gavin says he weighs seven and half pounds."

"I must have miscalculated," says Gavin hastily.

Happily at that moment the baby starts crying.

"He needs feeding," says Georgie. "Do you want to leave or

would you like to see him have his first breast feed?"

Nora is shocked. How casual these young people are about such things!

"Oh, we'll stay," says Marsha instantly. "Shall I pick him up and hand him to you?"

"If you want to."

Marsha gently picks up the baby. "Come along, sweetheart," she croons. "My, you *are* heavy!" She holds him at arm's length, and then turns to Georgie. "This is never a *premature* baby!"

"I assure you he is," says Gavin.

"Never! Don't treat me like an imbecile, Gavin. I'm not a nurse, but even I know he can't possibly be premature."

"Even the doctor himself was surprised..." begins Gavin desperately. But he stops, floundering, not caring for the Judge Jeffreys look on his mother-in-law's face.

"It's no use, Gavin," sighs Georgie heavily. "I knew it was never going to work."

"What wasn't?" demands Marsha.

"You're quite right, Mother, he is full-term, a couple of days late, in actual fact."

Marsha freezes, still holding the baby at arm's length. "I don't understand. I fail to see why..." Her voice fades away and her blood pressure simmers as the implications begin to filter through.

"Yes, that's right," continues Georgie wearily. "He was conceived before we were married."

*****

It is almost nine when Elsie next comes round, and the first thing she sees is the schoolboy doctor contemplating her, strumming his lips with his fingertips.

"I gather you've remembered your name," he says jovially, seeing her eyes open. "Excellent. Most encouraging."

"I've got to get out of here!"

"All in good time, Mrs Brannigan. We've been on to the Liverpool police to contact your husband. No doubt he'll come down and collect you."

"That bitch will never let him!"

"What bitch?"

"That bloody bitch he's living with."

The doctor looks shocked. "Oh, I see. It's like that, is it?"

Elsie sits bolt upright, wide-eyed. "My God, that's what's been bugging me!"

"Oh?"

"She's got me two boys. I've gotta go and get 'em!"

Elsie heaves back the bedclothes and starts to get out. The doctor tries to restrain her.

"Take it easy, Mrs Brannigan."

"Out of me way, sport!"

"Neeearse!" yells the doctor.

"Me clothes! Where's me clothes?"

"You're in no condition to—"

"You try stopping me! I know me rights."

The doctor blocks her path. They go into a clinch as Elsie tries to push past.

"Neeearse!" screeches the doctor.

"Lemme go! screams Elsie.

"Mrs Brannigan, you can't travel all the way from Brighton to Liverpool in your condition."

"Brighton?" Elsie stops struggling. Her lips curl menacingly. "Don't you try kidding me, sport. I know where I am."

"You do? Where then?"

"Wagga Wagga."

"Wagga Wagga?" The woman is wandering in her head.

A nurse comes galloping up.

"Help me get her back to bed," cries the doctor.

"Come along, dear, easy does it," coos the nurse.

Elsie puts up a valiant resistance, but she is still feeling woozey and collapses back on the bed.

"My poor boys," she moans. "My poor poor boys."

"There now," says the doctor kindly. "You have a nice little rest. Not to worry. We'll let you know when we hear from Liverpool."

"Gotta go...gotta go..." repeats Elsie, like an old gramophone winding down.

"The poor woman is far from right yet," mutters the doctor

to the nurse as they move away. "Appears to be suffering from some sort of delusion. She thinks she's in Wagga Wagga."

"Where's that?" asks the nurse.

"No idea. Zululand, I think. She seems to have developed a strange accent, so maybe she is a Zulu."

Elsie sobs herself back to sleep.

*****

At the Fendleton Manor Country Hotel Len finally surfaces around nine. As always it takes him a minute or so to collect his wits, but when he does he sits up in horror and stares in disbelief around the big bedroom, with its smart decor and simulated antique furniture.

So it wasn't some hideous erotic nightmare he'd had. He really did rescue that loony farmer's wife from her raving husband, made a balls of changing the car wheel, walked with the woman in torrential rain to this hotel, agreed to share the room with her. *And...?*

Did he or didn't he? He hasn't a clue. He recalls trying to help her rise from her knees, and has some vague notion he fell on top of her – but then what? In the hope of jogging his memory he turns to look at her.

Except that she isn't there to look at. The space is empty. Probably she's in the bathroom, he thinks. But no, the door is open and the light off. Then she must have gone down to breakfast on her own.

He is relieved. He can wash and dress in peace. He swings his legs to the floor and is shocked to find that apart from his socks he is completely naked. How did that come about? He vaguely remembers being swathed in towels, but they are nowhere to be seen.

He looks round for his clothes. His jacket shirt and tie are over the back of a chair but his underwear seems to have disappeared. Then he spots it, draped over a radiator under the window. As he pads round the bed to retrieve it he comes across the two towels strewn across the carpet.

My God, whatever *did* happen last night? He must have been pretty far gone, although he doesn't recall drinking all that much. There was that bottle of Johnnie Walker, he seems to remember, and eventually sees it standing on the dressing table. It is empty.

But under the bottle there is a note scrawled on a piece of hotel notepaper. He picks it up.

Dear Mr Scaly,

Being a true Christian woman and a dutiful wife I have decided to return to my Man, brute and drunkard though he be. I thank you for coming to my rescue in my hour of need. You are a gallant gentleman, Mr Scaly, a Night in Shining Armour. I shall never forget you, or our lovely time together. May the Lord go with you.

Yours very truly,
Alice Isobel Potts (Mrs)

Len's relief is enormous, even though she has failed to leave the promised contribution to the cost. At least now he can forget her and concentrate on getting back on the road and driving on to Benthaven. If the car is ready, that is.

Hurriedly he gets dressed, not bothering to wash and shave, and makes his way down to reception.

"How can I help you, sir?" asks the receptionist, all bright and smiley.

Len begins to explain about the car, but he doesn't get far. "Ah yes, Mr Scally, your car is all ready for you."

Len brightens. Fortune seems to be smiling on him for once.

But not for long.

When the receptionist presents him with his car keys, she also presents him with two accounts, one for the hotel accommodation and one for the repair of the car, the amounts of both making Len blanch.

But when he reaches for his wallet and finds it is missing, Len more than blanches – he staggers, grips the desk for support. The receptionist notices.

"Is anything wrong, sir?" she asks.

"My wallet! It's missing!"

"Indeed, sir?" She's heard that one before.

Len slaps, pats and taps each of his pockets in turn. No wallet. He can't understand it. He had it last night – or did he? "I think I must have left it the bedroom," he tells her. "I'll just pop up and see."

"Shall I just look after your car keys then, sir," offers the receptionist, holding out her hand, "until you return?"

Len hands back the keys and returns to the bedroom, searching frantically, but without success. He *must* have had it, because he paid the night porter for the whisky from it. Or has that Potts woman nicked it? Surely not! A good Christian woman like her?

But what does he do now? All his cash and credit cards are in that wallet. But his cheque book and the cash for Colin, he realises, thanks to Nora's insistence not to keep everything together, are in his suitcase. And his suitcase is still in the car – or should be!

Down to Reception he goes again.

"I think my er...wife must have taken my wallet when she left," he explains anxiously to the girl.

Before the receptionist can respond, a man emerges from behind the scenes who apparently is the manager.

"Trouble, sir?"

Len explains the situation. The man listens with supercilious disinterest.

"Then perhaps we'd better go and get your suitcase from the car, sir," suggests the manager.

Off they go together to the car, which Len is only too relieved to see is standing in the forecourt on four good tyres. He's even more relieved to find his suitcase intact in the boot.

"I suggest you take the case to your room to open, sir," says the manager when they are back in Reception, mindful of other guests in the vicinity. "Then, perhaps you'll return as soon as you can and settle these accounts?"

"Um," says Len, only too pleased to escape.

"I'll just hold on to your car keys for the moment then, sir, until you return. Just a routine precaution, you understand, sir,

I'm sure." He has a charming smile.

Len returns to Room Thirteen feeling like a hunted criminal, but at least he has his case, and in it, safe and sound, his cheque book and Colin's money. In it also are his toiletries, which, now he knows he has the money to pay his debts, he feels emboldened to use. They can wait for their money until I've had a wash and shave, he thinks.

While he does so his mind reverts to the mystery of his wallet. He finds it hard to believe Alice Potts took it. She is certainly a bit nutty, but he can't believe her to be dishonest.

Feeling more in command of himself Len goes down to reception again, armed with two cheques he has written to meet the bills. When he's settled them he intends going in for breakfast to which he feels entitled, since he is in fact paying for two.

He is glad to find the manager is engaged talking to a group of guests, so he goes up to the smiling receptionist and hands her the cheques. "There you are!" he says with satisfaction.

The receptionist takes the cheques and studies them. "Have you a cheque card or credit card to support these, please, sir?" she asks.

Len gapes. "No, they were in my wallet!"

"Can't accept cheques without a card, sir."

"B-b-but under the circumstances, surely...?"

The receptionist looks sorrowful, the smile gone. "I could ask the manager, but I very much doubt if he'd..."

So do I, thinks Len. There's only one thing for it – he'll have to dip into the cash he brought for Colin. And with painful misgivings this is what he does.

The smile returns. "Thank you very much, sir. Here's your receipts and car keys. Have a safe journey."

"After I've had me breakfast," answers Len sourly.

But before doing that he decides to phone Colin; it's pointless to go on to Benthaven with only fifteen pounds left of Colin's money. With no cash of his own he's going to need it to buy petrol to get him back home.

He goes to the payphone and calls the Ocean View.

"Oh, Mr Scally!" comes the unmistakable voice of Mr Pertwee. "Mr Stilwell said he was expecting y'the noo."

"I'd like to speak to him," says Len.

"He's not here. He's gone to Brighton to look for his wee wife."

With all his own problems Len's forgotten that Elsie has gone missing. He expresses his great concern at this unhappy event and asks Mr Pertwee to tell Colin about his own misfortunes and that he will phone again later from home.

Len enjoys his breakfast. Now his troubles are over he feels quite pleased with himself. On the whole he handled the situation pretty well. It'll be something to yarn about to his cronies at The Mason and Magpie. What he'll tell Nora, of course, is another matter.

When he's finished his breakfast Len returns to the bedroom to collect his case and finds the chambermaid there, doing the room.

"Are you Mr Scally?" she asks the moment she sees him.

"Yes – why?" He's surprised she knows his name.

"Have you lost anything, sir?"

"Lost anything?" Len has to think for a moment. "Yes – me wallet!"

She delves into the pocket of her overall. "Is this it?"

Len feels a hundred years younger. "Where did you find it?"

"In the bed."

"In the bed! How did it get there?"

She grins. "If you don't know, luv, then I certainly don't!"

Len is profuse in his thanks and even gives her a fiver as a tip. His faith in humanity is restored. He's also glad Alice Isobel Potts (Mrs) hasn't stolen it. He'd rather his memory of her remain untarnished.

So after profusely thanking the chambermaid again Len picks up his suitcase and departs the Fendleton Manor Country Hotel and sets off for home.

It's a relief to be behind the wheel of his old Escort again. He's been very lucky to extricate himself from what promised to be a very nasty situation. But he still has to decide what he's going to tell Nora. The truth, of course. But not the *whole* truth! She would never understand about Alice Potts. What he must do, he decides, is simply to tell her the truth, but without mentioning her.

He finds his way back to Newbury and on to the M4 without difficulty. He'll be home in less than an hour with any luck. But Lady Luck is still not smiling upon him. As he changes gear to climb a hill the clutch goes limp. He pumps furiously at it with his foot. He is slowing, the car not responding to the accelerator. Toots from behind.

Frantically he swerves over on to the hard shoulder and stops.

*****

Colin is sitting beside Daphne in Mr Pertwee's white mini-van on their way to Brighton. Boss is behind them, panting down their necks, and staring at the road ahead like a back-seat driver.

Despite his anxiety about Elsie, Colin is conscious of Daphne's shapely jean-clad thighs beside him. He stares determinedly at the road ahead. Think of her as a pillar-box or something, he tells himself, anything but the gorgeous girl you've already seen more of than you're entitled.

"You really think Boss might pick up Elsie's scent?" he asks to divert his mind.

"M'father thinks so."

"Well, he should know. He's certainly knows how to train dogs."

"Aye." Daphne glowers at the road. "And he dinnae do a bad job on me, neither."

"Whatcha mean?"

"Wael...y'know..."

"Being strict with you and that?"

"Aye, and trying to run m'life for me. Trying to make me do what *he* wants. He dinnae care what *I* might want."

"Mustn't let him do that."

She jerks the van to a halt as traffic lights turn red. Daphne's driving tends to reflect her mood. "He's going to take up dog training when he's sold the hotel," she adds as they sit and wait.

"I know."

"Aye, but he wants me join him and be his kennel maid."

Colin can't help laughing. "You, a kennel maid!"

"He's determined on it."

"You'd be pretty good at it. But you won't, will you?"

"Och no!"

"What *will* you do then?"

"I'll go and live with Carlos."

Colin has forgotten all about Carlos. "Did he turn up the other night – after I left?"

"No, he dinnae, the sod." The van jerks off again as the lights turn green. "But I'll get him. I'm going to see him this afternoon. I'll soon sort him out."

"But isn't he still going with that other girl – the one he was all over at The Black Spot?"

"Cheryl? Aye, but I'll get him back."

She will too, Colin thinks. Personally, he can't see why Daphne is so taken with Carlos. Despite his good looks, Carlos seems a weak slimy sort of character to him.

"Y'dinnae blame me?" asks Daphne, glancing at him.

"No, not if you're really sure that's what you want. Good luck to you."

"Thanks."

"Look," says Colin after a pause. "I haven't really apologised to you for coming to your room like that the other night. I should have known better. I just didn't know what I was doing."

"Och, not to worry. I led you on."

"Shouldn't have fallen for it, though, a man of my age. After all, I've got a son older than you."

She glances at him again. "Y'don't look old enough to have a son my age!"

"Compliments will get you everywhere," grins Colin.

"What's he like?"

"Who – Boris? A bit of a disaster to be honest. But I must say he's settled down a bit since he's had this part-time job in a market garden. He seems to have taken to it, oddly enough. But when he's not working he's either blaring us out with Radio One or roaring round the town on his motorbike."

"Och, I love motorbikes. I'm going to have one mysel' when I get away from m'father."

If she drives a bike like she drives this mini-van, thinks

Colin, they'd better start clearing the roads right now.

Daphne suddenly signals right and turns off the main road into what appears to be a supermarket.

"Where we going?"

"I have to collect provisions from the Cash and Carry, dinnae I say? It willnae take a minute."

Colin speeds up the process by helping her to load the provisions into the back of the mini-van, and then they drive on into the centre of Brighton and park in the multi-storey car park where Colin and Len had their encounter with Jaspar and Pug. Colin prefers not to recall all that. It was the start of all his troubles.

They walk down to the entrance of Hambledon's, Boss straining impatiently on his lead.

"I'll just go and have a word with the manager first," Colin tells Daphne, "and find out exactly what Elsie did after I left. You mind waiting here?"

"Och no. Take y'time."

Full of grim determination Colin plods his way to the manager's office on the top floor and demands to know what happened to Elsie. The manager knows nothing about the incident and calls in his Security Chief, who comes ambling into the office fingering his black moustache nervously.

"Oh, I remember her," says he. "She was the woman who had her holdall nicked."

"She's not a woman," objects the manager, "she's a customer."

"Whichever. Her old man went chasing through the store like a madman after a suspect. On the CCTV."

"That was me," growls Colin.

"So I told her to stay put until he came back."

"Quite right," nods the Manager.

"But he never did."

"No, cos he got mugged, didn't he?" snaps Colin. "Found himself in bloody hospital."

"Not my fault." There is a note of insolence in the Security Chief's voice. "Nothing to do with me."

The manager becomes angry. "The point is a customer has disappeared. We can't have customers disappearing like that.

What happened to her after hubby shot off in pursuit of the suspect?"

"She waited."

"I know she waited, I told her to," grinds Colin. "But what happened to her after she finished waiting?"

The Security Chief glances apprehensively at the manager.

"Answer the question," he orders, like a judge.

"She continued to wait until closing time, and since her old man failed to return I escorted her out of the building and told her to wait outside until he turned up."

"What!" explodes Colin. "With no money? Not knowing what had happened to her old man?"

"How was I to know he'd get himself mugged?"

"It just happens," seethes Colin, "that I am also a security man, with a big chemical company. Our job is to *protect*, mate, and that includes caring for those in distress, be they customers, employees, truck drivers, or even sales reps."

"True enough," nods the manager.

"And you left her standing outside the store all alone and penniless!"

"Told her to go the police station if her old man didn't turn up," protests the Security Chief. "Said they'd see her safely home. Told her how to get to the nick and everything."

"Well, she didn't get there. Disappeared, mate, that's what she did. Vanished into thin air. Hasn't been seen or heard of since."

"Very unfortunate," murmurs the manager.

"Unfortunate! I'll sue the pair of you for everything you've got if anything's happened to her!"

With that Colin storms out of the office and back to the waiting Daphne, beside himself with fury and anxiety.

"I dunno," he moans to her. "Fancy leaving her standing there with no money nor nothing! Calls himself a security bloke! I'll get him struck off!"

Daphne listens patiently, full of sympathy.

"So now what do we do?" he asks when he's run out of steam.

"There's still Boss. He might just pick up her scent."

Colin stares at the dog doubtfully. Boss stares back, panting and looking expectant. "Nothing to lose, I suppose."

"Did y'nae bring that item of her clothing?"

"Oh! Ah!" He delves in his pocket and produces one of Elsie's bras.

Daphne dangles it in front of the dog's nose. Passers-by stare. "Find her boy! Find her!"

All eager, Boss sniffs around the store's entrance, dodging this way and that, getting in people's way. Then he suddenly takes off down the pavement, dragging Daphne after him. Colin follows hopefully.

But then the dog halts abruptly, turns tail and charges off in the opposite direction. He halts again, looks puzzled and turns back again in the other direction.

"Can't make up his bloody mind," moans Colin.

"She must have walked up and down a wee while," observes Daphne.

Boss pauses, looks bewildered, gives it up as a bad job and turns his attention to the post of a bus stop.

"Och, come *on*, Boss, do y'stuff!"

She again dangles the bra in front of the dog's nose.

A passing youth leers at her. "Not my size, dearie."

"Bog off," growls Daphne.

But Boss shows no interest in the bra and concentrates on the bus stop.

"It's no good," sighs Colin. "Can't expect it after so long and with people passing up and down and that."

"Rained all yesterday too. So what will y'do?"

With a mighty effort Colin forces himself to concentrate, be the detective. "Got to look at the situation logically, Daph. We know she got this far, was standing here on her own with no money when the store closed. We don't know what she did next, but we *do* know what she *didn't* do. She didn't go to the police. She didn't land up in hospital. And she didn't arrive back in Benthaven."

He pauses, not sure where to go from there. Then he has an idea.

"Supposing it was you," he says to Daphne. "What would you have done?"

"Hitched a lift back to Benthaven," she says instantly.

Colin blanches. That's one scenario he's trying not to contemplate. "Well, she didn't get there, so let's hope she didn't. What else?"

"Taken a taxi and got m'father to pay the fare for her at the hotel."

"She didn't do that either. Anything else?"

"Walk back."

Another undesirable scenario. "Doubt it. She's not that fond of walking. Anyway, she'd have got there by this time."

"Wael..." Daphne is running out of inspiration. "Nicked a car and driven back?"

"Elsie can't drive. Anything else? *Think*, Daph!"

Daphne thinks, but no new inspiration arrives.

Colin feels a cold sweat creep over him. His worst fears are confirmed. "So," he says, trying to remain calm, "we know she didn't end up in hospital, nor take a taxi, nor a bus, nor did she go to the police. That means she either hitched a lift or walked. I knew it! Either way she's in real trouble, Daph, she's got to be. Come on, let's get down the bloody nick. I'm going to give them buggers what for."

"Wait!" exclaims Daphne, restraining him.

"What?"

"Did y'nae tell me this morning there was some woman in hospital who'd had an accident on a stolen push-bike?"

Colin pauses. "Yes, but it can't be Elsie. She hasn't ridden a bike for years. Besides, that woman was supposed to have lost her memory or summat."

"Exactly! That's probably why you haven't heard!"

Colin jolts. "You mean she could have pinched the bike, had an accident and lost her memory?" Torrents of hope surge into him. Just the sort of madcap thing Elsie might do, he thinks.

"Daphne," he cries. "You're a genius!"

*****

Marsha is glaring at her daughter, momentarily speechless, her mouth hanging open as if her jaw spring has suddenly snapped.

"Conceived before you were married?" she manages to

repeat.

"In plain terms, Mother," sighs Georgie, "we did it before we got married, and I got lumbered, hence the shotgun wedding."

"Oh Gavin! You naughty boy!" cries Nora, not sure if she's ashamed or proud of him.

"Are you telling me," demands Marsha in a voice straight out of the freezer, "that you deliberately came all the way to this...to this *place* to have my very first grandchild with the deliberate intention of deceiving me into believing the child is premature?"

"We did it for your sake, Mother."

"*My* sake!"

"To save you embarrassment of course! The embarrassment you'd feel when your posh friends realised your virtuous daughter had her first baby after only seven months of marriage. Their wagging chins would have had a field day!"

Marsha glowers. "Georgina, neither my friends nor myself are the prudish fuddy-duddies you appear to think. We are perfectly well aware of the change in attitude towards such things."

"Yes, but you don't approve," retorts Georgie.

"That is not the point. It has to be accepted as a fact of life these days. What grieves me very much is that you should choose to engage in this elaborate deception rather than tell me about it. Am I such an ogre that you are unable to confide in me?"

"Yes, Mother, I'm afraid you are."

"That's a monstrous thing to say!"

Georgie relents slightly. "Well no, I don't mean that. Look, all we were trying to do was to save a lot of fuss and bother. We simply thought that taking it all round it would be best if we came away for me to have the baby and at the same time have a belated honeymoon, so to speak. We were hoping to surprise you with the baby when we got back, and by simply saying it was premature, hoped it would prevent a lot of awkward questions and everyone would be happy."

"You could never have made me believe that baby to be premature!" objects Marsha.

"Oh, I don't know. By time we arrived back home there'd have been little difference. Premature babies catch up pretty quickly, you know."

"I reckon it would have worked," chimes in Gavin, "if it hadn't been for the scare about the breach birth."

Georgie glances at him sourly. "And you phoning home like that in a blind panic."

"Well, I didn't think they would—"

"I know you didn't." Georgie sounds derisive.

Marsha contemplates her daughter and son-in-law with dissatisfaction. "Well, I have to say I'm most disappointed in you – both of you. It was a very selfish and thoughtless thing to have done. You have no idea the shock it gave us."

"I *did* say there was nothing to worry about," says Gavin defensively.

"Nothing to worry about! My dear boy, for someone as bright as you it is unbelievable that you're so naive when it comes to things of everyday life. Of *course* we were worried! Everything to do with babies is worrying!"

"Well, I'm sorry," mumbles Gavin. "I just didn't realise."

Marsha seems mollified by his apology and slews her eyes from him to the baby. "Well, no harm done, I suppose. Except, of course, Nora and I have had to endure a long, tedious and exhausting journey to this benighted place, and for nothing. And now we are having to face a similar journey back." The sight of the sleeping peaceful baby takes the defrosting process a stage further. "At least we've had the pleasure of seeing the little mite on his first day of life, which makes it all worthwhile, wouldn't you say, Nora?"

"Oh definitely!" Nora's in no doubt.

"Look," says Gavin, hoping the worst is over, "why don't you both stay on for a while now you're here? Enjoy the baby and have a bit of a holiday?"

"That's not possible, I'm afraid. We must leave as soon as we can. Olly will be back from Singapore tomorrow, and Nora no doubt is anxious to continue her interrupted holiday in Brighton."

This cues Gavin to play his trump card. He intended to keep it until he got home, but feels his tarnished image could do with a little burnishing right now. "Actually," he says, trying to sound casual, "there is one other piece of good news we have for you."

Marsha eyes him sharply. "Oh yes? And what's that?"

"I've been promoted."

"Promoted?"

"By the bank."

"Oh Gavin!" Nora fairly whoops with joy. "You clever, clever boy!"

Marsha sounds less impressed. "Well, that is good news, I have to say. My congratulations."

"What are you going to be?" asks Nora. "A manager or something?"

Gavin grins. "Hardly! Actually, I won't know for sure until I'm transferred."

"You're being *transferred*?" Marsha takes more interest.

"Yes, to another branch."

"And where's that, may I ask?"

"Brighton."

*****

The next time Elsie surfaces the ward is full of activity. Surgical trolleys are being wheeled up and down like prams. Patients chat and wander about. Nurses hold wrists and wave thermometers.

When she opens her eyes Elsie is aware of activity by the bed opposite to her own, and she watches through slit eyes as the Sister brings in an old lady into the ward accompanied by a middle-aged woman carrying a black case, and deposits them by the bed.

"Here we are, Mrs Brand," says Sister, pulling the curtains around the bed. "If you'd just like to get undressed and hop into bed…"

The old lady looks terribly frail to Elsie, incapable of hopping over a matchstick, never mind into bed. Sister hustles off but leaves a bit of a gap between the curtains, and Elsie watches as the old lady slowly undresses and the woman with her opens the black attaché case, extracting a bottle of Ribena, grapes, a dressing gown and a nightie. The woman silently helps the old lady on with the nightie and deposits the clothes she has just removed into the case.

"Into bed with you," says the woman.

"I wanna wee," cries the old lady.

"Oh Ma! You've just been!"

"I wanna go again!"

"Can't you wait until..."

"I wanna go bad!"

"Oh, all *right*! Come on then, let's see if we can find a lavvy."

Elsie watches while the woman helps the old lady on with the dressing gown and they go off together in search of a toilet.

By the time all this has happened Elsie is wide awake and the idea that there is something very urgent she has to do hammers in her brain once more. And she remembers what it is! She has to get back to Liverpool to rescue her two sons from the clutches of that woman. She's got to get out of here right now, but how?

The answer to that is staring her in the face.

Up she rises from her bed, weaves her way with uncertain steps across the ward and slips behind the curtains. With the speed of a quick-change artist she is off with her nightdress and on with the old lady's clothes. They are much too short for her lanky frame and make her look like a schoolgirl from St Trinian's, but she couldn't care less. She has to get out of this place and back to Liverpool just as fast as she can, that's all she cares about.

She snatches up the other woman's handbag from the bedside locker, shuts it in the black case, picks the case up, and after a quick look between the curtains to make sure the coast is clear, walks nonchalantly out of the ward.

"Oi!" shouts a patient from the ward. "Nurse! Nurse!"

Elsie hurries through the maze of corridors, oblivious of where she is going, the shouts of alarm receding into the distance. Presently she spots an arrow pointing to the exit, and following it, eventually finds herself outside the hospital in the hazy sunshine. She's made it!

The fresh air clears her head still further. She must push on, she thinks, before they catch up with her. She continues as rapidly as her unwilling legs will permit, down unfamiliar streets, not knowing where she is heading. She's only been to Wagga Wagga a couple of times before, when Brig brought her to his flat in that noisy sports car of his, so she has no idea how to find the station, or even if there is one.

Her legs are beginning to fail, so when she comes to a bench in some sort of open square, she sits down and takes stock of the situation. She needs to find the station, but has she the money for the rail fare? She opens the case and looks in the handbag. There are several notes in the purse. It should be enough, she thinks.

As she is sitting there a van passes by. 'Brighton Carpeting Co' it says on the side. *Brighton?* The name makes a sonar sounding into the depths of her mind. Someone mentioned Brighton to her recently, she vaguely remembers. It was that doctor, insisting she was in Brighton not Wagga Wagga. He must be mad! The only Brighton she's heard of in Australia is Adelaide way, and she's never even been there! Yet somehow the name Brighton makes her feel uneasy; it has a disturbingly familiar ring.

She closes the case and gets to her feet. She's got to find the station, that's what she's got to do.

"Excuse me," she says to a burly man carrying an Asda bag who is passing by, "but can you tell me where the station is?"

"Station?" says the man in a broad Welsh voice. "Sorry luv, but I'm a stranger here myself, see."

Elsie next asks a woman with a double pushchair in which identical twins are screaming their heads off.

"The station?" queries the woman, not pleased at being stopped. "Shut up, you two! Let's see... Rikki, stop doing that! Oh, that way. Turn right up West Street. Stop it, I said! And straight on, can't miss it. Rikki, I shan't tell you again!"

Elsie is heartened. She picks up the case and walks in the direction indicated by the woman. Sure enough, she comes to the station and joins the queue in the booking hall.

"Liverpool, please," she says when her turn comes.

"Single or return?"

"Single." She opens the old lady's purse.

"Going today?"

"Now."

"Sixty-two pounds twenty," says the booking clerk.

"Pounds?" Elsie is puzzled. "You mean dollars."

"I mean pounds," responds the clerk. "Them things you've got in your hand."

"But we changed to dollars years ago!"

"Not yet we ain't. Bloody Euros, maybe." My God, thinks the clerk, you don't half meet 'em in this job. "Let's see what you've got there, shall we?"

Elsie holds out her hand for him to examine her money.

"You from the States?" he asks.

"No, I'm a Pom."

He looks at her in surprise. A real nutter here! "Well, whatever you are, you're not going to get to Liverpool on this lot. You've only got thirty-three quid. Ain't you got any more?"

Elsie delves in the purse. "No."

"Credit card? Rail card?"

Elsie shakes her head.

"Traveller's cheques?"

She shakes her head again.

"You've had it then. Sorry, luv. Next!"

Elsie wanders away in despair. Now what does she do? She is still feeling a bit dozy, and her head is pounding. She'll have to go back to the hospital, that's all she can do. But she'll be in dead trouble if she does, walking out like that, pinching the old lady's handbag and clothes. In despair she wanders on, not knowing or caring where she is going.

Suddenly she finds herself confronted by the sea. There it is large as life, grey and green, cut almost in two by a pier. This *can't* be Wagga Wagga! It's miles from the sea – that much she knows for sure!

She wanders on along the sea front. Holiday coaches line the road. Perhaps she could get to Liverpool by coach – it would be cheaper. She might have enough money for that. There must be a bus or coach station somewhere. She asks several passers-by but no one seems to know. She is feeling really desperate now. Here she is in some sort of resort, presumably Brighton, since several passing buses have Brighton on the front. But how has she got here? What happened to her? She's never been to Adelaide in her life, not with Cliff, not with Brig, she feels positive about that.

Then a mini-bus passes by with the name 'Benthaven' on the front. That also has a disturbingly familiar ring to it, but in what connection she hasn't a clue. Could she have been there with Brig? She has no recollection of having done so. Tantalising snippets begin to flit into her mind – playing the organ somewhere, a bald-headed man with horn-rimmed glasses, sunbathing on a pebbly beach. Confusion mounts to an almost unbearable level. What is happening to her? Who is she? What is she? Where is she?

She tries to make her mind focus on what she has to do and that is to get the hell out of this place, wherever it is, and get to Liverpool.

Then she suddenly finds herself confronted by what seems like a mirage; mysterious oriental domes appear to be hovering above the rooftops. Elsie stops dead, blinking in amazement.

"I've seen them things before," she says aloud, "and not long ago either."

She continues to stare, riveted to the spot, cudgelling her brains as wisps of memory come and go. A vision of a vast four-poster bed invades her mind.

"The King's Bedchamber!" she exclaims. "I saw it with somebody!"

But who was it? A woman, she feels sure. Further flickers of memory float before her eyes like clips from films – a red and white holdall, a little man with a strong Scottish accent, singing in a pub, dancing in some psychedelic disco – that bald-headed man again! – and a big-breasted girl with stubbly hair and 'Bristol Rovers' emblazoned on her T-shirt who was dancing with... Inexplicably, acute anger rises in her. That cow! She was trying to get off with her husband! *Husband?* Not Cliff, not Brig – what the hell was his name? Is his name! She can see his fair hair, his blue eyes...

Still standing staring at the domes the picture slowly begins to fill in, bits of it anyway.

"Brighton!" she exclaims out loud. "I'm in England, not bloody Australia!"

"Just as well to know that," grins a callow youth who happens to be passing by.

The present gushes into Elsie's mind like water into a bath.
"Oi!" she calls after him.
"What?"
"Where do I get the bus for Benthaven?"

Chapter 15

By mid-morning on Thursday, Oliver Bloom has just about wound up his affairs for what he now vows shall be his last visit to Singapore, or to any of these far-flung exotic places. The golf course is definitely beckoning.

He despatched the new receptionist Akita from his bed as early that morning as was seemly. She didn't appear reluctant to go. In fact, he realised later she was damned glad. After having observed his reaction to the news of Rosemary's untimely death, Akita might well have guessed the reason for his reluctance to indulge in further lovemaking.

He lost no time in making discreet enquiries from Rosemary's colleagues as to the cause of her death, but no one seemed to know, or if they did, weren't prepared to say. Perhaps Akita was wrong, he thought hopefully. Rosemary had been a clean wholesome kind of girl, but, although it hadn't worried him at the time, she had relied on the Pill rather than use condoms.

He resists the urge to rush round to the nearest doctor for a check. For one thing there isn't time if he is to catch his plane back to London, and for another he'd much prefer to consult a British doctor; but not his own GP in Brockbury, needless to say. What he plans to do is to spend Thursday night in the bedroom reserved for his use at the Heathrow Skyfly Hotel, as he often does, and then consult a doctor privately in London the next morning instead of driving straight home. He'll have to let Marsha know, of course, fabricate some believable yarn to cover his delay, probably say he's going to visit Rosemary's parents in Wimbledon to offer them the Company's condolences on their daughter's sad and untimely demise.

But when he phones home there is no reply. He is a bit surprised; in England it is three in the morning. But he's not unduly concerned. Marsha has probably gone to see her sister in Cheltenham and decided to stay the night.

When his plane finally takes off for Heathrow, and Singapore is a rapidly diminishing spot below, Oliver is glad to just sit back in his seat and do nothing. He feels weak, weary and worried. His innards are still playing him up and his whole body feels as if it has been filleted. He knows little if anything about AIDS, but he's got it into his head that a feeling of lassitude is one of the symptoms. He won't feel happy until he's seen the doctor and at least knows the truth.

What a bloody fool he's been! He should have known he couldn't keep up this sort of life indefinitely without running into trouble. Well, it's over, regardless of whether or not he has AIDS. He'll hand in his notice tomorrow morning. At least Marsha will be pleased about that.

With a sigh he opens the magazine on gardening he has bought at the bookstall instead of the more salacious reading matter he normally indulges in on these long flights. The sooner he accustoms himself to the idea of a quiet suburban existence the better. But the plane has scarcely attained its cruising altitude before his head slumps forward and he dozes off.

The route of his flight to Heathrow is via Hong Kong, and he sleeps soundly until the plane touches down. While he is waiting for it to take off again he tries once more to read his magazine, but soon closes it with a sigh. He can't imagine himself spending the rest of his life, long or short, growing roses and radishes. He's still only in his middle fifties, for God's sake! He's still got something to offer the world, surely.

"Hello, Olly!" exclaims a familiar voice. "What are you doing in this neck of the woods?"

He looks up to see a large man in a smart business suit and a Churchillian scowl on his face plonking himself in the seat next to him. It is none other than George Bollinger, Chief Executive of Regal Chemicals plc, Fertiliser Division.

"George!" Oliver assumes his convivial business personality. "Long time no see."

"No," agrees Bollinger. "Business pressure. No time to attend meetings somehow these days."

"Me neither."

Both men are members of the Brockbury Masonic Lodge. The doors are closed and the aircraft begins to trundle its way to the main runway.

"Been stirring up the Hong Kong Skyfly, I suppose," says George, strapping himself into his seat.

"No, the Singapore actually."

"Ah. How are things there these days?"

"Chaotic as ever – the hotel, I mean. Making a profit, though. Singapore itself is on the up."

"Glad to hear it."

"Been to Hong Kong on business?" asks Oliver.

"What else?"

"How do you get on with the Chinese?"

"Don't ask! Well, reasonably, I suppose – better than we expected. Even so, we've decided to pull out."

"Really? Because of them?"

"No, not entirely. We were damn fools to have opened a branch here in the first place. When you think about it Hong Kong isn't exactly a place in dire need of fertilisers."

"But you've got the whole of China as a market on your doorstep, surely?"

"That's what we thought, but Head Office in its wisdom has decided otherwise. They want out. I've just had the disagreeable task of informing the staff they're redundant. Damnable job telling people they're redundant. One feels one is playing God." George Bollinger sounds as if he's about to burst into tears.

"I know what you mean," says Oliver sympathetically, although he has never found it a problem firing people.

"Still, it's an ill wind, as they say. At least it means it's one less of these damned long flights to make. I suffer terribly from jet lag, don't you?"

"One never gets used to it," agrees Oliver. "Not good for the system."

"Too true. Too true."

Oliver, not a man to miss opportunities, sees one here and loses no time in seizing it.

"As a matter of fact..." he begins with an appropriate air of reluctance, "I decided only this morning to chuck my job and retire."

"Really? Surprised to hear you say that, Olly. Thought you lapped up this kind of life."

"Well..." Oliver stretches himself languorously in his seat. "Not getting any younger, George. Anno Domini and all that. Got to respect the old body. Besides, it's not fair to Marsha, being alone so much, especially now Georgina is married and away from home."

"How is she, by the way?"

"Georgina? Great, great. Expecting a baby in August."

"Oh really? Give her my felicitations."

"Will do. Will do. Anyway," adds Oliver quickly, not wanting to stray from the point, "I want to have more time to spend with my family, so I'm thinking of taking early retirement, putting my feet up for a bit."

"Don't blame you. Wish I could myself. But it's a pretty big leap for you, isn't it? From your hectic lifestyle to nothing, so to speak?"

"Well, I'll get used to it. Mark you, I don't intend to idle the rest of my life away. After a rest I intend to find myself a desk job locally. Not quite ready for the rubbish tip. I feel I still have quite a lot to offer."

"Of course you have, Olly, man of your ability and experience."

The plane has reached the runway and is poised to take off.

"Actually," says Oliver when he judges the moment to be ripe, "I was wondering if by any chance there was a slot I could fill in your outfit."

Bollinger turns his cod-like eyes to look at him. "At Regal Chemicals? Well, I wouldn't know about that. We're—"

"As one Mason to another?" There is an impish twinkle in Oliver's eyes.

"Always possible, I suppose. We could certainly use some new blood. A man of your capabilities could be handy. See what I can do. No promises, mind."

"Of course not, jolly good of you, George. Much appreciated."

The plane's engines roar into life. For all his years of air travel Oliver has never overcome his dread of the take off. But this time he doesn't even think about it. Suddenly he is feeling pleased with himself. He has done the right thing. He has made a quick, clean decision, and now he can look forward to a new and challenging future. If he lives long enough, that is.

*****

In the private clinic on Thyros the euphoria over the newborn babe has done much to mend Marsha's mood. It has occurred to her that the young couple's attempted deceit over its birth may prove to be no bad thing after all. As Georgie pointed out, it will certainly save her having to make embarrassing explanations to her friends and may even bring her some sympathetic attention.

And so, with much hand-waving and blowing of kisses from the door of Georgie's private room, Marsha and Nora, accompanied by the much relieved Gavin, take their leave and make their way in relative harmony down the long passage towards the hospital's exit.

"Yes," says Marsha, "I still think the name Jonathon is the most suitable name for him. So long as he doesn't get called Johnnie, or Jonty. And certainly not Jack."

"Jack Scally rolls off the tongue best," says Gavin.

"But it lacks dignity, dear. It would suit a manual worker quite well, but he'll be destined for better things, I trust. I think Jonathon Oliver Scally would sound quite impressive."

"It would be nice if 'Len' could be included in his name," says Nora, who's feeling a bit left out of these momentous deliberations.

"We mustn't burden the poor mite with too many names. Jonathon Oliver Leonard Scally is rather a mouthful, don't you think?"

"I don't think that matters," says Gavin, bravely taking his mother's side. "His full name is only likely to be used on official documents, like death certificates."

"Well, you must discuss it with Georgie, dear. It's for you two to decide, after all. We are only making suggestions."

They are approaching the clinic's entrance where a woman is on her hands and knees scrubbing the steps. A graphic 'Wet Floor' sign stands close by with a warning in Greek.

"On the whole I'm glad we came," says Marsha, eyeing the woman disdainfully and giving her a wide birth. "At least we know all is well, despite your rather shameful deception."

"We meant it for the best," says Gavin.

"I realise that now, dear. Well, we'll say no more about it."

"Are you quite sure you both won't stay on for a few days?"

"We'd love to, but I must get home for Olly. He'll wonder what has happened to me if I'm not there."

"He'll be happy to hear the news."

"I'm sure he will. And about your promotion. Brighton, you say?"

"That's right."

"Then that settles it. I shall definitely insist Olly retires now, and we'll move to Brighton as soon as—"

Marsha never finishes that sentence.

Instead, she slips and does a purler to the bottom of the slippery steps.

*****

On the bus on the way back from Brighton to Benthaven, Elsie's memory has mostly returned, but not entirely, nor all that accurately. She thinks her husband's name is Conrad and that she is on holiday here with him and their friends, Ben and Cora.

But struggle as she may she can't remember how she came to be in hospital. Someone there told her she'd run into a traffic signal on a push-bike, but that's a load of balls. She doesn't even possess a bike! And where's Conrad, and Ben and Cora? Why hadn't any of them visited her in hospital, brought her flowers or fruit, or at least sent her a 'Get Well' card? If that's all they think of her, well, sod 'em!

Mr Pertwee is at reception welcoming two new guests when she stumbles into the foyer. He gapes in amazement when he sees her, standing there in the old lady's half-zipped-up skirt and a jumper so short it doesn't even cover her midriff.

"Mrs Stilwell! Y've been worrying us! Where have you been?"

"That's what I'd like to know," snaps Elsie.

"Where's Conrad?"

"Conrad?"

"Me husband!"

"Och he's gone to Brighton with Daphne to look for—"

"Daphne!" That's a name to shift the most stubborn amnesia. Oh yes, of course! That bloody bitch! Fire kindles in Elsie's eyes. "So he's finally pissed off with her, has he?"

"Mrs Stilwell, *please*!" Mr P. glances nervously at his new arrivals.

She shoves him to one side and heads for the stairs.

"Y'll be needing the key," he calls after her.

With a Basil Fawlty genuflexion to his new guests Mr Pertwee hurries after her with the key.

"It's not what y'seem to think," he whispers urgently. "They went to—"

"Sod 'em!" snarls Elsie.

She snatches the key from his hand and charges up the stairs. She is still seething when she reaches the room.

"That's it!" she cries, slamming the black case down on the bed. "I've bloody had it. I'm off!"

Then she glimpses herself in the mirror.

"Good God! I look like a bloody scarecrow!"

Savagely, she peels off the clothes then promptly bursts into tears, slumping down on the bed in total despair. She sobs and sobs and sobs, until she eventually reaches the snivelling and snuffling stage. What have I done to deserve this? she moans to herself. They don't care about me. All Conrad thinks about is that girl. And Ben and Cora, they've gone off to see them bloody kangaroos, I bet!

With sudden resolution she jumps to her feet, her eyes like steel.

"Right!" she cries. "*That's* what I'll do!"

She swings open the wardrobe doors, takes out a pile of her clothes and selects something to put on – it has to be her pink beach trousers and a top, since her other clothes are still at the hospital. She swings over to the dressing table, empties her underwear on to the bed, hurries into the bathroom, sweeps up her toiletries and tosses them on to the bed. Then she dresses (no bra? – well, sod it), brushes her teeth, applies her make-up, then stops and looks round.

What else?

Money! She's going to need money. She opens the black

case she took from the hospital and takes out the handbag. Thirty pounds! That's not going to get her very far. Then she discovers a credit card in a pocket of the old lady's purse in the name of L. D. Brand. She doesn't fancy using that, but the poor old soul isn't going to need it for a bit, and she'd only use it herself if she had to.

What else? Her shoes! She's not going to put the old lady's shoes back on; they've almost crippled her already. So she goes to the wardrobe to get a pair of her own. It is while she's bending down to pick them up that she spots Colin's wallet strapped to the underside wardrobe shelf. So that's where he hid it, the bugger!

Ripping it off she takes it to the bed and empties out the contents. Among the various documents is Colin's money belt. It's certainly stuffed full of something. She pulls out wads of notes and stares at them in dismay. She's never seen bank notes like these before, big white things. But bank notes they certainly are. 'Promise to pay Bearer the sum of Five Pounds' they read. Perhaps she's forgotten what five-pound notes look like – anything is possible with her dodgy memory. And there on the bed, too, lies her old passport. She snatches it up, a glint in her eyes.

"Right!" she exclaims, stuffing the notes and passport into the handbag. "That's it!"

She throws as many of her clothes and other belongings into the case as will go in, and takes a final glance around the room. It looks like a refuse tip but she doesn't care. Then she spots the old lady's clothes on the floor. She feels guilty. She ought to let her have them back, just in case she ever did leave hospital.

So she grabs a pen and scribbles a hasty note. 'Please return these clothes to Mrs L. D. Brand at the hospital with my apologies. Will refund money when I can.'

She puts the clothes in a neat pile on the bed, and is just tucking the note between them when there is a knock on the door.

"Piss off!" she yells.

"Mrs Stilwell, it's Mr Pertwee. May I nae have a wee word?"

"Go away!"

"But it's important!"

He is about to knock again when the door flies open, not to let him in, but to let Elsie out. She slams the door after her and slaps the key into Mr Pertwee's hand.

"Will you kindly inform Conrad I've left!"

"But y'dinnae understand!"

Elsie's in no mood for understanding anything and pushes past him, marching off towards the stairs, the black case rigid in her hand.

"But where are y'going?" calls Mr Pertwee, galloping after her.

"Australia!" she shouts back.

*****

At that very moment Colin is sitting with Daphne in the mini-van in the hospital car park, festering with frustration.

After she had made her staggering deduction that the woman with amnesia could be Elsie, Daphne had driven him straight round to the hospital.

Yes, the lady on reception confirmed, there had been a woman admitted on Tuesday evening who'd been involved in an accident on a push-bike.

"Are you Mr Cliff Brannigan?" the receptionist asked.

"No, I'm her bloody husband," growled Colin.

The receptionist rang the ward sister, and was told her to send him up.

"She was admitted as Jane Doe," said the ward sister. "Then she remembered her name was Elsie Brannigan and gave an address in Liverpool."

"That's her!" Colin cried.

"But she said her husband's name was Cliff Brannigan."

"She was confused. Her former husband was Cliff Brannigan. And it's Liverpool, near Sydney in Australia she was on about not Liverpool on the bloody Merseyside."

"I see," said Sister, not seeing at all.

"It's *my* Elsie all right," Colin insisted. "I want to see her right away."

"You can't. She's left."

"What!" Up went Colin's BP. "You mean you discharged her in that condition?"

"No. She absconded." The ward sister was tight-lipped. "She stole a poor old lady's clothes and a purse containing thirty-three pounds, ninety-seven pence. The police are after her for theft. It caused a major disruption in my ward, I can tell you. Doctors' rounds were all late as a result."

"And when exactly did all this take place?"

"Over two hours ago – about ten, I suppose."

"Ten! She could be anywhere by now!"

Furious that he'd found Elsie and immediately lost her again, Colin rushed back to the mini-van where Daphne is still patiently waiting.

"Bloody hospitals!" he rants. "You'd think they could manage to hold on to their patients. Talk about security! I mean, how can someone like Elsie manage to walk out disguised as an old lady and get away with it?"

"The mind boggles," grins Daphne.

"I dunno. I dunno." Colin scrapes back his fair hair in despair.

"Och, the police will soon find her. They'll want her for theft now."

"God, that's another thing! She must have been desperate to pinch that money! In her right mind she'd give it away, not pinch it. What the hell am I going to do?"

"Y'can only go back to the hotel and wait. She might find her way back, y'never know."

"How can she? She seems to think she's in bloody Australia!"

Daphne starts the mini-van's engine. "Wael, I must get back, anyway. I want to catch Carlos before he goes out for the afternoon."

"Can't think why you're bothering with him," says Colin pettishly, fastening his seat belt.

"I love him."

"Love him!"

"Aye, just as you obviously love y'wife."

He looks surprised. "Reckon you must be right, Daph. Love's a bugger, ain't it?"

As soon as she draws into the forecourt of the Ocean View, Colin is out of the van and chasing up the stairs to the bedroom in the forlorn hope that Daphne may be right and Elsie has found her way back. His hopes were further raised when he'd noticed the bedroom key wasn't on the board.

At the top of the stairs he runs into, of all people, Billy Greenhorn. He'd forgotten all about him.

"Goood aafternooon," beams that gentleman.

"You seen my wife?" demands Colin.

Billy looks astonished. "Why no! I thought your good lady was missing."

"So she bloody is, mate."

He pushes past him and hurries to the bedroom door. He turns the knob. It gives. The door is unlocked!

"You there, Els'?" he calls as he pushes the door open.

No answer. He goes into the room and stops transfixed when he sees the state of it.

"'Ullo, 'ullo! We've had visitors!" he exclaims aloud.

He stares in disbelief at the drawers hanging open, the gaping wardrobe, the clothes and shoes strewn everywhere. His eyes fall on his document case lying open-mouthed on the bed.

The old fivers! He spots the money belt – empty! The bastards have even swiped the old fivers!

He flops on to the bed. He is so distraught he doesn't notice the old lady's clothes with Elsie's note tucked in them on the bed beside him. This is the last straw. As if he hasn't enough troubles already without being robbed! Well, he thinks grimly, at least they didn't get away with any cash they could use – there wasn't any to get away with.

But how did they get in? His policeman's curiosity makes him go to the door to examine the lock. No sign of damage. The thief must have used the key. The door was unlocked, he recalls. Probably just helped himself to the key off the board in reception. Easy enough.

Then he remembers seeing Billy Greenhorn at the top of the stairs. What was he doing up here? Surely that bumbling old fool couldn't have done it? Or could he? That beaming face has been haunting him ever since he first saw it.

"My God, I know who he is!" he cries suddenly, leaping up.

He's off down the stairs regardless of his still-aching back. He can't have gone far, Colin thinks. He dashes into the lounge, but it is empty. He crosses the foyer, and as he opens the dining room door, walks slap bang into Billy.

"Come out of retirement then, have we, Reggie? Back to the old tricks, eh?" Colin pushes him back against the wall amid the greenery. "Should have recognised your bloody mug before – seen it on the walls of the nick enough times."

Billy's mouth opens but nothing comes out.

"Now you listen. I've had a real bellyful these last few days and I'm in no mood for a lot of mucking about, so just hand it over, eh?"

"W-w-w-what?" stutters Billy.

Gangster-fashion, Colin grabs him by the tie and forces him up against the wall. "You heard what I said!"

Enter Mr P. from the kitchen, carrying a fistful of cutlery. It clatters to the floor when he sees them. "Mr Stilwell! What are y'doing?" he cries.

"Are you aware," Colin bawls at him, "that you are harbouring a wanted criminal in your hotel?"

Mr Pertwee's jaw seizes up. Words won't come.

"This bugger's none other that Reggie the Rifler, well-known thief and conman. He's just done-over my bedroom!"

Mr P. puffs up like an adder. "Thief!" he screams. "Are y'mad!"

"Mad? I'm bloody furious!"

"Let him go or I shall call the police!"

"Great! You do that. I can't wait to get him behind bars."

Give him his due, Mr P. valiantly tries to haul Colin off Billy, but he's no match for an ex-cop. Pinning Billy to the wall with one hand, Colin shoves Mr Pertwee off with the other, sending him sprawling across a table, dragging off the tablecloth, and with it the jam jar of artificial carnations thereon.

"Reet!" declares Mr P., rising from the debris. "That settles it. I have made allowances for your behaviour in view of y'various misfortunes, but I cannae have m'father-in-law treated in this fashion. I am sending for the police."

With dogged steps he makes for the door.

"Wait!" shouts Colin suddenly.

Mr P. turns. "Aye?"

"Did you say your *father-in-law*?"

"Aye, m'wife's father."

"I know what a father-in-law is," growls Colin. "Don't you try kidding me, mate. Your wife's a Scot!"

"Aye, so was her mother. But her father's from London."

Colin gawps and swallows hard. He can't believe it.

"*And*," adds Mr P. triumphantly, "he's *not* a common thief. Before he retired he was a much-respected impresario, y'ken?"

"Then that makes him Daphne's grandfather!" It's all beginning to make sense.

"Aye, that's reet."

Colin turns a questioning gaze on Billy who nods vigorously. It's hard to believe but he feels it must be true.

"Sorry, mate. Case of mistaken identity. You're the spitting image of Reggie the Rifler." He smoothes down Billy's jacket and straightens his tie. "No hard feelings, eh?"

Billy, too dazed to answer, shakes his head and beats a hasty retreat.

"Mr Stilwell," says Mr P., molto agitato, "I cannae permit this to go on. I'll have to ask y'to leave."

"Look, mate, I'm sorry, I really am. All this trouble over me wife and that has got me all mixed up."

"Aye, I understand you're not y'wee sel', but—"

"Look," interrupts Colin, "somebody's done over our room. I've just been robbed of over five hundred quid in old fivers, so you'd better call the police just the same."

"But are y'sure your wife didn't take it when she left the noo?"

"Whatcha mean?"

"When she left just a wee while ago."

Colin jolts as if he's been electrocuted. "You mean she's been back here?"

"Aye, did y'not know?"

"No, I bloody didn't! Where is she now then, for God's sake?"

"She left again."

Colin is thunderstruck. "You mean she came back here then went off again? Why the hell didn't you stop her?"

"I tried to. She was very upset. I tried to explain. She wouldnae listen." Mr P. splays his hands.

Colin heaves his shoulders in despair. "I dunno. I dunno what's happening any more."

"I'm sorry. I couldnae stop her, she left in such a hurry."

"Did she say where she was going?"

"Aye – Australia."

"Australia!"

"Aye. But she was very confused y'ken. I dinnae believe she meant it."

"*I* believe it," says Colin grimly.

*****

Len is back home, safe and sound.

Both he and his Escort were hauled off the motorway, and the garage soon informed him that his clutch cable had gone. He was faced with the alternative of either leaving the car with them until a new part could be obtained, or having a breakdown service vehicle convey it back to Brockbury for the job to be done there.

When fully awake Len is no fool. Being little more than thirty miles from home he phoned his own garage run by a crony of his, whom he knew would come out in his breakdown vehicle and convey both himself and the car back at a fraction of the cost this garage would probably charge.

And so, after a long wait, he was eventually driven home in style in the back of the breakdown vehicle's cab, along with two dogs and the proprietor's six-year old granddaughter, and with his Escort firmly tethered behind.

And now he is languishing in the bath. He has taken this unprecedented step because he was feeling so demoralised, dirty and done in when he got home. He is hoping that the hot water, laced with a liberal helping of Nora's Tesco Creme Bath Lotion, might somehow soak away the series of costly misfortunes that have befallen him.

But, in fact, as he lies there reflecting on the events of the past two days, he again feels quite pleased with himself. It has been a real adventure, and he reckons he's come out of it pretty well, even if it has proved a costly exercise. *And*, he reminds himself with satisfaction, he's done it without any advice or instruction from Nora.

Thinking of Nora makes him wonder how she is getting on in Greece and when she is likely to arrive home. He is concerned now about the Snooker Final due to take place at the Sports and Social on Saturday. What with not knowing when Nora is likely to be back, Elsie apparently missing, and Colin stuck in Benthaven penniless, he can't see how they can possibly hope to make it. He reckons it'll either have to be cancelled or postponed. But first, he'd better get on and ring Colin, as he told Mr Pertwee he would, and find out what the latest situation is down there.

So he clambers out of the bath, has a shave and redresses, but as he's lumbering down the stairs to phone Colin the phone beats him to it and starts chirping. That'll be him now, he thinks.

But it isn't.

"Hello, Dad!"

"Gavin! Where are you?"

"Still in Greece."

"What's happening? How's things going?"

"Great. We thought you'd like to know Georgie gave birth to a baby boy earlier today."

"She did? That's wonderful! I bet your mum's pleased."

"Over the moon."

"Everything okay? Both doing well?"

"Fine! No problems at all."

"So when's your mum coming home?"

"She's just left. She was going to phone you herself, but they had to hurry to catch the ferry."

"Any idea what time they will get home?"

"Well, that's the problem. You see, Marsha's had a bit of an accident. She slipped on the hospital steps and sprained her ankle. Nothing too serious, fortunately, but it's very painful for her to walk, and she doesn't want to more than she can help, obviously. So what Mum wants you to do is to take the car to Heathrow and meet them."

"Me go to Heathrow!"

"If you leave soon you should be there in plenty of time.

Their flight from Athens is due in there at eight twenty."

"But I can't! The car's in dock, the clutch cable's gone."

"Oh! That's awkward. Well, can't you hire a car?"

"*Hire* one!" The very suggestion appals him. "I'm not driving a strange car all round Heathrow! Your mother would have forty fits if I drove Marsha back in a strange car!"

"Well, couldn't you get someone else to drive you? What about Colin?"

"He's still in Benthaven."

"Oh. Can't one of your other friends take you?"

"I can't expect them to take me all the way to Heathrow at a moment's notice! Can't they get a taxi or something?"

"They could, but we've no means of letting them know you can't meet them. They'll be waiting for you at the airport, not knowing what's happening."

"They shouldn't go making these arrangements without making sure I'm able to do it!" Len is really angry for once.

"I'm afraid it was my idea in the first place, Dad. I was just trying to help Marsha. Look, the only thing I can suggest is that you try phoning Heathrow and see if you can get a message conveyed to them when they arrive."

Len doesn't fancy having to do that. "But we can't be sure they'd get the message – you know what these places are."

"Well, it's either that, or get there yourself somehow or other."

Len heaves a long-drawn-out sigh. "I suppose I'll *have* to hire a car or summat. All right, Gavin, leave it with me. I'll find a way of getting there."

"Sorry about this, Dad. I was just trying to be helpful."

"Well, you should check before you go making arrangements for other people."

"Yes, you're right. Sorry." Gavin is very contrite.

"What time did you say they get there?"

"20.20 hours – twenty past eight tonight."

"All right. I'll think of something. Don't worry."

When he's put down the phone Len loses no time in reaching for the whisky bottle. This demands some heavy thinking. It never rains but it pours, he moans to himself, as he slumps into his armchair. He's never been to Heathrow but from what he's seen of it on the telly it's a pretty chaotic place. He wouldn't fancy driving there in his own Escort, never mind in some hired car. And having bothered his old crony at the garage once already today, he can't expect him to turn out again to take him. Nor does he fancy phoning Heathrow to get a message given to Nora and Marsha. If they didn't get it there'd be hell to pay.

But who else can he get to help him? He sits and thinks long and hard, long enough for the whisky to lubricate his imagination. There's just one person who might. It's a very long shot, but worth a try. He gets up and goes to the phone to ring Cyril.

Chapter 16

Boris has acquired a puppy since Colin and Elsie went away on holiday. Cyril's little bitch Tina had a litter a few weeks back. Boris watched the process with solemn fascination and followed the puppies' progress with such interest that Cyril was moved to offer him one of the litter for a pet.

As a result Boris no longer goes tearing off at nights with his mates. Nor does he have them round his dad's house creating mayhem. Instead he devotes himself to the puppy, getting up at unheard of hours to walk him, clearing up puddles and piles from Elsie's carpets, searching for something suitable for the little creature to sleep in, which in the end turns out to be an old holdall he found down in his dad's shed.

He has decided to call him Renwick, for no better reason than that he happened to notice the name above a shop front when he first brought the little creature home, tucked in his motorcycling jacket. The name seemed to suit the black, snub-nosed little devil, Boris thought.

He is sitting on the settee watching with fascination as Renwick makes short work of shredding today's copy of the *Sun* when the phone cheeps. Normally he wouldn't bother to answer it, but this afternoon he thinks it could be Cyril.

"'Ullo?"

"Boris?"

"Yer."

"It's y'dad."

"Whacha want?"

"Listen. I'm in dead trouble. It looks as though Elsie has gone mad."

"You've found her, then?"

"Eh? Well, yes and no. Found out eventually she'd had an accident on a push-bike and lost her memory. But it must be more than just that. It seems she came back to the hotel while I was out looking for her, packed her bags and told everyone she's off to Australia."

"Go on?" Boris finds this mildly interesting.

"I've got to try to stop her, but the trouble is I'm skint. I've only got ten quid. You got any cash there?"

"Dunno."

"Well find out! Let me know how much. I'll hold."

Boris plods up to his room and counts the wages he's received from Cyril and what remains of his unemployment pay.

"About sixty quid," he tells his dad on his return.

"That all? Well, it'll have to do. Now listen, I want you to drive down here right away and bring that money and any other money you can lay your hands on. Got that?"

"Yer. Where to?"

"Benthaven, of course!"

"Where's that?"

"Near Brighton. Look, you'd better write it all down. Get a pencil and paper."

"Right."

Colin gives him detailed instructions of where to come and how to get there. "Sure you've got all that?"

"Yer."

"Leave as soon as you can and don't hang about. On the other hand, don't go mad and get yourself killed. Now what I intend to do is this. You get here as soon as you can, then I'll take over and drive us straight to Heathrow."

"Heathrow?"

"The airport, you fool. If she's going to Australia she'll be heading for Heathrow, won't she?"

"Might go to Gatwick."

Colin hasn't thought of that. "No, she'll go to Heathrow cos she knows it. That's where she went from years ago. Anyhow, that's our best bet."

"Could have already left by the time we get there."

"Shouldn't think so. She'd have to be damned lucky to get a flight that quick. We'll have to take our chances. All I know is that I've got to do me best to stop her."

"It's me day for going to Cyril's tomorrow."

"Then you'll have to cancel it. Ring him and tell him a family emergency has cropped up."

"Right."

"Look, don't let me down, will you? I'm depending on you."

"That makes a change."

"Don't be sarky. See you soon."

Boris is not averse to this unexpected piece of excitement. He wouldn't be averse to driving to the North Pole so long as he could do it on his motorbike and with Renwick in the sidecar.

Without even bothering to clear up the confetti the puppy has made of the newspaper, he dons his cycling clobber and prepares to leave.

Then he remembers he hasn't phoned Cyril. Patiently he removes his helmet and picks up the phone. But the line is engaged.

He tries again – still engaged.

"Oh, sod it."

He slams down the phone, replaces his helmet, puts Renwick in his holdall and leaves.

*****

For once, Cyril is neither in the bath nor washing his feet when the phone goes. He's just made himself a cheese and pickle sandwich and happens to be passing the phone, or he'd have left it for Glennis to answer.

"Bupp's Market Garden," he says, taking a bite of his sandwich.

"Hello, Cyril – it's Len."

"Hello, Len. How be?"

"In a bit of a fix, Cyril. Hoping you can do me a big favour and help me."

"Favour?" Cyril's on his guard. "What sort of favour?"

"You remember I told you Nora has gone to Greece with Marsha Bloom cos there was a bit of a panic over Georgie and the baby?"

"Oh ar! How's things now?"

"Fine! The baby's arrived. No problems after all, it seems."

"Fancy! Hear that, Glennis? Nora's a grandma at last!"

"Trouble is," continues Len quickly, before Cyril gets too

carried away, "Nora and Marsha are on their way home now and Nora wants me to meet 'em at the airport cos Marsha's ricked her ankle or summat. Only thing is, me car's in dock – clutch cable's gone. Was wondering if there's any chance you can take me in your Land Rover."

Cyril chokes on his sandwich. "Oh, dunno about that..."

"Wouldn't bother you," Len goes on, "only I can't let 'em know I can't make it, see, cos they're already in the plane on their way."

"Oh, I dunno…"

"I'll pay the petrol and everything," adds Len.

That makes a difference. "Well...have to see what Glennis says."

"You do that."

Cyril perches his sandwich on the table by the phone while he goes into the living room where Glennis is watching telly and licking a walnut whip.

"Boy or girl, is it?" she asks.

Cyril starts. "He didn't say."

"Well ask him, will you?"

"In a minute. He wants to know if I can take him to meet Nora, cos his car's conked out."

"Coming back from Greece, is she?"

"Ar, I suppose."

"With the baby?"

"Dunno."

"When does he want you to go?"

"This evening, I think. He's paying and that."

Glennis licks her fingers as she finishes off the walnut whip. "Don't see why not. Nothing much you have to do, is there?"

Cyril brightens. He fancies a bit of a change. "Nothing Boris can't do tomorrow."

"What about your arm?"

"Reckon I can manage." He's not going to miss the chance of a free outing because of that.

"There you are then. Make a little break for you, so long as you're not too late back."

"Ar."

"So tell him yes, and find out about the baby."

Cyril returns to the phone and takes another bite of his sandwich before speaking.

"You there, Len?"

"I'm here."

"That'll be all right then. Shan't be too late back, shall us?"

"Shouldn't be. Plane arrives a bit after eight, so we should be back by half ten. Course, the plane could be late and that."

"Don't forget to ask about the baby," calls Glennis.

"Is it a boy or a girl?" Cyril asks Len.

"Um...boy, I think."

"It's a boy, Glennis!"

"What they going to call him?" shouts Glennis.

"What's his name?" asks Cyril.

"Dunno, didn't say. Look, we'd better get on. We've got to get to Heathrow and there might be traffic hold-ups."

"Heathrow?" Cyril's heard of it. "Near London, ain't it?"

"That's right, and it's five now. We ought to try to get away in an hour, so can you come to collect me about six? Give ourselves plenty of time."

"Right you are."

"Thanks. Much appreciate it, Cyril. See you soon."

The mention of London has given Cyril another buzz. His mind flits back to the good old days when he was doing his National Service in the Army. He'd been a bit of a lad then, spending much of his leave up the West End, going to saucy shows and generally having a good time. He hasn't been there since and wouldn't mind going back to see how it's changed. Not that he's likely to have the chance. Pity.

He lights his pipe thoughtfully and goes into the living room, leaving his cheese and pickle sandwich by the phone.

*****

Due to their last-minute booking, Marsha and Nora are not sitting together on the flight from Athens to Heathrow. As a result Nora is feeling even more nervous than she did on the outward flight, having some skeletal drop-out of a young man sitting next to her instead of the reassuringly substantial Marsha.

Nor has the journey from Thyros by boat and hydrofoil

proved easy with Marsha hobbling along with two aluminium walking sticks bequeathed to her by the hospital, and with Nora herself having to do all the porterage. But now the aircraft is fully airborne and seat belts unfastened, she is feeling more relaxed and able to think happily about her first grandson and dream about his future.

At least she is until the young man next to her becomes a bit chatty.

He looks up from the tomb of a book on his lap with a big sigh and snaps it shut. "Travelling by air is incredibly boring, don't you find?" he says to Nora in an educated voice. "One feels it is a golden opportunity to catch up with one's studies, but when it comes to it one is unable to concentrate. At least, that's what I find."

"Can't be easy," says Nora, not knowing what else to say. She is surprised to find him so well spoken.

"I'm Wallace, by the way. Everyone calls me Wally, of course." He extends a long, tapering hand finished off with grimy fingernails. "How do you do?"

"Pleased to meet you." She feels honour-bound to take the hand. It feels like a flabby piece of steak.

"Just returning from your holiday?" asks Wally, after a brief interlude during which he took off his steel-rimmed glasses and wiped them with a crumpled handkerchief.

"Well...not exactly. Me daughter-in-law has just given birth unexpectedly to me first grandson while on holiday in Thyros and we've been to see them."

"Really? How exciting for you! So he'll be a little Greek – not a little Turk." He laughs at his own attempt at a joke. "Perhaps that, too!" he adds.

Nora is all set to acquaint him with the details, but Wally seems to have other ideas.

"Thyros..." he says reflectively. "Not one of the more interesting islands, archaeologically speaking. Seems to have taken a back seat during classical times. Been occupied by some state or other over the centuries – Minoans, Persians, Venetians and the rest." He pauses to tap the book on his lap. "I'm an archaeological student, you see."

"Fancy!" Nora's not too sure what that means.

"I'm just returning from a dig on Aegina. Now there's a fascinating island! Silver coins were minted there, you know. And some of the finest sculptors worked there..."

And Wally is off on his own subject. Nora tries to listen politely and nods in what she hopes are the right places, but soon her eyelids begin to droop.

Then Wally abruptly changes the subject.

"It appears your friend has had an accident. Nothing too serious, I hope?"

Nora starts. "Oh! No, not really. She slipped on the hospital steps and hurt her ankle."

"Not broken?" Wally is full of concern.

"No, no, but very painful."

"I'm sure. I noticed at the airport you were having to carry all the luggage. It looked much too heavy for you."

"Well, I managed." She is pleased to receive a little sympathy for a change.

"If you like..." continues Wally diffidently, "when we reach Heathrow I'll procure a trolley. I've only got my haversack, so there would be plenty of room for your cases, and I'll push it for you."

"Ooh lovely! Thank you very much!"

"And perhaps you'd like me to changes places with your friend now, so that you can have a chat about your new grandson?"

Nora is all too happy to accept. Baby Jonathon is much more interesting to talk about than archaeology. But what a nice considerate young man, she thinks. You can never go by appearances.

*****

Elsie is standing in the Departures Hall of Terminal 2 at Heathrow airport with her case at her feet. She looks and feels completely lost. It's like some vast shopping arcade, so different from when she was last at Heathrow all those years ago, when she returned from Australia after Cliff had turned her out and Brig had deserted her for the Outback.

She has slept most of the way up in the train from Brighton, but she is still feeling dozy and confused, her memory still irritatingly coming and going. She's not even sure what she's doing here, why all of a sudden she felt it so vital to go to Australia.

What she does know is that she is hungry. She can't remember when she last had anything to eat or drink, but she's certainly in need of something now. Among the myriad of signs confronting her she spots one pointing to pubs and restaurants and follows it, her case feeling ten times its weight as she lugs it wearily up the steps.

There isn't a lot of choice at the cafeteria, but it will do. She grabs a tray and helps herself to a slice of Quiche Lorraine and a cup of coffee, then goes to find herself a seat.

The cafeteria is almost empty. A sprinkling of people, waiting for their flights, are trying to fill the vacuum between one life and the different one to come with food and drink. Elsie finds an empty table close to one where two airhostesses are involved in earnest conversation. She feels the world to be pressing in on her, squeezing out what little energy she has left. She makes an effort to sort out in her mind what made her come here. It was this overwhelming impulse to go to Australia, of course, which seems to be diminishing by the minute. She realises now her boys are almost grown up and leading their own lives over there, her desire to rescue them from Cliff and that woman being a nightmare from the past. But she would like to see them again, even so, and now she's come this far, she thinks she may as well make the trip.

But what about Colin and that girl? Colin? That's right, his name is Colin, not Conrad. If only she could remember what all that was about! And her accident, how she had come to be on that push-bike? She touches her head. It is still very tender, still aching.

These questions revolve in her mind without let-up, but no answers come. Heaving a heavy sigh she picks up her knife and fork and nibbles at the quiche. At least there is one thing about which she is certain; she cannot possibly face flying straight on to Australia, not tonight, anyway.

She pushes aside the quiche and takes a sip of her coffee without bothering to put in the cream from the little plastic carton. The coffee is lukewarm by this time. She pushes it aside again and returns to the quiche. So what is she going to do? What she craves for more than anything is oblivion, to escape from this whirligig of dislocated thoughts for a bit longer, in the hope that the next time she wakes it will have stopped and she will be able to think more clearly.

A hotel, that's what she needs, somewhere to put down her head for the night, then decide what to do in the morning. But has she the cash? She's got all those five-pound notes she found at in the hotel bedroom. Or did she imagine them? She can't be sure of anything at the moment. She opens her bag. Yes, there they are, and the old lady's credit card in the name of Mrs L. D. Brand. She'll have to use that.

A spurt of resolve brings her to her feet and she begins to make her way out of the cafeteria.

"Where's the nearest hotel?" she asks the woman at the cash desk, who is sitting idly reading a magazine.

"We're surrounded by 'em, luv."

"But how do you *get* there?"

"On the Hotel Hoppa. Go to the Hoppa info desk down in the Arrivals Hall and take y'pick. They'll sort you out. Just follow the signs."

Elsie does, and books herself a single room.

"Take the bus with yellow on the side," says the girl on the desk, "just outside there."

She finds the bus and heaves herself aboard.

"Let me take your case, dear," says the driver. "You look all in. Had a rough trip?"

"You could say that," says Elsie.

She plants herself thankfully in the nearest available seat, not noticing two men in business suits sitting further back. But one of them sees her and finds her face familiar. At length the bus moves off, deftly weaving its way through the dense traffic around the airport, through the approach tunnel, around roundabouts, before eventually pulling up in front of an imposing twenty-odd-storey slab of a building.

"Skyfly International Hotel," announces the driver.

*****

Daphne Pertwee is boiling over like an old tin kettle. She's on her way back to the Ocean View in her dad's mini-van after going to see Carlos at the Craxton Hotel, where he works as a waiter.

Or did.

"He's left," the head waiter told her.

"Left? Y'mean gone out?"

"No, I mean left. Bunked off. Gone back to Spain, and good riddance."

That was when Daphne started to boil.

"Gone back to Spain! When did this happen?"

"Only this afternoon, about an hour ago. Said he was going to get married."

"Och, I dinnae believe this!"

"Straight up. On his way to Heathrow right now."

"The scumbag!" spumes Daphne, savaging her gears. "He'll nae get away with that!"

She skids to a standstill in the Ocean View's forecourt, jumps out of the van, charges up the stairs as if she's on an assault course, and slams the door of her room so hard that she wakes her dad, who's having forty winks on the bed in the room opposite to hers, as he usually does prior to preparing the evening meal for his guests.

Mr Pertwee sits bolt upright on his bed, listening. Now what? he wonders, hearing the commotion coming from his daughter's room. He knows Daphne has a fiery temper which lies dormant most of the time, but once roused is liable to erupt in a spectacular and even dangerous volcanic display. He hasn't forgotten the occasion when she threw a freshly made sherry trifle from the sweet trolley at him, and followed it with a rain of bananas, oranges and apples.

Daphne has become a wee problem to him. All these doubtful friends she goes out with to these dens of iniquity, sneaking in at ungodly hours. He doesn't believe it when her grandfather reports it's all harmless fun and there's nothing to worry about. He's heard what goes on in these places, and it's not what he wants for his lovely Daphne.

If *only* he could sell the hotel and set up his dog-training centre in the highlands of Bonnie Scotland, well away from all these temptations. She would be much happier, he is sure. She loves the dogs and is so good with them. And if he's to make a go of it, he will certainly need her.

But the hotel isn't selling. Only people who can't afford to buy it, like that Stilwell fellow, are showing any interest. Perhaps he should consider lowering the price still further, but he can't really afford to do so.

The bedroom door suddenly bursts open and there stands Daphne, red of countenance and with a rucksack humped on her back. Mr Pertwee leaps up. It is unseemly for his daughter to see him lying on the bed in his underwear. He hastily covers himself.

"Y'should have knocked before—"

"I'm leaving," announces Daphne.

Mr P. forgets his state of undress. An instant thunderstorm darkens his face. "Och, no y'not!"

"Och, yes I am!"

"I'll have nae more of this nonsense! Go back to y'room and prepare y'sel' to serve dinner!"

"I'll do no such thing. I'm leaving."

"Y'll do as y'told!" Mr P. fairly dances with paddy.

"Not this time, Father. Y'cannae make me, I'm old enough to please mysel'. I'm off to Spain."

"Spain!"

"Aye, to marry m'lover."

"*Marry...?*" The words won't come. He rises to his full insignificant stature. "You'll do no such thing, m'lassie! Back to y'room!"

"Balls," says Daphne.

"I'll nae have that language in this hoose!"

"You'll nae have to. I'm off to Heathrow reet noo, and y'cannae stop me. I'll no longer have y'bossing me aroond, Father, telling me what to do and say. I've had it! I'll be off and oot of y'hair just as soon as I've said goodbye to Mother."

Exit Daphne in a whirlwind.

Mr Pertwee rushes to the door after her. He is halfway along the corridor before he realises he's still in his underwear and hastily backtracks into the bedroom, just in time to hear a thunderous roar coming from outside the window. As he frantically struggles into his trousers he stares out to see what it is.

A Kawasaki ZXR 400 motorbike with a green and yellow sidecar attached is roaring into the hotel's forecourt and comes to a stop in the parking space reserved for Billy Greenhorn's Merc.

*****

Mr Pertwee isn't the only one to hear the roar, but to Colin the sound is all too familiar. He leaps up from the armchair in the lounge, where he has been impatiently waiting for Boris to arrive with his money, and angrily rushes out.

"You bloody idiot!" he yells. "I meant you to bring the *car* – not that rattletrap!"

"Then you should have bloody said," responds Boris unconcernedly as his head emerges from his helmet.

"You should have bloody known! You expecting me to bump all the way to London on that thing?"

"Suit y'self."

"You brought the money?"

"Yer."

"Well, that's something. But I suppose you realise what this means? I'm not driving that thing, so you'll have to go on all the way to Heathrow."

"Easy." He can drive his bike till doomsday can Boris. No problem.

"There won't be time for you to rest or nothing, it's getting on for six already."

Boris doesn't answer but ambles round to the sidecar and hauls his puppy out of the holdall by the scruff of its neck.

Colin goggles. "What's that!"

"Renwick."

"It's what?"

"Renwick, me puppy. Cyril give him me."

"Ye gods and little fishes! That's all I need – a bleedin' puppy to nurse all the way to London. Why the hell didn't you leave him at home?"

"Got to be fed and that."

"Then you should have left him with Cyril."

"No time."

Colin sighs. "Well you can't take him into the hotel. There's a couple of thundering great Alsatians in there. They'll have him for supper."

"Got to take him for walkies," grunts Boris.

Colin's eyes widen so much they're in danger of falling out. "*Walkies*?" Is this really Boris, son of Colin? "Well, there's no time to take him far. We've got to get cracking."

Mr Pertwee comes tearing out of the hotel, staring around frantically.

"Have y'nae seen her?" he demands of Colin.

"Seen who?"

"Daphne."

"No, mate."

Mr P. looks both relieved and puzzled. Then he turns an unfavourable eye on Boris. "I'm afraid there are no vacancies here," he snaps, "so perhaps you would kindly remove that...vehicle from my premises."

"Eh?" says Boris.

Colin is indignant. "No need to talk to him like that – he's my son!"

"Och! So sorry...I dinnae know." Mr Pertwee splays his hands.

"He's come to take me to Heathrow, see if I can find me wife and stop her taking off for Australia."

"Aye, of course." His words are automatic. He is still looking around for Daphne.

Even so, he doesn't see her when she comes striding out of the hotel, looking as if she's off on a hiking holiday.

But Colin sees her and looks at her attire in surprise. "Hello! Where you going?"

"I'm leaving," she grunts.

"Och, no y'not!" cries Mr P.

"Och, yes I am!" cries Daph.

"Don't you contradict me, m'lassie! Back to y'room the noo! Get ready to serve dinner."

"Drop dead."

The colour of her dad's face suggests he might. "I willnae have y'talking like that! Back to y'room, do y'hear?" He gives her a violent shove, hotelwards.

Daphne pushes him back. "Och, get lost!"

"Back to y'room. Do y'hear! *Do y'hear!*"

Mr P. pushes her again. Daphne retaliates. A shoving competition is in danger of developing. Excitement mounts. Renwick supplies a complementary chorus of soprano yapping, joined by a basso profundo obligato from the hotel.

"'Ere," intervenes Boris, placing his massive body between them. "Back off, you." He gives Mr P. a push that makes him reel backwards.

Mr Pertwee recovers himself but stays his distance. "Mind y'own business!" he yells.

"Now then!" warns Colin in his policeman's voice. "Can't have none of this. What's going on?"

"She's going to Spain after that Spanish heathen," cries Mr P.

"He's not a heathen, he's a Catholic!"

"Worse still!"

Daphne turns to Colin. "Y'see what I mean? M'father''s nothing but a bigoted ass!"

"I'll not have y'call me..." Mr P. is beside himself and again tries to reach Daphne.

"Back off, I said," growls Boris, barring his way.

"I don't get it," says Colin to Daphne. "I thought you were going to see Carlos at—"

"Och, I did go. But he's left. He's going back to Spain and marrying that bitch, Cheryl."

"Marrying her, eh? You can't go chasing after him in that case."

"He'll nae marry anybody but *me*, I promise you that!" Daphne is quite definite about it. "I'm on m'way to Heathrow to stop him."

"Och, no y'not!" yells Mr Pertwee.

"Och, yes I am!" yells Daphne.

"That's enough!" Colin is in his element. It's like being back on the beat, preventing an affray. "She's over age," he tells Mr P. "You can't stop her. It's the law, even if you think it's a bloody stupid thing for her to do."

"It's nae stupid!" cries Daphne.

"I told you, he's not worth it, Daph. If he's decided to marry that other girl, there's nothing more you can do. That's it. End of story."

"Never! I love him! I love him! I cannae live without him! I'll nae let him marry that cow. Never, never, never!"

High drama indeed for a Thursday evening in Ensdale Terrace. Mr P. looks anguished, Colin perplexed. Boris is entertained. Better than the rubbish he sees on TV.

"Well, you'll have to sort it out between yourselves," says Colin. "I got me own problems. Got to get to Heathrow meself."

"Y'nae going to Heathrow y'sel'?" exclaims Daphne.

"Elsie's got it into her head she wants to go to Australia. Got to stop her."

"Och, would y'nae give me a wee lift?"

"Over my dead body!" cries Mr P.

"Can't give you a lift." Colin points to the motorbike and sidecar. "No room in that damn thing."

"Could ride pillion," suggests Boris, chuffed to think someone actually wants to ride on his bike.

"Och, greet! *Please!*"

Colin scratches his head. "Well, I dunno..."

"*Please!* I helped y'this morning, remember?"

"True, all right then. But you go in the sidecar, I go on the pillion."

"Done," says Daph.

"Got to give Renwick his walkie first," says Boris.

Colin points to the ground. "No need, he's already done it."

"On m'forecourt!" screams Mr P.

"Let's go," says Colin.

Daphne piles into the sidecar, stuffing her rucksack into the toe. Boris puts the holdall on her lap with Renwick in it.

Mr Pertwee watches dementedly. "Och, Daphne, dinnae go!" he pleads. "What am I to do? What aboot the wee dogs?"

Daphne ignores him. Boris re-helmets himself. Colin climbs on the pillion. The Kawasaki roars into life, does a deft U-turn in the forecourt, and roars off, narrowly missing Billy Greenhorn's Merc as it returns from The Fisherman's Float, where its owner has been revitalising the parts that were reached by Colin when he duffed him up.

*****

In the kitchen of the Ocean View, an emergency meeting immediately takes place.

Present: Alec Pertwee, Moira Pertwee, Billy Greenhorn, Boss and Bess.

Mr P. loses no time in opening the proceedings. "That Stilwell fellow has taken her with him to Heathrow," he raves at his wife.

"Don't shout, Alec," she responds. "I'm not deaf."

"But she's going to Spain after that Spanish waiter!"

"I know. She told me."

"Then why did y'nae try to stop her?"

"*Me*, stop her? What you expect me to do aboot it? You're to blame. You're the one who's been coming the heavy father."

"I've only been trying to bring her up in the reet and proper way."

"And a fine job you've made of it! I hope you're proud of yourself."

"But what am I to do?" wails Mr Pertwee.

"What you've got to do right now is to hire someone to wait at table, that's what you've got to do."

"I dinnae mean that. I cannae just let her go, I cannae!"

"She's already gone. We've got dinners to serve shortly so I suggest you lose no time in taking over her work, and start by taking Bess and Boss for their evening walk."

The mention of the magic word brings the two dogs to their feet, flapping their tails expectantly. "Och, no, no, no! I cannae rest until she's back. I cannae let her throw her life away! I'm going after her."

With sudden resolve he leaps up from the waste-bin upon which he has been perching and lunges towards the door.

"You're wasting your time, Alec," retorts his wife scornfully. "She'll take aboot as much notice of you as an elephant does a tic."

"But I must try! I cannae rest until I've tried!"

Mrs Pertwee appeals to Billy, who is standing appraising the situation in his usual beaming manner but minus his Guinness glass. "For God's sake, Father, try to din some sense into him!"

Billy nods. "It's no good, Alec, no good at all."

"I dinnae care! I must try!"

Mr Pertwee rushes out of the kitchen followed by the two animated Alsatians.

Moira Pertwee follows, equally animated. "That's reet, walk out just at dinner time! Don't mind me!"

"Get y'father to help oot!" Mr P. is raiding the till on the reception desk, pocketing wads of notes.

"What! The guests won't get their dinners till midnight if *he* does it!" Mrs P. glares at her father derisively.

"Then call in Mrs Huggings," seethes Mr P.

He slings on a coat, snatches an umbrella from the stand and stamps out, the dogs following him.

"Stay!" he commands, seeing them. Boss and Bess stop, not exactly pleased.

"Guard!"

They sink down at the bottom of the stairs, resigned. It's a dog's life.

Billy ambles up, the irate Moira following.

Mr Pertwee marches off to his mini-van.

"For God's sake, Father," cries Mrs P, "do something! Go with him, try to knock some sense into *both* of them! Daphne might take more notice of you than him, the stupid blundering fool!"

"But you'll need me to—" begins Billy.

"I'll manage. Go on!"

Billy beams and nods; a break is always welcome, even from a life of Guinness.

He's just in time to catch Mr Pertwee as he's reversing out of the forecourt.

"Not to worry, Alec," he says as he climbs into the passenger seat. "She'll listen to me."

The mini-van shifts off with a jerk.

Heathrow looks like having a busy evening.

Chapter 17

"Look!" cries Nora. "Dear old England!"

She feels like breaking into 'The White Cliffs of Dover', but there are no white cliffs to be seen. Instead, she says wistfully, "I wonder if we'll pass over Brighton."

Marsha grunts as she tries unsuccessfully to reach down to soothe her damaged ankle.

"Funny about the bank moving Gavin there," continues Nora. "Bit of a coincidence really, us being on holiday near Brighton and that."

"You know what it's going to mean, don't you?" sniffs Marsha. "Now we've finally got our first grandson we're not going to see anything of him."

"Oh, I know." Nora is well aware of that. It's the one fly in the otherwise highly beneficial ointment that has been applied to her today.

"At least it's done one thing," continues Marsha. "It's definitely made up my mind for me that Olly has to retire. We'll go and live in Brighton, as I've always wanted. No doubt Georgie will go back to nursing as soon as she can, so she'll need someone to look after the little mite. There'll be no question of him being left in charge of one of these baby-minders, nor any other such person. One hears such dreadful things these days, doesn't one?"

"Oh, I know," says Nora again. And that's another fly in her ointment, she suddenly realises, Marsha moving out of Webbley Park just as she is hoping to move in. But despite everything Nora's mind is still ticking over as brightly as ever. "I've been thinking," she says. "It's possible we might be moving to Brighton as well."

Marsha looks at her sharply. "Oh, really?"

"Course, it's by no means certain at the moment, but we've heard the private hotel where we're staying in Benthaven is up for sale, and it occurred to us we might take it on and run it ourselves."

"I see." Marsha sounds disdainful and none too pleased.

"Not just me and Len, of course," continues Nora. "We couldn't afford to buy it on our own. But our friends are interested too, so we might go in with them."

"Really."

"It makes sense if you think about it. Elsie's worked in restaurants and that, Colin knows all about security, there's not much Len don't know about bars, and I can deal with the accounts side of things. So I don't see why we shouldn't make a go of it, do you?"

Marsha takes a middle line. "Possibly."

The announcement is made that they are beginning their descent into Heathrow, to fasten their seat belts and not to smoke. Marsha has trouble fastening her seat belt across her bulky body. Archaeologist Wally leans across to her.

"Allow me, madam," says he with a winning smile.

"I can manage thank you," answers Marsha in her imperious way.

"Worst part of the trip, the landing, I always think."

"H'mp," grunts Marsha.

Nora grips the arms of her seat, shuts her eyes and prays her newly gained grandmothership is not about to be abruptly terminated. It isn't. The plane makes a smooth landing and trundles its way to Terminal 2.

"Shall I try to obtain a wheelchair for you?" asks Wally, as Marsha is hobbling up the plane's gangway.

"No, thank you!"

When they eventually reach the luggage hall Wally instantly procures a trolley and helps Nora heave the cases off the carousel, then puts them on the trolley along with his rucksack. With Marsha walking with the gait of a tortoise, and at roughly the same speed, they proceed solemnly towards Customs.

"If you have nothing to declare," says Wally, "we can follow the green signs."

"We haven't," affirms Marsha.

"Great," says Wally. "So 'Green' it is."

But they haven't proceeded very far before a burly white-shirted Customs Officer, who is standing to one side with his arms folded and eyeing the departing passengers with apparent disinterest, suddenly springs to life and bars their way.

"Would you step over here a moment please?" says he.

"What, all of us?" asks Wally.

"If you don't mind, sir."

Marsha draws herself up on her walking sticks. "We have nothing to declare, we haven't bought anything."

"This way, please." The Customs Officer indicates the way.

"I really fail to see the point of having a way through for people with nothing to declare," complains Marsha as she hobbles along, "if you intend to stop them anyway."

The officer makes no comment but leads them to a long bench where he mutters a few words to an officer behind it who nods and looks grave. For no apparent reason Wally and his rucksack are moved further down the bench, out of earshot.

"This is an outrage," declares Marsha. "Have you nothing better to do than embarrass upright citizens like my friend and myself?"

An officer with a beard, who'd look more at home on the bridge of a battleship, approaches Nora and holds up a card up for her to read. "Have you read and understood this, madam?"

Nora nods dumbly. She's read it but not understood it.

"Have you anything you would like to declare?"

"Haven't bought nothing."

"Is that your case?"

"Yes," mumbles Nora.

"Would you mind opening it, please?"

Nora couldn't have felt guiltier had it been full of bank notes. Clumsily, she fiddles with the zips and locks.

Marsha is going through a similar ordeal with a weedy-looking officer, but her reaction is much less docile.

"I'll have you know young man that I sustained a very painful injury while I was away which is not being helped by having to stand while you waste your time and the nation's money treating me like a common criminal."

"Bring the lady a chair, Maureen," sighs the officer.

"I prefer to stand, thank you."

Nevertheless, Marsha sits when the chair is brought.

"Will you open the case, please?"

"I warn you it is very full. I shall expect it to be repacked precisely as it is."

"Just open it, if you don't mind."

With a sniff of exasperation she opens the case. A bottle of bath oil springs out and rolls across the bench. She seems to have brought with her the entire contents of her bathroom.

The officer examines each item in turn, tapping it, sniffing it. He rifles through her underwear, delves into the pockets of a jacket, feels around the lining of the case.

Marsha's face blotches with indignation. "I hope you are satisfied, young man?"

"That gentleman who is accompanying you," says the officer, "would he be your son?"

"My *son*? Certainly not! If he were, he wouldn't appear in public looking like a putrefying fish."

"Some other relative then, or a friend perhaps?"

"Neither, I'm relieved to say. He merely offered to help us with our luggage, which I suppose at least shows he has some consideration for the infirm."

"I see." The officer studies her searchingly. "May I just take a look at those walking sticks, please?"

"Whatever for? They're not mine, strictly speaking. They were loaned to me by a Greek hospital, which I have every intention of suing for negligence, having caused me to fall on their slippery steps."

"If I may just take a look?"

She thrusts the sticks at him. He examines them closely, pulling out the rubbers from the bottoms and peering up the hollow tubes.

"What do you think I am?" demands Marsha. "A drugs runner?" It isn't until she's said it that it occurs to her that that is exactly what he *does* think.

The officer hands the sticks back to her without comment. "Your handbag please, madam."

"My *handbag*!" She sounds like Lady Bracknell.

"If you please."

Marsha makes a sound somewhat similar to Mr Pertwee's 'Och!' but much more sharp, and thrusts her bag into his hands.

The Customs Officer looks in the bag, extracts her passport

and reads it. "I'll retain this for the moment, madam."

For once Marsha is beyond speech, a condition she is not programmed to sustain too long.

The officer glances up the line at his colleagues and they seem to engage in some kind of secret signalling.

"I must ask you to come with me, madam," he says.

"Come with you? Where? Why?"

"Our enquiries are not yet complete. We may have to carry our investigations further. Help the lady to her feet, Maureen."

A similar requirement is made of Nora who is too far gone to protest.

"What's happening?" she quakes to Marsha.

"Search me," growls Marsha, unaware of her unfortunate choice of words. "They want to waste more of our time and money, no doubt. I shall be reporting this, have no fear."

Still complaining, Marsha hobbles after the Customs man, Nora following, terrified out of her wits and clutching her handbag.

"I trust all this is not going to take long," continues Marsha. "We have someone meeting us, you know. He will be terribly worried if we fail to put in an appearance."

"If you will give us his name we will ensure that he is informed you have been delayed," says the officer.

Marsha and Nora are put in separate rooms, which scares Nora even further and infuriates Marsha to the point of apoplexy. "I will not be treated in this fashion," she rages. "We are honourable and upright citizens. My husband is a highly respected businessman, and have no doubt he will take this to the highest authority – to the House of Lords if necessary."

"Wait here, please," says the officer, unconcerned. "Someone will be along presently."

The doors are shut on them but not locked. Nora finds herself in a plain-walled, windowless room containing three chairs and a table, and a single strip-light above. She has seen this sort of room on the telly, but never has it occurred to her she would find herself shut in such a place.

She hasn't a clue why she's here, even though the officer has tried to explain. She feels lost, alone, wanting Elsie there to share her woes.

She stands miserably in the middle of the room, twisting her sweat-soaked handkerchief.

"Never again," she vows. "Never ever again."

*****

"Will Mr Len Scally, meeting flight OA282 from Athens, please go to the Information Desk," requests a metallic girl's voice all over Terminal 2. "Mr Len Scally to the Information Desk."

But Mr Len Scally isn't there to hear it. At this moment he is in Cyril's Range Rover, just emerging from the tunnel leading into the airport, and is staring round distractedly for somewhere for Cyril to park amid all this chaos.

"Long stay or short stay?" asks Cyril who has spotted the signs.

"Short stay, short stay!" cries Len.

With his pipe between his teeth firmly pointing the correct direction, Cyril grimly follows the signs to the Short Stay 2 car park and stoically sends the Range Rover up the spiral ramps in bottom gear until he finds a vacant slot near the top of the building in which to park.

When they finally come to rest, they both slump back in their seats, traumatised.

"We're late," says Len. "Nora's going to be hopping mad."

"Couldn't be helped. All that traffic and that."

"Better get moving, though." Len opens the Range Rover door none too enthusiastically.

"Ar, suppose so."

Somehow they manage to get themselves across to the main building complex and find themselves in Terminal 1.

"Well I never!" Cyril stands and gapes in amazement. He's never seen such a melange of bustling activity before. Puts Piccadilly to shame, he reckons.

Len is floundering. Where does he start? What does he do? "How the hell are we to find 'em in this lot?" he asks.

"Dunno." But Cyril is feeling brighter than Len at the moment. "Information place over there. Better try that."

When he manages to gain the attention of a smart-looking

girl with over-painted cherry-red lips, Len tells her he's come to meet a Mrs Nora Scally and a Mrs Marsha Bloom.

"Where have they come from?" asks the girl.

"Greece."

"Where abouts in Greece?"

"Dunno." Then Len remembers Nora saying. "Athens, I think."

"Which airline?"

"Airline?"

"Olympic Airways, BA or what?"

"Um…dunno!"

"Do you know the flight number?"

"No."

"What time was the flight due?"

"Can't remember." Len is feeling a bit of a lemon. "I think she said eight something."

The girl bunches her cherry-red lips and taps on her keyboard.

"Well, there is Olympic Airways flight OA282, arrived a few minutes ago at Terminal 2, and British Airways flight BA763 due at Terminal 3 at 21.07. Take your pick."

Len remembers it was eight something. "Must be the first one."

"Terminal 2 then."

"Terminal 2?"

"This is Terminal 1. You'll have to go to Terminal 2. Follow the signs."

They do, along a long, dim passageway with its moving walkway. Cyril eyes it all in wonderment. He's never seen the like. He's finding it exciting and he's glad he came.

They find themselves in the Arrivals Hall of Terminal 2. It is surprisingly quiet. There is a man sweeping up.

"Is this where the planes from Athens come in?" asks Len.

"Don't ask me, mister, I only work here."

Len looks around forlornly. There is no sign of Nora and Marsha.

"Look at the monitor," advises the sweeper-upper. "See if it's on there."

Len hasn't noticed the TV screens before. He peers at one.

"Rome, Frankfurt... Yes, there it is – Athens, flight OA282, arrived 20.20."

"That's twenty past eight," he translates for Cyril's benefit. "It's nearly twenty to nine – they should be here."

"Well, they ain't," says Cyril.

"Must be late. Have to wait, then. Might as well take a seat."

Cyril pulls out his pipe and pouch. Len sits with his legs stuck out, contemplating his highly polished shoes.

*****

"Long stay or short stay?" shouts Boris over his shoulder at Colin on the pillion as they emerge from the tunnel leading to the airport.

"Short stay, you moron!" Colin yells back. "We're not taking off for a holiday in the Bahamas!"

Boris follows the sign for Short Stay 2 for no reason other than it seems easier than Short Stay 1. The roar of the Kawasaki as it ascends the concrete ramps reverberates like Concorde taking off. Boris has to go almost to the top of the building before he finds a vacant parking lot, not far away from a Range Rover, which he would have recognised had he happened to spot it.

Colin peels himself off the pillion. The ride has done nothing for his aching back.

"Come on!" he cries. "Let's see if we can find her."

Boris grabs Renwick from the holdall Daphne has been nursing, and sets him on the ground.

"He'll want to go, I 'spect," he says.

"He's not the only one," growls Colin. "He'll have to wait, like the rest of us."

Boris puts Renwick back in his holdall and they all trail over to the complex of buildings and find themselves in Terminal 1.

Colin looks around, dumbfounded. "God Almighty! How are we to find Elsie in this lot?"

"Information desk," says Daphne, who has travelled this way before.

When they manage to gain the attention of the girl with the cherry-red lips, Daphne puts her question first and asks for the time of the next plane to Spain.

"What airline?" asks the girl.

"Any airline."

"Destination?"

"Och, wherever the next plane is going."

The girl taps away. "Flight IB3671, 21.00 hours, destination Madrid. Terminal 2. But it's too late to board it."

"No matter, he could be on it." Daphne turns excitedly to Colin and Boris. "I must awa', I might catch him yet. Thanks for the wee lift. I love you both!"

She waves a kiss and she's gone, knapsack on her back.

"Good luck!" Colin calls after her.

Now it's his turn with the cherry-lipped girl, and he asks her when the next plane to Australia takes off.

"Which airline?" asks the girl.

"Any airline."

"Destination?"

"Er…Sydney."

The girl taps away. "BA3857, 21.10 hours, Terminal 4. But it's already boarding."

"Don't matter. Reckon that's the one. Come on, Boris."

Boris starts; he's been watching the girl's cherry-red lips with fascination as she rapped off the information. They reminded him of close-ups for toothpaste commercials he's seen on the telly.

"Did you say Terminal 4?" Colin turns back to ask the girl, having realised he hasn't a clue where it is.

"That's right. You need to take the courtesy bus. Just outside, the stand right at the far end."

"Come on," Colin says again to Boris. "I reckon we might catch Elsie yet."

When they find the stand after many more enquiries, there is no bus waiting.

"How often do these bloody buses run?" growls Colin.

"Dunno."

Colin stumps up and down, not only with impatience but also because he's bursting.

So is Boris, but he stands stolidly. In the holdall he is clutching, Renwick is also bursting.

*****

Nor are they the only ones. Len and Cyril, waiting in the Arrivals Hall of Terminal 2 for Nora and Marsha to put in an appearance, are both pretty desperate too.

"Better not both go together," says Len, "in case they turn up. You go first."

By the time they've both found the toilets and managed to find their way back a further ten minutes has elapsed.

"Still no sign of them then?" asks Len as he resumes his seat.

"No. What we going to do, then?"

"Dunno. Better give 'em a bit longer I suppose."

Len sits silent, staring moodily at his polished shoes.

Cyril once more lights up his pipe and watches the smoke begin its long voyage to the ozone layer. "You remember the old Imperial Airways?" he says after a bit.

Len nods disinterestedly.

"Croydon where they went from, wan't it? Bit different to here. Amazing how things have changed. This place didn't exist then. Bloody marvellous, though."

No response from Len.

"Them big planes – jumbos and that – dunno how they make 'em stay up there. And all them gadgets these days – electronics and that – bloody marvellous! Different world."

"Um," says Len.

"'Spect London's changed a bit too. Ain't been there since I did me National Service, y'know."

"So you said." Len is hoping stave off another bout of nostalgia from Cyril. He's been treated to a surfeit of it all the way from Brockbury.

"Used to come up with the lads when we were on leave. Had some good times, I can tell you. Course, that was before I was married and that. You come to London at all these days?"

"Haven't been for years. Used to come up quite a lot. Nora liked looking round the shops, going to shows and that. But she won't come now. Says it's got too costly."

Cyril nods dolefully. "The old Windmill still going, is it?"

"Dunno." Len's not into that sort of thing.

Cyril relights his pipe thoughtfully. "Y'know, I've been thinking. When I get that bit of a windfall from the sale of Dad's house, reckon I *am* going to retire. Sell up the business and move right away. Go and live in a city where there's summat going on. Enjoy life a bit before I turn me toes up."

You'll have to get a move on then, thinks Len.

"Reckon I made a big mistake going in for market gardening. I'm a town bloke at heart. Seemed a good idea at the time, though, fresh air and that. Glennis was all for it, of course, being a country girl. Suppose I let her talk me into it."

Len is surprised by this admission. "Thought you enjoyed the open air life."

"Novelty wears off after thirty-odd years. Get fed up with it, same thing day after day. More in life than just cabbages and caulies. You've been at Regal Chemicals some years, ain't you Len? Don't you ever want to give it up and do summat different?"

"Suppose so." But Len would really rather give it up and do nothing, except go to the pub.

"Trouble is, Glennis is bound to be agin it. Still, she's had her way all this time so I reckon it's time I had a bit of me own."

"Fair enough." But Len isn't paying attention. He is getting worried about Nora and Marsha. "It's gone nine," he frets. "I wonder what's happened to them."

"'Spect they missed the plane," says Cyril.

"Shouldn't think so." Nora never misses anything.

"Course, could be on that other plane."

"What other plane?"

"What that girl said. Nine summat."

Len starts. He's forgotten about that. "Could be. We'd better hang on a bit and see if they are. Should be here soon."

"Different Terminal, though, wan't it?"

"Terminal?"

"Ar, what that girl said. Terminal 3, she said."

"You sure?"

"Ar. Terminal 3, that's it."

Len suddenly panics. Supposing they're waiting for him there! "Reckon that is what must have happened. We'd better get over there pretty damn quick!"

They follow the signs for Terminal 3.

*****

A white mini-van emerges from the tunnel leading to the centre of Heathrow Airport. Mr Pertwee looks round frantically.

"Where do I go now?" he demands of his father-in-law.

"Short stay car park," says Billy. "Short Stay 2, usually more room. Follow the signs."

Billy Greenhorn is no stranger to Heathrow. He's got a little bolthole in Malta where he sojourns during the winter months.

With reluctance the mini-van climbs the ramps of the Short Stay 2 car park building and comes to rest beside a Kawasaki motorbike with a green and yellow sidecar attached.

"That's it!" cries Mr Pertwee. "That's the motorbike they brought her in! We might catch her yet. Come on!"

But when they emerge from the car park he stops dead, perplexed by the conglomeration of buildings confronting him. "Och, we'll n'er find her here in time!"

"Yes we will," says Billy confidently. "Let's try Terminal 2."

*****

It has gone ten past nine when Nora and Marsha eventually emerge into the Arrivals Hall of Terminal 2.

Nora could have kissed the bearded Customs Officer when he came into that horrid little room and told her she was free to go. He was profuse in his apologies for the inconvenience. They had to be satisfied she and Marsha weren't in league with the young man who was with them, he told her. They've had their eye on him for some time. Apparently Wally has interests of a less cultural nature in addition to archaeology, and attached himself to them in the hope of not being spotted. But Customs have found what they were looking for and Wally is now under arrest.

Marsha received the news of her release with less gratitude. She was past remonstration by this time and her face was a lump of solid granite, apart from her jaw, which worked silently from side to side, like a cow chewing the cud.

Not since her courting days has Nora looked forward to seeing dear old Len's hangdog face so much, and as she emerges into the Arrivals Hall, she gazes around eagerly for her first glimpse of it.

But neither dear old Len nor his hangdog face are to be seen.

"He's not here," she says, her affection swiftly turning to aggravation.

Marsha's grunted response implies that she never really expected he would be.

"Could have just popped to the toilet," says Nora hopefully. "Better sit down and wait a bit."

Marsha hobbles to the nearest seat and slumps down. "We'll give him five minutes," she snaps.

"I don't understand it," says Nora. "I hope he's all right."

Her aggravation with Len has now turned to anxiety. She immediately imagines he's had an accident. Without her at his side he's probably got himself killed driving like a madman on the motorway. She can just see him lying in the mortuary, shrouded in white.

"Men," grunts Marsha. "You'd have thought the Good Lord would have found a more satisfactory means of procreating the human race other than by lumbering us with men."

"I wonder what could have happened to him," frets Nora, not immediately concerned with the Good Lord's works. "What are we going to do if he doesn't turn up?"

"I know what we're going to do. We're going to Olly's hotel for the night. I've had more than I can put up with for one day."

They sit silently for ten minutes, but no Len.

"That's it," says Marsha. "I'm waiting no longer."

"But what about Len?" protests Nora. "We can't go and let him find us gone."

"My dear, that is easily taken care of. Come with me."

Marsha struggles to her feet and toils towards the Information Desk on her sticks, Nora following, pushing the trolley heaped with their luggage.

"This lady wishes to leave a message for her husband who is coming to meet her," states Marsha in her most authoritative voice to the young man behind desk. "Would you please let her have a pad and pen?"

"Certainly, madam."

Nora is supplied with these necessary materials.

"What shall I say?" she asks.

"Say that since he has apparently been delayed in coming to meet us we have gone to the Skyfly Hotel, and would he please join us there immediately."

While Nora is laboriously writing out the message Marsha issues further instructions to the young man.

"Would you please put out a call for a Mr Len Scally to come and collect the message, and keep doing so until he finally does?"

"How do we get to the hotel?" asks Nora once all this is taken care of.

"Quite simply, my dear. We take what they call the Hotel Hoppa, although why they can't spell the word 'hopper' in the accepted manner, I shall never understand. Follow me."

*****

Colin's impatience has turned to anger. The courtesy bus taking himself and Boris to Terminal 4 seems to be taking the scenic route.

"This can't be right!" Colin bawls at Boris when he realises the bus is heading for the M4 motorway. He charges down the bus and accosts the driver. "We *are* going to Terminal 4, I suppose?"

"Yus, mate."

Not entirely convinced, Colin sways back down the gangway as the bus branches on to a slip road and starts meandering out over the airfield, past what looks like a tip for discarded aircraft.

Boris is gazing out of the window with interest. Worth coming for, all this, he thinks. "Wouldn't mind being a pilot and that," he mutters when Colin flops down beside him.

"*You!*" His dad is scornful. "If you flew a plane like you drive that bleedin' bike you'd end up on the moon!"

Colin keeps peering out of the window for some sign of the

Terminal.

"Where the hell is this place, then?" he fumes as the bus rattles on. "In bloody West Africa?" Then he spots a large long building looming up. Ah, that must be it, he thinks.

But no, the bus goes off at a tangent, back into the wilds. "My God, Elsie'll be in Australia before we even reach the bloody Terminal!"

But seven interminable minutes later the bus comes to a standstill. "Terminal 4," announces the driver.

Colin is first off the bus. Boris lumbers after him clutching his holdall and cycling helmet.

"Come on! It's ten past nine. The bloody thing will have gone!"

"Could be late leaving," observes Boris.

"Don't you believe it! Not with the sort of luck I've been having lately."

And he is right. The girl behind the desk informs him that Flight BA3872 for Sydney has just taken off.

"Was my wife on it?" demands the exasperated Colin. "Mrs Elsie Stilwell – or she might be calling herself Mrs Elsie Brannigan."

"I really couldn't say, sir," says the girl disdainfully.

"Well, can't you find out?"

"We don't divulge that sort of information for obvious reasons."

"What obvious reasons?"

"Security reasons."

"Bugger security!" That's the second time in a week that Colin has buggered security. "Surely a man has a right to know if his wife's on a plane?"

"Sorry, can't help you." The girl turns abruptly to her next customer.

Colin doesn't know what to do with himself. He frets and fumes, blaming everyone he can think of.

Then Renwick, fed up with his long incarceration in the holdall, starts whining.

"Can't you shut that animal up?" barks Colin.

"He wants to do his business."

"He can't here!"

But it's too late. Boris has already taken Renwick out of the holdall and the little dog loses no time in relieving himself.

Colin looks round furtively. "Let's get the hell out of here before someone sees!"

"I wanna go meself," says Boris.

"Me too," says Colin. "Come on."

*****

When Len and Cyril arrive in Terminal 3 they learn the British Airways flight from Athens has already landed five minutes before.

"Shouldn't have to wait long then," says Len. "We'll soon know if they're on it."

They sit. Len contemplates his polished shoes. Cyril pulls out his pipe and notices with concern he's running out of baccy. He lights up just the same.

Time ticks by.

"Nora must be thrilled," says Cyril eventually.

"What about?"

"Being a grandmother and that."

"Um." The baby is the least of Len's concerns at the moment.

"Grandkids can be a perishing nuisance mind, when you're getting on."

"'Spect so."

"Still, the women are mad about 'em. Keeps 'em happy, I suppose."

Len nods but doesn't answer.

More time ticks by.

"Yup," says Cyril presently "women don't seem to be interested in nothing but kids. You take Glennis. Soon as we were married she couldn't wait to have 'em. Then when she'd had 'em, kept on about having grandkids. And now she's got 'em she can't wait for the little buggers to grow up and give her greatgrandkids. It never ends, Len. Just when you think it's over, it starts all over again. Can never rest, women. No peace and quiet for long."

"Um," says Len again, but with more feeling.

"Tell you this much, once Dad's house is sold I'm retiring and we'll move right away from all these kids. Made up me mind to it. Going to have a bit of life meself for once."

Wish Nora would bloody hurry up and come, thinks Len.

A trickle of tired-looking travellers begins to emerge.

Len scrambles to his feet. He's feeling as tired as the travellers, and a good deal thirstier. "Come on, let's hope they're among this lot. I shan't be sorry to get home."

They stand and watch as the trickle becomes a flood and the flood becomes a trickle again, and until it eventually peters out altogether.

"Now what do we do?" asks Cyril.

"I dunno. Just don't understand it." In desperation Len tries to think back to what Gavin said on the phone. If only he'd written it down! "Y'know, I reckon it *must* have been that other plane. I'm damned sure Gavin said it arrived at eight something."

"Weren't there though."

"No, but they could be by now. Could have been held up or summat. Reckon we ought to get back there and make sure."

*****

It is coming up to nine thirty when Billy Greenhorn leads a despairing Mr Pertwee into the Departure Hall of Terminal 2. The announcement for Mr Len Scally to report to the Information Desk is being relayed, but both of them are too intent on their own business to recognise the name.

Billy leads the way to the Information Desk.

"Where are we going?" asks Mr Pertwee.

"To find out the times of the planes. Where is it Daphne's heading for, do you know?"

"No, I dinnae."

The young man behind the desk tells them the last plane has left ten minutes ago. That was for Madrid.

"She's gone!" wails Mr Pertwee. "I shall nae see m'fair sweet Daphne again!"

Billy lays a reassuring hand on his son-in-law's arm.

"I doubt it, Alec. She can't be on that plane. She'd have to check in an hour before it left and she wasn't that much ahead of us."

"Y'mean she must still be here?" Open-mouthed and bright-eyed, he stares around frantically.

"Somewhere," says Billy. "But where?"

"We'll find her. We'll search every nook and cranny until…"

Dry of Guinness, Billy's mind is quite sharp. He ignores Mr Pertwee's ravings and asks the clerk the time of the next plane to Spain.

"Where for?" asks the clerk.

"Anywhere."

"09.05 hours tomorrow. Barcelona."

Billy turns to Mr P. triumphantly. "That's the one she'll try for!"

"Och, but she'll ne'er be staying here all the neet!"

"She can't stay here. It'll be closing soon."

Mr P. looks hopeful. "Then perhaps she will give up and go back home!"

Billy shakes his head. "More likely she'll stay the night somewhere and catch that flight in the morning. Best for us to come back then and catch her before she does."

Mr Pertwee is horrified. "Y'mean, go home and come all the way back in the morning?"

Billy beams. "Of course not, Alec! We'll go to a hotel. I'll take you to the hotel I stay at when I return from Malta. You'll like that."

"A hotel! But will it nae be a wee bit expensive?"

"Just a little. But worth it, surely, to save Daphne?"

"Aye. Aye, anything to save m'wee sweet Daphne."

Billy beams. Guinness is looming. "Come on then, we have to take a bus."

*****

"What do we do now, then?" asks Boris as he stands next to his dad in the Gents at Terminal 4.

"Don't ask me. All I know is what I'm *not* going to do."

"Yer? What's that?"

"Ride all the way home tonight in that bloody sidecar of yours."

"Whatcha going to do, then?"

"Have a bloody drink and think about it. Didn't I see a bar or summat out there somewhere? Let's go and find it."

"Suits me," says Boris.

That doesn't take long. Drinking holes have a natural gravitational pull for both Colin and Boris.

"You get 'em," Colin tells his son. "You've still got all the money."

"You look after Renwick, then."

Colin finds himself a seat and sits down thankfully. His back is aching like mad. He feels done in, done up and done for. And at the end of it all he's failed to stop Elsie catching that plane. If she *did* catch it, he wonders suddenly. He knows nothing about catching planes but he's heard of 'stand-by'. Perhaps she couldn't get on that plane and is 'standing-by' until she can. He feels more hopeful. Come to think of it, you probably can't jump on a plane, just like that.

And another thing – how did she think she was going pay the fare? There couldn't have been enough money in that handbag she stole to get her to Australia, and if she thinks she's going to use them old fivers, she's got another think coming. Should have thought of all this before, he scolds himself, instead of haring off in a panic. She could be back in Benthaven right now, might even have gone back home for all he knows.

Boris joins him with the pints and a couple of packets of crisps. "Dear beer here," he grunts as he sits down.

"Cheers," says Colin automatically.

"Cheers," says Boris.

They savour the first sips of their pints.

"Reckon we're here on a wild-goose chase," says Colin.

"Yer? How's that, then?"

"Cos she couldn't have had enough money with her to pay the bloody fare to Australia!"

Boris ponders this. "Dunno why she wanted to go to Australia in the first place."

"Well, she did. Don't ask me why."

"You two have a row or summat?"

"Yes – no, not exactly. It's a long story. She had this accident and hit her head on a traffic signal and ended up in hospital. Lost her memory, they said, but I reckon it did more than that – could have sent her a bit bonkers."

Boris nods, seeming to imply that with Elsie it wouldn't take a lot of doing. He surreptitiously feeds Renwick a crisp. "Who was that girl then?"

"What girl?"

"That girl we gave a lift to."

"Oh, Daphne. She's the daughter of that twit Pertwee who was trying to stop her. She thinks she's got the hots for some Spanish waiter who's suddenly decided to return to Spain, and she's chasing after him, the silly bitch."

"Go on?" Boris munches a crisp thoughtfully. "So what you going to do about Elsie, then?"

"Been thinking about that. Don't think it's possible she could have been on that plane, so I reckon she's either gone home or back to Benthaven. Hope so, or she could be in real trouble."

"So what we going to do? Can't stay here."

Colin sips his beer thoughtfully before answering. "Find somewhere to kip for the night, I suppose, and see how things are in the morning – if we've enough cash, that is. How much money did you bring with you?"

"Dunno." Boris feeds Renwick another crisp.

"You must have some idea!"

"Well, a hundred and summat altogether." Boris feels in the pocket of his jeans for his crumpled wallet.

"Don't start counting it here! You don't know who's watching. If you've got a hundred that should see us through."

Renwick, who apparently has developed a taste for crisps, starts yapping for more. Heads turn, wondering where the yapping is coming from.

"Shurrup!" Boris growls at the holdall.

Colin glances around nervously. "Dogs not allowed in here, I reckon. We'd better bugger off."

The courtesy bus, once it arrives, seems to take far less time on the return journey than it did going, but on the way Colin asks the driver about somewhere to stay the night.

"You want the Hotel Hoppa, guv. Get off at Terminal 1 and go to the reservation desk. They'll fix you up."

And when they reach Terminal 1 that is what they do.

"One double bedroom at the Skyfly International," the girl tells them. "Take the yellow bus."

For once the bus is standing there waiting. Colin climbs aboard wearily but thankfully. Boris follows, clutching his precious holdall in one hand and his helmet in the other.

And who should be sitting halfway down the bus but Daphne, Mr Pertwee's wet-eyed daughter, weeping buckets over her bare plump knees.

*****

Len and Cyril have scurried back to the Arrivals Hall of Terminal 2 brimming with high hopes of finding Nora and Marsha waiting for them.

No such luck.

Cyril lifts his old trilby and scratches his bald pate. "Well, I dunno."

"Nor do I," says Len grimly.

"What do we do now?"

"Nothing we can do. What I do know is I need a drink."

"Good idea." Cyril points with his pipe. "Saw a sign there to restaurants and pubs and that."

Len has already spotted it earlier but hasn't had the nerve to take advantage of it. "Reckon we deserve it," he says. "Come on."

In no time at all they are both sitting with their pints before them.

"Dear beer here," grumbles Len as he plonks the drinks on the table.

"Cheers," says Cyril.

"Cheers," says Len.

They savour the first sip of their pints.

"So what you reckon's happened to 'em?" asks Cyril.

"Dunno. *Must* have missed the plane. Bit worrying."

Cyril opens his pouch and scrapes the last microscopic residue of tobacco into the bowl of his pipe. "Perhaps they've gone down in the drink."

"Don't say that!" Len has been thinking the same thing himself. "No, no, couldn't have done. There'd have been an announcement or summat. Besides, we know the plane landed."

"They must have missed it then."

"Suppose so. All the excitement over the baby and that, I 'spect."

"Might as well go home then. Can't stay here all night. Glennis'll be crawling up the wall."

Len ponders. "Let's give it until ten. If they haven't turned up by then, we'll go."

"Ar," says Cyril, lifting his pint. "Good idea."

But they don't have to wait that long.

"Will Mr Len Scally please go to the Information Desk?" comes the metallic plea out of the air. "Mr Len Scally to the Information Desk."

"That's you!" says Cyril, taken aback.

"Um." Len can't take it in at first either. "It must be Nora! Come on!"

"I've only just started me beer!"

"Can't be helped. Have to leave it."

At the Information Desk the young man hands Len Nora's note. Len reads it, a puzzled frown on his face.

"They're at a hotel," he tells Cyril.

"Go on! What they gone there for?"

"Don't say. We've got to go there to pick 'em up. Got to get a bus to get there or summat."

They follow Nora's instructions out to the stand where the yellow Hotel Hoppa is just returning from having conveyed Colin Stilwell and son, plus Renwick and the overwrought Daphne, to the Skyfly Hotel.

Len and Cyril climb aboard and wait patiently for the Hoppa to take them to the same destination.

Now it looks as if it's the turn of the Heathrow Skyfly International Hotel to be busy.

Chapter 18

In her bedroom on the fourteenth floor of the Heathrow Skyfly Elsie awakes with a start. She was in Australia, dreaming she went to Cliff's house to reclaim her two boys and was accosted by that bitch Maisie, who hurled a boomerang at her, which came up from behind and hit her on the head.

Her eyes blink open, and she gazes around the tasteful but impersonal bedroom, wondering where she is, striving to remember how she got there. Slowly it returns. She's at Heathrow, *en route* for Australia, but she is still very hazy as to why. Something to do with a tiff she had with Colin at that grotty seaside resort, whatever it's called, on the south coast.

She looks at the digital clock built into the bedside table. 22.01. She's been asleep for six hours! She's feeling rested, calmer in her mind, even though her body feels weak and her stomach empty. She needs food, that's what she needs – and a good stiff drink.

She hauls herself off the bed and wanders into the smart, tiled bathroom, with its gleaming taps, luxurious apricot-coloured towels and whirring extractor. She'll have a shower, freshen herself up a bit, then go down to see if she can find food and drink. But at this hour? Well, it's a big posh hotel, so she should be able to.

The shower is heavenly. Goodness only knows when she last had so much as a wash, and as for her hair – well! She takes advantage of the sachet of shampoo and the hair-dryer provided. Her spirits begin to rise. She could quickly get used to this kind of life.

Feeling like a film star in a movie Elsie returns to the bedroom wrapped in a huge bath towel. The next question is what shall she wear to go down for this meal? She opens the old lady's case she brought with her, but its contents do not look very promising. She'd just chucked in a wild assortment of garments when she left the Ocean View and nothing seems to match up. She's brought the top of her best trouser suit but not the trousers! But she has got her Spanish-style dress, the one the silly bald-headed man admired so much at that disco. It is all crumpled and stained, but it will have to do.

As she gets dressed she remembers more clearly what happened at the disco. The bald-headed man, Billy something or other, had taken her back to the hotel in his posh car because Colin had been lusting after that Scottish tart, whose name she's forgotten again. What happened after that until she woke up in hospital is still a blank. But bits and pieces are certainly coming back and she is feeling less vulnerable, more assured.

When she is ready Elsie checks the old lady's handbag to make sure she has enough cash for a meal and a drink. Doubtful! Well, if necessary, they'll probably add it to the bill. She leaves the bedroom and makes for the lifts.

In the Skyfly the restaurants, bars and shops and other facilities are situated on the mezzanine floor. Soft music plays. The simulated marble floor gleams. Islands of plush furniture on thick carpets abound. Gilded signs point to the toilets, hairdressers, pharmacy, florists, 'The Beer Barrel', 'The Trafalgar Trattoria', 'The Nelson Restaurant', 'The Breakfast Bar' and 'The Snappy Snax Bar'.

For Elsie the choice is easy. She makes for The Beer Barrel. It is dimly lit, with a ceiling vaulted like the inside of a beer keg. The seating is arranged in intimate alcoves, each with its own shaded lighting. She hasn't been anywhere so lush for many a long day, not since she left Australia.

Elsie perches herself on a stool at the bar and decides to order a double vodka to drink while she studies the bar menu.

"Coming or going?" asks a man sitting on the next stool, attracted by the flouncey, Spanish-style dress.

"I wish I knew," says Elsie.

He laughs. "I know the feeling."

Conscious of the man watching her, Elsie keeps her eye riveted on the menu.

"I should avoid the Chef's Special," he advises. "You could try the Escaloppina Don Camillo though. Can't go wrong with that. The chef's Italian."

Being unfamiliar with the exotic dishes listed on the menu

Elsie decides to have the Escaloppina. Then she downs her remaining vodka in one gulp.

"You needed that!" grins the man. "Jock! Give the lady another!"

"No! No really!"

"Go on! Nice just to have a chat for a few minutes."

What the hell, thinks Elsie. Suddenly she realises she hasn't really talked to anyone since leaving the hospital. Might help her get back to normal. "A small one, then."

"So, are you flying off or coming back?" asks the man.

"Flying off. Sydney."

"Sydney! Oh, I know Sydney. Great people the Sydneysiders. Holiday, is it?"

"Sort of. My two sons live out there. I'm going to—" Elsie stops abruptly as her memory does a somersault. More pieces are falling into place.

"Oh my God!" she cries.

The man looks alarmed. "What's the trouble?"

Elsie clamps a hand to her forehead and sways on her stool.

Fearing she is about to swoon, the man leaps up and puts his arm around her to steady her. "Jock! A brandy for the lady. Now!"

"I'm okay – honest." She tries to wave off the brandy.

"You'd better sit down somewhere." He leads her to the nearest vacant alcove and tenderly sits her down on one of its sumptuous seats. "Here, drink this."

"I'm all right now."

"Drink it just the same. Pull you round."

Elsie can't say no to a buckshee brandy, even if it is on an empty stomach. The man watches anxiously.

"What's the date?" asks Elsie suddenly.

"The date? Of the brandy, you mean?"

"No, today's date."

The man consults his watch. "Fifth of June."

"Bloody hell!"

"Why? What's the trouble?"

"What's the time?"

He consults his watch again. "Half past ten."

"It's too late now." Elsie seems distraught, close to tears.

"Too late for what? What's the trouble? Can I help?" He puts his hand over hers. It is large, warm and strong.

"No no. It's just that…well, I've just remembered it was my eldest son's eighteenth birthday two days ago. I was going to phone him but I had an accident and couldn't. He'll be thinking I've forgotten him."

"And he's in Sydney?"

Elsie nods miserably.

"It'll be morning there. You could phone him."

"It's too late. He'll have gone to work."

"Could you fax him or send a message on the Internet?"

"Oh, no!" Such things are beyond Elsie's ken.

A waitress comes up. "One Escaloppina Don Camillo?"

"For the lady." The man presses Elsie's hand. "Now eat up and don't worry. If you're flying out there tomorrow you might as well wait until you get there and tell him what's happened. He'll understand."

"Suppose so. You're very kind." Elsie looks up at him. It is the first time she's really taken notice of his face. It seems vaguely familiar. A distorted image of a bald-headed man with horn-rimmed glasses appears before her eyes, like on a TV screen that needs tuning.

"Don't I know you?" she asks.

He laughs. "That's supposed to be *my* line!"

"No – I mean it."

"I'm quite sure I wouldn't have forgotten you if we'd met before."

Elsie tussles with her recalcitrant memory. Surely he is that man she'd danced with at that disco who had driven her back to the Ocean View. Whatever is his name? She'd remembered it earlier.

Then it comes. "I know who you are! You're Sergeant Bilko!"

The man roars. "I'm afraid I haven't that honour, my dear. No, my name is Oliver – Oliver Bloom."

*****

"Oh my God, it's a double bed!" cries Colin. He doesn't

fancy spending the night in the same bed as Boris.

"You go and sleep in the single room then," growls Boris. "Daphne can come in here with me."

He looks at his son in disbelief. "That's the first time I've known you want to be with a girl! Don't tell me you fancy her."

"She likes dogs. Renwick took to her."

"As good a reason as any for wanting to sleep with her, I suppose. Anyhow, you'd better forget it. You saw what a bloody awful state she's in over that Spanish bloke."

Boris switches on the radio. Radio One blares forth.

"Turn that damn thing off!"

"Renwick likes it. Keeps him quiet."

"Bugger Renwick! Let's have a bit of peace and quiet, for God's sake." Colin turns off the radio then slumps on the bed in despair. "I dunno, what a bloody awful day! Charging round Brighton all the morning, having an up-and-downer with old Pertwee, Daphne behaving like a drunken cow over that Spanish git, then having to bump all the way here on that bloody bike of yours! I'd have been better off riding a bronco from some rodeo, I can tell you! And after all that we still haven't the foggiest what's happened to Elsie, if she's halfway to bloody Australia or holed up alone, God knows where. And to top it all, here we are in some ritzy hotel with hardly enough money to pay the bill!"

"Should have gone back home," says Boris as he takes Renwick out of his holdall.

"What, in that contraption of yours with my bloody back! It's a wonder I can still walk." He rubs his back unconsciously. "And there's another thing," he goes on. "What the hell has happened to Len? He was supposed to be going to Benthaven with money for me but never turned up. What else is going to happen, I wonder?"

He stops suddenly, looking even more frenzied. "Great gobstoppers! What day is it today?"

"Thursday."

"It's that bloody Snooker Final on Saturday! Well, we're never going to make it, that's for sure." He takes out a hanky and gives his nose a hefty blow. "And for Pete's sake take that flamin' dog off the bed! He'll be piddling all over it before we know where we are, and we'll end up sleeping on the bloody floor!"

"He's got to go somewhere. Can't stay in the bag all the time."

"Well, put him in the bathroom. Can't come to much harm in there."

"He'll be lonely. Can't he have the radio on?"

"No, he bloody can't!"

"I'd better sit in there with him then, keep him company and that," says Boris as he takes Renwick to the bathroom.

"Don't talk so wet. You'd think it was a baby the way you carry on."

"He'll pine on his own," says Boris, coming back.

As if to prove it Renwick sets up a whine fit to curdle the blood.

"For crissake, shut him up! He'll get us chucked out."

"I told you."

"You'd better bring him back in here, I suppose. But you'll have to clean up if he makes a mess."

Colin eases off his shoes with an expression of sublime relief. His feet are hot and the soles irritating like mad.

"He's thirsty," says Boris as he returns again with Renwick in his arms.

"Give him some water then."

"Nothing to put it in."

"Use the ashtray, you berk."

Boris bumbles off to the bathroom to fill the ashtray with water. "He's hungry, too," he says when he returns.

"So am I," grunts Colin, rubbing his feet. "He'll just have to starve – like us."

"He's got to eat."

"Well, he can't. Nor can we, not at the prices they'll charge here. We'll probably end up doing the washing-up as it is."

"Might manage a sandwich and a drink."

Colin stops rubbing his feet and looks at his son. It is very tempting. "Could run to that, I suppose," he concedes. "Trouble is, the bar could be closed. Still, it's worth finding out."

When Renwick has finished sloshing water all over the bedroom carpet Boris puts him back in his holdall.

"You can't take him down there, if that's what you think."

"He'll pine and whine if we leave him up here."

"Then we'll have to go down separately. You go first."

"Don't fancy going down there all on me own."

"Have to, if you want to eat." But Colin is not too keen to do that, either. This posh place intimidates him. "Suppose we could have it sent up, but it'd probably cost a bomb. Waiter would want a five quid tip for a start."

"Daphne could look after Renwick," suggests Boris.

"Come off it! In her state she couldn't look after a bloody goldfish."

"She likes Renwick. He'll comfort her."

"Well, we'll try her if you like. Only let's get cracking in case the bar shuts."

Into the holdall goes Renwick, and they're off.

Where did you find that holdall, anyway?" demands Colin while they are waiting for the lift.

"Down the shed."

"Down the shed? That's Elsie's old one; she's been going mad looking for it. What was it doing down there?"

"Dunno. Had your old tools in it and that."

Colin sighs. "You know what? If she hadn't lost it, I wouldn't have had to buy her another one, and none of this would have happened."

"Dunno whatcha mean."

"Oh, never mind."

There is a discreet ping and the lift doors opens. A man dressed like an Arabian sheikh steps out. He glances sharply at the squirming holdall Boris is clutching to his chest.

When they reach Daphne's room Colin taps on the door and announces himself in a soft, coaxing voice. He can't help remembering the time he tapped on her bedroom door at the Ocean View.

"Go awa'!" cries Daphne, from within.

Poor Daphne, she's in a terrible state. Shakespeare couldn't have concocted a more poignant drama than that of Carlos skipping off to Spain with her ex-mate, Cheryl, and Daphne just failing to stop them by a matter of minutes.

"We don't want to disturb you," coos Colin through the door. "We were just wondering if you'd do us a favour."

"Go awa'!" wails Daphne again.

"I've got Renwick here," shouts Boris. "Want you to look after him for a bit, like."

"That's right, tell the whole bleedin' hotel we've got a dog," grinds Colin.

But to his surprise the door opens an inch and Daphne's face appears. It's so blotched with tear stains it looks as if it's been camouflaged.

"We're just popping down for a beer and a sandwich," Colin whispers urgently. "Wondered if you'd look after the dog for a few minutes."

"You wanna come?" Boris asks her suddenly.

"Och, no!"

"Got to eat. No good not eating."

"I couldnae. I'll nae eat again!" She snatches the holdall and slams the door.

"I'll fetch you up a sandwich," bawls Boris through the door.

No response from Daphne.

"Come on," urges Colin. "Let's go."

They take the lift down to the mezzanine floor.

*****

"Mrs Bloom! How lovely to see you!" exclaims the Skyfly receptionist, lying through her teeth.

"Good evening, Barbara," answers Marsha, without enthusiasm.

"But you are walking on sticks! Whatever happened?"

"The result of an unfortunate accident in Greece."

"Oh, I *am* sorry!"

"And as a result of which," proclaims Marsha, "we have decided to stay here tonight, since the person who was to meet us has failed to put in an appearance. I shall stay in my husband's room, naturally, but perhaps you would kindly provide a single one for my companion here, Mrs Scally."

"Of course, Mrs Bloom," says Barbara, consulting her computer. "That will be Room 1734 on the seventeenth floor."

"Oh my!" exclaims Nora. She's never slept so close to God

before.

"*Should*, by any chance," continues Marsha, "a Mr Len Scally arrive asking for us, perhaps you would be good enough to direct him to Mrs Scally's room?"

"No problem, Mrs Bloom."

Exaggerating her limp for the benefit of the receptionist, Marsha leads Nora towards the lifts. "I suggest that, before we bother looking for your room, we go to Oliver's room just to freshen up, then come straight down again to provide ourselves with some much-needed nourishment before everything closes down."

Oliver's room, kept private for his personal use, is on the top floor. One of his perks as a VIP is that his wife is also allowed to use the room and has a key of her own, which she sometimes uses when she visits London, something that is a source of anxiety to Oliver, since it means she is liable to turn up at some inconvenient moment.

And this looks like being one such occasion.

"You see that, Nora?" declares Marsha as soon as they are in the room. "There's Oliver's travelling bag. He told me he was arriving back from Singapore Friday, but he's already back, no doubt with the intention of spending tonight here with some woman."

"Well I never!" Nora is appalled.

"You see what I mean? He's devious. He knows more tricks than a dog in a circus. Well, he's done it this time. He'll be retiring forthwith, whether he likes it or not."

Nora simply cannot believe it. Oliver Bloom, the confident, ebullient businessman whom she so admires, has been proven to have feet of clay.

"Aha!" cries Marsha suddenly as she picks up a small package lying on the corner of the dressing table. "Look what we have here!"

"What is it?" asks Nora.

Marsha hands her the package.

"'Jiffys'," reads Nora. "'Three Assorted Flavours.' What are Jiffys?"

"Condoms. Surely you know that?"

Nora doesn't know where to put her face.

"There you are, then," Marsha says with satisfaction, pocketing the Jiffys. "He can't wriggle out of this. Come, let us freshen up a little and then go down to do battle."

*****

"Excuse me," says Len to the Skyfly Hotel receptionist, "but I have a message that says Mrs Nora Scally is here."

"Mrs Scally?" Receptionist Barbara is a bit slow on the uptake. She has a lot on her mind, not least the presence of Mrs Bloom in the hotel.

Len hands her Nora's crumpled note to read.

"Oh, Mrs Scally! She's Mrs Bloom's friend, isn't she?"

"That's right." Len is relieved. At last they seems to be getting somewhere.

"She's in Room 1734. Take the lift over there to the seventeenth floor."

"We've found them at last," Len says to Cyril who is gaping round at the opulent foyer, with its bright lighting, spreading palms and simulated waterfall.

"Don't like heights," says Len when they emerge from the lift on the seventeenth floor. "Makes you feel queer." He hasn't forgotten his visit to the Post Office Tower.

When he knocks on the door of Room 1734 there is no response. "Not there," he says superfluously after several knocks. "Now what do we do?"

"Wait, I suppose," says Cyril.

Len props himself against the doorpost; he's feeling weary as well as giddy. The thought of the journey back home in Cyril's Range Rover appals him. He'd like to put his feet up and have a nap – not to mention a drink.

But Cyril is still lively enough. He walks up and down the corridor, looks out in wonder at the panoramic view of London from the window at the end and stares with mystification at the pictures on the corridor walls.

"Don't understand it," says Len when Cyril returns.

"What's that then?"

"Why they've booked rooms for themselves. Don't need rooms if they're coming home with us, do they?"

"'Spect they want to put their feet up for a bit, have a wash and that."

"Cost a bit just to do that." Len sounds doubtful.

Cyril pulls out his pipe and pouch, stares forlornly at his empty pouch and absently knocks out the pipe into a potted plant. "What we going to do then?"

"Don't ask me. Have to wait, I suppose. They must be here somewhere."

"Gone down for a meal or summat, I 'spect."

"Probably."

"Could do with summat meself. Didn't finish that drink we had before, did us? Is there a bar in this 'ere place?"

"Sure to be. Might not be open, though." Len looks at his watch. "It's gone half past ten."

"Could go and find out. Better than just standing here. Might even see 'em down there."

"True..." There's nothing Len would like to do more, but he's afraid Nora will be mad if she comes back and finds he's still not there. But he reckons he's earned a drink.

"Okay, we'll go. Better make it a quick one, though."

*****

"'The Beer Barrel'," reads Colin, staring up at the twirly red illuminated sign above the entrance. "This'll do us."

"Looks a bit posh," observes Boris.

"Dear too, I 'spect. Can't be helped. Come on."

They grope their way through the semi-darkness to a vacant alcove. "You get 'em," Colin tells his son, flopping thankfully on to the plush seating. "You've still got the money. Don't go and spend it all, mind. Got to be careful."

While Boris goes off to the bar Colin leans back and closes his eyes, and soon the dim lighting and the soft background music have a lulling effect, making him feel drowsy.

Until Boris awakens him by plonking two tankards of beer on the table. "Sandwiches are coming," he says. As he sits down Boris puts a fistful of paper napkins on the table.

"What you brought all them for?" demands Colin.

"For the sandwiches. Ordered four. Gonna take one up for

Renwick and one for Daphne."

"How much did that lot cost?"

"Dunno. About eighteen quid."

"Eighteen quid! We're never going to have enough to pay for the bloody room!"

Boris couldn't care less. He lifts his tankard. "Cheers."

"Cheers." Colin sips the beer gratefully, even so.

The sweet strains of 'Ramona' soothingly pervade the air. Colin cocks an ear.

"That's one of them old tunes Elsie plays," he says.

"Go on?"

"And she plays it a bloody sight better than that! Didn't tell you, did I? Some bloke at the hotel – Daphne's grandad in fact, you'll be interested to know – says Elsie has quite a future playing the organ. Says she could turn professional and that."

"Go on?" says Boris again, not listening.

"Used to be a talent-spotter or summat. Queer bloke, mind. Wouldn't think he was into that sort of thing. Billy something or other. Looks just like Sergeant Bilko."

"Who's Sergeant Bilko?"

"Used to be on the telly, before your time."

Without warning Boris gets to his feet.

"Where you going now?"

"Get some mustard – for them sandwiches."

While Boris is away Colin becomes fretful again about Elsie. In her state she could be in trouble wherever she is. God knows what might happen to her if she's already left for Australia, and if she hasn't she could be wandering the streets, lost, even huddled up in some doorway like an old bag lady, no money except for them useless old fivers. Would happen just when it looked as if she could become famous playing the organ. Sod's law, he thinks angrily.

It is quite a long time before Boris returns holding a fistful of mustard packets, but he doesn't sit down. Instead he stands staring at his dad with a kind of mesmerised look, which for Boris should be construed as one of bafflement.

Colin looks up. "What's the matter with you?"

"Dad, I've just seen Elsie."

"What! Where?"

"Over there."
"You sure?"
"Yer."
Colin rockets to his feet. "What did she say?"
"Didn't speak to her."
"Why ever not?"
"She's with a bloke!"
"Bloke? What bloke?"
"Some bald-headed git with glasses."

It is too dim in The Beer Barrel for anyone to see Colin's face change from white to burning red.

"Don't need telling who *he* is," roars Colin. "Where is the bugger?"

"Over there."

Colin charges over.

Sure enough there sits Elsie, a bald-headed man with glasses emptying a sachet of Demerara sugar into her coffee.

"Well, well, if it isn't Sergeant Bilko!" cries Colin. He couldn't sound more triumphant if he'd been accompanied by a fanfare of trumpets.

"Conrad!" cries Elsie.

"So *this* is what it's all about. Now I get it! Now I see it all! Off to Australia are we? All that guff about amnesia, and all the time you're off with this bugger!"

Shocked, scared and scandalised, Oliver jolts to his feet. "I think there must be some—"

Colin leans over the table and grabs him by his old school tie. "Don't try gabbing your way out of this one, mate! You're caught in the act – end of story!"

"There's some mistake," cries Oliver in a voice that sounds as if he's gargling. "My name's not Bilko, it's—"

"Tell that to the Marines!" yells Colin.

He gives Oliver a violent shove back into his chair.

Except that he mis-aims, and Oliver hits the arm of the chair, loses his balance and ends up on the floor.

*****

"Goood eevening," Billy Greenhorn greets receptionist

Barbara. "Have you two single rooms for tonight, please?"

"Sorry, sir, all singles are taken. We are almost full, but we do have a double room on the fourteenth floor. It *is* twin bedded," she adds, eyeing Mr Pertwee distastefully.

"That will do nicely," beams Billy.

"Fourteenth floor," moans Mr Pertwee as they are soared heavenwards by the lift. "I dinnae call this a hotel."

"Not your sort, Alec. But unlike your place it makes a handsome profit."

"Aye, and it doesnae care how it makes it, nae doot. It is a hotbed of immorality, y'can smell it."

"It's a transit hotel and provides a necessary service. They get all sorts, of course, but it is well run. You might pick up a tip or two while you're here."

"Och, I'll nae want m'hotel to be like this. I'll nae sacrifice m'principles on the altar of money."

They arrive at the fourteenth.

"You'll never be a successful business man, Alec," says Billy as they meander down the corridor looking for Room 1479, "until you learn that morals and money don't mix." Quite the philosopher is Billy – when he's sober.

"I dinnae care aboot money, nor the hotel. I'm determined to return to the clean, pure air of Scotland and train m'dogs, just as soon as the hotel is sold."

"But it's *not* selling, is it? And it won't unless you do something to cheer it up. And don't forget, even training dogs is still a business and has to be run like one."

They find Room 1479. When they enter Mr Pertwee looks round at the beige walls, beige carpet, beige bedspread and a beige picture depicting a misshapen boat in a misshapen harbour. "Och, I dinnae like this! My rooms are much more attractive."

"I'll grant you that, Alec. But alas, they're not situated at Heathrow Airport."

Mr P. pokes his head into the bathroom and sees his reflection in the mirror. He is horrified. "Och, I missed m'shave this evening! And I havenae m'shaving kit."

"There's barber's shop here."

"And no pyjamas!"

"Sleep naked," says Billy, beaming at the prospect.

"Och, I couldnae do that! I'll have to sleep in m'underclothes."

"There's a shop below where you can buy pyjamas."

"I'll nae be buying pyjamas just for one neet!"

Billy beams with amusement. "Suit yourself. Well, don't know about you, Alec, but I need a drink. And I'm missing your Lancashire hotpot for once. There's a little pub below. Let's go down and see what's doing."

"How can I eat with m'Daphne gone!"

"She hasn't gone. I told you, she couldn't possibly have caught that plane. We'll find her in the morning. Come on, you look in need of a stiff drink."

He does too.

"Aye, well it's been a terrible, terrible day. But I couldnae go down there. I couldnae, not for all the whisky in Scotland."

"Then we'll get something sent up."

"Och, no!"

"Yes we will. I'm starving."

Billy grabs the phone and asks for Room Service.

But Mr Pertwee is having second thoughts. "Och, I'll never sleep in m'underwear! I'll *have* to get some pyjamas."

Billy puts down the phone. "Splendid! We'll get you some from the shop, then go to The Beer Barrel."

"But I need a shave!"

"Well, go to the barber first then, if you must, and get one."

"But he won't be open at this hour."

"Alec," sighs Billy, "this place never closes. Let's go and find out."

*****

When Marsha and Nora issue from the lift on the mezzanine floor, Nora stares about spellbound.

"My!" she exclaims. She's never seen the like of it before.

"He'll be in The Beer Barrel," declares Marsha grimly. "This way."

Without understanding this strange statement Nora follows Marsha as she forges ahead on her sticks. But Marsha stops abruptly and points with a stick as she sees a limping figure emerge from The Beer Barrel. "Well, well, speak of the Devil!" she murmurs with obvious satisfaction.

Oliver is in disarray, his old school tie askew and his glasses awry, a bloody handkerchief wrapped around his thumb. He is walking directly towards Marsha and Nora, but is too concerned with his own unhappy state to notice them.

When he draws level Marsha holds out one of her sticks, barring his way.

"Good lord, Marsha! What are *you* doing here?"

"You may well ask."

"And Nora! What a delightful surprise!"

"*Is* it?" Marsha is wearing her granite look.

"Of course it is!" He struggles to regain his *savoir faire*. "But you're using sticks, my dear. Whatever has happened to you?"

"And you are limping," retaliates Marsha. "What has happened to *you*?"

"Oh, I...er...tripped. Clumsy of me, but it's nothing. But how come you are both here?"

"Nora dear, I wish to speak to Oliver privately for a few moments. Perhaps you'd like to go on in and order me a double whisky and something for yourself. I won't be long."

"No need for that," says Oliver gallantly. "I'll buy you both drinks. Come on."

"No, I wish to speak to you first."

"Oh. As you wish, my dear." He looks nervous. "Afterwards then."

Nora is only too relieved to escape. Disappointed as she is in Oliver, she feels sorry for him having to face the broadsides Marsha is about to release.

"What's this all about?" he demands anxiously.

"Let us sit down." Marsha hobbles to the nearest deep-buttoned brown sofa and sits down carefully. "You told me you weren't returning from Singapore until tomorrow," she says.

"Oh, that!" Oliver feels more confident. "That's easily explained. I had to come back early because I have some business to attend to here in the morning."

"Really? And what business might that be?"

"Just one of those things; nothing of any interest to you, my dear."

"Tell me."

"It's really not important."

"Tell me," persists Marsha.

Oliver takes off his glasses and polishes them with the corner of his blooded handkerchief.

He's playing for time, thinks Marsha.

"Well, if you really want to know, Rosemary Woods – you wouldn't know her – she's a receptionist at the Singapore Skyfly, or rather was, until she died suddenly the other day. It is my disagreeable task to go and see her parents in Wimbledon in the morning to offer the Company's condolences and to finalise the arrangements for the poor girl's body to be flown home."

"I see. And do you always go to see employees' relatives when they die?"

"Sometimes. It depends. Look, what's all this—?"

"And what about tonight?"

"Tonight?"

"What company business have you to attend to tonight?"

"None, of course. I'm perfectly free tonight, if that's what you mean."

"Then why do you need these?"

Marsha holds aloft the packet of condoms for Oliver, and the world, to see.

Oliver gulps and looks round frantically. "For God's sake, Marsha, put them away!"

"Not until you tell me why you've got them."

"Well obviously for us."

"*US!*"

"Of course! I was only thinking on the plane coming back we seldom do it these days, what with me being away so much and all our other commitments, so I thought perhaps it might be nice if—"

"But we haven't needed to take precautions for more years than I care to remember." Marsha's voice is at a low temperature. "So why suddenly start now?"

Oliver's vocal chords seize up. Then he laughs nervously. "Ah, I understand now! You think there is someone else tonight

I want them for! No, no, I assure you, it's nothing like that. They're for us."

"Olly, I wasn't born yesterday. Why should we need to use them all of a sudden?"

"Well, I'm not sure, to be honest. I suddenly felt it might be wise to take precautions."

"Precautions? Against what, pray?"

"You know the sort of thing, Marsha."

"Tell me."

Marsha is still holding the condoms aloft. Out of the corner of his eye Oliver has just spotted George Bollinger's head appear at the top of the escalator that leads up from the reception to the mezzanine floor. On his arm is a buxom, bejewelled woman in black.

"Marsha, do put those things away. People will see!"

"Tell me," insists Marsha.

"Well you know the sort of thing," he says hastily. "Diseases. So much of it these days."

"Are you inferring," grates Marsha, "that I might have some disgusting disease?"

"No, no, of course not!"

"If there is one thing of which you may be sure in this uncertain world, Oliver, it is *that*. Unless, of course, it is *you* who has given it to me."

George Bollinger and his lady are moving in their direction, Oliver notices with alarm. He makes one of his famous lightning decisions. "Okay, Marsha, you win. I admit there has been the odd woman – it's virtually impossible to avoid it in my kind of job. But I'm perfectly healthy, I assure you. Now for God's sake put those things away!"

"And I assume these were intended for 'the odd woman' tonight?" asks Marsha, keeping the condoms aloft.

"No, no, of course not! You're not going to believe this, but it was only this evening, coming home in the plane, that I made up my mind to give the whole rotten business up. I've decided to retire."

"You're right, Olly, I don't believe you." She lowers her arm, even so.

"It's absolutely true!" He is keeping his eye on the

approaching Bollinger. "Suddenly this morning I felt totally sickened by my whole lifestyle. People think it's a glamorous life, but it's no way to live, you know, jetting around the world all the time, spending lonely nights in impersonal hotel bedrooms."

"*Lonely?*"

"Yes, lonely! And if not, then one is consumed by guilt. And, believe it or not, another reason I stopped over here tonight is to hand in my resignation in the morning."

Marsha is faltering. "Well, I'd like to believe you, Olly, but you're such a—"

"Put those damn things away," he whispers urgently, "because, as it happens, here comes someone who can prove to you that what I am saying is absolutely true."

Bollinger and his lady, *en route* for the lifts, have drawn level with them and he gives Oliver a passing nod.

"I say, George," cries Oliver, springing to his feet. "I don't think you've met my wife, Marsha. Darling, this is George Bollinger, Chief Executive of Regal Chemicals at Brockbury. We sat together on the plane back."

Not having time to put the condoms into her bag, Marsha hurriedly slides them on to the sofa, behind her.

"Charmed," says Bollinger gruffly, taking her hand but none too pleased at having his evening disrupted. "And this is Gloria, my...er...wife."

"I have just been telling Marsha," continues Oliver, "about my decision to chuck my job. I was talking to George about it on the plane, darling," he explains smoothly, "and he tells me there may be a vacancy for me at Regal Chemicals – a nine-to-five desk job."

"Indeed!" The sun breaks through on Marsha's face.

"No promises about that mind," warns Bollinger.

"No, no, naturally. As we agreed, I'll give you a buzz once I've worked out my notice."

A curt nod from Bollinger as he begins to move on.

"Actually," adds Oliver hastily, "we were just going into The Beer Barrel for a nightcap. Perhaps you'd both care to join us?"

Bollinger looks down at the lady on his arm for her reaction, hoping she'll refuse.

"That would be lovely," says Gloria, looking up at him with limpid eyes.

"A quick one, then," he grunts. "We're planning on having an early night."

*****

In an alcove of The Beer Barrel a 'Grand Reconciliation' is taking place between Elsie and Colin, but not before there was a chaotic period during which vitriolic verbalisation was exchanged by all concerned.

After Oliver's purler over the arm of his chair, people jumped to their feet, Elsie screamed, the bartender rushed over with the intention of ejecting Colin by the scruff of his neck, and would undoubtedly have done so had Colin, being more experienced in that kind of activity than the bartender, freed himself and immobilised the bartender in an armlock.

Witnessing this adroit piece of manhandling on Colin's part also immobilised Oliver's desire to punch Colin on the nose. Instead he resorted to angry and persistent declamations to the effect that he was *not*, never had been, never would be, and hadn't the slightest desire to be, Sergeant Bilko; and that if Colin thought that he was in any way interested in Elsie beyond wanting to help a lady in distress, purely out of the goodness of his heart, then he should attend the nearest hospital for a brain transplant.

For the second time in half a day Colin found himself apologising over and over for a case of mistaken identity. "Sorry mate, sorry mate, no hard feelings," he kept saying, and offered to buy his victim a conciliatory drink.

But Oliver was more concerned with his tattered dignity and stamped, or rather limped, out of The Beer Barrel in high dudgeon, clutching the handkerchief round his bleeding thumb. Naturally, had he known Marsha was lying in wait for him outside with her warpaint on, he would have undoubtedly accepted the drink in preference.

Watching two men embroiled in such an altercation over her did Elsie the power of good, and after Colin had quickly placated the bartender and things had settled down again, she waxed hot with adoration for him, calling him her shining knight, proclaiming her admiration for the timely way he had rescued her from the clutches of that bald-headed beast. Never again, she vowed, would she doubt his love for her.

Colin was close to tears with love and relief. He held her close, whispering tender reassurances into her ear. She must never again doubt his undying love for her, he insisted. Never again would he let any bald-headed man come between them.

"Nor any lynx-eyed Scotch bitches," Elsie reminded him.

Nor that, he promised, not, he sought to convince her, that there had ever been a serious threat of such a thing happening. Elsie was the only one, his life, his all.

"Four beef sandwiches!" yells the waitress, who has been wandering around in The Beer Barrel's gloom trying to locate the purchasers.

"'Ere!" shouts Boris.

He has been sitting, beer tankard in hand, watching and listening to this lovey-dovey display between Elsie and his dad with nausea and scepticism. If this is love, give him the *Sporting Life*.

"Going to take up Renwick and Daphne's sandwiches," he says, lumbering to his feet.

Elsie pricks up her ears. "Daphne? She's *here*!"

"Yer," says Boris. "Came up with us on the bike."

Her tears have not entirely washed the flint away from Elsie's eyes. They glint with fury as she shoves Colin away from her. "You filthy bloody rotten...!"

Colin glowers at his son. At this moment Boris would make a substantial javelin target.

"Hold y'horses, Els'! Hold y'horses! It ain't what you think."

"Get *off* of me!" screams Elsie.

"But she *asked* us for a lift, isn't that right, Boris?"

"Right," says Boris.

"She's madly in love with some Spanish git. She asked us to give her a lift here so she can try and stop him before he flies off to Spain. Isn't that right, Boris?"

"Right," says Boris.

381

"But the plane had gone when she got here, so she's catching the first plane to Spain she can get on tomorrow. Right, Boris?"

"Right," says Boris.

"So you see, that's the end of her, my darling. She'll be gone for ever, finished and forgotten."

Elsie's mind is back in the blender, too shattered to bother further. "Is that really true?" she asks wistfully.

"True," confirms Boris.

"Cross me heart," says Colin with appropriate actions.

Boris picks up three beef sandwiches. "I'm off," he grunts. "Renwick'll be missing me."

"Who's Renwick?" asks Elsie.

*****

It is not only the waitress who has to feel her way about in the dimness of The Beer Barrel, Nora does too. But she isn't searching for the purchasers of beef sandwiches, she is looking for somewhere for Marsha and herself to sit. The Beer Barrel has suddenly become crowded due to an influx of knapsacked teenagers.

Nora teeters along on her weary, swollen feet, holding a small tray on which stand Marsha's whisky and her own gin and tonic, her handbag swinging like a pendulum from her forearm. She can't find an alcove available with more than one free seat. In the end she has to settle for one where a couple are snogging in the dimmer recesses of the alcove and the rest of the seats are free.

"Excuse me," says she, "do you mind if I share your table?"

"Feel free," says the man without looking up.

Carefully Nora lowers the tray of drinks on to the table, but her handbag slides down her arm as she does so, jolting the tray and spilling some of Marsha's whisky.

"Damn," she mutters. She looks round for something to clear up the spill. "Excuse me," she says again, putting her handbag on the table, "do you mind if I use one of your paper napkins to clean this up?"

"Feel free," says the man again.

But out of the corner of his eye he has seen the bulky handbag, and it seems all too familiar. He looks up.
"Good God! Nora!"
"Colin!"

*****

Len and Cyril look up at the squiggly red 'Beer Barrel' over the entrance.
"Looks a bit posh," says Cyril.
"Um," says Len. It's not his idea of a pub either. "Still, it'll have to do."
"Ar."
They venture in and make for the bar.
"Want summat to eat?" asks Len when they've ordered their pints.
"Could do with a bacon sandwich."
"You'll be lucky." Len grabs the bar menu.
Cyril peers at it over Len's shoulder. "Don't understand it. It's in French or summat."
Len doesn't understand it either. No fish and chips or egg and bacon. Nor is he smitten with the prices. "Don't think I'll bother," he says.
"Nor me. Could have a bag of crisps, I suppose."
"Good idea."
Armed with their beer and crisps they look round for somewhere to sit.
"Bloody full," moans Cyril. "Fancy, at this time of night!"
"Let's just sit at the bar," says Len, spotting a couple just vacating two stools.
"Good idea."
They perch themselves thankfully on the stools.
"Twenty to eleven," moans Len, looking at his watch. "It's going to be gone one at least before we get home."
"Glennis ain't going to be pleased. Said we'd be back by midnight."
"Better phone her, hadn't you? Let her know we've been delayed?"
But Cyril doesn't fancy using one of these new-fangled

payphones. Not like pressing button A in the old days. "No, he says. "Won't hurt her to worry for a bit."

They sit, drink, munch and wait. Mantovani's sweet melodies continue to play softly. Len isn't enjoying his pint at all. He feels ill at ease in this place and is feeling homesick for The Mason and Magpie.

People begin to drain away. They sit on.

*****

"It's like midnight in here," Marsha complains to Oliver as they enter The Beer Barrel with Bollinger and his good lady in tow. "What's the matter – can't they afford stronger bulbs?"

"Surveys have shown most people prefer lighting in bars to be soft," explains Oliver.

"Then they should provide torches. How else are we supposed to find Nora?"

"You will once your eyes have become accustomed."

"I'm not grovelling around in this murk looking for her," says Marsha. She takes a mighty breath and booms. "*NORA!*"

Nora cannot help but hear. She stops in the middle of crowing to Elsie and Colin about her first baby grandson. Once she had recovered from the shock of meeting up with her old friends in such a remarkable way she seized the first opportunity to impart her glad tidings, although not before Colin has acquainted her with all that had happened to Elsie and himself, and how it is they have come to be there.

"*NORA!*"

Nora jumps to her feet. "*HERE!*" she cries, holding up her arm like a football referee showing a yellow card.

Marsha comes hobbling up. "Ah, there you are."

She sits down next to Nora while Bollinger holds her sticks.

"These are friends of Oliver's," she explains to Nora. "Mr…ahm…Bollinger…"

"George," says Bollinger.

"…and…ahm…"

"Gloria," says Gloria.

"Pleased to meet you," says Nora.

Full stop.

For when Bollinger sits down and a little light is shed upon his congested countenance, Nora, Elsie and Colin all gawp incredulously as they recognise him as none other than their illustrious boss from work, the Chief Executive of Regal Chemicals plc, Fertiliser Division.

George Bollinger isn't given to gawping, but if he were he would have gawped. But instead his mouth tightens with aggravation and disbelief. He immediately recognises them. George never forgets a face.

"Don't I know you?" he growls, not wishing to display this asset too readily.

"I'm Nora Scally, sir, from the Accounts Department."

"So you are!"

"And Elsie Stilwell from the Canteen and Colin Stilwell from the gatehouse."

"Yes, yes," he says impatiently. He's already recalled seeing Elsie on the Hoppa Bus and her extraordinary behaviour at the New Year's Eve party at the Sports and Social. Then, to hide his embarrassment, and also to prove that he does his homework by reading the works newspaper, *Regal Fortunes*, he turns to Colin and barks, "Stilwell? Aren't you one of the chaps in the Snooker Final on Saturday night?"

"That's right, sir," says Colin, resisting the temptation to salute. He just about manages to disguise the shock he feels at the mention of the Snooker Final. He'd completely forgotten about it again.

"I hope you're practising your shots, man. I expect an exciting match. Time those two chaps Hodge and Cooney were given a thorough thrashing."

"Do our best, sir."

"That's the spirit! Shall enjoy seeing it."

"Are you going to the match then, sir?" ventures Nora. She didn't know it was customary for the Chief Executive to be there.

"Of course. Never miss it. Best game there is."

"What game is that?" asks Oliver as he rolls up with the tray of drinks.

"Snooker, man, what else?"

"Great game, great game," enthuses Oliver, handing out the

drinks. "Love it."

"Got some damn fine players at our place. This chap here is playing in the Doubles Final on Saturday. You ought to come and see it."

"Love to." Oliver looks at Colin and is shocked to realise he's the brute who molested him only minutes before. "You!" he exclaims.

"We meet again," grins Colin. "No hard feelings, eh?"

"Forget it," snaps Oliver. He's only too happy to do so. The less Marsha hears about that episode, the better.

"This is Elsie and Colin Stilwell, the friends we went on holiday with to Brighton," Nora explains to him. "We've just run into them here by pure chance. Isn't that amazing!"

"Unbelievable!" But it makes Oliver uneasy. There have already been too many disconcerting incidents this evening for his liking.

With Oliver momentarily preoccupied with these thoughts, Marsha takes the opportunity raise her glass. "Let us drink to the new baby!" she booms.

"Baby?" queries Oliver, coming round. "What baby?"

"Your first grandson." Marsha is watching his face to assess his reaction. "Of course, I haven't had a chance to tell you about it, have I?"

Oliver is a bit slow on the uptake for once. "You mean, Georgie has already had her…?"

Marsha nods in the style of a royal assent.

"But that's great!" There is no doubting his delight. "Absolutely fabulous! When did this happen?"

"Last night in Greece. That's where Nora and I have been. We've just arrived back."

"But I thought it wasn't due until…"

"It was premature." She's already finding this a useful excuse. "That is why we went out. But all is well. Georgie and Gavin now have a bonny baby boy!"

"A boy!" Oliver is beside himself. "You hear that, George, I'm a grandad!"

"Congratulations," growls Bollinger.

"This calls for a celebration, a *real* celebration. Champagne! Hold on, I'll go and get a magnum – *two* magnums!"

Oliver is up and off to the bar in a trice, all his troubles put on hold. It's the best news he's had for many a day.

"Champagne, Jock!" he tells the barman. "*Two* magnums!"

"Sorry, Olly. Gone eleven. Bar's closed."

"Aw, c'mon. This is a celebration. I'm a grandad!"

"Sorry, no can do. More than me job's worth."

"Bugger that! I'll square it with…"

In his aggravation Oliver thumps the bar, and jerks the arm of an old chap sitting on a stool beside him, face upturned as he drains the last drops of beer from his glass. The jerk is all it needs to send the old chap's trilby hat floating to the ground.

"Sorry, old fellow," says Oliver, a gentleman first and last, as he retrieves the hat.

Oliver gives the hat a perfunctory brush with his sleeve and hands it back with one of his winning smiles.

"Ta," says the old boy.

His drinking companion, becoming aware that something is happening, vaguely recognises Oliver's voice and bestirs himself sufficiently to look over at him.

"Oliver!" he cries.

"Len!"

Jock the barman takes advantage of this diversion to pull down the bar grille.

Chapter 19

Boris, with a plate of beef sandwiches in one hand and a couple of tins of Heineken plus a pot of mustard in the other, has to kick Daphne's bedroom door with his foot to make his presence known.

"Go awa'!" cries Daphne.

"Brought Renwick his dinner," shouts Boris.

"Don't care. Go awa'!"

"Got to have his dinner. Ain't had nothing since breakfast." He forgets about the crisps.

No reply.

Boris kicks the door loud enough to wake the whole hotel. "Open up!"

"Go awa'!"

"Not till he's had his grub." Boris can be as obstinate as the next man when he sets his mind to it. He kicks the door again.

The door opens two inches.

"Och, let me have it then!" She thrusts out a hand.

He ignores the hand. "Brought a beer and sandwich for you too."

"Take it awa'. I couldnae eat a thing."

"Got to eat."

So saying, he gives the door a shove with his shoulder before Daphne can resist.

"Hey!"

"Got to walk Renwick after he's had his grub," explains Boris, marching into the room.

Renwick, previously occupied shredding toilet tissues, goes mad on seeing his master.

"Shurrup, you little bugger," growls Boris, picking the puppy up by the scruff of its neck, "or it'll be the knackers' yard for you. Behave and you can have a nice beef sandwich."

Despite her grief Daphne watches with fascination as Boris opens a sandwich, removes the beef and lays it on an ashtray.

"Y'really love that wee puppy, don't you?" says Daphne.
"Yer."
"Och, if only someone loved me like that!"
"Eat your sandwich."
"I cannae eat a thing. Give it to Renwick."
"Eat it!"

He shoves a sandwich into her hand, then sits down on the edge of the bed and watches Renwick making short work of the beef.

With the sandwich in her hand, Daphne can't resist biting into it. Boris picks up the third sandwich and they sit silently side by side on the bed watching Renwick.

"So whacha going to do then?" he asks after a bit.

"I'm going to kill m'sel'."

"Go on?" He shows about as much surprise as if she'd said she was going to vacuum the carpet. "How you going to do it then – gas, gun or rope?"

She looks at his deadpan face, unsure if he's serious or joking.

"Trouble is, you ain't got none of 'em here. I'd lend you me razor, but I ain't got it with me."

"You're a bit of a weirdo, aren't you?"

"Can't chuck yourself out of the window, either, cos you can't open it far enough." He leans forward and gives Renwick a bit more meat from his own sandwich. "Course, you could electrocute yourself in the bath, if you know how."

"Shut y'face," snaps Daphne.

Boris wipes his huge fingers with his napkin and reaches down for the tins of Heineken. He opens one. "'Ere, drink this," he tells Daphne.

"Y'don't understand, do you? Have y'nae been in love?" Daphne says, taking the tin.

Boris shakes his head as he opens his own tin; after witnessing the charade between Colin and Elsie he's glad he hasn't.

"It's the very divil. Y'cannae resist it. Nothing else matters. Y'have to follow where it takes you. Can't help it."

"Go on?"

"Och, y'making fun if me. You'll find oot one day."

When Renwick has finished pushing the ashtray around the room and licking the carpet, Boris gets up and takes the ashtray to the bathroom to fill it with water.

"Fancied a barmaid once," he says as he comes back. "Didn't fancy me, though. Girls don't. Soon got over it."

"That's sex, not love."

"Yer?"

"Love won't let go, wrings y'out."

Boris finishes off his Heineken and lumbers to his feet.

"Taking Renwick for his walkies now. Wanna come?"

"Och, no."

"Do you good. Fresh air and that."

"I dinnae want fresh air."

Boris picks up Renwick. "C'mon, you bugger, walkies time."

He dumps the puppy in the holdall, and then takes Daphne's jacket from the back of a chair and chucks it at her.

"Put it on. 'Spect it's cold outside."

There's something about this huge terse fellow that compels her to obey. She puts on her jacket and follows him to the door.

"You can kill yourself when you get back," he says.

*****

Meeting up with Len and Cyril at the bar and feeling obliged to ask them to join them, Oliver wonders when his celebration party is going to stop growing. Not that he is sorry. The more the merrier, he thinks. It all serves to distract Marsha from dwelling on his infidelities.

Nor does the refusal of the barman to supply him with champagne daunt him. He's just had a great idea. Oliver is a dab hand at beating trouble. It's his job, if not for much longer.

"Great to see you, old chap!" he assures Len, thumping him on the back. "We've all been very worried about you. Nora will be jolly relieved, I can tell you. And you're just in time to join us. We've got quite a party going. There's something super for us all to celebrate, as you'll see."

He glances at Cyril doubtfully, but leads them both through the gloom to the alcove where the rest of his party is still sitting, supping their drinks.

Nora's first reaction on seeing Len is one of anger. "What time do you call this?" she demands. "What happened?"

"Car broke down," he answers defensively. "Had to get Cyril to bring me in his Range Rover."

She is furious. The last person she wants to see there is Cyril, with his long face and trilby hat. But she dare not vent her feelings, not in front of this austere company.

Oliver comes to the rescue.

"Len's here, safe and sound, that's all that matters," he comforts her. "Now listen. We can't let this incredible occasion come to a premature end just because the bar is closing. So what I am going to do is see if we can continue our celebration elsewhere – in the Trafalgar Room, if it's available."

"I think," intervenes Bollinger, "that if you don't mind we'll give it a miss. We need to get to bed."

I bet, thinks Oliver, eyeing Gloria. But he says. "Oh, c'mon, George, don't split up the party quite yet. I'm sure Gloria will sleep better for a glass of the best champagne, won't you, Gloria?" He gives her one of his never-failing. prize smiles.

"Oh, I love champagne," murmurs Gloria, squeezing Bollinger's arm.

"Ten minutes, then," grunts the Chief Executive.

"Splendid! Now talk quietly among yourselves while I go and make the arrangements."

Before anyone else has the chance to demur he's off as fast as his limp will allow down the escalator to Reception. He finds it momentarily unattended, so goes behind the desk into the inner sanctum where Barbara is sitting on a stool sipping a Dry Martini.

"Hi, Barbara!"

"Your wife is here," responds Barbara in a voice drier than her Martini.

"I know, one of those things. It's off for tonight, I'm afraid. Sorry. Another time, eh?"

He had arranged to spend the night with Barbara as his one last fling, a sort of Don Juan swansong.

"Look, I've got a bit of a party going – a celebration, as a matter of fact. I've just learned about the birth of my first grandchild."

"So far as you're aware," comments Barbara acidly.

"Now, now!" He wags a finger and grins. "The point is, I want to know if the Trafalgar Room is available tonight."

"Haven't a clue. You want me to check, I suppose."

"If you wouldn't mind. Sorry to be a pest."

She heaves herself off her stool and slumps out to tap her computer.

"You're lucky, it's free."

"Great! Now be a luv and arrange for two magnums of the best champagne to be sent up there – no, you'd better make it three – and some lovely strawberries and cream to go with it. And some nibbles of some sort – enough for ten people. And charge it to me – Expense Account, of course."

Oliver opens his wallet and slips her a fifty-pound note. "And have a little celebration yourself on me."

*****

With Renwick safely tucked out of sight in his holdall, Boris and Daphne descend the escalator from the mezzanine floor, past the Skyfly Hotel's liveried doorman, and out into the cool night air.

Once in the dimness of the car park, Boris releases the puppy from his prison. "Walk, you bugger," he growls.

Daphne and Boris saunter silently to the far perimeter of the car park and over the grass towards the hotel's boundary at the edge of the motorway.

"Dad found Elsie," Boris tells her after a bit.

"Och, I'm glad. Where was she?"

"In the pub. She was with some bloke. Dad thumped him one."

"Good for him."

"Only it wasn't the bloke he thought it was."

Daphne laughs. "Whatever happened?"

"Bit of a bust-up. Dunno what it was all about really."

They walk on silently, Renwick making meteoric orbits over the grass.

"I like y'father," says Daphne presently.

"All right, I suppose."

"He must love his wife very much. He dinnae know what to do with himself when she went missing."

"Fight like cat and dog at home."

"Wael, that shows they're human."

"Yer. Suppose."

"Nae like *my* father."

"That little geyser who was yellin' at you?"

"Aye. He treats me as if I'm still aboot seven. Disapproves of everything I do."

"Strict and that, is he?"

"Strict! I cannae even go to a disco without he sends m'grandfather along to spy on me."

"Go on?"

"M'grandfather's a funny old buffer, but he doesnae split on me. He likes a good time himsel'. But I know this much, I'll nae go back home, ever."

"Unless it's in a coffin," says Boris.

They have reached the hotel's boundary and they just stand, watching the motorway traffic whizzing by.

"Have you a job?" asks Daphne.

"Yer – part-time. Market garden. Digging up spuds and that."

"Do you like it?"

"All right. Better than being stuck at home all the time."

She nods understandingly. They continue to stand there, staring at the traffic while Renwick sniffs in the long grass. "Course," says Boris meditatively, "you could always throw yourself under one of them trucks."

"Och, give over!" laughs Daphne. "Y'sound as if you want me to kill mysel'."

"Only trying to help."

They watch solemnly while Renwick strains over his job and then wander back slowly towards the hotel.

"I bet y'girlfriend doesnae know what to make of you," says Daphne presently.

"Told you, don't have a girlfriend. Cos of the bike."

"Och, rubbish! Girls love bikes. They're greet. I'd have one meself but m'father willnae hear of it."

"Don't need one where you're going."

She laughs again and pokes him in the ribs. "Will y'nae keep on aboot it! Y'know very well I'll nae kill mysel'."

"What *will* you do then?"

"Go to Spain as I said, find Carlos and marry him."

"Suppose he's already married with fifty kids?"

"Then he'll have to get unmarried. He promised to marry me, so that's what he'll do."

Boris ponders this. "Don't understand. Don't seem worth it, going all that way just for some bloke. Plenty of blokes here."

"Wael, that's what love does to you."

When they reach the hotel Boris grabs Renwick and stuffs him back in the holdall. They walk calmly through the foyer and on to the escalator leading up to the mezzanine floor. But Boris makes the mistake of putting down the holdall on the escalator step while he blows his nose, and doesn't realise he's failed to zip up the top of the bag.

Renwick is out in a jiff and tearing helter-skelter across the shiny mezzanine floor.

"Come back 'ere, you bugger!" bawls Boris.

Round and round the floor scampers the little dog. Boris lumbers after him. Daphne tries to grab him as he comes round after every circuit. Boris puts two fingers to his mouth and emits a shrill whistle, but all to no avail.

Renwick continues his circuit at a speed that would do him credit at Brands Hatch. Passing guests stop to stare. Security is alerted. Daphne, too intent on trying to trap the little dog, fails to notice her father and grandfather emerging from a lift and making their way towards the barber's shop.

Renwick avoids Daphne on his umpteenth circuit by leaping on to a sofa where, to his delight, he finds a small packet, which he quickly seizes between his teeth and darts off with, just as Daphne is about to pounce.

But he makes the fatal mistake of taking his new-found treasure to a corner behind a potted palm, no doubt with the intention of ripping it to pieces. Boris comes up on one side of the potted palm and Daphne on the other. There is no escape.

It is Daphne who finally succeeds in grabbing him by the scruff of his neck and hauling him up from the floor.

"What *have* y'got there?" she says, wresting the slimy packet from between his teeth. "Och y'naughty boy! At your age too!"

"What is it?" asks Boris.

"Condoms!" laughs Daphne. "Here, you have them. You'll have to find yoursel' a girlfriend now."

"*DAPHNE!*" The cry comes from behind her, full of outrage and censure.

Daphne spins round. "Father!" she gasps.

And there stands Mr Pertwee, with Billy beaming mildly in surprise. Having found the barber's shop closed they were making a beeline for The Beer Barrel when they came upon the commotion.

Hearing Daphne so much as utter the word 'condom' is enough to rocket her father's blood pressure.

"Y're no daughter o'mine, y'filthy slut!" he raves.

"Good," responds Daphne.

"Y'coming home with me the noo. I willnae have y'consorting with the likes of him!"

"Y'silly old fool, I'm nae consorting with him nor anybody else. I'm in love, can y'nae understand? I'm going to Spain and I'm going to marry Carlos."

"Never, never, never!" Mr P. seems fully determined. "Y'coming home with me, m'lass—"

"Sod off!"

"I willnae have y'using—"

"Why can y'nae *understand*, Father?" Her voice is as heavy as Nelson's Column. "I'll nae come back, ever. I've finished skivvying for ye. It's over, finished, done with, do y'get m'drift?"

"There'll nae be skivvying once the hotel is sold. I'll be needing y'to help train the dogs in Scootland."

"Aye, still skivvying, no doot. No, Father, I'll never be y'kennel maid, nor y'kitchen maid, nor y'chamber maid, nor y'bar maid, nor, if I can help it, an old maid. So y'can go piss y'sel'!"

From his stance it looks as if Mr Pertwee might do just that. He can't believe that the sweet, wee bairn he dangled on his knee can now be so horribly crude. And in public!

"Daphne," he pleads, "y'mustnae talk like that! Come home! Let us start again, a new life in bonny Scootland..."

Mr P. gabbles on, trying to paint a seductive picture of a dog's life in the glens, while Daphne spits unseemly epithets at him, like pips from a peashooter.

As befits a grandfather, Billy Greenhorn does his best to pour balm on the festering situation with words to the effect that this kind of ding-dong will get them nowhere, and a drink or two followed by a good night's sleep might promise a more satisfactory outcome.

With an exasperated "Och!" as breathy as the hiss of a steam engine, Daphne seizes Boris by the arm and stalks off.

Mr Pertwee chases after them, arms outstretched and pleading woefully, and manages to grab Daphne by the tail of her tartan shirt.

This is too much altogether for Boris, who seizes Mr Pertwee's arm and flings it aside.

"'Ere," he warns. "Back off!"

A nasty moment.

In his frenzied condition it looks as if Mr Pertwee is about to assail this King Kong version of the human species, but mindful of their previous encounter only hours earlier, he stands, a desolate figure, as he watches his beloved Daphne striding away from him as if into the sunset.

*****

After obtaining the key to The Trafalgar Room from the sour Barbara, Oliver Bloom is making his way back to The Beer Barrel with almost a spring-like step. The news about his first-born grandson has had a rejuvenating effect on him. That, and a series of good belches brought on by a liberal dosage of Wind-eze, which miraculously disposed of the horrible sinking feeling he's been suffering in the pit of his stomach.

I feel fine now, he tells himself, never better. I don't think I can have possibly contracted that terrible disease.

When he reaches The Beer Barrel, now closed, he finds his party all standing in a group outside, as if waiting to have their photo taken.

And a right motley lot they look, he thinks. Marsha, resting on her sticks looking like the Wooden Horse, Nora with her drooping handbag, Len of the doleful countenance, Cyril looking like a startled peasant, Bollinger a scowling sentinel with the willowy Gloria at his side, that bastard Colin fawning over his wife, Elsie, who looks as if she is liable to snap in half at any moment.

"We're in luck folks!" he cries as he approaches them. "Bubbly all round – in The Trafalgar Room! This way."

It is as he is ushering them all to the lifts to convey them to The Trafalgar Room on the top floor that they encounter the distraught Mr Pertwee with Billy, who is leading him hopefully towards The Beer Barrel, following their encounter with the errant Daphne.

Nora is the first to recognise them.

"Mr Pertwee!" she gasps.

"Sergeant Bilko!" cries Colin.

"Mr Greenbum!" exclaims Elsie.

Oliver stares in amazement. "These people friends of yours?" he demands.

"Mr Pertwee owns the hotel we're staying at in Benthaven," Nora explains excitedly. "Well, fancy you being here!"

"And he's the bloke I thought *you* were!" exclaims Colin, pointing at Billy.

Oliver doesn't find that too much of a compliment.

"We're just on our way to get a drink," says Billy.

"They're closed, mate," Colin tells him.

Billy's beam dips.

"Join *us*!" cries Oliver expansively. "We're having a celebration!"

"Och, I couldnae," wails the bereft Mr P.

"Oh come on! The more the merrier! We'll make a night of it! Plenty of champagne and strawberries for us all."

Billy's beam is restored. "How very kind," he says.

*****

As the lift whisks Daphne and Boris skywards, Daphne is still breathing like an asthmatic bull.

"I'll nae speak to him again!" she seethes. "Him and his Lancashire hotpots and suet dumplings!"

She is still simmering when they leave the lift.

"Bloody dogs! He's mad! You heard what he said, wants me to give up m'life just to be his bloody kennel maid!"

"Wouldn't mind being a kennel maid meself," says Boris.

She glances at him and scratches her left breast vigorously. "You're welcome," she grins.

"Thought you liked dogs."

"Aye, dogs. Not manipulated puppets."

When they arrive at the door of her room, Daphne says, "Well, thanks for standing up for me doon there. You should be a minder, not a kennel maid."

She unlocks the door and opens it. Boris hovers.

"You going to kill yourself now, then?" he asks.

"Och, dinnae y'start that again!"

"Only I was wondering if you'd look after Renwick a bit longer like. Dad's got the key to the room, see, and I can't take Renwick back down there again."

She gives him a quizzical look and scratches her breast again.

"You got fleas or summat?" he asks.

"What you mean is you want to come back in," she says, ignoring the remark. "Come on, then."

Once in the room Boris releases Renwick and then stares at the chewed-up packet of condoms still in his hand.

"You reckon he's made holes in them things?" he asks.

"Why? Y'want to find out?" asks Daphne dryly.

Chapter 20

"My, oh my!" cries Nora when she sees the opulent splendour of The Trafalgar Room.

It is all done out in green and gold. Glittering chandeliers hang from the ceiling. The walls are covered with striped Regency wallpaper, on which hang specially commissioned oil paintings of the Battle of Trafalgar.

Her exclamation echoes around the room, which is empty apart from the tables and chairs neatly stacked at the far end, along with an organ, shrouded in its dust cover.

Elsie soon spots the organ and the confusions of the day instantly evaporate.

"Does it work?" she asks Oliver.

"Should do. Why, can you play it?"

"Oooh yes!"

"Great! Just what we need." He whips off the dust cover and plugs in the organ. "All yours!"

That's Elsie settled for the night – well, for the time being, at least.

"Come along, gentlemen," Oliver calls out. "Lend a hand with the chairs and tables. Eleven chairs in a cosy ring, if you please, and a couple of tables in the middle."

Once all is in place, Oliver solicitously helps his wife to settle herself in one of the chairs. "I think you'll find that comfortable, my dear. Allow me to relieve you of your walking sticks."

"Don't fuss, Oliver. I can manage."

Nora plonks herself on the chair next to Marsha. "Well, this is very nice I must say. What a lovely room! It's very generous of Oliver to do all this."

Marsha laughs scornfully. "He's just showing off, and I don't suppose for one moment he'll pay for it all."

Elsie soon gets under way, and a vibratoed version of 'Ramona' echoes through the room. Billy Greenhorn soon joins her, leaving Mr Pertwee, still in a state of shock over Daphne, sitting limply on his chair.

Bollinger, looking bored, sits himself next to Gloria, who is finding this turn of events much more fun than having sex with the old buffer with whom her agency has lumbered her. "She's not a bad organist, is she?" she says.

Bollinger grunts. The grind of heavy machinery is more like music to him than this racket. "I sing, you know," continues Gloria. "I'm training to be an opera singer in my spare time." Being a call-girl is simply the least tiring and the most lucrative way of paying for her lessons.

Bollinger doesn't even bother to grunt this time.

Gloria jumps to her feet, tra-laaing 'Ramona'. "I'm going to join them. Do you mind?"

"Don't be long then," he warns. "We're leaving as soon as we can."

Unable to sit still without his pipe, Cyril is mooching around the room pondering the paintings of the Battle of Trafalgar.

Colin and Len, overjoyed at being together again, stand talking animatedly about their respective experiences since they last met, until Nora, demanding they come over to join her, interrupts them.

"That's never his wife Mr Bollinger's with, surely?" she whispers to Len as he sits down.

Len looks vacant.

"Course it's not," says Colin for him. "It's some fancy woman, I bet."

A bored-looking waiter pushes in a food trolley, laden with enough champagne, strawberries and cream, and canapés to feed the five thousand.

"Put it all on the tables, Sam," orders Oliver. "Easy does it. That's the way!"

He takes a tenner from his wallet and rewards Sam, who shoves it in his 'tip' pocket and goes his way, contented.

Oliver claims the attention of his guests by tapping the side of an ice bucket with a spoon. "Come on, folks! Time to wet the baby's head!"

The music stops. The songsters take their seats. Champagne corks pop. Glasses are charged. Oliver plays the host.

"Ladies and gentlemen – friends – thank you for agreeing so readily to attend this very special occasion. I gather you've all had a pretty hefty day, so I'll be brief, but surely this must be a unique occasion, and we really can't allow it to pass uncelebrated, if only because of the amazing sequence of events that has brought us together in this fashion, so amazing in fact that one can't help feeling it must have been pre-ordained."

"Get on with it, man," mutters Bollinger impatiently.

But Oliver is well and truly launched. He goes on to inform his captive audience that there are three specific items of wonderful news he would like them to raise their glasses to, first and foremost of which must surely be the birth of a son to his lovely Georgie and her splendid husband. He pauses a moment and turns to Marsha. "Do we know what they intend to call him, my dear?"

"Jonathon," says Marsha firmly.

"To Jonathon, then. May he have a long, happy and successful life!"

"To Jonathon!" comes the echo.

"God bless the little mite," adds Marsha.

A sober moment as the champagne is savoured.

"Oooh, lovely!" cries Nora, who is rapidly acquiring a taste for bubbly.

"Not bad," agrees Bollinger. For free champagne of this quality it is perhaps worth delaying getting to bed.

Secondly, Oliver tells them, it is only this *very day* that he has decided to take early retirement. "I am not proposing a toast to myself," he adds hastily, "but I'd like you to raise your glasses to my dear wife Marsha, who has been urging me to retire for so long, and has waited so very patiently for this day to arrive. To *you*, my dear!"

Murmurs of "Hear, hear!" and "Good luck."

"Did I tell you Marsha and Oliver are moving to Brighton when he retires?" Nora whispers to Len.

"Um," says Len.

"And thirdly," Oliver persists, "let us not forget the rising generation. Nora has told me that Gavin informed her when she and Marsha were in Greece that his bank is promoting him, and that he is to be transferred to its Brighton branch. Those of us who know him will agree it is a well-deserved promotion, and all of us, I'm sure, wish him the very best of luck in what promises to be a glittering career."

More champagne passes the increasingly eager lips of the celebrators. Even Mr Pertwee, who has scarcely allowed enough champagne to be poured into his glass to inebriate a wasp, drains the dregs and wishes he'd accepted more, a wish instantly granted by Oliver, who, magnum in hand, magnanimously recharges the glasses of one and all.

"Help yourselves to strawberries," he cries when he eventually sits down.

Hands stretch out. Speedy plate depletion sets in.

Nora is already feeling a little squiffy, just enough to give her the courage to let off the squib she's just manufactured in her head.

"Mr Bollinger," she calls across to that austere gentleman, "is it true there are going to be major redundancies at the Plant?"

Bollinger sits up as if a red-hot iron has been shoved up his backside.

"Only we heard a rumour about it only the night before we went on holiday," she elucidates.

"Mrs…ahm…Scally," growls Bollinger, "this is not the time to discuss Company business."

But 'Shop Steward' Scally is not put off so easily. "Don't want to *discuss* it, sir, we don't want to bore your…er…good lady here…" She stares meaningfully at Gloria. "We just need to know if it's true or not, cos we've got to make some big decisions about our futures and that."

The bloody woman's trying to blackmail me, thinks Bollinger. She knows damn well Gloria's not my wife. But he wouldn't be the Chief Executive of Regal Chemicals plc, Fertiliser Division, if he didn't know how to slink out of a tricky one like this. "I'm sorry, I'm not at liberty to comment. All I *am* prepared to say is that I have just returned from Hong Kong where I've had the disagreeable task of having to tell all our employees there that the branch is to be closed down and that they are redundant."

"Hong Kong?" echoes Colin. "You mean it's the Hong Kong people who are being made redundant, not us?"

"I can make no further comment."

"There you are!" exclaims Nora. "What did I say? Trust old Frank to get it wrong."

Bollinger makes a mental note of the last remark. He can guess who 'Old Frank' is – the Company's bloody chauffeur.

"But he was so sure—" begins Colin.

Bollinger holds up his hand. "Not another word! We really must be going. Come along, Gloria."

"Don't break up the party just yet, George!" cries Oliver. "The night is young and we still have oodles of champagne. Let's make a night of it! We've got our music maestro here – and very good she is too – and one of the best dance floors in London all to ourselves, so let's make use of them both!"

"Ooh, let's dance, George!" cries Gloria, squeezing Bollinger's arm. "Just one, mmm?"

"Well, if you must." Bollinger is starting to mellow now the champagne is circulating his body.

Elsie returns to the organ and revs up with 'All By Yourself in the Moonlight'. Billy Greenhorn follows her to the organ. Gloria drags Bollinger on to the floor.

"What a shame about your ankle, my dear," says Oliver to his wife, "otherwise we could have had a dance. It is years since we have."

"You know perfectly well I'm no dancer," says Marsha irritably.

"Even so, on an occasion like this..." He looks round for an alternative partner. The choice isn't spectacular – just Nora. But protocol demands. "Nora, my dear, shall we dance?"

"Oooh! Lovely!"

Oliver whisks her on to the floor. Marsha watches them superciliously; at least Oliver is unlikely to make a pass at Nora, she consoles herself.

Mr Pertwee is becoming drowsy as the champagne soothes his tortured soul. Cyril, lost without his pipe and missing his customary evening meal of a chop and chips, helps himself to more strawberries.

"Well, that's a relief, anyway," Colin says to Len, as he also helps himself to more strawberries.

"What is?"

"It's not us who's being made redundant. Rotten luck for Hong Kong, though."

"Um." Len's not too worried about Hong Kong.

"Pity in a way. Was quite looking forward to a change of job and that."

Nora soon returns from the dance floor, red-faced and out of breath. "Oh my!" she gasps. "That was lovely!"

"Allow me to top you up," invites Oliver. Without waiting for a response he refills Nora's glass, and while he's at it, those of Mr Pertwee, Cyril, Len and Colin.

Elsie modulates into 'Three O'clock in the Morning'. Bollinger, who is finding the feel of the small of Gloria's back sexy through her slinky dress, insists on a further wheel around the floor.

"Oliver," says Nora, having regained her breath, "I'd like your advice on something."

"Of course, my dear! Anything."

"Our friends and Len and I are thinking of going into business together."

"Really? What sort of business?"

"The hotel business."

Both Len and Colin jerk up. Stop press news to them.

"Private hotel, that is, the hotel where we're staying in Benthaven. Mr Pertwee's hotel, in fact."

"Thought you were dead against that idea," protests Colin.

"I wasn't *dead* against it," Nora retaliates. "It was only because we were going to move to Webbley Park. But now Gavin and Georgie are going to Brighton, it's different. It makes good sense. I mean, we can all stay together and that, and as Mr Pertwee here wants to sell the hotel and train dogs, we'll be doing him a favour. Isn't that right, Mr Pertwee?"

This is enough to haul Mr P. back from his suicidal meditation. "Aye! Aye, that's reet!"

"So what you think, Oliver? Do you think it's a viable proposition?" Nora makes herself sound businesslike, despite her increasing desire to titter.

Oliver takes on a serious air and looks knowledgeable. "Very old British tradition, guest houses, private hotels, that kind of family business," he observes, staring at the twinkling chandelier above his head. "Struggling a bit these days, I believe, but still popular with some holidaymakers. They rely heavily on the Tourist Information Centres for business, of course, and it also depends where the business happens to be situated. But down on the south coast it should be a reasonably safe bet."

Coming from Oliver these are words of honeyed sweetness to Nora. "That's what *I* think!" she claims triumphantly.

"Yes, but it must have a bar," says Len, who is also trying to appear businesslike.

"I agree," says Colin. He turns to Mr Pertwee. "That's where you went wrong, mate, if you don't mind me saying so."

"I'll have nae to do with the demon drink on principle!" cries that person, taking a gulp of his champagne.

"I'm afraid principles and business don't mix," Oliver informs him, echoing similar sentiments expressed to Mr P. by Billy only a short time before. "The modern tourist expects guest houses to be licensed and to have all the basic amenities of a big hotel, en suite rooms, tea-making facilities and so on."

"Well, the Ocean View's got most of 'em, except the bar," says Colin, his old enthusiasm for the project returning with a vengeance. "Reckon you could easily put one in that lounge."

"Don't forget the cost," Len reminds him.

"Wouldn't cost much. And pay for itself in no time."

"True. Got to have enough capital, though. Important to have enough capital."

"Quite right," agrees Oliver. "Can't run a business on a shoe-string."

Elsie launches into 'Empty Saddles'.

It is a favourite of Colin's and it gives him a Nora-like inspiration. "Tell you what, Elsie could play the organ in the evenings! People like live music and that."

"Oooh, lovely!" exclaims Nora, wishing she'd thought of that herself.

"Not a bad idea," says Oliver. "An Organ Bar, but you'd need a bit of variety as well – a singer or a comedian."

"A cabaret!" cries Colin. The champagne is firing off his little grey cells like nobody's business. "Come to that, we could turn it into a nightclub! A casino, even!"

"With strippers and that," adds Cyril as dormant yearnings rush to the surface.

"I'll nae have m'hotel turned into a den of vice!" cries Mr Pertwee, mortified by these suggestions.

"I should think not!" growls Marsha. She has been listening to all this with mounting distaste.

Shades of The Black Spot pass before Colin's eyes. "Well, not a nightclub maybe. Got to keep it respectable and that."

"Absolutely!" agrees Oliver. "Keep it select. Aim for the richer middle classes and charge high. Do help yourselves to strawberries everyone – don't let them go to waste."

"That's settled then," says Nora, accepting the invitation. "It looks as if we'll be buying the Ocean View from you after all, Mr Pertwee."

But Mr Pertwee is having second thoughts. "Och, I dinnae know aboot that. I dinnae feel like selling anymore."

"Not selling!"

"Without m'Daphne I havenae the heart."

"But you must sell now!"

"Thought you were so dead keen on setting up this dog's home," says Colin.

"Training centre," corrects Mr P., not so heartbroken he can't be bothered to have things right. "Aye, but it will ne'er be the same without her."

"Tell you this much, mate, you're a bloody sight better at training dogs than running a hotel." Colin turns to Oliver. "Amazing the way he's got them dogs trained, I tell you."

"Yes," agrees Nora, "that is certainly his...ahm...his what'sit..." The champagne is getting in the way of her words.

"Métier?" offers Oliver.

"Yes, er…that'll do."

"You're verra kind, but without m'Daphne..." Mr P. splays his hands in despair.

"Cheer up, mate," says Colin. "She ain't in Spain yet. She could change her mind by morning. You've still got time to make it up with her, tell her you forgive her and that."

"You really think so?" His hopes seem to rise a notch.

"You must," says Nora, to whom the champagne has also brought inspiration, " cos I've just thought of the ideal place for you to train your dogs."

Colin is surprised. "You have? Where's that?"

"Cyril's place."

Cyril drops the strawberry he's just popping in his mouth.

"You want to retire and move, Cyril. So if you sell to Mr Pertwee and he sells to us, think of the time and expense that would save!"

"Certainly would," nods Colin.

"Great idea!" cries Oliver.

Mr P. is not too sure. "Aye, but is it in Scootland?"

"It's near Brockbury," says Nora, as if there's nowhere better. "Nice little town. Good place for business and that. Cyril's market garden is absolutely ideal."

"But without m'Daphne, I doot if I can—"

"She'll come round, mate," Colin assures him. "Leave her to me. I'll make bloody sure she does."

Nora can't believe it. "Isn't it exciting! We'll all be living in Brighton together! You'll be able to be our business advisor and that, Oliver."

"Glad to, Nora, glad to." Not exactly what he has in mind for his retirement, but it's better than gardening. "Come along, everybody, let us raise our glasses to this wonderful new venture!"

*****

In Daphne's room, several floors below, the inevitable has occurred. One of the condoms in the packet chewed by Renwick was blown up and found satisfactory, so put to its intended use.

And now Boris, bemused by this swift and perplexing turn of events, lies in bed staring at a painting on the opposite wall, which appears to depict a row of strangely coloured blocks, while Daphne nestles in the crook of his arm, inscribing magic circles around his nearest nipple as she has seen girls do on the telly. Across their feet lies Renwick, flaked out after all his excitement.

This is only the second time Boris has made love. The first was to a girl named Cynthia he'd met in a disco. That had proved a protracted and clumsy exercise, not worth all the aggro in his opinion. But tonight with Daphne it was more in the order of a tornado, which has battered his life to pieces. If he's ever going to settle down, as his dad keeps on to him about, then Daphne has to be the girl.

"That supposed to be a row of houses?" he asks suddenly.

"What?"

"That picture."

Daphne surfaces momentarily to look at it. "Och, no! It's an abstract of some sort."

"Looks like a row of old houses to me."

"You're nuts." She snuggles down again and runs her hand over his chest. "Still, you're one hunk of a man – like a big, friendly old bear. Or you would be if y'had more hair on y'chest. A bare bear!" She laughs and tweaks his nipple.

"'Ere!"

"Funny – Carlos is a wee weed but he's as hairy as a gorilla."

Boris doesn't answer. He doesn't want to know about Carlos. He's more concerned with his own thoughts, which chug along like some old trawler.

"I suppose the name Boris suits you in a way," murmurs Daphne. "It makes you sound like a Russian. But I think I'll call you Yogi – or Teddy. Which would y'prefer?"

"Don't care."

"I'll call you Teddy then, it sounds more cuddly."

"Gorrit!" exclaims Boris suddenly.

"Got what?"

"That old house. That's the place!"

"What old house?"

"Nora Scally's."

"You mean that old girl with a face like a haggis?"

"Yer."

"What about it?"

"Her dad died, see, and left her this old house. Bloody dump it is, but I reckon it'd do us for a start. Might get her to rent it to us dirt cheap."

Daphne raises her head again to stare at him. "Are you serious?"

"Yer."

"Are y'suggesting we live together, or is this supposed to be a proposal of marriage?"

"Proposal."

"Och, get on!"

"What you say?"

"I'll have to sleep on it."

So saying, Daphne turns and snaps off the bedside light.

"You want me to go?" asks Boris.

"Suit yoursel'."

Boris doesn't move. He lies in the darkness, his thoughts chugging along. If Cyril does decide to retire, he thinks, I wonder if he'd let me run the market garden, then if he does move, we could live in his bungalow. Daph could start a kennels, do dog training and that. Don't suppose Cyril will retire, though. Pigs might fly...

Thoughts turn into dreams. Neither of them are aware of Renwick jumping off the bed. The puppy sniffs around the room until he comes across Daphne's discarded clothing lying on the floor, whipped from her during the tornado. Renwick reckons they'll do him very nicely and scratches himself a snug little hollow.

*****

Back in The Trafalgar Room there is a lull in the proceedings so that organist Elsie can catch up with her quota of champagne and strawberries after having played unceasingly for the dancers for almost an hour.

"We haven't told Elsie the news," says Nora, once everyone is seated and supplied with further refreshment.

"What news?" demands Elsie.

"We've agreed to buying Mr Pertwee's hotel and we're going to run it between us."

Elsie looks vacant. "Hotel?"

"You remember," says Colin. "The Ocean View, where we're staying in Benthaven. It was my idea in the first place. I said if we were all made redundant it might be a good idea if we clubbed together with Len and Nora and ran the hotel between us."

"*That place!*" Visions of snarling dogs and unnegotiable stairs rear up in Elsie's mind.

"It makes sense now, see," says Nora, "now that Gavin and Georgie are moving to Brighton. And since Mr Pertwee wants to sell and go and train his dogs and that, it's the obvious thing to do. You think so too, don't you, Oliver?"

"Absolutely!" cries Oliver.

"Over my dead body," snaps Elsie.

"Aw, c'mon Els'," pleads Colin. "It's a good idea. It's all arranged."

"Don't *I* get a say in it then?" Two rosy spots appear on Elsie's cheeks.

"Well, you were busy playing. We were going to—"

"I'm never going back to that bloody hole, I'll tell you that now!"

A ripple of anger passes over Mr P's grief upon hearing his hotel called a bloody hole.

"But it's a good idea, Els'," protests Colin. "I know we're not being made redundant after all, but it's a chance to do something different, start a fresh life and that."

"Bugger that!" Elsie scrambles to her feet. She's on her high horse, and off at a gallop.

"Where you going now?" he cries.

"For a pee!"

Colin starts after her. "Wait...!"

"I'll go," volunteers Nora. "Leave her to me."

She rises nobly. The Trafalgar Room spins a bit, but she follows Elsie, managing to maintain a stately gait.

Had there been a three-legged stool in the powder room Elsie would have undoubtedly collapsed upon it in floods of tears, but in its absence she locks herself in the toilet and does her blubbing there.

Nora utilises the time while waiting for Elsie to come out by dowsing her increasingly blotchy face with water. But Elsie doesn't emerge, She's having one of her sulks, thinks Nora. She knocks on the toilet door.

"Come on!" she calls with Marsha Bloom authority.

"Piss off!"

"Now then! I'm ashamed of you, letting me down like that

in front of me friends. And that disgusting language! Whatever will they think of us?"

This is enough to make Elsie forget her self-pity. It turns to hot anger. "You bleedin' stuck-up selfish old snob!" she screeches.

With a liberal quantity of champagne inside this is too much for Nora. "And you're a common ignorant old fart!" she bellows back.

A cut and thrust battle ensues through the toilet door, both sides jabbing away with grievances stored up over a decade of friendship.

But Nora is still sober enough to realise that this is no way to deal with Elsie. She needs to be craftier. So she shuts up and waits, sloshing more water on her face to cool herself down. Gradually Elsie's violent abuse subsides, replaced by bouts of moaning, and at length, by bitter weeping.

When Elsie has reached the snivelling stage, Nora coos through the door. "It was your lovely organ playing that helped us make up our minds. Oliver thinks it would be wonderful if you played the organ at our hotel in the evenings and that. You'd be a big attraction, bring in the customers. Oliver thinks we could—"

"Oliver thinks! Oliver thinks!" mimics Elsie.

"Well, he does! He should know. He's very impressed with the way you play, very impressed indeed." Nora believes in larding it on. "He says we ought to put in an organ bar specially for you."

"Oh yeh? Don't you try smarming *me*!"

"I'm not! It's the truth."

"If I play anywhere it'll be at the Blackpool Tower, not in some grotty guest house!"

First Nora's heard about Blackpool Tower. But her little grey cells aren't yet entirely pickled in alcohol. "Oh, no doubt you will one day. But you've got to start small like everybody else. 'Spect even Reginald Dixon started small."

Silence from behind the toilet door.

"Elsie?"

The toilet flushes.

Nora smiles. "Come on out. Everybody's waiting for you to

play again. We want to have a sing-song."

Elsie comes out with set lips, for once her face not camouflaged by streams of eye shadow. "Did he *really* say them things about me?" she mutters.

"Scout's honour."

Elsie seems mollified, until she sees her face in the mirror. "Christ Almighty!" She opens the handbag she filched from the hospital – and pulls out the old lady's compact. But with it comes a roll of the old fivers she took from under the wardrobe shelf when she left the Ocean View.

"Wherever did you get *them*?" demands Nora suspiciously, remembering the fivers she discovered herself in her dad's old house.

"Found 'em." Elsie sloshes her face with water.

"*Found* 'em? Where?"

"Dunno. Can't remember."

Nora cocks an eye to take a sly peek into the open bag. "You got a lot more of 'em in there!" she can't stop herself exclaiming. "Must be hundreds of pounds worth! You must remember where you got 'em, surely?"

"Well, I don't," snaps Elsie, fiercely rubbing her face dry with a handful of paper towels.

"And that's not your handbag. I *know* your bag. Where did you get it?"

"Mind your own business!" Elsie mouths the words at her in the mirror.

"Just trying to help," says Nora primly, " cos we don't want you getting yourself into trouble or nothing. You're a valuable asset now."

As she dabs powder on her face from the old lady's compact, Elsie pokes her tongue out at Nora's reflection. "You're not talking me into buying that bloody hotel, if that's what you're trying to do," she snaps, "so forget it."

"I'm not trying to do any such thing!" protests Nora, looking affronted. "Anyhow, we'd better get back. Come on, they're waiting to have a sing-song."

"I mean it! I'm not going back to that bloody hole."

"All right! All right! We'll talk about it tomorrow."

"No, we won't!"

"Oh, come *on*! Let's get back."

Elsie feels too confused and exhausted to protest further, and lets Nora drag her back by the arm to the waiting company.

"Here we are, safe and sound," announces Nora as she settles back in her seat. "Elsie's feeling a bit tired, but she's going to play for one last sing-song."

"Excellent!" proclaims Oliver.

Billy beams with pleasure. "This good lady has kindly agreed to sing us a solo," he says, indicating Gloria. He turns to Elsie, looking anxious. "That's if you're not feeling too tired?"

But where playing the organ is concerned Elsie can keep going until the cows come home.

"Do you know 'All in the April Evening'?" asks Gloria.

"You sing it, I'll play it," says Elsie shortly.

Gloria hums it, or something like it.

"Oh, that old thing! Come on."

So off to the organ they go, Billy in train.

The others sit and listen, or rather, pretend to listen. Bollinger is beginning to drift off. Cyril is doing likewise, his empty pipe which he has taken to sucking, falling from his lips. Len has already drifted. Colin, worried that Elsie won't agree about the Ocean View project, stares at his champagne for inspiration. Mr Pertwee has returned to his doleful meditation. Marsha, too, has shut her eyes but is not falling asleep. She is imagining herself cradling the newborn babe in her arms. Oliver, determined to keep his party alive, recharges glasses.

Nora, now wide awake, looks at Colin. "Elsie's got a lot of them old five-pound notes in her handbag," she whispers. "Wherever did she get 'em from?"

He gulps. The moment of truth! But now is not the time for confessions. "No idea," he mutters.

"Hope she didn't pinch 'em. That's not her handbag she's got, either."

"Hers was pinched. It was in that holdall, remember?"

"Yes, but that's not a new handbag. It must be somebody else's."

"Well don't ask me," says Colin testily. "You know what Elsie is."

"*All in the April evening…*" warbles Gloria.

Roused from her reverie, Marsha groans. For an avid listener to Classic FM, this is Murder One.

"M'dear mother used to sing that to me when I was a wee bairn," Mr Pertwee tells her, also roused by Gloria's rendition. "She also used to play the bagpipes, y'ken?"

Marsha glances at him sharply. "Your *mother*?"

"Aye, m'mother, God rest her dear wee soul."

The silly old fool is drunk, thinks Marsha.

"Och, whatever happened to the innocence of youth?" he wails suddenly. "When I was a bairn we were all so innocent, brought up to fear the Lord and respect our elders."

Marsha's sentiments entirely. "Very true," she nods.

"The young no longer fear the Lord. I blame the telly mysel'. All sin and vice! The Devil stalks the earth!"

Mr Pertwee rants on.

"*The Lambs were weary and crying...*" warbles Gloria soulfully.

Bollinger groans audibly. He's going to demand a refund from the agency for supplying him with this woman.

Nora nudges Len. "Come on, wake up! Try to show some interest!"

But Len isn't interested. Instead he thinks about Alice Potts and can't believe all that has actually happened to him.

Cyril scrabbles about on the floor retrieving his fallen pipe, his trilby falling off in the process.

At last Gloria stops, flushed of face, breathless and expectant. There is desultory clapping.

"You sing beaootifully!" beams Billy, for whom champagne is proving an effective substitute for Guinness. "You should take it up professionally, dear lady."

"Do you really think so?" says Gloria, eyes shining.

"Indeed I do! Indeed I do! The Opera House is where you belong. And I can help you! I used to be an impresario. I still have contacts. I'll give you my card."

Gloria is overwhelmed by gratitude. Perhaps her life as a call-girl will be over sooner than she anticipates.

"Let's have our sing-song now!" cries Nora, hoping to avoid an encore.

"Yes, indeed!" exclaims Oliver. "C'mon folks, gather

round!"

But only Nora and Oliver himself join Gloria and Billy at the organ. Elsie strikes up again with 'I Don't Know Why I'm Happy, I Only Know I Am'.

The champagne is getting to Marsha by this time, and she'd rather like to take a little nap, but Mr Pertwee won't let her.

"I have given the best years of m'life to that wee lassie," he wails, "and she repays me by running after a Spanish waiter! I dinnae understand it. She'd be so much happier with mysel' and the dogs in Scotland than frying onions in Spain."

"*Show me the way to go home,*" roar the revellers. "*I'm tired and I wanna go to bed…*"

"It is very hard when the young leave the nest," agrees Marsha, reminded of her own grief when Georgie left home.

"Aye, especially when they cannae fly."

Marsha is beginning to feel sorry for herself. "Would you describe me as some sort of monster, Mr Pertley?"

"Pertwee. But please call me Alec."

"Alec, then. But you wouldn't say I am a monster, would you?"

He lifts his eyes to look at her. Perhaps there is some physical resemblance, he thinks, but he's too much of a gentleman to say so. "Och no! Not at all!"

"My daughter says I am."

"*The more we are together, together, together,*" chant the choristers. "*The more we are together, the merrier we'll be…*"

"My daughter thinks I'm a harsh old fuddy-duddy," Marsha goes on, tears springing to her eyes.

"The young are so ungrateful," sympathises Mr P.

"I have done everything to give her the best possible start in life – a good education, a decent religious upbringing, every consideration she could reasonably expect…"

"I know, I know," he condoles, nodding despondently.

"And yet – and yet – despite all the love and care I have shown her, she tells me today she was too frightened – too *frightened*, mark you – to tell me her baby was conceived out of wedlock. For a loving mother to be told that I find rather sad, Mr Pertley."

"Verra sad, verra sad." He and Marsha are rapidly becoming

soulmates.

"What was right is now wrong," pronounces Marsha suddenly, "and what was wrong is now right."

"Aye...aye...aye," he sighs on an intake of breath.

"*O, ye'll tak' the high road, and I'll tak' the low road,*" sing the songsters, "*and I'll be in Scotland afore, ye...*"

This rouses Mr P. from his dolorous deliberations. He starts to sing along in a quavery voice. "*On the bonnie bonnie banks...*"

And this is enough to make Marsha dab away her tears and reach for another strawberry.

"Auld Lang's Syne!" cries Mr Pertwee suddenly when they finish. "Let's have Auld Lang Syne!"

"Great idea!" cries Oliver. "C'mon folks, form a circle, join hands! All of you now!"

All reluctantly obey, except Marsha, who continues to sit contemplating life's injustices as she might a sepulchral mound.

"*Should auld acquaintance be forgot...*"

"Sing up, darling!" cries Oliver, noticing Marsha sitting alone. "I know you can't come and join us because of your poor ankle, but sing up just the same!"

She manages a weak smile and reluctantly starts to sing in a tuneless undertone.

"*We'll tak' a cup o kindness yet, for AULD...LANG...SYNE!*" They end in one almighty roar.

And upon that triumphant note Elsie promptly flakes out over the organ.

Chapter 21

Late the next morning a bizarre motorcade departs from the forecourt of the Skyfly Hotel.

A Rolls Royce, driven by Old Frank, the Company chauffeur, who has risen at four in the morning in order to collect the Fertiliser Division's Chief Executive from Heathrow, heads it. Alone in style in the back sits George Bollinger.

Next comes a London taxi hired by Bollinger to convey Gloria back to her Pimlico flat.

Then comes Oliver's BMW, with the man himself at the wheel. Next to him sits Marsha, and in the back, Len and Nora.

They are followed by a white mini-van, driven by Billy Greenhorn. Mr Pertwee sits beside him, looking as if he's just suffered a bereavement, which in a manner of speaking, he has.

A mud-splattered Land Rover comes next, with Cyril at the wheel, his now-filled pipe and his hat both at a jaunty angle.

Finally comes a motorbike with a green and yellow sidecar attached. It is a grim Boris at the helm. Colin is on the pillion, and Elsie in the sidecar with Renwick in his holdall on her lap.

Conspicuous by her absence is Daphne.

Boris slept heavily in her bed until nine, and when he did wake up there was no Daphne beside him.

But on the bedside table was a note, written in her large scrawling hand on a piece of the Skyfly Hotel's smart notepaper.

Dear Teddy,

You are a yummy piece of brawn, but to be frank I can't say I fancy spending the rest of my life in some crummy terraced house.

Besides, it wouldn't be fair to expect you to bring up the wee bairn I'm carrying. So I'm off to catch up with the little bugger's father.

Sorry. Thanks for the support and bliss.

Love, D.

So now it's Boris who's feeling suicidal. For two pins he'd run his bike straight into that HGV in front of him. But he has Renwick to consider, not to mention his bike. He's through with women, though. When he gets home he's going straight round to see his old mates again and get pissed.

*****

Billy Greenhorn is driving the mini-van as if it's Concorde, but Mr Pertwee doesn't appear to notice, or rather, to care. His 'Great Sorrow' has reached its tragic climax. His lovely Daphne has gone forever.

It was during a very late breakfast in the Snappy Snax Bar that the final nail was driven home by Colin, who was thoughtful – or perhaps thoughtless – enough to inform him of his daughter's condition.

"Probably all for the best, mate," Colin tried to console him. "Reckon she's done the right thing in the circumstances. Baby needs a father. She'll settle down now, you'll see. Probably come home on visits and that, invite you out there for holidays. Could be worse."

But Mr Pertwee remains inconsolable. "I'll nae take up m'dog training now," he laments as Billy jets him back to Benthaven. "Without m'Daphne it'll ne'er be the same."

But Billy, being sober, is full of ideas this morning.

"Has it occurred to you, Alec," he says as he honks a slowcoach in front of him, "that if Mohammed won't go to the mountain, perhaps the mountain should go to Mohammed?"

Mr P. looks vague. He couldn't care less about Mohammed or his mountain.

"What I mean is, have you thought of going to Spain

yourself and running a dog centre *there*?"

The very thought is enough to jerk Mr Pertwee out of his gloom. "Never! Never, never, never!" He's seems pretty positive about that.

"It's a pity it's not bulls you train," observes Billy. "You'd be able to make a fortune then."

Mr Pertwee is not amused. His chin drops back on his chest. He looks the picture of misery.

Billy jerks into the fast lane. The speedo shudders into the nineties. "So what *are* you going to do?" he asks.

"I dinnae know. I really dinnae know. Stay where I am, that is all I can do."

"But you've agreed to sell."

"Aye, well I've changed m'mind. I willnae sell to that Stilwell fellow. He'll turn the place into a den of vice."

Billy is silent while he digests this. "He's right about one thing, Alec. If you're going to stay there you'll really have to put in a bar."

Mr Pertwee heaves a long, long sigh. "Aye, wael, maybe. If I must."

Billy beams. That sounds more promising.

But Mr P. is soon back with his 'Great Sorrow'. "I doot if I'll ever hear from her again!" he wails.

"Oh, look on the bright side, Alec. She'll probably send you a postcard from time to time."

*****

Of all the departing company it is only Gloria who has greeted the new day with outstretched arms.

She and Bollinger had finally rolled into bed at four in the morning, but it proved to be all the rolling that was done. Bollinger behaved like a naughty little kid about her having yowled – as he called it – so long with Elsie at the organ and would have nothing to do with her, even though by this time Gloria herself felt quite in the mood. Not that it bothered her at all, and she was certainly not in the least concerned when he'd curtly despatched her after breakfast without so much as a parting kiss.

As the taxi whisks her back to her apartment Gloria's mind is not on the past, but firmly on the future. Her days as a call-girl, glamorous though they may be at times, are definitely numbered, that bald-headed man with glasses last night had as good as said so. But she can't remember his name. It is all rather hazy.

Then she smiles and opens her little black, velvet bag. There, next to the tiny broach Bollinger brought back for her from Hong Kong as a gift, lies the visiting card. 'Billy Greenhorn – Impresario', it reads.

She takes it out and kisses it.

*****

Cyril is also in a buoyant mood as he turns his Land Rover in the direction of home. He hasn't enjoyed himself so much for many a year. But his optimism is quickly dampened when he realises he'll soon have to face Glennis.

He'd completely forgotten about phoning her to say they'd been forced to spend the night at Heathrow and she is probably worried out of her wits. Nor will she exactly be pleased when she finds Boris hasn't turned up for work this morning, as he should have done. In fact, she'll be hopping mad, he thinks. She'll be waiting for him behind the kitchen door with the frying pan at the ready.

In order to allow Len and Nora to sleep together, he'd taken over the single room Marsha had originally booked for Nora, and he'd had a great time making himself numerous cups of tea with the facilities provided while flicking through the countless TV channels, none of which he is able to obtain at home, but wishes he could.

Yes, he thinks, as he bumbles along in the slow lane, I am definitely going to retire and live in London, or at least in some big city where there's a bit of life.

Glennis won't like it, of course. She'll want to retire to the Valleys, or some remote spot where there is even less life than in Brockbury. Well, she'll have to put up with it. She's had her way all these years, now it's his turn.

He'll have to be very careful how he goes about it, of

course. Bide his time, not mention moving to London and that until she's got over last night and is in a good mood. If he'd thought of it earlier, he'd have brought her back a box of chocolates.

*****

In the back of the Company Rolls, George Bollinger is staring moodily at the dandruff on the collar of Old Frank's uniform.

Thorough balls-up last night, he muses. Should never have let that Bloom feller cajole me into going to that bloody celebration. All Gloria's fault, her and her bloody yowling. The Royal Opera is welcome to her.

His mood deepens further when he remembers about that Scally woman trying to worm information from him about the redundancies by hinting to tell his wife about Gloria. At least he'd managed to sidestep that one pretty adroitly. Letting them all assume it was just the Hong Kong branch that was being closed down and not the whole Fertiliser Division was a pretty nifty piece of thinking on his part. By the time the closure is eventually announced it won't matter what she says. He'll have gone himself.

"What the hell's the matter with your ears?" he barks suddenly at old Frank in front.

"Me ears, sir?" Old Frank unconsciously fingers his left one.

"They've grown ten times their size, man!"

"Sir!"

"That's due to listening to other people's private conversation, no doubt…"

"I-I don't understand…"

"…and then tittle-tattling it all over the bloody Plant!"

The car gives a Rolls Royce of a lurch.

"But I never, sir! I never, honest!"

"Don't argue. You're fired!"

George Bollinger feels a lot better for that.

*****

In Oliver's BMW all the occupants are silent.

Oliver himself is intent on making a futile bid to pass the Rolls. He's feeling vexed. His intention to visit a London doctor this morning for a health check has been thwarted by the presence of Marsha and the Scallys. Not that he's too concerned. He's feeling so much better, thanks to Wind-eze, and he's convinced himself his health hasn't suffered at all as a result of his cohabitation with the unfortunate Rosemary in Singapore. He's much more vexed because in his panic he's promised Marsha he would retire, and now it will be very difficult to wriggle out of it. He was a fool to have made such a big thing of it last night.

Marsha sits beside him, eyes firmly shut. She is furious with Oliver because he has failed to hand in his notice as he promised he would. He couldn't, he'd told her over breakfast, because his boss was away on a fishing trip in the Outer Hebrides, but he'd see him as soon as he got back.

Marsha is unconvinced. He's trying to get out of it, she thinks. He's hoping by dragging it out I'll lose my determination. No way. We're retiring to Brighton, and that's that. Georgie is going to need me to look after baby Jonathon while she's at work, and I'm going to be there to make sure he's brought up in a proper Christian manner.

In the back seat Nora is remarkably silent. She is suffering from a hangover, her normally agile mind stubbornly stagnating in a sludge of pain. Even the prospect of managing the Ocean View has momentarily lost its appeal. She is trying to focus on the new baby, to think of some extra little gift to give him when he arrives home from Thyros. But her mind won't function. She is longing only for the moment when the Paracetamols she took in place of breakfast take effect.

Len, although silent out of habit, is wide awake. Not having drunk all that much by his standards, he hasn't suffered a hangover. But his thoughts are sombre. In the cold light of day the idea of the four of them running the Ocean View seems to him to be absurd. Quite apart from the financial risks, he can see no sense in embarking on a lot of hard work and worry when he is due to retire. The whole point of retirement is to be able to take it easy. He has to find a way of weaning Nora off the idea.

But after his masterful handling of the Alice Potts affair and its aftermath, he is feeling much more sure of himself. If Nora makes a fuss, he tells himself, he'll just have to put his foot down with a very firm hand.

*****

The motorcycle and sidecar approaches a notice announcing: 'Services 1 Mile'.

Out shoots Elsie's arm from the sidecar and she tugs violently at the hem of Boris's leather jacket.

"Stop there!" she yells, pointing frantically at the sign.

"Not yet! Only just started," Boris yells back.

"Stop! I want the toilet!"

Elsie woke this morning in a state of acute anxiety about her bowels. She hasn't been since God knows when. Unfortunately, her Lactulose is still languishing in the en suite bathroom of Room Six at the Ocean View. It was ready-for-all-emergencies Nora who came to her rescue, providing her with Sennakot, of which Elsie took a liberal dosage and is now suffering the consequences.

As soon as Boris pulls into the services, Elsie jets off to the loo. Colin and Boris stand waiting amid the gaming machines and milling children.

"So you spent the night with Daphne," says Colin with a note of envy. He hasn't had a chance before to privately quiz his son on this remarkable event.

"Yer," growls Boris. "Then when I woke up she'd bloody gone."

"That's how it goes, mate. That's life. Reckon you had a lucky escape though, if she was already pregnant and that. No wonder she wanted to catch up with that Carlos bugger."

"Yer."

Colin is feeling sorry for his son, but also relieved to think at last Boris is showing an interest in girls. "Never mind," he consoles him. "There's plenty more fish in the sea."

"Yer, and they can bloody stay there."

Elsie comes reeling out of the Ladies, shattered but successful.

"I need a coffee after that," she mutters.

"We've only just had breakfast," protests Colin. "Besides, we're skint, remember? We ain't got a dime between us after paying for that room at the hotel."

"I got some cash," says Boris, producing a small wad of tenners.

"Where you get them?" demands his dad suspiciously.

"Daphne left 'em to pay for her room."

"What! And you didn't pay it?"

"Forgot."

"You bloody fool! That's all we need!"

"I was upset."

"Not as upset as me! Well, we're not going back now to pay it. Suppose we'll have to get Mr 'Fix-it' Oliver to sort it out with the hotel when we get home and pay him back."

"We going to have coffee or not?" demands Elsie.

"Might as well, I suppose."

In the cafeteria it is Boris, the man with the money, who's elected to get the coffee.

"And bring me back a doughnut," Elsie calls after him. "I'm starving."

Elsie and Colin settle themselves at a table, Renwick in his holdall at their feet. Elsie opens her borrowed handbag and starts dibbing into it.

"What you looking for?" asks Colin.

"See if I've got enough money to pay for that doughnut."

"Good grief, don't bother about that now! I'll sort it all out when we get home – if we ever do."

But Elsie continues to delve, pulling rolls of the old fivers out of the bag and putting them on the table.

Colin starts with alarm. "And put them things away! You don't know who's watching."

Elsie picks up a roll and looks at it as if it's a holy relic. "I wish I could remember where I got 'em."

"Staring at 'em won't help. Put 'em away!" He doesn't want her remembering where she found them, not at this moment in time, nor at any other, come to that.

"*Must* have got 'em from the hospital, I suppose." Elsie stuffs the notes back in the handbag. "Best thing I can do is return 'em when I send the bag back."

"You can't do that!"

"Why not?" A dangerous challenge in Elsie's voice.

"What I mean is, you might remember later where you did get 'em," Colin explains hastily. "Then it'll be too late to do anything about it."

Boris arrives back with the coffee and doughnut. Elsie loses no time in taking a bite.

"It's the only place I could have got 'em," she says with her mouth full. "If only I could remember better."

Colin feels guilty. He ought own up, but again he feels it is not the moment for complicated explanations. He'll tell her when they get home.

"Can y'spare a bit of that for Renwick?" asks Boris.

"Get y'own bloody doughnut!" flares Elsie. "And while you're about it, get me another one."

Boris shrugs and mooches off again.

"And don't be all day," Colin calls after him. "Got to get home. Len and I got to get some practise in before this bleedin' Snooker Final tomorrow. Not that we stand a chance in hell of winning it, but we've got to put on a bit of a show with old Bollinger being there."

"You and your bloody snooker," says Elsie, licking the jam off her fingers.

When Boris returns with two more doughnuts he pulls a bit off one and feeds it to Renwick in the holdall.

"Don't go and let that goddam dog escape again," warns Colin. "We don't want a repeat of last night's fiasco."

"Don't keep on," grunts Boris.

"And that bloody dog better not start tearing up the happy home, neither," says Elsie, tucking into her second doughnut. "If he starts peeing all over my carpets you'll wish you'd never been born."

"Whatcha so worried about? You'll be moving soon," he growls. It's dangerous to criticise Renwick.

"Moving? I'm not moving! If anybody's going to bloody move it's you."

"But Dad said you're all going to run that hotel together or summat daft."

Dawn breaks over Elsie's mind. What with her dodgy memory and constipation she's forgotten all about the elaborate plans of the night before.

"Then Dad can forget it. I'm not running no bleedin' hotel and that's flat!"

"But you agreed last night!" exclaims Colin, appalled.

"That was last night."

"Aw c'mon, Els'. It's all fixed up. We're going to take over Pertwee's hotel and he's going to buy Cyril's market garden for dog training."

"So what?"

"But you were so keen, once you got used to the idea – playing the organ to the guests in the bar and that."

It's a wonder Elsie doesn't throw the remains of her doughnut at him. "I'm not playing an organ for a lot of old fuddy-duddies. If I play any bloody organ other than me own, it'll be at the Blackpool Tower. So you can put that where the monkey puts his doughnuts!"

Elsie has spoken.

Chapter 22

Glennis isn't behind the kitchen door with the frying pan when Cyril arrives home; she's out in the yard waving a spade.

"Where the hell have you been?" she yells at him.

"Heathrow – told you."

"All this time? Doesn't take a day and half to go to Heathrow and back!"

"Nora got held up by the Customs and that. Thought she was a drug-runner or summat."

"Don't talk wet!"

"'S true!"

"Then why didn't you phone me?"

"Couldn't. Met up with some folks Nora knew at the hotel. Didn't get a chance."

"At what hotel? You trying to tell me you spent the night at a hotel?"

"Had to, see. Nora and that other woman was all shook up and that."

"And there was I phoning the police thinking you'd had an accident!" Glennis is furious. If she wasn't so tired from digging Cyril would be feeling the sharp edge of that spade. "I suppose this hotel didn't run to a telephone?"

"Course it did. Right posh place, I can tell ya. But there was this bit of a do and I didn't get the chance."

"What sort of a do?"

"Celebration and that, for the new baby, champagne and strawberries. Grand, it was."

At the mention of the baby Glennis melts like ice cream in an oven. "For the baby! Oh, I see! There's lovely! Why didn't you say so?"

"Cos y'didn't give us a chance!"

"Oh, come on in and tell me all about it. Like a cup of tea, would you? And something to eat?"

"Wouldn't mind a bacon sandwich."

Back in the old familiar kitchen with its groaning Aga and smell of frying, Cyril looks back with longing to the glitz of the Skyfly Hotel. He's going to sell this dump to that Scotch bloke and get to London just as quick as he can.

Glennis quizzes him about the baby as she busies herself with the bacon sandwich, asking him all kinds of clinical questions about the birth and about the hotel celebration. Cyril does his best to answer, and what he doesn't know he makes up. When it comes to the bit about Nora and the others buying the Ocean View, Glennis stops her busying about and sits down.

"You mean they're going to buy a hotel in Brighton?"

"Yus. That's what they said."

"Never! Nora couldn't afford to buy a hotel, love you!"

"They're going to club together like, the four of 'em."

Glennis considers this silently, and then goes to the Aga to make the tea. "Then they must be mad, that's all I can say."

"One thing, though," says Cyril, deciding the moment is ripe to make his stand. "The bloke they're buying the hotel from is interested in buying this place. He wants to turn it into a dog's home."

The Aga sizzles as Glennis pours the water on to it instead of into the teapot. "Turn this place into a dog's home? Never!"

"One of Nora's bright ideas."

"Would be. Trust her to interfere."

"Well, she knows you want me to retire and that. Not a bad idea, if y'think about it."

Glennis manages to make the tea and brings it over to the table. "But what about all the produce – and the orchard? All the dogs would be piddling against the trees! Wicked shame that would be."

"Ar, well I thought we might sell the orchard separate like. Make a bit extra that way."

This mollifies Glennis a bit. She plonks a large rasher of bacon between two hunks of bread and shoves it in front of him. "Not such a bad idea, I suppose. Time you retired. Get away from this place."

"Oh ar. See a bit of life while we can. Go where there's summat going on and that. London or someplace."

"London! God love you, I don't want to go to London!"

"Plenty to do there. Different life. You wanna see it. We ain't lived yet, Glennis, I tell ya."

"I don't call that living! No, if we move from here it's back to the Valleys. Nice little cottage in the mountains. Good clean fresh air."

Just as Cyril's been dreading. "Long way from all the family and that," he parries.

"No more than in London!"

But Glennis falls silent as she pours the tea. Cyril bites into his bacon sandwich with what's left of his brown, stained teeth. He's had it, he thinks, fatal to have mentioned the family.

"No, we mustn't move too far away," says Glennis, eventually. "All the family's in these parts see. Got to stay close or we'd never see them. No, what we must do is to go and live in your dad's old house. Have it done up, see, then we'd have plenty of money to enjoy ourselves. Yes, that's what we'll do."

Cyril reaches for his pipe. He knows his destiny is sealed.

"I'll give them bacon rinds to the birds," says Glennis, snatching up his plate.

*****

"No place like home," says Nora as she opens the front door.

Amen to that, thinks Len.

Despite the luxury of Oliver's BMW, neither of them enjoyed the journey very much. Oliver drove like a madman and Marsha sat mute, scarcely responding when Nora tried to talk about the idea of moving to Brighton.

Len's first job is to put the kettle on. Nora inspects the mail that has accumulated. Apart from the gas bill it is all junk mail and charity appeals, which she promptly tears up.

"You'd better find out if the car's repaired yet," Nora tells Len, seeing him idly waiting for the kettle to boil. "We're going to need it for getting back to Benthaven on Sunday."

"It won't be ready. They said Monday at the earliest."

"Try just the same, you never know."

Dutifully, Len tries. The car isn't ready.

"Now what are we going to do?" moans Nora.

"No problem. Colin's already agreed we can go back to Benthaven in *his* car."

"He has?" Nora is surprised Len's made such an arrangement without her prompting. "That's all right then. But we're going to have to do something about that car. Must have one that's reliable. Trouble is the cost."

Len goes over to the boiling kettle and makes the tea.

"Biscuit?" asks Nora, reaching for the tin.

Len shakes his head.

"Better have one. I know we had a late breakfast, but it's a while to supper and we've had no lunch." She plonks a couple of digestives in front of him.

Len doesn't argue.

"Well, what a week it's been!" she continues as she sits herself at the kitchen table. "Good job we didn't know what we were in for when we left last Saturday."

Amen to that, thinks Len again.

"Still, it's all worked out for the best. All's well that ends well, as they say. It's wonderful news about the baby. We're grandparents! Aren't you thrilled?"

"Um." Len spoons his tea.

Nora rattles on about the baby and her visit to Thyros. Len wonders where she gets the energy after what she's been through the last few days. He's feeling dog-tired himself and still worried sick about the Snooker Final tomorrow.

"I expect the tea will be brewed by now," she prompts him.

Len obediently gets up and pours the tea. He's vaguely aware that he's slipping back into his old ways, but he can't be bothered to make a stand. Not at the moment.

"Can't get over all of us all meeting up like that last night," Nora resumes as she sips the tea. "Fate, that's what it was. It was meant to be. We're meant to take over that hotel, obviously. When we get back to Benthaven on Sunday we must discuss it with Mr Pertwee. We might as well get things moving." She pauses to take another sip of her tea.

Len rouses himself. The moment has come! If he's to stop all this nonsense, the sooner he does it the better.

"Ah, that's good!" cries Nora. "There's nothing like your own tea, I always say. The Greeks haven't a clue how to make it.

They give you a glass of hot water and you have to dunk the teabag in it!"

"Y'know, I've been thinking," says Len, girding up his loins.

"What about?"

Len frowns into the bottom of his cup as if trying to read the non-existent tea leaves. "This hotel idea. I'm not sure we ought to go through with it."

"Of course we must go through with it! No point in moving to Webbley Park with Gavin and Georgie moving to Brighton. We'd never see the baby!"

"Bit risky, I'd say. Stand to lose most of our savings. We're too old to start in a business we know nothing about. Don't want a lot of worry and hard work at our age."

To his amazement Nora agrees, thus making marital history.

"That's true, I suppose. I've been thinking much the same meself."

Len feels emboldened. "No, the best thing we can do is stay here, then we can—"

"Oh, I'm not staying *here*," declares Nora roundly. "What we've got to do is to find ourselves a nice little bungalow down there close to Gavin and Georgie, then we'll have time to help look after the baby and that."

Having unexpectedly cleared the first hurdle Len is now faced by a much more formidable one. But it is now-or-never time.

"Ah, well now, I'm not too sure about that either," he ventures, sounding a bit like Oliver.

Nora pulls down her skirt, preparing to do battle. "Oh, and why not?"

"Well..." Armed with his new-found confidence Len stakes all. "I mean, we shouldn't move there just to be near Gavin and Georgie. We've got to let them lead their own lives now, cut the apron strings and that."

Wrong words, Len. He knows it, but it's too late.

"Whatcha mean, *apron strings*!" Nora's voice rises an octave. "I ain't never tied him to me apron strings!"

"No, no, no, I didn't mean that—"

"And what about the baby? With him down there and us up

here we'd never see him!"

"Course we would!"

"Typical of you. Having your first grandchild don't mean a thing to you!"

"That's not true!"

"All you're interested in is snooker and going down..."

"No! Just listen a minute—"

"...The Mason and Magpie. So long as you've got a beer mug in your hand..."

"Just *listen*!"

"...you're happy. You don't care about the baby or nothing except..."

"Will you *LISTEN*!"

Len thumps the table so hard the cups jump.

So does Nora.

"Look," he goes on, his heart pounding like a ship's engine, "we shall no sooner move down there than the bank will most likely move Gavin somewhere else – could even be abroad. We can't keep chasing after them – couldn't afford to for a start."

Nora has slipped up and she knows it. This possibility hasn't occurred to her. "But what about the baby?" she wails. "Georgie is going to need someone to look after him when she returns to work."

"Marsha can look after him, can't she, if they move down there? And if they don't Georgie will have to do what other working mothers do and farm him out. Or better still, stay home and look after him herself as she should."

"But we'll never see him! I was so looking forward to..." Her voice trails away, and to Len's surprise and alarm, she bursts into tears. It is the first time he can recall Nora crying since she lost her handbag in the Chamber of Horrors, years back.

"What we have to do," persists Len, thumping the table with the side of his fist like a politician, "is to *stay put*!"

"Oh, I don't want to stay here," she snivels. "I want a nice little bungalow."

Len is feeling victory slipping from his grasp. He's no match for a wailing woman. But he's not giving up.

"Now listen," he says, lowering his voice. "Since we know

now we're not going to be made redundant, the sensible thing is to stay here until we retire, which isn't long off. Then we'll see how we're placed, and if Gavin seems settled and that, perhaps we'll move then."

Nora clambers to her feet without answering. He thinks she's going to stump out on him. But no, she goes to the kitchen drawer and takes out a tissue to dry her eyes.

Len feels heartened. "It makes sense, see," he goes on, " cos that way we can afford to buy a brand new car, have holidays and that..." Len's eloquence dries up on him.

Nora dabs her eyes and looks up. "Well, that's true, I suppose. We could go to Greece! Treat Gavin, Georgie and the baby to a holiday with us. Gavin knows the ropes there and—"

But before she can wax too enthusiastic the phone interrupts them.

*****

Colin was scarcely in the door before he phoned Len.

"Got home safely then, mate?"

"Just about," says Len. He's still shaking from his up-and-downer with Nora.

"Look, what about this bleedin' snooker match? Better get in some practise, hadn't we?"

"Suppose so."

"What about if we go down the Sports and Social tonight for an hour, about seven, say?"

"Dunno about that." Len couldn't hit a snooker ball for love nor money at the moment. "Can't we leave it to the morning? Feel fresher then."

"True. Come to think of it, I doubt if me back would stand it after riding on that bloody pillion." Suddenly he is deafened by the banshee wail of a vacuum cleaner whining into action. "Call for you about ten tomorrow, then," he bawls into the phone.

Elsie has discovered the litter of newspaper left by Renwick in the living room, which Boris failed to clear up before his hurried departure for Benthaven. She rants and raves at the top of her voice as she pulls and shoves the cleaner hither and thither.

Boris makes good his escape by taking Renwick for a walk. Colin makes his by driving into town to obtain some much needed cash and to inform the bank about his stolen cheque book and credit cards, hoping to God those two thugs haven't already emptied his account.

When he gets back Elsie is still whining away and has extended her activities as far as the dining room.

"Get out of me bleedin' way!" she yells at him.

Being no peace downstairs to do anything with Elsie jabbing the cleaner here, there and everywhere, Colin makes for the sanctuary of the bathroom with the whisky bottle in his hand, as he's done many times of yore. He's hoping the whisky will ease his back and revive his flagging spirits.

Elsie roars her way into the hall, then when she sees the pile of mail picked up by Colin and dumped on the hall table when he first came in, she lets the cleaner sigh into silence.

She is hoping there might be a letter to say she's won a new car in some magazine competition she entered, but this time she is disappointed. There's only the gas bill, which she shoves in her apron pocket and forgets all about, and several charity appeals. Elsie can't resist the round eyes of the children staring up at her so appealingly. Her heart melts. She'll send a generous donation. Once she has some money to send, that is.

Up in the bathroom, having had his quick nip, Colin is in the middle of washing away the grime of the journey back from Heathrow when the vacuuming stops. Safe to go down, he thinks. But he's only just left the bathroom when it starts up again, and he finds his way blocked halfway down the stairs by Elsie and the cleaner.

"Turn that bloody thing off!" he bawls at her.

"What?" She stops the cleaner.

"Look, there's no point in doing all that now. You're only going to have to do it all over again when we get back from Benthaven."

"I'm not going back to Benthaven."

"Don't be daft! Course we've got to go back- we've got another week's holiday to come."

"I told you. I'm not going back to that place again!"

"But we'll have to! I've agreed we'd take Len and Nora in

our car, cos his is off the road."

"They can bloody walk."

On goes the cleaner.

"Don't be like that!" shouts Colin. "It's all fixed up!"

"You go on your own then, and I'll stay here. And good bloody riddance!"

"Aw, c'mon, Els'! We've got to see about this business of buying the hotel."

The cleaner stops again.

"How many more times have I got to tell you I'm not going back to that dump never ever again!"

The cleaner whines into action once more.

"For God's sake, stop that bloody row!" He grabs the machine and turns it off. "Now listen, you're dead beat, we both are, after what we've been through lately. And you've had nothing but a doughnut to eat all day. We need to eat!"

"You'll have to do the bloody cooking then!"

On goes the cleaner.

"All right, I will!"

But it's not Colin's métier, cooking.

He stumps down the stairs and out of the front door, and off to Friddle's for fish and chips.

Chapter 23

Saturday, the day of the 'Big Event', the contest between the holders Sid Cooney and Malcolm Hodge, and Len Scally and Colin Stilwell for the Regal Chemicals plc, Fertiliser Division Snooker Doubles Trophy, dawns bright and sunny.

Len is ready, willing and waiting when Colin calls round for him at ten. An early night, followed by a solid ten-hour sleep has done wonders for him. His self-confidence has also received a substantial boost by the successful outcome of his skirmish with Nora over the Benthaven venture. His one regret is that he hasn't stood up for himself more in the past. But marital harmony has been restored and he feels they can now both look forward to a rosy future. One further test of his new-found courage remains, however. He has to tell Colin the Benthaven venture is definitely off.

Colin is also feeling refreshed after a good night's sleep and is in a grimly determined mood. To his surprise Elsie hasn't relented on her determination not to return to Benthaven. He isn't looking forward to telling Len. He probably won't yet. There is still a chance Elsie will change her mind.

They walk silently for a while down the old familiar streets of the estate towards the Sports and Social Club, Colin with his long, gangling, flat-footed stride, Len's short legs having to work overtime to keep up with it.

"Nice to be back," Len ventures presently.

"Too true, mate, after what we've been through. Never thought we'd ever make this bloody snooker match, to be honest. Amazing how things work out. Don't reckon much for our chances tonight, though."

"Bit of practise this morning will help," says Len optimistically. "Change might have done us a bit of good."

"Might have. Can only do our best, any road. Trouble is old Bollinger wants us to give Cooney and old Hedgehog a thrashing."

"Well, you never know."

They walk on silently.

"Sorry about having to use your car tomorrow," says Len after a bit.

"That's all right, mate. Bloody cars always let you down when you need 'em most. Only trouble is Elsie's changed her mind again about going back to Benthaven. Won't even go back there to finish her holiday."

Len looks up at him in astonishment.

"But not to worry," Colin goes on. "You know Elsie, her bark's worse than her bite. She'll probably change her mind again before the morning. And if she don't, I'm coming anyway, so no problem."

Len is amazed. "You mean you're coming on your *own*?"

"If I have to. For one thing I want to suss that hotel out a bit if we're going to buy it and run it. Want to get old Pertwee to knock a bit off the price, too."

"But if Elsie's turned against the idea we can't—"

"Aw, she'll come right enough once she sees we mean business. Have no choice, will she, once I've sold the bloody house?"

Len can't believe it, and can't bring himself to tell Colin the Benthaven venture is off anyway; and since they have now reached the Club, he's not sorry to postpone having to do so.

"Well, better see what form we're in," growls Colin.

But it is not to be.

When they reach the snooker room there is no snooker table! They're told it's been transferred to the ballroom in readiness for the 'Big Event' and no one is to touch it.

"Bloody hell!" exclaims Colin. "Now what do we do?"

"Forget it," says Len. "Have to take our chances. The bar's open, let's go and have a drink."

They lose no time in doing that.

A cricket match is in progress on the playing field, and since the sun is warming up they take their pints and park themselves on a bench to watch.

"Going to miss all this when we go to live in Benthaven," says Colin.

"Um," says Len.

"We're going to miss the snooker too, I reckon."

Len nods.

"No time for games once we take over that hotel. Suppose we could turn one of the rooms into a snooker room. We'll need some sort of relaxation and that. Guests could use it too."

Len doesn't answer. Here's his chance to tell Colin the whole business is off, but he still can't decide how to do it.

"Hey!" cries Colin suddenly. "How's this for an idea? Suppose we turn the hotel into a snooker club! There ain't one in Benthaven, we know that only too well."

"Well..." Len is taken aback. He's not expecting new propositions.

"Damn sight less like hard work than running a hotel, I reckon. What you think?"

Len takes a long draught of his beer before answering. "The women wouldn't wear it," he says at last. "Be nothing for 'em to do, would there?"

"That's true, I suppose." Colin looks disappointed. "Got to consider them, of course. Best to stick to the hotel idea then."

Len thinks he sees a loophole. He girds up his sagging loins. "Well..." he begins.

"Butterfingers!" yells Colin suddenly, as a fielder drops a catch. "Sorry, mate. You were saying?"

Len takes a deep breath. "Well...I've been thinking."

"What – about the hotel?"

"Yes. If we're not going to be made redundant, see, we won't be getting redundancy pay, so we'll have quite a lot less capital than we thought. It'd make a big difference, bound to. Make it a pretty dodgy proposition financial wise."

Colin gapes. "You mean – we ought to drop the whole idea?"

Len nods dolefully, holding his breath.

Colin's emotions fly into disarray. Disappointment and anger predominate, but mixed in are feelings of relief. "I thought you were all for it," he objects half-heartedly.

"I am – or was. But I mean, what with the shortage of capital and Elsie not being keen and that, it's pretty risky. We've got to be practical."

"Well, I dunno about that! I mean, got to take a chance in

this life sometimes, otherwise it ain't worth living."

"True, but you've got to do it young. Not so easy when you're getting on a bit, with responsibilities and that."

Colin heaves a mighty sigh. "Bloody sod, living, ain't it? By the time you know what you really want to do, it's too late to do it!"

"That's life," says Len soberly.

"Well, I dunno," Colin, sighs again. "Suppose you're right. Got to be careful. Can't afford to go wrong. And with Elsie the way she is it could be a bit tricky, I must admit."

Len quietly lets out a long, long breath of relief. "Her memory all right now, then?" he asks, to change the subject.

"Pretty well, pretty well. Comes and goes a bit. She still can't remember how she came to be on that bike. She vaguely remembers being in hospital and that, then nothing till she found herself at Heathrow. Queer, ain't it? Probably just as well, though. What you don't remember can't bother you." He's thinking of the old fivers.

Len nods in commiseration. "Very nasty for her."

"Howzat!" yells Colin suddenly. "Old Bert's a pretty good bowler, ain't he?"

They watch in silence as the batsman walks slowly back to the pavilion, looking crestfallen. There is desultory applause. Len opens his blazer and leans back to enjoy the sun, which is warming up nicely.

"What about Nora?" asks Colin suddenly.

"What about her?"

"She's dead keen on this hotel caper now. Won't she do her nut when you tell her it's all off?"

"Don't think she'll worry all that much." Len is on his guard.

"But she was all for it yesterday. Dead keen."

"Well, what she's suddenly realised is that if we move down there to be near Gavin, we'll no sooner get settled than the bank will go and move him somewhere else."

"Could well happen, I suppose." Colin finishes off his beer. "Another, Len?"

Len looks at his watch. "Better not. Players will be going in for lunch shortly, I 'spect. We'd better be getting home."

"Suppose you're right."

Reluctantly they drag themselves to their feet. "One thing about it," says Colin as they wend their way back to the clubhouse, "the weather's improving. Forecast's not bad, either. Perhaps we'll be able to enjoy the rest of our holiday." He grins wryly. "At least it can't be much worse than the first week, can it?"

"Wouldn't lay a bet on it," says Len.

But a self-satisfied smile spreads over his face. He's done pretty well. It couldn't have worked out better.

I should have been a diplomat, he thinks.

*****

The hour has arrived for the 'Big Event'.

The ballroom is all tricked out television style. The table stands proudly in the middle of the floor, with special lighting installed above to improve the vision for the contestants. In each of two corners there are two chairs, both with a table between them, upon which there is a jug of water and tumblers. The trophy stands garlanded with flowers. Seats have been ranged on three sides for the spectators. Even video cameras have been installed to record the 'Great Event' for posterity, together with an electronic screen for keeping the score.

Elsie and Nora arrive early. They have walked to the Sports and Social with their contestant husbands, and now as VIPs for the evening, take their seats in the front row. Nora is wearing her navy-blue dress, which, despite all her efforts, is looking a bit sad after its trip to Greece, so she has put on her best pearl necklace in the hope of cheering it up. Elsie would have put on her Spanish-style dress, but that, she feels, is now well beyond rejuvenation. So instead she is decked out in her gold-sequinned trouser suit, the one she usually wears at Christmas time.

Oliver and Marsha are also coming, and even Boris and Cyril, but they won't be arriving until later because Boris is collecting Cyril and leaving Renwick with Glennis for her to look after.

Elsie's mood hasn't improved. She is still fed up with Colin. He's told her that the buying of Ocean View is off, but that he's still determined to return to Benthaven for the rest of the holiday. And she still hasn't forgiven Boris for lumbering her with Renwick, who persists in messing up the house again as fast as she can clean it. Just her luck that Daphne girl turned Boris down flat, she thinks. Couldn't really blame her, though.

"Oh my!" exclaims Nora, highly impressed with the set-up. "They certainly do things well, don't they?"

"Don't pay me membership money to be wasted on all this sort of nonsense," grumbles Elsie.

"Well I think it looks very nice."

There is an uneasy silence. Elsie opens her handbag – still the one she filched from the hospital – and produces a packet of liquorice allsorts.

Nora cocks an eye into the handbag. "What you done with all them old fivers then?"

"Got rid of 'em." Elsie shoves the liquorice bag under Nora's nose.

"You did! How?"

"Sent 'em to Children in Need."

"You sent all them old fivers to Children in Need! Whatever for?"

Elsie doesn't answer but chobbles her liquorice allsort aggressively.

"Don't see much point in doing that," says Nora.

"Why not? 'Spect they'll find a use for 'em."

"Don't see how."

"Well, I've got rid of 'em, that's all I care."

Nora sometimes wonders about Elsie. Fancy giving away hundreds of pounds, even if it is in old fivers!

The seats are beginning to fill. Nora watches the people coming in. So does Elsie, and her mood isn't exactly improved when she spots Rachel and Nerina among them. Come to see Colin play, she thinks grimly. If they think they're going to get their talons into him again, they've got another bloody think coming!

"Len tells me you're not going to come back with us to finish the holiday in Benthaven," says Nora presently.

"Oh yes I am!" snaps Elsie.

"But I thought—"

"Well you thought wrong." Seeing Nerina has made Elsie realise the danger. "You don't think I'm going let Colin loose in Brighton on his own again, do you?"

Another uneasy silence.

"Did I tell you Marsha and Oliver are coming this evening?" asks Nora unwisely.

"Big deal! You expecting me to curtsy or something?" No softening Elsie's mood tonight.

But Nora intends to have a go. "Oliver was very taken with your organ playing," she continues. "Most impressed he was."

"So you keep saying. Fat lot he knows about it."

"But everybody's impressed by it. You really ought to take it up, make a lot of money for yourself. That Billy what's-his-name should know, being a talent scout and that."

"That silly old fool don't know his arse from his elbow. Look at the way he thought Bollinger's bit-on-the-side could sing! Bloody sparrow can sing better than her."

"Well, I like your playing, anyhow," says Nora, helping herself to another liquorice allsort from Elsie's packet.

Enter Oliver and Marsha.

Up rises Nora, waving frantically. "Coo-eee! Over *here*!"

Oliver comes up, flawlessly attired in a smart, dark lounge suit, followed by Marsha, who is still hobbling but now reduced to just one walking stick. She is wearing a long shapeless black sack, but has put on a glitzy jacket over it as a concession to the occasion.

Nora brushes cheeks with Marsha and receives a generous hug from Oliver. Elsie just grimaces at them both.

"How's your ankle?" Nora asks Marsha immediately.

"Painful," she answers shortly. "The doctor says it will take time."

Oliver takes his seat next to the one reserved for George Bollinger when he arrives. "I trust your men folk are all revved up and ready to do battle," he says to Elsie and Nora.

"I very much doubt it," says Elsie sourly.

Nora is not having that. "Do their best, I'm sure. Got to make allowances, not being able to practise and that."

Cyril and Boris arrive and take their places on the further side of Nora. Glennis has had Cyril put on a collar and tie, and his twenty-year-old best suit, but his trilby remains firmly on his bald head. Boris has made no such concessions and is still in his jeans, T-shirt and trainers.

"Managed to get here in time then," says Nora to Cyril.

"Ar," mutters Cyril.

Three minutes to go and the Bollingers arrive. He's all togged up in an evening suit, but looks flushed and dour. His wife, a gawky lady, is bedecked in a Laura Ashley evening gown and is trying unsuccessfully to appear gracious.

Elsie perks up a notch. "I wonder if she knows about her old man and that Gloria woman," she whispers to Nora.

"Ssssh!" Nora gives Bollinger a scared glance.

But things are happening on the ballroom floor. The referee, Steve Harptree (Engineers), has appeared, looking a bit like a magician in his evening suit and dandy white gloves. He surveys the set-up critically, and goes to the table to inspect it closely.

Then he addresses the audience.

"Ladies and Gentlemen, may I have your attention please?"

He welcomes one and all to the Snooker Doubles Final and expresses his delight at having the Chief Executive in their midst, which produces a half-hearted round of applause. It is to be the best of seven frames, he tells them, between the holders, Sid Cooney (Works Lab) and Malcolm 'Hedgehog' Hodge (Dispatch), against the challengers, Colin Stilwell (Security) and Len Scally (Accounts).

Nora preens when Len's name is announced, and glances round proudly at Oliver.

The defenders, Cooney and Hodge, enter first. Cooney is mean and lean, with a beaked nose. Hodge is massive with a huge bristly beard. This earned him the nickname among his work mates of 'Hedge', which soon became 'Hedgehog'.

The challengers, Colin Stilwell and Len Scally soon follow. Colin looks handsome, with his broad shoulders and golden hair gleaming under the bright lights. Len looks professional in his crimson and gold waistcoat, brilliant white shirt and Dennis Taylor glasses.

Seeing Colin look so impressive sends Elsie's spirits up another notch. She joins vociferously in the applause that greets them. So does Nora. Oliver roars his encouragement.

"SILENCE PLEASE!" calls the ref.

Cooney cues off and they're away.

"Excuse me, but would you mind removing your hat?" hisses a voice behind Cyril.

Nora is perched on the edge of her seat and is sweating already, despite her deodorant. Elsie's mood spirals up dramatically, and she unconsciously delves into her bag of liquorice allsorts as the game moves into action. Oliver leans forward, watching critically. Marsha sits silent, totally mystified. Bollinger looks redder than ever. His lady wife looks bored.

Cooney and Hodge win the first frame, but Colin and Len take the second, thanks to a magnificent break of fifty-seven by Len.

"He's pretty good, isn't he?" says Oliver, turning to Nora when the frame is over.

"Oh, *very!*" Nora's cup brimmeth over. Perhaps, after all, she did the right thing in marrying Len Scally. More to him than meets the eye.

But Cooney and Hodge take the third frame and the fourth, Colin and Len coming back by winning the fifth.

Then comes the interval.

Bollinger and his wife discreetly leave the ballroom for private refreshment. He's not chancing that Scally woman telling his wife about Gloria. The others make for the bar, except for Boris, who unexpectedly mooches off on his own.

"Jolly exciting stuff," declares Oliver as he hands them all their drinks.

"Better than the telly," observes Cyril, pulling out his pipe. He's really caught up in it all.

"I have to admit," booms Marsha, "that I find it all rather boring."

"That's because you don't understand it, my dear," Oliver tells her.

"Reckon I'm going to take it up meself when I retire," says Cyril.

Nora glances at him in surprise. "You've definitely decided to retire then?"

"Oh ar. See a bit of life before I turn me toes up."

"And Glennis don't mind going to live in London?"

Cyril pulls at his left ear and looks doleful. "She reckons we ought to go and live in Dad's house, do it up and that, cos she wants to stay near the kids."

Nora's cup brimmeth over even more. That's the problem of that old house settled then. "Told you that was the thing to do, Cyril. Then if Mr Pertwee does buy your place, you'll have plenty of money to enjoy yourselves."

"Ar, well Glennis don't want to sell it, see. She says the best thing is if we keep it, like, put someone in charge – Boris if he's interested. Course, I'd keep an eye on it a bit. Give me an interest, she says, and keep the money rolling in. So I 'spect that's what we'll do."

Truth be told, he knows that's what they'll do.

The mention of Boris has made Elsie realise he isn't at the bar soaking up the booze. She looks around and eventually spots him chatting up Rachel and Nerina. That improves her mood even more. Keep 'em away from Colin, she thinks, and wonders if Boris could be interested in either of them. So long as he's not thinking of bringing her to live with them!

Due to the Final having not been expected to run the full seven frames, the odds being on Cooney and Hodge winning easily, the interval is strictly limited to fifteen minutes and when the buzzer goes people are hurriedly ushered back to their seats.

"Give it to 'em, Col!" yells Elsie as the player's reappear to enthusiastic applause.

"Hammer 'em!" bawls Cyril.

"SILENCE PLEASE!" shouts the ref.

Len cues off for the sixth frame.

Gasps of "Ooooh!" as Hodge misses an easy shot, and Colin comes to the table to make a splendid twenty-eight. Cooney replies with a thirty-seven, but Len, surprised by his own excellent form, clears the table to even the match.

Tremendous applause. Elsie and Nora hug each other like a couple of school kids. Oliver jumps up and down in his seat. Even Marsha feels caught up in the excitement. Cyril claps his bony hands until they sting. Bollinger becomes redder than ever. Only Mrs Bollinger retains a queenly presence.

"QUIET PLEASE!" calls the ref.

Three frames all. Everything depends on the final frame.

But alas, the waspish Cooney takes charge of that, and Colin and Len lose it by ninety-four to seventeen.

Bollinger steps down to present the trophy to the winners and has a word of commiseration for the losers.

"Damned fine effort," he tells them.

"We'll beat 'em next year, sir, don't you worry!" Colin tells him confidently.

You won't have the chance, thinks Bollinger, but is merciful enough to keep that to himself.

And, so a good time is had by all, be it by celebrating their victories, or drowning their sorrows.

The End